Tomorrow,
The Killing

Daniel Polansky

HODDER

First published in Great Britain in 2012 by Hodder & Stoughton
An Hachette UK company

First published in paperback in 2013

1

Copyright © Daniel Polansky 2012

A CIP catalogue record for this title is available from the British Library.

ISBN 978 1 4447 2136 2

Printed and bound by CPI Group (UK) Ltd, Croydon, CR0 4YY

Hodder & Stoughton policy is to use papers that are natural,
renewable and recyclable products and made from wood grown in
sustainable forests. The logging and manufacturing processes are expected
to conform to the environmental regulations of the country of origin.

Hodder & Stoughton Ltd
338 Euston Road
London NW1 3BH

www.hodder.co.uk

To the Sibs, in order of appearance: David, Michael,
Marisa and Alissa.

I

Man is a puerile creature, easily misled by the superficial. Some fool from the neighborhood, a mark you wouldn't trust to clean a chamberpot, comes up to you on the street in a clean suit and you find yourself ducking your head and calling him sir. It works backways as well – that selfsame halfwit puts on a uniform and gets to thinking he's hard, wraps up in a priest's vestments and mistakes himself for decent. It's a dangerous thing, pretense. A man ought to know who he is, even if he isn't proud to be it.

I tugged loose the collar of my dress jacket and wiped sweat from my brow. It was a hot day. It had been a hot week in a hot month, and it didn't look to be getting cooler. The drawing room wasn't built for the wave that had baked the city this last month, left wells dry and stray mutts foaming in the alleys. Though for the inhabitants of the mansion I supposed the drought was more a question of ruined outfits and canceled garden parties – what was life and death in Low Town was an

1

inconvenience in Kor's Heights. Even the weather afflicts the rich differently.

Which is to say it wasn't just the heat making me sweat, nor my raiment. I didn't like being here, didn't like heading this far north, not before nightfall, not at all if I could help it. Even the densest member of the city guard could figure I wasn't native. So when the footman had come knocking at the door of the Staggering Earl the day prior – not a runner asking for a few fistfuls of product, not a contact begging a favor – but a full-fledged steward, dressed in crimson livery and looking as out of place as an abbess in a whorehouse, I'd nearly sent him home. But curiosity made me open his message, that almost virtue which leads men to ruin and scrapes the ninth life off cats. The letter requested my attendance at a meeting the next morning, and it was signed 'General Edwin Montgomery', and by the time I got to the end of it I was wishing one of the local thugs had upended the emissary before I'd found another way to fuck myself. Given what was between us, I couldn't very well refuse his entreaty – though looking back on how things unfolded, it would have been better for everyone if I had.

It probably doesn't need to be said that I'm no great respecter of authority, nor of that particular brand of idiots who had sent me and several hundred thousand other souls out to die during the Great War – but Montgomery was all right. More than all right, he was a fucking legend, maybe the only man who'd ever borne high rank who deserved it. Most of his colleagues hadn't ever so much as seen the front, happy to set their headquarters in captured châteaux, working their way through the enemies' wine cellars and tallying up casualty rolls in grim little ciphers. After it was over, when the glow of victory began to fade and the backlash against the high brass crested, Montgomery had been one of the few whose name never started to rot. At one point there had been talk of making him the Minister for War, maybe even High Chancellor. But then, we'd all hoped to be something else, at some point.

I hadn't seen him for more than ten years. I hadn't ever

anticipated our meeting again, and was far from thrilled to find myself wrong.

I stifled an urge to roll a cigarette and tried not to fidget in my chair. Montgomery's servant, a densely built Vaalan, watched me from his position in front of his master's door. He was a military man, that was easily caught, from his proximity to the general and the coiled vigor of his physique. His eyes were etched unforgiving below the granite ledge of his forehead. His face seemed well suited to taking a beating, and his arms and shoulders well suited to delivering one. In short, I didn't imagine he had trouble chasing vagrants away from the back door – but, as with all of us, age was gaining. His hair, snipped low in a regulation short-cut, was more salt than pepper, and if only the faintest hint of flesh covered his dense core, still I suspected it was a half-stone more than he'd ever carried.

His name was Botha. I was impressed with myself for remembering it, given that I'd met him all of twice. In fact, I was having difficulty squaring our relatively limited acquaintance with the bleak stare he was aiming in my direction, the sort one reserves for the man who raped your sister, or at least killed your dog.

'Been a while,' I offered.

Botha grunted. I got the sense that as far as he was concerned, the pause could have extended out a good ways longer.

'You think you could rustle me up some finger sandwiches? The little ones, with cucumber and a bit of mutton?'

Having perfected his indifference against actual arrows, their rhetorical equivalent had little effect. He scuffed an imaginary bit of dirt off his shoulder.

'Isn't it appropriate to offer refreshments when entertaining guests?'

'You aren't a guest,' he muttered, the barest break in a steady and uncompromising countenance.

'Well, I'm here, aren't I? That would make me company or family, and either way I'd like a finger sandwich.'

A bell rang from within the room, so I never did get to find out whether I had done enough to rile him. But I wouldn't have bet against myself – I can be an aggravating motherfucker when I set my mind to it. Botha opened the door and slipped inside. He came back out after another moment, then waved to me.

'I'd tip you, but I'm all out of ochres, and I wouldn't want to insult your service with silver.'

'Maybe I'll get compensation some other day,' he said, slipping out sidelong as I brushed past him.

I stopped short, both of us squeezed awkwardly into the doorframe. 'I'm diligent in repaying debts.'

He allowed me to pass, then ducked his shoulders and nodded, mimicking the actions of a servant. The master of the house awaited, and I headed inside to meet him.

The study looked like what it was. Ebony bookshelves ran to the corners, filled by an appropriately dignified selection of leather-bound tomes. A stone fireplace took up most of the back wall, even its memory too hot for the day. A solid, uncluttered desk stood in the center, and the man himself sat behind it. It was a nice set-up – for the price of the furniture alone you could buy a half-square block of Low Town. But for a man whose wealth could have afforded him the most opulent luxuries, it was distinctly in the low key.

I'd met the general in Nestria some fifteen years prior, though I didn't imagine he remembered it. He'd toured the lines one night when I was sitting guard. That was during the first winter of the war, when you could never build a fire big enough to ward off the cold, and the first thing you did on waking was check your toes for frostbite. He'd come pacing in from the darkness, only an adjutant for company, dressed like any one of us grunts, shit on his boots and a greatcoat covered in mud. It had meant something to me. It had meant something to a lot of us.

The general was past middle age when he'd held a command during the war, and true to form, the years hadn't left him any younger. But neither had they taken from him the towering sense of self-possession I'd noticed even during the first few seconds I'd seen him, trudging through the icy rain – as if the weather, not to say the enemy, were factors beneath his contempt.

If anything age had sharpened it, the gradual withering of his body rendering clearer the absolute control that he maintained over it.

Of said body itself, there was little enough to comment. Youth provides in humanity the widest conceivable stretch of offerings, but time wears down this disparate variety into a handful of basic archetypes. By which I mean Montgomery looked like an old man – wisps of white attached to a leathery crown, the bones of his arms sharp beneath his shirt, a mouth you might suspect occasionally lent itself to slobbering. He wore a dark suit, less gaudy and better fitting than my own, though like me he was sweating through it. For all that though, his eyes were cool and sharp, and I didn't forget that sitting in front of me was a man whose word had once determined the fate of nations.

Botha closed the door behind me. Montgomery moved to stand, but I gestured him back into his chair and quickly took the seat across from him.

'It's been a very long time,' he said. I wasn't sure from his tone how he felt about it.

'Quite a while.'

'You look well,' he said.

'Thanks,' I said. 'You also.'

Two lies, and we weren't even through the pleasantries. 'Can I offer you anything?' he continued. 'A cup of coffee, perhaps? I don't suppose Botha offered you any.'

'He might have neglected that courtesy.'

'He was a better soldier than he is a domestic. Not much for etiquette, but a real terror with a flamberge.'

'I can imagine,' I said, and I could.

There was a pause while he worked up an appropriate line of small talk. I didn't envy his task – I'd done little in the time since we'd seen each other that was appropriately alluded to in casual conversation.

He settled on the basics. 'Is there a wife to ask about?'

'There is not.'

'Children?'

5

'None I'll admit to.'

It was my turn to play interrogator, but I kept quiet. I had a pretty good idea how the general had been this last decade, and I had a pretty good idea who was responsible for his unhappiness. Or I thought I did, at least.

After a while he realized I wasn't going to carry my end, and he stumbled forward banally. 'Damnable weather isn't it?'

'The flies seem to enjoy it.'

'Do you feel close kinship with the insects?'

I shrugged. 'People are a lot like flies.'

'How so?'

'We both die easy.'

The general swallowed my ugliness in a well-rehearsed guffaw. It was one of the hallmarks of the upper class, the ability to laugh away discomfort. I was acting badly but couldn't seem to stop myself. In preparation for this discussion I'd put away a half vial of pixie's breath, the illicit upper that I dealt when I wasn't using, but the buzz had long drained away. 'Perhaps you could tell me what it is I can do for you, General.'

'To the point, I can appreciate that. I'm sure you've got other things to do than sit in a hot room with an old man.'

Actually my plans for the rest of the day involved doing as little as humanly possible, a laborious exercise I intended to attempt with the aid of a suitable selection of narcotics. But he was correct in deducing that I wanted out as quickly as possible – of the neighborhood, the house, his presence.

There was an awkward pause while he inspected me with a queer and uncomfortable intensity, as if uncertain of my faithfulness. I wanted to tell him to go with this instinct, but before I could say anything he opened a drawer in his desk and took something out from the bottom of it.

'This is my daughter,' he said, sliding the object across the desk. 'Her name is Rhaine, after her mother, who died bringing her into the world.'

It was a heart-shaped locket, a shell of gold wrapped around a thumbnail portrait. I snapped open the catch. Miniatures are

6

a particularly inaccurate way to represent a fragment of reality. A square-inch oil, detail blurred to ambiguity by the requirements of size and the demands of an abstract notion of beauty. I thought it altogether unlikely that the subject of the sketch bore the slightest resemblance to the painting I held in my hand.

There was no great likeness between the general and his issue, but then the girl in the pendant must have been five decades younger than the man who sat across from me. And in fairness the dominating feature was her hair, red as the last moment of sunshine before evening, and time had long ago bleached the general's own locks. Apart from that she looked like everyone looks in a portrait: pearl skin, a slender nose mimicking the arc of her neck. The one quality offering a nod to her ancestry was her striking blue eyes, evidently a Montgomery family trait.

'She's lovely,' I said, though given the source I wasn't altogether sure that was a welcome compliment.

'She is indeed,' he said. 'She's also vain, willful, spoiled – and missing.'

I figured the last the most pertinent. 'How long?'

'Two days.'

'I notice you didn't say taken.'

'No, I didn't. I have reason to believe she departed of her own accord.'

'That would be?'

'We had a . . . row, I suppose. We've had a lot of them lately, but I'm afraid this was the breaking point.'

'I'm sorry to hear that, General,' I said. 'But the young are as quick to rage as they are to reconcile. I'm sure she'll show up soon.' Though of course I wasn't sure of that at all.

'I don't think so. She's headstrong, like her father.' Primed, he managed to continue without my assistance. 'She finished her schooling six months ago – an education, I assure you, that was as expensive as it was irrelevant. The interim since her graduation has been . . . trying for the both of us. She's not content to be married off, and while I don't blame her, I'm not sure sleeping

7

till mid-afternoon and shouting at the staff is a better substitute. Truth told, I'm not sure either of us knows what to do with each other.'

This was more information about the family Montgomery then I felt I needed. 'Be that as it may, General, I'm not sure what part I could play in your domestic issues.'

He pulled himself up in his seat, not so easy a task, given his age. 'I have reason to believe that she's somewhere in Low Town, hiding out. I want you to find her, and I want you to tell her . . . I want you to ask her to return.'

I scratched at the beginnings of a beard. 'What makes you think she's in Low Town?'

'If she had stayed within Kor's Heights, within her old circle, I'd know about it. And the nature of our fight led me to believe that she had taken it upon herself to look into something in your borough.'

That was indecipherably vague, but upon consideration I didn't think I wanted clarification. 'I don't work for the Crown any longer, General,' I said.

'So I've been informed.'

It wasn't much of a secret – though I doubted the general had an exactly accurate conception of my new slate of duties, or he would have sought help from a more appropriate source. 'And missing persons isn't my bailiwick these days.' Never was, really – even when I'd worn the gray I'd been more involved in making them disappear. 'I'm sure if you contacted Black House, they'd be happy to help you with your problem.'

'They would, they would indeed – they'd be happy as hell to help, to track down Fightin' Ed's wild daughter, and to remember it as long after as they'd need to.' He shook his head. 'I've had enough dealings with the Old Man to last a lifetime.'

'If it's discretion you're worried about, there are any number of firms who can offer it. I could give you the names of some reputable men.'

'I don't want discretion,' he said, not quite testily, but with less friendliness than he'd been offering. 'I want silence. I don't want the whisper, the hint of this, ever to get out – I want it never to have happened, and none of the bigger operators can promise that.' After a moment he cooled himself down a little, wiping at the flecks of spittle that had formed beside his mouth. 'Besides, I'd heard that you were the man to speak to about what goes on in Low Town.'

'And who'd you hear that from?' I asked. I had trouble believing the general spent much time in rooms where my name was bandied about.

'Iomhair Gilchrist,' he said, and smiled at my reaction. 'You don't much care for old Iron Stomach?'

'Oh, I wouldn't say that. If the Creator hadn't given us dung beetles, we'd have to spend a lot more time cleaning our shoes.'

'He's not a regular at Sunday dinner. But his avarice makes him easy to predict. I'm rich, he knows it, and that keeps him in my stable.'

'All the money in the world wouldn't buy him a spine – he's a coward, and useless in a pinch. Even if you could trust him not to screw you, you still couldn't trust him not to screw up.'

He nodded, not like he agreed with me, but like it didn't matter. 'Whatever else he is, he knows his business, and his business is knowing people, and he says you know yours.'

That was quite a little play on words, though I figured it was best not to call him on it. 'As flattering as it is to hear Iron Stomach thinks so highly of me, the fact remains, finding lost children isn't my line.'

I got the impression that Montgomery had expected this conversation to go easier. He took a long breath and rocked back in his chair, marshaling his forces before returning to battle. 'You never met Rhaine, did you?'

I had perspired through my shirt. I figured if I sat here much longer I'd soak my way through the overcoat as well. 'Not that I recall.'

'When last you and I met she would have been a child. In many ways I suppose she's still a child now. Roland quite doted on her. So did I. There were times when it seemed it was the only thing

9

the two of us could agree on. And of course she returned his affection. After his death I fear it turned to adoration. The longer he's been gone the more closely he resembles a saint.'

I concentrated firmly on the window behind the general, dull with dust and the glare of the sun.

'He always spoke highly of you, Roland. Even when he had little good to say of the Crown, of Black House in particular – he always spoke very highly of you.'

'That's nice to hear,' I said. It was the least definite statement I could think of.

'Yesterday I asked Iomhair for the names of three men who were solid enough to find my girl, and whom I could expect not to put my business out into the street. When yours came back at the head of that list, I must admit that . . .' he groped silently for words. It was clear the general was not one generally given to strong displays of emotion – I found myself wishing he'd hewn closer to his traditional habit of restraint.

'I'm not a religious man, you understand. But somehow when I saw your name I couldn't help but feel that the Daevas had some hand in it, in bringing you back into my life after such a long absence.'

I was far more keen to see the hand of the infernal in our renewed acquaintance than the divine. 'Roland was a friend,' I said. The fact that this was one of the few truths I'd bothered to tell over the course of the conversation was not lost on me. 'And if I thought I could help you, I wouldn't hesitate. But I'm not the sort to promise something I can't deliver, and I can't deliver this. I don't know Rhaine, don't know her habits, associates, don't know anything about her. Low Town is a big place, and even I don't have ears in all of it. And say I found her, what then? I've no leverage to force her to return, and cruel though it may be, the law wouldn't allow me to drop her in a sack and carry her here by force.' Laying them out like that they seemed like good excuses, not excuses even, explanations. I hoped he'd take them. 'I'm sorry, sir – but there just isn't anything I can do for you.'

10

He settled his antique body back into his chair, his face a shadow of what it had been a scant moment earlier. Nothing like breaking an old man's heart before lunch. 'Of course,' he said, his voice indistinct. 'I understand. Forgive me for wasting your time.'

'It was no trouble,' I returned, and then, wanting to say something to steady him, 'It was good seeing you again, General. I have . . . fond memories of you, and your son.' We were back to lies. I did have happy memories of Roland – but they were mixed evenly with some very terrible ones.

He didn't seem to hear me, which was just as well. The leather seat stuck to my ass as I stood. 'I'll take my leave of you, then.'

He nodded a farewell, lost in thoughts far from happy.

The palm of my hand was settled against the brass door handle when the image of a man flashed through my mind. A man who looked something like the general, but with the same shock of auburn hair as the woman in the locket I'd left lying on the table. His eyes were bright as a torch, the kind of eyes you'd follow anywhere – wild eyes, dangerous eyes, eyes that promised you things you shouldn't believe in.

'I could keep my ears open,' said the idiot in the badly tailored suit. 'I'm not promising anything, but . . .'

Montgomery shot up from the table, nearly sprinting towards me, forgetting his age in the excitement. 'Damn decent of you, damn decent of you!' He pressed the locket into my hand, and his grip was firm. 'I'll pay you anything you need, you don't worry about that. Just send me a bill and I'll cover it, double it – anything you need.'

At that moment I needed to get the hell out of his house, and I was about to do so when something occurred to me. 'One more thing, General,' I said. 'What was the fight about?'

The happy set of his face flushed away. 'It was about her brother,' he answered. 'And the circumstances of his murder.'

I left without saying anything further, through the parlor and past Botha's scowl, out the long hallway that led to the front room, through the gilded door and into the street. The sun shone down on a man who wished he'd had the last five minutes to do over again. Wished he'd had more than that, really, but who'd have settled for the last five minutes.

2

I t was hotter back in the old neighborhood than it had
been at the general's, hot enough to dry up what little
legitimate commerce existed and throw a pretty good dent
in the illegitimate businesses as well. I managed to make it all
the way back from Kor's Heights with nothing more than a half-
hearted catcall from a fabulously decrepit whore. I gave her an
argent and told her to get out of the sun.

I felt a brief moment of relief as I slipped into the confines
of the Staggering Earl. There wasn't much to be said about the
establishment of which I was half-owner. It was an unexceptional
neighborhood bar in an unexceptional section of Low Town –
ugly, threadbare, and catering to a class of customer straddling
that narrow line between rough and outright criminal. But it was
cool, and that was something. Actually, with the weather hot
enough to bake bread, it was a lot.

It might have been enough if Adolphus, my partner and the
nominal head of our enterprise, had been around to pour me a

draft of ale. But he wasn't. Nor was Adeline, his wife and the person actually responsible for the bar's solvency. The common room was empty, rows of rough-hewn tables leading to a long counter and the private area behind. After a moment I heard voices wafting in from the back, and, curious, followed them to their source.

When I'd first met him, back during the half-decade we'd spent murdering people in the service of our country, Adolphus had been as impressive a physical specimen as one could have put eyes on. Well enough over six feet that there was no point in measuring him, with a pair of arms the size of a thick man's legs and a back broad enough to run a cart over. Admittedly, his face was acne-scarred and homely, but the head it was attached to was set so far in the air that you barely noticed. He'd mustered out looking much the same, though now absent an eye courtesy of a Dren crossbow. Thirteen years of soft living and frequent sips from his tap had wilted him into something more believably a member of the human species. But he still looked like he could toss a cow over a wall, if for some reason he had been inclined to do so.

He was laughing when I came in, dominating the three men surrounding him as much by his brio as his size. It took me a moment to place them. Once I did, it took considerably less time for a scowl to work its way across my face.

'Hello, Lieutenant,' Hroudland began, quick with the pleasantries. 'It's been a while.' He held out his hand. After a moment of looking foolish, he put it away.

'Has it? I hadn't realized. I suppose I don't find myself thinking much about you.'

Hroudland nodded sadly, like he had hoped for better from me but had learned not to expect it. 'An unfortunate state of events. Because we at the Veterans' Association are thinking about you, you and all our other brothers, whose services to Throne and Country are being forgotten by the current administration.'

Hroudland was the very prototype of a mid-ranking officer,

more an abstract ideal than a fully realized human being. Give him a problem to solve and he'd solve it, and never waste a moment's thought on why it needed to be solved. He had a sharp enough mind, but he kept it in its case unless ordered otherwise. I didn't much care for him, but compared to his fellows I'd have been happy to cut my hand and swear a blood oath, kiss him on the cheek and call him brother.

Ten unfortunate years I'd known Roussel, and still the incongruity between his boyish face and his long history of violence left me slack-jawed. Rare amongst the population of the Empire, the coming of the war had been a singular blessing for the young Rouender. It was one shared by the stray dogs of his neighborhood, which, prior to his enlisting, had occasion to find themselves strung up and dissected, intestines stretched along the sidewalk and sweetmeats poked at with thin instruments of metal. The business of the front meant that Roussel had become a killer before his sixteenth birthday, but he wouldn't have lasted a virgin much longer even in civilian life. And though he came up barely to my shoulders, and had the blue eyes and pinked cheeks of a china doll, still he was the one I watched. The fact that Hroudland outranked him wouldn't mean anything if he got it in his head to hurt someone.

Rabbit was, by contrast, basically what you'd expect in a one-time infantryman and present-day thug. A series of wooden blocks stacked atop each other, the topmost a mass of scar tissue and tattered cartilage. Beaming through that last was a smile which held firm in sunshine or storm, when cutting a throat or disposing of a body. His nickname was a product of the sort of caustic humor common in the ranks, for if ever there was a man who bore less resemblance to the gentle lapin, I had trouble imagining him.

'What's with the monkey suit, Lieutenant?' he asked.

'On Sundays your wife and I have dinner, and I like to look my best.'

Rabbit laughed, belly juggling on his sturdy frame. 'I never married.'

'That's too bad. Everybody should have a wife. Then again, I suppose long years of barracks living, cheek and jowl with the creamy bud of Rigun manhood, might have given you an aversion to the fairer sex.'

Roussel started at that, mad eyes inching their way toward trouble, but Rabbit stole his thunder by laughing again, laughing and shaking his head in a friendly sort of way. 'I forgot how funny you are, Lieutenant.'

'Only when you're around. Once you leave I go back to drinking myself silent. While we're on the subject, mayhap you could enlighten me as to when exactly to expect your retreat. The bar isn't open yet, and anyway we keep a pretty exclusive entrance policy.'

'Come on now,' Hroudland said. 'We're all soldiers.'

'Did the High Chancellor start another war while I wasn't looking?' I smiled something that wasn't that. 'Either way, I think I've put in my time – which means whatever the hell you may be, Hroudland, *we* aren't anything at all.'

This was too much for Roussel. He tightened his fingers around the hilt of the short sword he had thus far, through an astonishing act of will, managed to keep sheathed.

'None of that,' Hroudland said, having spent enough time with the boy-sized lunatic to know without looking he was trending towards violence. 'The lieutenant was only joking. He likes a good joke, the lieutenant, and we like the lieutenant, so we don't mind. The lieutenant's a smart man, real smart – and he knows we're looking out for him and his interests, knows without the Association to make sure the Crown played straight, they'd strip us of everything we got, and see us out in the street.'

'I'm not sure I'm so savvy as you think.'

'Then it's a good thing we stopped by to educate you,' and for the first time a hint of steel edged itself into his voice.

'That reminds me, Hroudland. I'm behind on my dues.' I reached into a back pocket and came out with a tarnished bit of copper, then flipped it to him. 'That ought to cover it – in perpetuity. Don't imagine there'll be a need to come round again.'

Hroudland looked at it for a moment, deciding whether or not to push his play, but whatever their purpose was in coming here, it hadn't been to start a quarrel. And anyway, between me and Adolphus he probably figured he didn't have the brawn to chance it. So he closed his hand around the coin and put it away with a smile. 'We weren't here to see you, Lieutenant – that was just a happy accident. We're here to see the chief.' He gave Adolphus a friendly nod. 'And the Hero of Aunis knows he's welcome at a meeting anytime he chooses to show.'

He gestured to his boys and they followed him out. Rabbit had the same steady grin he'd worn the entire time, that he'd have continued to wear if things had gone in another, less amiable direction. Roussel looked like a child who'd dropped his sucker, sad to have lost what would likely be the day's best chance to make something bleed.

I rolled up the cigarette I hadn't been able to smoke at the general's, and added in a little dreamvine for wise measure. Adolphus stood mute, his face red and anxious. For someone I had once seen break a man's back between his hands, he had a real dread of interpersonal conflict.

'What the fuck were they doing here?' I asked finally.

'Just checking in. Wanted to see what I thought about this new bill the Throne's jammed down our throats.'

'Is that what they told you?'

'You don't believe it?'

'If Hroudland told me we'd see sun tomorrow, I'd take my winter coat out from storage.'

'They aren't all bad. Rabbit's a friendly enough fellow.'

'He get those scars being friendly?'

'They're soldiers,' Adolphus said, imbuing the last word with a reverence that turned my stomach. 'Just like us.'

'Spare me the brothers-in-arms bullshit. They impressed a fifth of the population – you think maybe a few bad apples crept in?'

He shrugged, not wanting to argue the point, but I wasn't

willing to let it go. 'You remember what happened the last time the Association had any power?'

This was enough to calcify his vague sense of dissent. 'Roland Montgomery was a good man.'

'With some bad ideas.' It was an unfortunate coincidence that had brought him to my mind twice in the span of as many hours – or so I thought to myself at the time.

'He was right about standing up for ourselves, not letting them take advantage of us,' Adolphus said. 'The Throne's got no business trying to tax our pensions.'

The war ended and a couple of hundred thousand men were dumped unceremoniously onto the streets of Rigus. Men wounded in mind and body, lacking practical skills beyond ditch-digging and murder. Some turned to crime, more to rattling tin cups on street corners. It started to look bad, the capital choked with the broken bodies of ex-heroes. Perhaps the wiser amongst the ministers began to wonder what would happen if their one time army decided to take up their old trade – a concern stoked when Roland Montgomery founded the Veterans' Association, in large part to convince his former comrades to do just that. Reparations were starting to come in, for once the Crown's treasuries were flush. It seemed prudent to give some modest percentage of the Dren's money to the men who had won it.

And thus was born the Private's Silver, half from guilt, half from fear. A half ochre a month for every man who'd served until such time as they weren't alive to claim it. Not enough to start a business or buy a house or feed a family. Just enough to die slowly, two to a bed in a slum tenement, out of sight of passers-by. I thought it was a pretty crap exchange for what we'd given, and generally didn't bother to go down to the tax office and claim it. But for most of my comrades it was near sacrosanct, weighed out of all proportion to its actual value.

In the grand tradition of shortsightedness, the Crown had not bothered to consider what would happen when the war indemnity ran out, as it had some years back. With our coffers near to empty, the High Chancellor had started to call for taxing the

Private's Silver as regular income, a rather impressive bit of legerdemain by which the Throne would take back with one hand what it gave with the other.

'The government fucks people – that's what governments do. You shouldn't need that explained.'

Adolphus shrugged with a petulance inappropriate to his age and bulk. 'Ain't right that they forgot us so quick.'

'First taxes, now time? What's your encore? You going to track death to her lair, wrestle her into submission?'

Adolphus dipped his head warily. 'Shouldn't blaspheme like that. She Who Waits Behind might be listening.'

'She's always listening, Adolphus – and she sets her own pace.' I trampled my cigarette into the floor. It meant work for Adeline but it accentuated my point. 'Course, you go mucking about with the Association and you might get her to double time it.'

It was as good a line as any other to end the conversation on, and besides I had a full enough day left ahead of me. I left Adolphus to consider the error of his ways, or more likely why he had chosen to go into business with a gibbering asshole, and threaded the narrow stairway up to my grim, dingy room. Once there I changed back into my regular get up, and took a spare moment to fill my skull with pixie's breath before heading back out into the street.

3

There wasn't any part of soldiering I had great affection for, but if you put steel to my throat I'd probably single out that period where we weren't killing anyone as being the least horrible. It was brief, lasting only the few weeks it took to transport forty thousand men from Rigus to Nestria and shove weapons in our hands. And it was still an awful, awful way to spend time – lost days in the hot sun practicing movements with pike and blade, off hours listening to the chittering of the other idiots stupid enough to have enlisted. But still, it was a hell of a lot better than what came after.

We didn't know it the morning of the Battle of Beneharnum, of course. We were all operating under the vague suspicion that having learned nothing more than to stand in a line and point our spears in the same direction, such would be all that was required. Our immediate superiors, no crack strategists themselves, encouraged this sort of thinking, indeed seemed to labor beneath it. A strange lethargy had spread through the ranks, from the officers, who drank and gambled and generally made asses of themselves, to our regimental drummer boy, who couldn't keep a fucking one-two if our lives depended on it – which, as it turns out, they did.

I was a private back then, the lowest rung on a long fucking ladder. It wasn't a position that much suited me. We're all dancing on strings, but I prefer mine less visible. It's impossible to maintain even the common pretense of free will when every drop of your energy is spent at the discretion of men you never see, who seem as far above you as the Firstborn and his siblings – albeit possessed of a good deal less wisdom.

We'd been drawn up in formation since morning, packed against each other while the artillery corps wasted small mountains of iron in a futile effort to annihilate the opposing forces. The Great War would see a dramatic expansion of the role of cannon in combat, recent industrial advances having allowed for their mass production. Of course, you could build all the culverin you wanted, didn't mean much without anyone who knew how to aim them. It was one thing to show an illiterate peasant how to swing a piece of metal at his Dren equivalent, another to provide him with the training necessary to correctly sight ordnance. As the conflict progressed and the gunners had time to perfect their craft, cannon fire would come to be as deadly as the plague, and the whistling of shot would be enough to send a brigade of stout-hearted men diving for cover – but that day was far off. The soldiers manning our batteries seemed half-blind or fully retarded, and there was probably no safer place in Nestria than that occupied by the army some half-mile distant. For once the Dren were equally incompetent, and a solid hour passed while shot and metal shards buried themselves in the mud a few hundred yards in front of us.

If you're hoping for a treatise on military history, you're shit out of luck. I didn't know then and I don't know now what it was about Beneharnum that necessitated the death of ten thousand men, why this particular stretch of earth needed to be watered with blood. I suppose it was as good a place to die as any, and I never heard a man put six feet down complain about the spot.

Certainly the officer who gave us our orders did no great job of explaining the situation. He looked the part at least, seated atop a white destrier and gesturing dramatically with his cavalry saber, though with the artillery duel going on no one could hear a word he said. I assumed he'd been exhorting us to die for Queen and Country, and though I'd never met the old bitch and wasn't mad for what I'd seen of her kingdom, a half-hour later I nevertheless found myself in the front rank of her army, leaning against the twenty-foot spear I'd wedged into the ground and waiting to march on to death.

Next to me Adolphus was doing the same, though the sapling seemed insufficient for his bulk. In light of future events it's tempting to imbue our early relationship with more than casual importance, but the truth is back then he was just another face in the regiment, albeit one set substantially above the rest. I didn't know much about him and didn't want to – it didn't make sense to get too close to anyone, given the reasonable likelihood of their demise. You could hear the hills in his argot, a country boy grown up slinging mud or diddling cows or doing whatever the fuck farmers do, I dunno. He'd told me the first time he'd left his village was when he'd joined up, as anxious to get out of the provinces as I'd been to leave the slums.

The artillery barrage finally ended. Adolphus let a spiral of saliva fall to the ground. 'Hell of an overture.'

'Gorgeous,' I responded. Tough as scrap iron, the two of us. If we hadn't been holding our weapons you'd have seen our hands palsy.

We had good reason for it. The front row was not an ideal spot as far as safety was concerned. The rest of the line had been drawn by lots, but the two of us had volunteered, meaning we drew double pay and more importantly, by my lights, had a shot at getting noticed by the brass. I hadn't enlisted to spend my time at the bottom of the post – I wanted to make a name for myself, and that wouldn't happen if I spent my service cowering in the back.

Of course, my hopes for future advancement were contingent on surviving our encounter with the enemy, and as the drummer boy began to beat out an uneven rhythm I realized that was pretty fucking far from a deadlock. There were five rows of men with too much wit to take our place in the vanguard, and they fell in behind us, pikes straight in the air. Scuttling in lockstep across the battlefield, our ungainly hedgehog joined a hundred-odd others stretching out along either side of us, surely as curious a migration of bipeds as ever graced the surface of the Thirteen Lands.

Battles are often conceived of as duels between generals, a chess game played out in real time, and we pawns no more than the instrument of their designs. 'The Twentieth took the hill,' read the histories, a minor escapade barely warranting its single sentence. But let me tell you, if you were a member of the Twentieth you'd feel a hell of a lot different about the whole thing. 'What hill?' you might well find yourself asking, 'and where the hell am I taking it?'

In the front ranks of a vast agglomeration of men, the dust from their footfalls kicking up around your eyes and the hum of their breathing drowning out any other sound, you'd be lucky to recognize the approaching incline. And that's before you even hit the enemy, and your focus sharpens down to a pinprick. I've been in a lot of battles, and rarely in any of them did I have the faintest idea of what was going on. It's enough to know there's a man watching your back, and to spend any leftover energy watching theirs.

As the distance narrowed between us I caught sight of my opposite, the man whose job it was to oppose my passage, to wound and kill me if he was able. Sitting in camp you spent half the day talking about them, passing out bits of folklore disguised as wisdom. In time it became difficult to think of the enemy as being composed of individual particles, as if we had declared war on one vast but singular organism. In the face of the man ahead of me I recognized my error. Apart from the dye of his armor he was largely indistinguishable from any of the men I was marching beside, or indeed from myself.

It was a curious discovery, and not one I had time to contemplate. The weight of expectation, which is not to say duty, kept us moving forward. Fifty-odd paces out, at one with the rest of the rank, I brought my spear level.

The pike is an odd weapon. Useless as tits on a bull one-on-one, it presents an impermeable barrier if you can get it in the hands of a few hundred men sharp enough to point it in the same direction and stupid enough not to throw it away and go home. But that's pretty much all it's good for – it doesn't lend itself to intricate movements or much in the way of technique, you don't really wield it so much as hold it in place. I think we all had it in our heads that, at the final moment, the Dren were going to sprint forward onto the points of our weapons. They seemed to be operating under the same delusion, because a few feet outside of effective range both lines stuttered to a stop, and for one ludicrous moment I found myself wondering if maybe we'd all give up and go home.

Then the men behind us plowed forward, unable to see anything and thus immune to the sudden twinge of fear or humanity that had briefly halted our movement. I managed to keep myself standing but the end of my pike skipped upward harmlessly. Luckily the Dren marching counter to me was similarly inept, and his did the same. My neighbor to the left was not so fortunate, the head of a spear plunging through his leather carapace, the forward press of the men slowly skewering it through his chest and out his back.

The other thing about the pike is that it's about twenty feet long and only a few inches of it can actually hurt a motherfucker. If you miss with the point there's still a long way to go, staring at your opposite, both of you scared shitless. But it only lasts a few seconds before the inexorable momentum pushes you together, the mad scrum of flesh allowing for little in the way of maneuver.

Everyone around me was holding on to their spears like they were some sort of charm against death, but I figured fuck that and dropped mine, going for the long dirk in my belt. It was an awkward movement, my forehead pushing up against the Dren in front of me, but I managed it, reversing my hold and slipping the weapon into his gut, just above the groin, beneath the protection afforded by his armor.

Unlike most of my comrades, I'd killed before I'd entered the service, knew what it felt like to watch a man stare up at you blankly as whatever force animates him slips out of the hole you've made. But I'd always felt something of it afterward, could tell you every man I'd sent to meet She Who Waits Behind All Things, could tell you why I'd thought I had to send them to meet her. Not justify it – I won't pretend that – but explain it at least, beyond that he was wearing a different colored outfit than I was.

Of course in the thick of things the moment barely registered. The dagger rose a second time, falling into my counterpart as of its own volition. I watched him die with my head tucked against his, close as lovers. After the third blow he slid limply to the ground, and I wish I could say I felt something about it but the truth is at that point my blood was up so high all I saw was the next man in line, and I stepped over the corpse, on it really, and launched myself into the Dren behind him.

He was quick, and he caught the edge of my blade with the shaft of his spear, the weight of the men behind us locking our weapons together. I jerked the ridge of my brow against his nose, snapping the fragile bone and smearing blood against my skull, but he didn't drop, red leaking down over a rigid sneer. It was my introduction to what would rapidly become, along with the stupidity and gutlessness of the brass, the bane of my existence for the next five years – the legendary Dren grit, a willingness to endure pain and discomfort that seemed almost an inability to feel either, which ensured that every redoubt would be held to the last man, and to the last man's last breath.

But still, meat ain't stone, and I managed to hook his eye with my off hand, and he screamed and dropped his pike so as to keep himself from being blinded, and I wiggled my steel into the underside of his throat and moved on to the next one.

Whether because of the hole I'd made or some other factor I

could feel their line bending. Not see it, I couldn't see anything except what was directly in front of me and a few blurred motions from out the corners of my eyes – but sense it somehow, like a change in the wind. 'We've got them!' someone screamed, and I realized that it was me. 'One more fucking push!'

I might have been right about that, or I might have been wrong, I never had the chance to find out. Because in the scant second after I had spoken, as the long, snaking line of Dren began to buckle and turn, as victory seemed just at the limit of our grasp, the world ended.

So it seemed, at least. Practically speaking, the results of a well-formed battle hex are indistinguishable from a black-powder barrage. They both result in the destruction of wide sums of flesh, the scattering of bone and brain – but one peculiarity that accompanies the use of sorcery, or more accurately fails to accompany it, is sound of any kind. In contrast to the ear-shattering boom of cannon, a hex is utterly silent. From out of the corner of my eye I saw a light so bright it nearly blinded me. But there was no noise connected to it, nothing to alert one aurally to the holocaust that was taking place.

The vacuum was quickly filled with the shrieks of my dying countrymen, those lucky or unlucky enough to have found themselves on the outskirts of the explosion. Having avoided outright death they now found their limbs atomized away to nothing. Their cries were picked up a second later by the surrounding infantry, to whom the spell had done no direct damage but who were quick to realize that our ranks had been irreparably shattered, and our flanks were bare of support.

Prepared for this sudden attack, the Dren redoubled their efforts, straightening their formation against ours. The sudden disappearance of a substantial portion of our unit had opened up a little room in my peripherals, but I didn't have time to take notice, not with an approaching infantryman keen to square accounts for his two comrades. The end of my knife had broken off against the spine of the last Dren, and I discarded the remainder and dove shoulder first at his back-up, hoping to get within grappling range before he planted something sharp in my chest.

I had him on the ground, my hands squeezing the blood into his face and the life out of his body, when it occurred to me that the back ranks had been awful slow to come to my aid. As a last gasp escaped past his lolling tongue I took a quick look up and discovered with a sinking horror that the lack of attention came by virtue of there being no one around to provide it. Our line had broken, utterly, and apart from Adolphus there were none of us left standing. It seemed that while I had been caught up in strangling a man to death the remainder of our division had assessed the situation and decided that the course of greatest wisdom lay in vacating the area with all possible speed.

Warfare is based on a sort of mass hysteria by which the individual mistakes his own well-being for that of the collective, but as solid as the mania may seem on march, it punctures mighty quick in the heat of battle. One moment you're walking in lock-step, no more cognizant of your own particular existence than is a drop of blood filtering through the heart. Then some unfortunate setback occurs, entirely disabusing you of the absurd fiction that anything could possibly matter more than forestalling your own death, and you throw down your weapon and sprint for the back, willing to trample your fellow soldiers into the ground should they prove an impediment to your escape.

It's then that the rock-bottom of a man's character comes out, when you get to learn who it is you've been bunking and eating and shitting with. Though the battle was lost and our cause vanquished, you couldn't have figured it from Adolphus, for whom the defeat of our army had been forgotten in the sheer joy of combat. He let out a roar that would have done credit to a lion, shoved back the Dren who opposed him and laid out left and right with his pole, snapping the neck of one man and notching the brain-pan of another, cowing the surrounding infantry and earning us a brief moment of respite.

He was continuing forward even then, but I got a hand on the back of his armor, not enough to check his progress but sufficient to focus his attention on me. 'Adolphus!' I screamed, trying to make myself heard over the fray. 'We're done! Let's go!'

He gave a mournful look back at the enemy, a handful of whom had neglected to fall upon our fleeing comrades and were instead showing disturbing signs of renewed hostility.

'Now, Adolphus!' I said again, in what I would later come to think of as my 'command voice.' He gave a quick nod, and together we began to fall back.

The nature of a rout is that it sends the victors into nearly as much confusion as the vanquished, as if you threw yourself against a locked door only to find it giving way at your touch. Though our side had ceased even the semblance of being an organized body, the Dren seemed but little more ordered. Some were hot on the heels of our retreating fellows, hoping to down their quota. Some had already started on the grim but lucrative business of looting the corpses. And a great many, an astonishing percentage really, milled about in aimless confusion.

If you can maintain some sense of direction in such bedlam you've got an advantage, and between the two of us we managed a capable fighting withdrawal. I picked up a stray pike and held it parallel with Adolphus's, edging it warily at anyone who came too close, falling backwards gradually and with purpose. Mostly those Dren pursuing our shattered rear didn't bother with us, not when there were easier targets swarming all around.

The march in had only taken us ten minutes, but going back took us twice as long, three times, hell, five, I don't know. It seemed an eternity, dead and dying everywhere you looked, the population of a fair-sized town made into mounds of rotting flesh. And the screaming, by the Firstborn, the screaming. It was like a strong wind, thousands of men hurling their misery at you, their terror and hatred.

At one point I tripped over a corpse and added to the song, certain that Adolphus would prioritize his own survival over our newly minted friendship. But he didn't – he stood over me steady as a statue, and the enemy stayed clear.

Things eased off once we got back to the baggage train. The

29

Dren quickly lost interest in murder, turned to scooping up anything that could be eaten, drunk, sold or fucked. By nightfall we were five miles back from the front, trying to find our unit amongst the mass of broken men, the wounded dying unattended, the officers no more capable of offering succor than they had been of saving us from the catastrophe of the day.

And that was that – twenty minutes on a bright autumn afternoon sounding the death knell on set-piece warfare, of fluttering pendants, of regimental musicians beating the score, of cavalry charges and men in tight formation. From then on it was all shovels and trenches, dugouts of mud and shit, scorching in summer and freezing in winter, and of course, always wet. Tactics switched to dead sprints across the barrens of no-man's-land in the dark of night, armies of men as huge and profligate as locusts, suiciding themselves without order, purpose or reason.

4

There are vast swathes of the middle and upper classes who are born in the city, who live and work in Rigus all their lives, who marry and spawn seed and are buried beneath their fair portion of dust, and who never at any point set foot within Low Town. For these people, Low Town occupies a position analogous to an agnostic's view of hell – abstractly unpleasant, but unworthy of overmuch consideration, given the dim odds of ever finding oneself there. They come to think of it, if they think of it at all, as something extraneous, irrelevant to their own existence.

As widely held beliefs tend to be, this one is entirely false. Low Town is not separate from Rigus – neither its stray effluvium nor its bastard offspring. Low Town is the heart and soul of the metropolis, as much as the Old City with the palace and parliament, with its glittering citadels and wide lanes. The rich and well fed need Low Town as much as those who inhabit it, need a place away from the kindled lights, close enough to reach after nightfall but far enough away so the stink doesn't follow them home.

In the false distance between the two worlds the factor earns their supper. Say you're an uptown merchant or a baronet, and you find yourself needing a den for late-evening assignations, the ownership of which ought never find its way back to your wife – no problem, sir, not a problem at all. Hand over a few ochres and you'll get your little love nest, a quaint walk-up just over the line from Offbend, with nary a piece of paper to link you to it. And let's suppose, having acquired such a fine piece of real estate, you have an interest in filling it with a buxom lass and a few twists of dreamvine, or a comely youth and ouroboros root, or prepubescents and wyrm – well, your intermediate knows many different sorts of folk, sir, and would never grudge a fellow his pleasure. Not a decent, well-born sort such as yourself, sir. And continuing on with our imaginings, let's say your better half was to sniff out your paramour or grow suspicious as to where exactly her dowry is disappearing to, decides to make a nuisance of herself – then, as was said, sir, the factor knows all sorts of folk, all sorts of folk indeed, and he suspects he could help you out of that little difficulty as well.

It's a dirty sort of business, and even by common standards, Iomhair Gilchrist was a particularly unpleasant incarnation. Servile and treacherous, his sole constant an infatuation with short money that blinded him to the long. Too clever by half, and quick to forget he was a coward until things went to push. Odds suggested he'd end up dead in an alley, and I was always a little surprised to discover that coin unclaimed. Not that we'd ever had much contact – aside from his propensity for betrayal, I found him to be, on a personal level, as foul as a whore's privates.

But life's not all rosewater and sunshine, and so after I left the Earl I headed toward Gilchrist's office, keeping to the shade as best as I was able. He had lodgings on Apple Street, a fading structure sandwiched between two tenements. A newly painted sign above the door read, 'Iomhair Gilchrist, Factor. Private and confidential.' Beneath it, still visible despite the fresh coat, someone had scrawled 'cunt' in broad letters. I thought about knocking, but only briefly.

The room was an ugly shell of a space, though one could predict that from the exterior. What one could not have predicted was the sheer volume of clutter, as if a river of trash had overflowed its banks. Scattered across the desk in the center of the room, the chair across from it, the bench against a side wall and the floor itself were the end-products of a dozen full reams of paper – notes, text, receipts and letters, some settled high enough to serve as a perch, others more reasonably stacked no further than my shins.

Gilchrist sat on a stool behind the bureau, the one spot sufficiently empty of junk as to allow human occupation. Some part of Iomhair's success, to the degree that he could be said to have had any, stemmed from the fact that his body was not an accurate reflection of the vacuousness of his soul. Instead of a malformed figure, one found a plump, pleasant-looking Tarasaighn, ruddy-cheeked with a serious countenance. If there was nothing particularly distinguished about him, neither was one immediately overwhelmed by the inclination to beat him with the nearest blunt object. He had a bushy caterpillar of a mustache, which he rubbed at when he wanted to give the impression that he was deep in contemplation. It was an affectation of which he was perhaps too fond, and he tended to paw at it over-frequently, as if it was a stain to be removed through vigorous scouring.

He looked up as I came in, and though the heat had already set him to sweating through the homely tweed he wore, he seemed to leak another fluid ounce at my presence. 'Warden! How nice of you to come by and thank me for the recent avenue of employment I provided.' On the desk was a box of cheap cigars, and he opened it, picking one out for himself and gesturing for me to do the same.

I scooped the stack of paper off the chair opposite him and dropped it without preamble. Gilchrist winced as it hit the floor. 'Is that why I'm here?' I asked, taking the seat and ignoring the offered smoke.

'What other reason? And though your civility does you credit, it is of course quite unnecessary. I've always got my eyes out for any kindnesses I might do for such a dear friend, any minor services I might render one who has done so much for me.' Iomhair preferred to play both parts of a dialogue. 'I take the greatest pleasure in knowing I was able to have done a favor, however small.'

'Why the fuck . . .' I began, holding on to the last word for a long second, '. . . would you think you've done me any sort of favor?'

He licked a spread of spittle over his lips.

'Let me ask you a question, Gilchrist,' I continued, arching my back and stretching my arms wide, taking up as much room as I could. 'What was it about my resume that made you suppose I was keen to pick up a sideline tracking down missing nobles?'

'Everyone can use a little extra work.'

'Is that what you think? That I'm so hard up for coin I'd be willing to do anything for it? To what other ends has this misimpression set you? Have you been bandying my name about to the city as a ditch digger? Should I expect to be approached by any sodomite off the street, having been given your word that I'm the man to satisfy their twisted desires?'

His cigar rested unlit between his fingers. 'So you . . . turned him down?'

'There you go again, Gilchrist, thinking. How many times does that habit have to get you into trouble before you give it up?'

He laughed nervously.

'Tell me about Rhaine,' I said.

'Don't know what I can tell you, Warden. I never met the girl – I was just doing the general a favor. He's a war hero, you know.'

'That's the rumor.'

Iomhair nodded vigorously. 'A sad business, and hopefully one with a speedy resolution. I'll light a candle to the Firstborn, in hope the girl returns home.'

'Did you tell her that when you saw her?'

His eyes dodged away. 'I'm afraid I don't follow.'

To the general, Low Town was a dark and bottomless pool, and Rhaine had fallen into it. Probably the girl had said something to that effect as she'd stomped out, swearing she'd disappear without a trace, never to be seen again. No doubt she'd even meant it. But the simple fact is that such a thing is an impossibility – we leave ripples everywhere we go, and more so when we are unsure of our surroundings.

I'd been lying to the general when I said his daughter would be impossible to find – in fact, I assumed it wouldn't be particularly difficult, and not just because the heiress would have trouble blending in with the streetwalkers up on Pritt Street. Rhaine had stalked out of Kor's Heights with a head of steam and a few ochres in pocket change, and neither of those would last long. Once the reality of her situation sunk in, she'd go to ground in whatever hole she could afford, and she would make contact with the only person in Low Town whose name she knew.

'She came around yesterday?'

'Come off it, Warden. This sort of foolishness is unbecoming.'

'You guessed you'd up whatever reward you're going to get from Montgomery if she stayed missing a few more days. Probably you even took something from Rhaine herself to keep silent. If you were smarter then you are, you'd have made sure that list of names you gave the general didn't include anyone halfway competent. Though in due deference, you probably figured I'd go along with it, between the two of us we could string the man out for half his worth.'

The gradual pinkening of his fat face suggested I wasn't far off the mark. 'I simply can't understand where you're getting these absurd notions.'

'It doesn't matter why I think what I think, Gilchrist. You wouldn't be able to follow along anyway. What matters is that she did visit you, and I know it, and the more time you waste pretending otherwise the faster I start to lose patience – which if we're being honest, is not one of my stronger qualities anyway. So let's dispense with the pretense that you're an honest man, or that anything you've said to me up to this point is true. I won't hold it against you. In fact, if you come through for me now, I'll even try to score some coin for you, once I send her home.'

Between the promise of money and the flaccid nature of his character, Iomhair folded. 'She asked me about her brother. She said she wanted to know about what he was doing before he died.'

'And what did you tell her?'

'Not much. I didn't know much. I told her to go down and see the boys at the Association – they were the ones to talk to.'

The anger that I had been feigning flared to life. I tamped down on it. Getting hot never helps anything. 'You sent her to see the vets?'

I must not have done an absolutely successful job of keeping myself calm because his tongue seemed stuck in its depression, and it was a while before he stuttered out confirmation. 'Yeah.'

'By the Lost One, Gilchrist, sometimes I forget how fucking stupid you really are.'

I guess there wasn't much could be said to that. At least, nothing he could think of, or had the courage to speak.

'When did this interview take place?' I asked.

'Yesterday evening. I didn't think it would do any harm. Roland was the head of the Veterans' Association before he died, and Joachim Pretories was always his truest friend.'

I had no interest in setting Iomhair straight about the nature of the Association's activities, nor the character of their current commander. 'Where is she sleeping?'

'I don't know – I swear, she wouldn't tell me. You know I'd never lie to you.' As if he hadn't spent most of the conversation doing just that.

'Then I guess you'll need to find out.'

'How?'

'That's the nice part about not being a pawn, Gilchrist – you get to tell people what to do without working out how they'll do it.'

The truth was I didn't have much to hold over the man if he refused me – but he wouldn't, conditioned as he was to do the bidding of anyone who raised their voice. 'There isn't any need to let the general know I saw Rhaine, is there? I was going to tell him, really, I just didn't get the chance yet.'

'If you aren't going to smoke that,' I finished, nodding at his unlit cigar, 'you'd best put it back in its box.'

He looked down at the fat five inches trembling in his hand, and I bobbed on out.

5

The air in the Earl was so stale you could cube it and stack the pieces. I headed to the courtyard to draw myself a pint of water from our pump.

Wren sat cross-legged against the back wall, eyes closed as if in slumber. He had grown since I'd taken him off the street three years prior. As a child he had been lean and quick, light-skinned, dark-haired, and subtle as the night. As a youth he had turned gawky, and, cruel as it was to point out, acne-ridden. Though he ate three square meals and incessantly between them, he was as thin as he had been the day I'd found him loitering in an alleyway, and it sat worse on him than it once had. His limbs seemed overlong, like they were intended for a full-grown man but had been mislaid. I figured he'd grow into them, if someone didn't kill him first.

And someone might, for a lot of reasons. Because he had a sharp mouth and opened it around people who repaid insult with iron. Because despite my best efforts he still had only a dubious respect for the concept of personal property. But primarily because of the small blue light that swirled around his outstretched palm – speaking more accurately, because of his ability to produce it.

Most folk live and die without ever having any direct experience with the Art. They come to think of it like it is in fairy tales, rings that turn you invisible, incantations that make a man fly or transform shit to gold. Maybe during the harvest festival they give a hoarded argent to a traveling conjuror in exchange for a charm or a palm reading. Almost certainly, they gave their money to a con man, and are lucky to have found themselves cheated.

Because there is far more terror in the Art than wonder, and even as a child, when I'd counted amongst my closest friends perhaps the most powerful and certainly the most decent practitioner the realm had ever produced, I still didn't like it. Magic is a perversion of reality. Dabbling with it is, in my experience, a recipe for madness, or damnation.

Though in truth, the damage Wren might cause himself was not my primary concern. The Art was power in its most concentrated form, and the government regulated it zealously. At the first sign of the spark a practitioner was required to register themselves with the Crown, and anyone under twenty-five forcibly enrolled in the Academy for the Furtherance of the Magical Arts. Originally it had been a wartime measure, to fade away once the crisis with the Dren had passed. But of course, that's not the way things work – once authority is ceded to the Crown, nothing short of revolution is sufficient to claw it back. Indeed, in the years since the armistice the Crown's hold on the Empire's practitioners had only grown firmer. When it first started the Academy had been a finishing school for practitioners, its students in their late teens or early twenties, already long apprenticed to a master. These days the Academy was closer to a prison than a boarding school, raising the next generation of sorcerers to walk in lockstep with the Throne.

I swallowed my greeting once I saw the phantasm. Mind fixed

on his creation, Wren didn't notice my appearance. Even a basic use of the Art is taxing, and he was still an amateur – it took every ounce of concentration to maintain his working.

A long-handled axe was slung by the door, awaiting the next time Adolphus needed to chop wood. I slipped my palm around the butt and stalked the short distance between us, flipping it over so the blade was towards me. Then I rang the back end of it against the wall a few inches above Wren's head, the metal sparking off stone.

The light died stillborn and the boy leapt to his feet, but I was ready for him, discarding the axe and pinning his shoulders against the wall. 'Are you out of your mind?' I asked quietly, and despite the coolness with which I'd taken my quarry my heart beat a rapid staccato. 'Are you out of your fucking mind?'

He wouldn't look at me, his head swinging back and forth as if to some unheard rhythm.

'Do you have any idea how dangerous that is? What can happen if you miscalculate?'

'I know what I'm doing.'

I tightened my fingers around his collarbone. 'There are cells below the Bureau of Magic Affairs for people who knew what they were doing, knew what they were doing till they didn't. Maybe tomorrow I'll take you to see them, rows of lunatics shitting themselves and spouting gibberish.'

He stopped swaying long enough to sneer. 'You wouldn't get in.'

'No, I wouldn't – but they'd still be there, and you'll still be joining them if you keep acting the fool.'

'I'm careful. I don't try anything I can't handle.'

'You don't know enough to know that. And what if someone else had come by and seen you, as you were so bright you decided to try this outdoors? The Crown pays yellow for straight tips on children with the gift.'

'I'm not a child.'

'You act like one. How do you think it'd be telling Adeline that the gray are carting you off, remaking you into their tool, that she's

41

never gonna see you again?' I shoved him back against the bricks. 'The Art isn't a fucking toy – pull your pud if you need a diversion.'

Not so long ago this exchange would have been enough to set him running off to the streets, and I'd have to spend the next half week dodging the wrath of his adopted mother. But three years of domestication had worn him down enough to accept rebuke, or at least fake it.

'I want your word you won't try this shit again. Not on your own, not without a guide.'

'So find me a teacher.'

'Believe it or not, boy, your education isn't my sole priority.'

He gave a vague shrug, and looked to change the subject. 'How'd your meeting with the general go?'

'I'd comfortably assumed it'd be the worst part of my day, but you've gone and proved me wrong. Now do I have your word that you'll hold off any more experimenting, or don't I?'

He finally met my eyes. 'You have it.'

You can't trust an adolescent to keep a promise, they change too quickly – the person who gave his guarantee is dead twelve hours later. I'd need to do something to keep him satisfied. 'Adolphus will be home any minute. Get cleaned up, he'll need help with the dinner rush.'

Wren went inside and I finally got my water. It was warm, and brackish.

6

I was picking at the end of my chop steak when the girl on the picture in my front pocket walked into the bar. She scanned her surroundings before fixing on me, then approached with the sort of air that suggested her greeting would be less than cordial.

'I'm Rhaine Montgomery,' she said. 'What the hell do you want?'

Well, that was pretty fucking easy, I thought, and pushed aside my plate.

My tobacco pouch sat on the counter. I thumbed out a sheaf of paper and a few tufts, playing for time. The portrait painter had taken liberties, but then I guess that's what they're paid for. The woman in front of me was a far cry from the vision in miniature I had been given. Her face lacked any trace of softness, of the plump vitality that draws the male gaze. She was too sharp, too angular, her body a reflection of the belligerence her reputation spoke of and our short acquaintance confirmed. A crueler man than I might have called her boyish, and I imagined her childhood had contained no shortage of pimpled wits happy to plague her with similar epithets. Still, her scarlet hair was as striking in person as in oil, a vivid contrast with the blue of her eyes.

The longer the pause lasted the narrower these got, till they were little more than slits in a sea of freckled pink. 'Well? I asked you a question.'

'You look like your brother,' I opened.

Excitement spilled across her face, but she killed it quick, tightening her mouth into a sneer. 'You knew my brother?'

'I served under him during the war. I saw him around a little after that.'

She cocked her head as if to spear me. 'I don't believe you.'

'All right then. You look like your mother.'

Now she was thoroughly confused, so much so that for a moment she forgot even to be angry. Her face was more pleasant when it wasn't radiating antipathy. 'You knew my mother?'

'No, never met her,' I said, flagging down Adolphus. He sidled over from the other side of the bar and refilled my glass.

'Who's this?' His smile would have been charming if it hadn't been attached to the rest of him.

'She's our new barkeep. I'm sick of watching you drag your ass over here every time I need a beer.'

Adolphus looked her up and down. 'Not sure she's big enough,' he said. Then, to her, 'You think you could carry a half-cask up from the basement?'

'I'm not a barback!'

'No need to get huffy about it.' Adolphus winked his one good eye and drew off, chuckling.

I took a shallow drag off my cigarette while she composed her fraying nerves. 'Why are you looking for me?' she said again.

'Why do you think?'

'It's Father, isn't it?' She shook her head angrily. Petulantly, if you were inclined to be judgmental about it. 'Tell him he can stop worrying. Tell him I can take care of myself.'

'Can you?'

'I'm here, aren't I? I've made it this far.'

'So did he,' I pointed at a drunk passed out in the corner, his snoring interrupted by the occasional involuntary belch. 'But if we were kin I'd be concerned to hell.'

She had primed herself for a screaming match, and my refusal to offer a fight left her unsorted. Her shoulders slumped, pinned down by the day's length. 'What does he want from me?'

'The general? I think he'd like you to outlive him. It's a common hope of parents, I'm told.'

'And what of Roland?'

'I imagine your father would have liked him to do the same.' The longer the conversation lasted the more it was becoming clear I was not the ideal candidate to reconcile the Montgomery family, never having had a family myself, nor entirely understanding their purpose.

'You say you knew my brother.'

'I said that.'

'How well?'

'How well does anyone know anyone?'

'Did you think him the sort of man to end his life face down in the gutter, outside of a Low Town whorehouse?'

'I've known better men who died worse.'

That was close enough to an attack to allow her temper free reign. 'You can tell Father I'm not some child to get fetched by the help. You tell him I'll stay in Low Town till Roland gets justice, since he's not man enough to see it done himself.'

As she turned to walk away I closed the tips of my fingers around her wrist. 'Let me tell you something about the dead, as someone who's seen a few of them. They don't care what we do. They don't yearn for vengeance, and they don't hope for redemption. They rot.' I tightened my grip slightly. 'Stick around Low Town and you'll find out I'm right.'

She ripped her arm away with enough force that I worried she might have injured herself. Then she shot me a look that could have curled paint, and stalked off into the night.

I finished the rest of my drink and told myself to stay out of it, knowing I'd be too stupid to listen.

7

Roland Montgomery's birthday party was not my kind of scene.

This was a year or two after the armistice. I was a low-ranking agent, investigating crimes and punishing the guilty, or at least the unlucky. Roland was amongst the most beloved heroes of the Great War, and the Association rapidly becoming a political power. That ought to have been enough to mitigate against our continued interaction, even without the differences in our upbringing and social status. I suppose Roland's willingness to try and forge a friendship despite them was to his credit. But virtue and vice often walk hand in hand, and I sometimes wondered if his sense of egalitarianism wasn't an offshoot of his consuming love of being liked.

In later years, in my professional capacity as a purveyor of phantasms and herb-induced bliss, I would find myself in any number of upper-class debaucheries, half-orgies populated by the degenerated scions of the aristocracy. This was about as far from those as you could get. General Montgomery was old school, and though Roland's politics now ran to the radical, personally he was as little taken with revelry as his father. I suspected that this celebration was not of his making, that if his wishes had been taken into account the day would have come and gone unmarked.

A white canvas tent had been erected in the backyard, a term that hardly does justice to the virtual nature preserve that was the Montgomerys' grounds. The late spring evening was illuminated by white lanterns hung amidst foliage. The weather had been kind enough to go along with the proceedings, the night warm, the sky clear. A pleasantly bucolic scene, though the chattering of the insects was largely drowned out by the chattering of the guests. Waiters shoved trays of over-elaborate pastries into my face, diced quail spleens with candied almonds, goose liver dabbed atop thin-cut white bread, things that looked like food but somehow weren't quite. I got the sense that no one else was having a particularly good time, but then they'd all had more practice in faking it.

The young Rouender woman with whom I was nominally conversing had spent a good deal of money to look very cheap. She wore little in the way of clothing but a great deal of make-up, along with a selection of jewelry that weighed enough to drown a man in a gutter. Her name was Buffy or Minnie or some other jarring diminutive more appropriate for a child's doll than an adult. I'd long since stopped paying attention to her words, but their gradual increase in volume suggested her anecdote had reached its climax. I shook free of my thoughts long enough to catch the last sentence. 'It's just so hard to find a decent servant these days.'

'A constant struggle,' I agreed.

'You have no idea. And if you are lucky enough to find someone who knows what they're doing, good luck keeping her! I had the sweetest little girl, a half-Islander who could do the most amazing things with my hair. Five years I had her, and then one day she just disappeared, shipped out to the Free Cities with some . . . man she'd married.'

'After everything you'd done for her.'

'Exactly!'

Foremost what is hateful about the aristocracy is their fundamental meaninglessness – they do nothing and thus are nothing. On some dim level they seem to be aware of it, hence their refuge in petty intrigues and expensive narcotics, in nightly soirées and the occasional bloody duel. There's a frantic quality to their play, more distraction than recreation. If things ever stopped spinning long enough for them to take a look at themselves, half would end up taking a midnight dip in the bay.

'How exactly do you know Roland?'

'I served beneath him.'

She set one hand on my chest. 'We all so appreciate your sacrifice,' she said, blinking her eyelashes as if shooing away a fly.

I would never be categorized as handsome – a lifetime of scraps had been effective in defacing a physiognomy that would not originally have been mistaken for attractive. But there was a certain type of woman that seemed to find my alley-mutt face alluring, at least as a curiosity. And the uniform helped – the rich had no greater love of Black House than any other cohort of the population, but it was at least evidence that I had a real job, which I supposed made me something of a novelty.

'Is it true what they say about him, our Roland?'

I thought about that for a while. 'Yeah, it pretty much is.'

'What an honor it must have been for you, to be a part of his command.'

'Every moment a joy.'

'Tell me, what was it like? The war, I mean?'

I finished off what was in my cup. 'It was like something that you never feel like talking about.'

Her face turned from pink to bright red. The pink had been make-up, but the red seemed authentic.

'Where is the guest of honor, anyway?' I asked. I'd seen Roland briefly on the way in, he'd pumped my hand and told me we'd talk soon. That had been two hours prior, and so far his promise had been unfulfilled.

'I'm . . . not sure,' she said, eyes fluttering about the party for someone else to speak with.

'Perhaps I'll see if I can't run him down,' I said, disengaging.

Buffy or Minnie made no particular effort to dissuade me.

Somewhere in the vast estate surrounding me there was a fully stocked bar, but it was not in view, nor did the various waitstaff seem inclined to provide directions. This left me trying to get drunk on the house punch, a syrupy concoction ill-suited to my mood, which was bored trending towards bitter. It filled my bladder long before offering any sort of a decent buzz. As watering the greenery seemed likely to betray my upbringing, I found my way towards the powder room.

Business concluded, I detoured away from the party, bright lights and dull people. This was my second visit to the Montgomery manse. The first had been several months earlier, a dinner party to which I'd been invited. I'd sat at the far end of the table from Roland and his father, said little and enjoyed myself less. But it had given me a passing familiarity with the layout, one I put to good use in avoiding the gathering outside.

I wasn't exactly trying to snoop, but then I wasn't exactly trying not to either. As a member of the secret police I figured I had at least the license, if not the obligation, to figure out what everyone else was doing. And given the sensitive nature of the conversation, General Montgomery and his seed had done little to inure themselves from eavesdroppers. The door to the office was half open, and if they weren't yet yelling outright, it was clear the conversation was moving in that direction.

'They can't very well name me High Chancellor with my eldest child calling for the abolition of the damned monarchy!'

'There are more important things in the world than your political career, Father,' Roland said. His voice was calm but not quiet, and I thought I detected in it a hint of mockery.

'Like yours, for instance?'

'Like the interests of the men who served beneath my command.'

'And how are their interests served by you making trouble in the streets? By threatening the Crown and the government?'

'I'm simply asking that the Queen appropriately reward the men who died keeping her aloft. If she chooses to take offense, I can hardly be blamed.'

'Should she take offense at your marching armed through Low Town? Of instigating feuds with drug dealers and criminals?'

'I can hardly imagine the Throne would object to concerned citizens defending their families.'

'The Throne would object to your building a private army, regardless of who you choose to aim it at.'

'The Throne built the army, Father. I'm just borrowing it while it's not in use.'

There was a choking sound, then a long silence. When next the general spoke, it was with that studied composure that lies a short step from open rage. 'Flippancy ill-suits you, or the gravity of the situation. Pensions, almshouses, jobs – as High Chancellor I'll be in a position to provide these things. If you cared as much about them as you did your own grandstanding, you'd cease your provocation and fall in line!'

A movement in the shadows betrayed that I wasn't the only one interested in the goings-on of the Montgomery clan. Botha stood silently outside the study door, an impressive degree of stealth for a man of his size. I wondered what it meant that he hadn't bothered to chase me off. His smirk had worn a groove into his face – a bitter thing, devoid of levity.

I followed the hallway back toward the party, taking a seat on a small sofa near the exit. It was getting late, and unlike the rest of the attendees, I had things to do in the morning. I could hear Roland and his father continue with their dispute, the distance

I'd added made up for by the increase in volume. It was too garbled to make out specifics, and I didn't strain myself trying.

After a moment I noticed someone peering out from around the corner. A young girl, ten or twelve, I'm bad at that sort of thing. She had her brother's red hair and her father's fierce gaze.

I crooked one finger in hello. She scowled and approached me.

'It's my brother's birthday,' she said.

'Is that why all these people are here?'

'Of course,' she said, clearly thinking me very foolish. As a line, the Montgomerys had many virtues, but not one of them possessed anything resembling a sense of humor.

'Are you supposed to be up so late?'

'No one cares what I do,' she said.

At her age I had been five years on the streets, orphaned by the Red Fever, scraping by on theft and low cunning. It had been quite literally the case that no one cared what I did. 'Don't you have a nanny or something?'

'She thinks I'm in the privy.'

'A budding criminal genius.'

'I don't want to be a criminal,' she said.

'Most don't.' I very much had the urge to smoke a cigarette, but decided it was better not to offer the pubescent an opportunity to feel morally superior to me. We stared at each other for a while.

'Do you want to sit down?' I asked.

'Will you tell Father that I'm out of bed?'

'I won't.'

'Do you promise?'

'I promise.'

She rolled over the worth of my word. 'I shouldn't believe you,' she said. 'But I will.' She plopped herself next to me on the sofa.

'That's very kind.'

We sat quietly while the familial dispute worsened.

'My brother's a hero,' she said suddenly, as if expecting me to contradict her.

'I've heard that.'

'My father too.'

'That's the word.'

There was the sound of something breaking. One of the participants had thrown something against a wall. I assumed it was Edwin. He'd something of a reputation as a firebrand, despite his age.

'They fight a lot,' she said. 'I'm not supposed to know that.'

'I don't think either of us are.'

'If they're both heroes,' she asked, 'then why do they fight so much?'

'Heroes can't disagree with each other?'

'Of course not,' she snapped. 'Being a hero means you always know what the right thing to do is.'

'What if there's more than one?'

'There's only ever one right thing to do,' she said, the final moral authority on the subject.

'Often not even that.'

What little enthusiasm I'd managed to inspire in the girl dissipated quickly. She all but leapt up from her seat. 'I don't think I like you,' she said.

'A popular sentiment.'

She lifted her chin till it pointed at the ceiling, turned imperiously and marched back the way she'd come.

Free of the possible censure of a child, I smoked a cigarette and said a silent prayer for those poor fools who'd chosen to personally ensure the continuation of the species. It must be exhausting, having to pretend you had the answers. My position within Black House required a rather casual relationship with the truth, but even I wasn't forced to uphold such an absurd fiction every moment of the day.

I never ended up seeing Roland. A few minutes after Rhaine went to her bed I decided to head to my own. It had been a long trek to Kor's Heights, with little enough to show for it.

When the general had asked me if I'd met his daughter, I'd lied and said I hadn't. At the time I hadn't seen any point in mentioning our initial conversation, brief and meaningless as it was. Having had a follow up, I wasn't so sure. There seemed to be a great deal of the child I'd met in the woman whose life I was trying to save.

8

I awoke the next morning stewed in my own sweat, and well past breakfast.

I didn't mind. It was too hot to eat, too hot to do anything but lie in bed and be too hot. Sadly I didn't have that luxury, so I stretched myself into yesterday's shirt and dropped down the stairs.

Wren was hung over a table, naked from the waist up.

'I've got a message I need run.'

'Can it wait till the afternoon?' he asked. 'It's hot as hell out.'

'It'll only get hotter,' I said, and he pulled himself up off the wood sulkily. 'I need you to find Yancey. Ask him what he's got going on this evening. Tell him I'd like to pay him a visit.'

He smiled. He liked the Rhymer. Everybody liked the Rhymer. 'Where are you going?'

'I gotta make my tithe.'

He nodded sympathetically and went back to not moving. I watched him enviously, then slipped out the back.

The job of the city guard, contrary to popular belief, is not to stop crime. They do stop crime, albeit rarely and mostly by accident, but doing so is not their primary function. The guard's job, like the job of every other organism, singular or collective, is to maintain its existence – to do the bare minimum required to continue doing the bare minimum.

I'm in the same general racket, which is why once a week I nip over and toss the hoax a cut of my enterprises. Not a big one, but not a small one either. Enough for them to leave me alone and let me know if anyone is planning to do otherwise. Everybody in my line does, everybody who isn't a fool, everybody who wants to keep at it for more than a fortnight. Because while as a general rule the guard don't seriously concern themselves with catching criminals, they're apt to rediscover their zeal if they hear of anyone keeping too much of their own money.

Low Town headquarters is, befitting its inhabitants, derelict and unimpressive. Very little of the guard's earnings, from the official budget or that provided by me and my ilk, seemed to be going towards its upkeep. A sentry milled aimlessly about in the shadow of its three stone stories, a pair of which could comfortably have been removed without affecting life in the borough. A stoop led to a set of double doors, one to walk into with high hopes, and one to walk out of disappointed. I skirted the main entrance and went through the back, up a short flight of steps and straight to the Captain of the Watch, nodding at the duty officer on the way in.

Galliard's position required him to collect money and not rock the boat, and he was well suited to both. On a bad day he ate two meals between breakfast and lunch. Today was a good day, and he was polishing off a plate of smoked ham when I came in.

'Morning, Warden. Good to see you. Take a load off.'

I dropped into the stool opposite him. 'Captain.'

He pointed at the buffet, finger-fat jiggling. 'Fancy a bite?'

'It's a little hot for salted meat.'

'Not for me,' he said, lowering a sinew of pink-white muscle into the bulge of his neck. 'How you been?'

'Standing.' I took a pouch of ochres out from my satchel and set it on top of the table. 'You?'

'Sitting,' he acknowledged. He weighed the purse expertly in his hand, then tossed it onto his desk. When I was gone he'd redistribute it accordingly, slivers of my wealth going to the men above and beneath him, food for children and jewelry for whores. 'You hear the Giroies wiped out the James Street Boys? I didn't figure them for the balls to make that kind of play.'

The Giroies were an old school Rouender syndicate, had their fingers in some pies out near Offbend. In recent years they'd been struggling to keep themselves stable, their forces weakened after they went a round with the Association during the Second Syndicate War. 'Since Junior took over they've been thinking they're big time. You gonna do anything to convince them otherwise?'

He shrugged, though it was more effort than he was used to. 'Why?'

Why indeed. 'There's muttering that two Islanders got sent to Mercy of Prachetas with a rash that looked like the plague.'

He batted aside the suggestion with a wave of his flipper. 'Idle gossip. I talked to a man at the desk, said it was just another case of the flux. The seafarers need to stop drinking from fouled wells, though what with the heat I can hardly blame them.' Surprising thing about the hoax, they knew more than you'd credit them with. They just never bothered to do anything with the information. 'Course the plague ain't the only plague. There's been a buzz coming from the Association these last few weeks. They've got a rally scheduled next week over this thing with the pensions, gonna pull out all the stops.'

'I never understood the big deal about marching. I walk places all the time, no one gives me any credit.'

'Word is they told a crew of Courtland Savages to stop moving vine through their neighborhood. You know the Savages got Giroie backing.' Galliard slapped a pad of butter over a crust of brown bread, then expunged both with three quick bites. 'You were in the army, weren't you, Warden?'

'They wouldn't let me in, on account of I only got one arm.'

'If you're close with anyone over there, you ought to let them know they're starting to draw attention.'

'I don't have any friends left in the Association.'

'We've been getting feelers out from Black House.'

'I don't have any friends left there either,' I said, and that was an understatement. 'The vets been respectable a long time – they don't have the teeth to make trouble.'

'Maybe, maybe not. I don't imagine they've forgotten which end of the knife to hold, even if they've kept it sheathed the last few years.'

'Joachim Pretories ain't Roland Montgomery.'

'Let's hope he knows it,' Galliard said. From the open window I could hear two street children arguing over something. A brief scuffle decided the issue, the loser running off squealing. Galliard wiped his mouth with a napkin tucked into his collar. 'Maybe it's just the heat. Seems like the whole city's gone crazy the last few weeks. We picked another hooker out of the canal this morning. Third one this month.' He rubbed his hands against each other, crumbs falling to the floor, tits jiggling beneath his shirt. 'Things will get worse before they get better.'

'People say that – but in my experience things usually just get worse.'

Galliard chortled, then fell silent.

I stood to leave. 'Well then, I've my duties to attend to, as I imagine you've yours.'

The captain lifted his corpulent buttocks from his chair and shook my hand. 'Quite right, quite right. See you next week.'

'Next week,' I agreed, and found myself out.

9

I wasn't expecting to come back to the Earl and find Hroudland and Rabbit waiting for me at the bar. If I had, I probably wouldn't have showed – I'd have found my way to the docks, lit up a twist and hoped for a breeze.

They were the only people in there, the rest of the coterie out for the morning, trying to take care of a day's worth of errands before the sun made travel too uncomfortable. That meant I wouldn't be able to count on Adolphus's muscle if things went sour – but it also meant I didn't have to bother with any pretense of amiability. 'What the fuck do you want?'

Rabbit belched out a giggle, and Hroudland answered me with an easy lilt to his voice. 'You know, Lieutenant, there's really no need to begin the conversation in such a combative fashion.'

'I suppose that's something else we'll need to disagree on.' I rolled up a cigarette. The flare of the match was an unnecessary aggravation in the heat. 'Let me make it easy on you, because I know dialogue isn't your strong point. Adolphus ain't here.'

'Not looking for Adolphus,' Rabbit piped in, a smile swelling his lips, looking for all the world like a child spoiled with a secret. 'We're here for you.'

'Why, Rabbit, is that you over there? You cheeky devil, hiding in the back, so quiet I'd never even notice! And then you start dribbling nonsense and ruin the whole effect! You don't want to see me, Rabbit, because I don't want to see you. I was fairly clear on that point, last time we spoke.'

Rabbit laughed again, laughed and blushed, and Hroudland took over the reins. 'The big man wants a word with you.'

'I'm not sure who you're referring to.'

'Commander Joachim Pretories.'

'Is he really what you'd call big? Guess we've got a different sense of scale.'

'I don't want to argue with you, Lieutenant.'

'Well, I'm in no mood to dance, Hroudland – and since you don't want to argue and I don't want to dance, I'm not sure what's left for us.'

'The commander just wants a few minutes of your time. Surely that's not such a sacrifice.'

'You haven't factored in the opportunity costs – a few minutes of my time is like a decade to you or Rabbit. Who knows all the extraordinary things I could do with a half hour? Write a sonnet maybe, or find a cure for the flux.' I shook my head. 'If you think about it that way, it's actually quite a lot that you're asking – more than I feel like offering.'

'The commander said I was to insist.'

'He said you were to insist now, did he? You hear that, Rabbit? The two of you are supposed to insist.'

'That's what the captain said,' Rabbit agreed.

'That's what he said all right.' I stubbed out my smoke. 'You so sure you could compel my attendance?'

'No,' Hroudland said. 'Not at all. Which is why I'm hoping you'll do the smart thing, and come for a little walk with us, rather than push this into a direction it doesn't need to go.'

That was in fact the smart thing to do, even if it was Hroudland saying it. And if Hroudland wasn't sure he and Rabbit could force my attendance, I wasn't sure they couldn't. And it would be a damn stupid thing to die over, because I felt like taking the weather out on two men I vaguely disliked.

'You'll buy me an ice on the way over, Rabbit?'

Rabbit laughed, the same as he had with death thick in the air. 'Lieutenant wants to know if I'll buy him a ice!'

Rabbit was an easy audience. It was one of his few positive qualities.

The Association for the Advancement of the Veterans of the Great War – or the Veterans' Association if you were a fan of brevity, or simply the Association if you were really obsessed with the concept – was an institution claiming to represent those unfortunate souls who had found themselves manning the trenches during the Empire's last foray into mass suicide. It was founded by Roland Montgomery six months after the Humbling of Donknacht loosed a quarter of a million former soldiers back upon the homeland they had killed to protect. When Roland died two years later, it had been taken over by his long-time second, Joachim Pretories, and he'd spent the interim turning it into a respectable political power. For all its pretensions it was a typical corporate entity, nominally advocating for the rights and privileges of its members, in practice cadging for the few lucky souls at the top.

For a while it had been something else. But then things used to be different all over, back in the day.

They headquartered in an old banking house in Offbend, a few stones' throw from the Old City, or one really good throw for those well practiced in throwing stones. It was a beautiful structure, four floors of white brick on a cobblestone square. A wooden platform had been erected in the middle of the arcade, a focal point for their frequent rallies. A handful of men stood stiffly outside the entrance, their attempts at loitering spoiled by too many years in the ranks. They nodded at my escort and allowed us inside.

'I'll tell the commander you're here,' Hroudland said,

disappearing into the back. I took the time to inspect my surroundings.

The entrance hall was big enough to hold a few hundred people, though at present there were barely a dozen occupying it – apart from me and Rabbit, there were a handful of men seated at a long wooden table, waiting to cater to the needs of paying members. Trophies of our conflict hung on the wall, captured pennants and Dren weaponry, tapestries depicting major battles. I spent a moment inspecting these last, though I had trouble recognizing myself in the ranks of proud spearmen chasing the fleeing enemy into the distance, or in the mounted officers leading the charge. Hung over a huge fireplace was a portrait of the Association's founder, staring down at his children, blue eyes stern but supportive.

His father's name could have earned him a spot away from the front line and the dangers of combat, but that hadn't been Roland's way. Indeed, no promotion seemed sufficient to force him back from the front. By the time I'd met him he was well on his way from man to myth, and if the first had ended three years after the armistice, face down in the Low Town mud, the second had only continued to grow. A decade on and his was still a name to conjure with amongst anyone who'd ever served in the ranks.

Hroudland opened the back door and waved at us. Rabbit and I followed him down a narrow corridor, up a flight of stairs and past several more watchmen, stopping in front of the commander's quarters. 'Through here,' Hroudland said. 'When you're done we'll take you back to your bar.'

'Rough neighborhood like this, I need someone to protect my virtue.'

Hroudland shook his head, glad to have me off his hands. He opened the door and I headed inside.

Soldiering is not a profession that lends itself toward the glorification of violence, nor of those who practice it. The flux kills more men in an hour than the most skilled warrior could account for in the entirety of his bloody existence, and no amount of bravery or strength is proof against a stray artillery shot. Afterward, trying to impress a girl in a tavern, you might spin a yarn about some squadmate who could down a dozen Dren single-handed, might even say that squadmate was you. But at the time, while it mattered, you knew all that was nonsense. One sword doesn't swing the outcome of a battle – there were too damn many of us for any particular individual to play much import. A man was either solid – which was to say if he was next in line when you went over the top, you didn't check to make sure he followed – or he wasn't, in which case you hoped he'd die soon and leave the rest of the squad his rations. Anything beyond that was fodder for the broadsheets back home.

Even so, Pretories had acquired a reputation not simply for being a solid man, but an excellent one. I could remember Roland waxing poetic as to the number of times his life had been saved by the uncanny ability of his second-in-command that he feared for nothing so long as Joachim Pretories stood behind him. But then, Roland had said a lot of things.

Credit due, Joachim had kept himself together, a trim forty, the touch of gray in his hair offering an appropriate note of distinction. Of course that didn't mean the core hadn't rotted. Ten years playing politics is like five spent smoking wyrm, and though the grip he held out to me was attached to a sizable bicep, he had the smile of a man who grinned for a living.

'Lieutenant, good to see you again,' he said, walking me to his desk. 'Would you like some whiskey?'

'I've recently turned teetotal.'

'Water?'

'I've sworn that off as well.'

He took a seat across from me and poured a few fingers of liquor into his own glass. 'Hroudland said you weren't happy to have the boys round your place.'

'But you called me anyway. Guess that makes you a real glutton for punishment.'

'I've been called worse.'

'I'm sure that hurt your feelings. What is it you want me for, Colonel?'

'Commander,' he corrected.

'I didn't realize the Crown promoted decommissioned soldiers.'

'I'm the Supreme Commander of the Great War Veterans' Association, by the will of my brother soldiers.'

'I voted myself Emperor of Miradin, but ain't no one sending me any rents.'

'I'm having trouble figuring where this animosity comes from – I hadn't thought I'd done you any particular harm.'

'The world has been cruel to me, Joachim – I take it out on whomever I can.'

He backed off my abuse with a laugh, more evidence he'd turned politician. The man I'd known would have dropped me over half of what I'd offered. Or tried to. 'I'd hoped we could keep this conversation civil, but as it seems you're too busy for simple courtesy, I'll get right to the meat of it.' He poured whiskey through a forced grin, then set the glass back down on the table. 'Rhaine Montgomery,' he said.

Cold fingers ran up the base of my back, but they didn't show on my face. 'You'll need to add a verb for that to count as a full sentence.'

'I'm told she's in Low Town.'

'Were you?'

'And I'm told you're looking for her.'

'You're well informed.'

'Look, Lieutenant, there's no reason for you to play coy. I know that the general asked you to try and find his daughter and persuade her to come home. I know this because he told me. He told me because we've known each other most of my life, because his son was the closest friend I've ever had and the best man there ever was. We all want the same thing here.'

'Which is?'

'Rhaine out of Low Town. Back home, in Kor's Heights. Safe and free of trouble.'

That was certainly what I wanted, though I was unprepared to speak for anyone else. 'Who'd make trouble for her?'

'The world is a dangerous place.'

'I sometimes have that inkling.'

'Rhaine is . . . an impressive young woman. But she's out of her element, as would be obvious to any cutpurse who happens upon her.'

'So you're concerned that she might be mugged on the way to market?'

'This conversation would go much quicker if you stopped pretending to be a fool. Roland Montgomery was murdered by powerful men, men who feared his crusade would bring them to ruin. I don't imagine they've forsworn violence in the twelve years since his death, and I'm quite certain they'd happily send Rhaine to meet her brother, rather than see her make them any trouble.'

'On that at least, we very much agree.'

He nodded firmly. 'I called you here today to let you know that the Association stands ready to assist you in your task.'

'And what exactly is it you think you can help me with?'

'Have you met Rhaine?'

No point in being honest. 'I haven't yet had the pleasure.'

'She can be rather . . . single-minded in her thinking.'

'I'm getting that impression.'

'The point being, if you do find her, I'm not at all certain she'll listen to what you have to say. And if she doesn't, if you can't get her home, I'd like you to come back and tell me.'

'What would you do that I couldn't?'

'We're not entirely lacking numbers. The very least I can do is detail a few men to look after her. The greatest tragedy of my life was my failure to keep Roland safe. By the Firstborn and all his kin, I won't make the same mistake with Rhaine.'

Prevarication is not an easy thing to do competently, for all that most of us get plenty of practice. We blink, look away, scuff at suddenly discovered flecks of grime. And that's just with little things – 'I was at the bar with Seinfried all last night. I'll have those five coppers for you tomorrow.' Try lying for your life sometime, feel how tight your collar wraps around your throat, that desperate itch on the palms of your hands. Even people who are professionally dishonest usually don't have any particular talent for it, getting by on balls and vigor.

To do it right, I mean to do it really well, you've gotta believe. You've gotta wrap your arms around it, hold it with both hands, take it as a lover. You've gotta build the rest of yourself around this false core, till it's as automatic as breathing. Till if someone shook you awake in the middle of the night your first words would confirm white as black. Credit where it's due, Pretories had it down to a two-step. If I hadn't known otherwise, I'd have trusted him. It was impressive, in a certain amoral way.

But then, I wasn't exactly an amateur when it came to deceit. 'If it's all the same, I think I'd like that glass of whiskey now,' I said.

'Of course,' he smiled, and poured me a few fingers.

I drank it slowly, making a show of my concern. 'I didn't want this gig, Commander,' I said.

He nodded sympathetically.

'I've got my own work in front of me, and it doesn't include sprinting after a self-destructive heiress.'

'I don't imagine.'

'But the general needed something from me, and I told him I'd do what I could.'

'You're an honorable man.'

The bullshit was waist high and rising. 'The point being, I'm happy to let someone more competent take over, if I thought they could handle it.'

'Go on.'

'I've made some inquiries into Rhaine's whereabouts.'

'And?'

'Nothing yet, but something will shake out. In truth, I don't imagine finding her to be the problem. Convincing her to return – or protecting her if she won't go – that's going to be the sticky part. And I wouldn't turn up my nose at help, if it comes to that.'

'We'll be here to offer it,' he said, shaking my hand firmly and leading me to the door.

I stopped in the front hall for a moment, preparing to face the heat and staring up at Roland's portrait. It was life-sized, but somehow I remembered him as being bigger. One of the men milling about noticed my attention, propped himself up from where he'd been sitting, and approached me. No easy task, as he was amidst that unfortunate but sadly not uncommon coterie of veterans that had come back from Nestria with less body than they'd left. He took the hat off his head with the hand that wasn't crippled and held it to his chest. 'Hell of a man, wasn't he?'

I rolled my eyes and hurried out.

IO

The first time I had met Roland Montgomery he had come very close to killing me.

It was a year after the disaster at Beneharnum had proved the futility of waging warfare in ranked formation even to the most hidebound traditionalist. Tactics had developed accordingly – trenches were miserable, cramped and cold, but they kept you out of sight of any practitioners that might be waiting, and they were moderately effective against cannon. We'd long settled into the steady attritional warfare that had come to characterize the conflict, an endless succession of raids and counter-raids, of static lines and fighting rats for food.

Those of us in the ranks, that is – the brass still dreamed of a break out, of a sudden puncture to the Dren lines that would allow us to roll them back all the way to Donknacht. It was a fantasy which would take a long time to die, and would carry a hell of a lot of men with it.

My hopes of advancement had proved prescient, though I attributed that less to any particular genius on my part than to the decimation of the officer class during the opening phase of the conflict. If things continued at that rate they'd be making drummer boys into brigadier generals inside of six months. Even with my rapid rise through the ranks, my presence at the meeting was out of the ordinary. Calling a meeting of officers before committing troops to battle was a common enough activity, including anyone so far down the pole as myself was most certainly not.

But then, Roland Montgomery was no ordinary officer.

This was early on in his career, before his glorious charge at Gravotte carried the field, before he withstood seven weeks besieged in the Matz salient absent of outside support. The legend was in its infancy, but it was easy enough to see the seed. He was, first and foremost, strikingly handsome. It was the worst kept secret in the Thirteen Lands that the brass was thick with buggerers, and looking around at my fellow officers, there were no fair few gazing at the colonel with something more akin to adoration than respect. But even amongst those of us for whom a well-toned buttock was no particular object of affection, it was hard to miss the fact that Roland Montgomery seemed to have been hewn from marble rather than pushed out a womb. He radiated health and good cheer, no small feat given that he was effectively in the midst of an inconceivably vast infirmary, and we lost a hundred men a day to the flux. Added to that was his heritage, that he was the latest in a long line of Montgomerys that had pursued the Crown's enemies in foreign lands, that his father even then was held with something resembling reverence by large swathes of the ranks.

All of these were secondary, however, to the indefinable aura of certainty that he carried with him like a heavy winter cloak. Every motion he made and every word he uttered seemed to carry with it a sense of profound meaning, as if the Firstborn himself had decreed that, at this exact moment, Roland was to smile or shake his head or greet you. He was, in short, a man of destiny.

You strained to listen when he spoke, pushed past friends to approach him, found yourself held captive by the deep blue of his eyes and the unshaken strength of his convictions.

So contradicting the plan he had just put forth – suggesting that it might even be possible to contradict it, that he was capable of error even in theory – took a bit of firmness on my part. 'I'm afraid I have a concern, sir.'

It was also not an activity likely to gain me any friends. As befit my relatively lowly rank, I was in the back of the twenty or so soldiers clustered about the colonel. The front row was made up of men most similar to Montgomery, in background, position and pedigree. The terrible casualties we'd suffered had allowed a few of us to ascend to the middle rungs of the military hierarchy, but the upper echelons were still composed exclusively of aristocrats.

I tried not to hate them. That they were in Nestria at all meant something, when so many of their fellows had found convenient excuses for remaining at home – sudden injuries, unexpected nuptials. And I didn't imagine Roland would keep around him anyone whose courage or fortitude was suspect. But then, impartiality is not my strong suit, and I had to swallow down hard on my contempt to keep it from showing on my face.

They seemed in no hurry to extend me a similar courtesy. The man whom I would later come to know as Joachim Pretories swiveled an eye off the colonel, turned it nasty, and aimed it at me. The rest of his pack joined suit. If I had been operating under any illusion that my opinion was wanted, the black looks I got from Roland's inner circle were enough to convince me otherwise. I was not there to speak; I was there as a demonstration of Roland Montgomery's populist leanings, of the affection and love he had for his men, even for the lowliest of us.

By contrast, Roland himself seemed almost pleasantly surprised at my interruption. 'Of course, Lieutenant,' Roland said. 'Speak your mind.'

I cleared my throat uncomfortably. Back then I was still concerned with my thick Low Town patois, widely considered by the rest of the Empire to be somewhere between repulsive and incomprehensible. In later years I would come to recognize it as an asset, lulling my audience into a false sense of superiority. Most folk born north of the river Andel dismissed me after my first sentence, assumed I wasn't anything more than a thug, didn't learn otherwise till it was too late. But at that moment, surrounded by baronets and princelings, I was conscious of every dropped syllable and swallowed consonant.

I brushed towards the front, through a mass of men wishing me ill, toward the board and the map that Roland had been using to indicate our plan of attack. 'These six inches,' I said, pointing to a corresponding spot, 'are three hundred yards of muck, utterly without cover of any kind. This light brown shading,' I moved my finger a tick, 'an uphill slog that narrows the front to the point where our forces can be massacred in detail. And these markers here,' again shifting my aim to the blue pins meant to indicate the enemy forces, 'are at least three battalions of the most vicious, competent, battle-hardened souls the Firstborn ever saw fit to inflict upon our benighted world. A simple statement of the facts at hand should be sufficient to show that what you propose is, in short, impossible.'

No one said anything for a while. Most of them seemed to take the criticism as the product of sheer gutlessness. For a bare handful, perhaps, my words served reminder that their bodies were composed of flesh and sinew, as were the men in their command. Roland remained absolutely passive, his faint smile unaffected by my arguments.

It was up to his leader of cavalry, a major with the exhausting name of Conrad Baldwin de Camville, to take the offensive. By this point in the war it was long since clear that the continued existence of the cavalry arm was an anachronism – the best pedigreed stud in the Empire was useful only as a pack animal or fresh meat. For that substantial portion of the gentry who had grown up with a saber in hand and dreams of valiant charges in mind, this was a hard truth to accept. Conrad was very much one of those. He still wore the full kit, six-inch silver spurs on boots of freshly shined black leather. His jacket and pants were bright crimson, fringed with gold, and his sword had a pearl the size of a bull's eye set in the pommel.

'No one is suggesting that our objective will be gained without cost, Lieutenant,' he said, stressing the three syllables in my rank in a fashion more reserved for other, less flattering epithets. Traitor, for instance. Or child molester. 'But the ridge is the lynchpin of the entire area. Any hope of our regaining northern Nestria relies on taking it.'

'It is indeed, sir – and they hold it. They've held it for the last two months, and they've been strengthening it the entire time.'

Another one of Roland's cronies jumped in. 'What is this man even doing here? This meeting is for captains and higher.'

'Our captains keep dying in suicidal charges,' I said. 'I've been in operational command of "A" company for two months.'

'All our information is that the Dren have denuded their forces in that sector,' Baldwin continued without pause. I suppose it was the calvaryman's mentality, attack, attack, attack. It was more effective in conversation than in combat.

'I am that sector, Major,' I said. 'I sleep in its mud and get wet in its runoff. I've watched it day and night, and if the Dren are going weak-kneed on us, I've yet to see any proof.'

'Perhaps your eye isn't sufficiently trained to recognize the weaknesses in their positions.'

'Your own must be exceptionally keen, to make them out a mile and a half behind our lines.'

Baldwin bristled like he'd been spat on. I had gone too far, all but accused him of outright cowardice. The nobility's attachment to the duel had survived a year of mass murder that dwarfed anything the Thirteen Lands had seen in two millennia of recorded warfare. One would think that the sacrifice of a quarter of the nation's menfolk would have been enough to satisfy anyone's taste for bloodshed, but one would have reckoned without the bewildering stupidity of the aristocracy. Barely a week went by without two blue bloods squaring off against each other over some real or imagined insult. It seemed a great deal of trouble to take for little enough reason – if you were so desperate for oblivion, all you needed to do was step ten feet outside of the forward trenches and wait for a Dren bowman to notice you.

Roland put one hand on my would-be killer's shoulder, and brought him back down into his chair. 'Peace, Major, peace. The lieutenant is simply doing what we've asked of him.' Like a weeping child at a mother's touch, Baldwin slipped swiftly from furious to pacified. 'Please continue with your assessment of the situation, Lieutenant,' Roland said, turning back to me.

'I've made it, sir. They'll have the high ground, and they'll be waiting for us.'

'We'll have the numbers!' Baldwin insisted.

'But we won't be able to use them – we'll get funneled through the defile, and their cannon and missilists will pick us apart. That's the best-case scenario. Worst case, they've got a practitioner or two stashed away, just waiting for a chance to erase us *en masse*.'

For a brief moment the assemblage put aside their desperate desire for glory and considered the grim possibility I'd put before them. The war had begun with the Throne calling for twenty thousand volunteers. After Beneharnum they'd called for another fifty. Seventy thousand proved to be the total number of suicidally foolish men living in the empire proper, so they moved comfortably into conscription. After six months we had a quarter of a million men beneath the colors. The Dren followed suit, and by the end of the first winter our respective forces had spread across the continent, choking the hills with trenches and blockhouses.

But while you could always cull up another ten thousand warm bodies to press into service, bog farmers and penny tailors, supporting them with fully trained practitioners was another story altogether. The Academy was a partial answer, funneling through anyone with a spark of talent, going in children and coming out weapons. But even so, there were never enough to adequately support the vast forces, and you never knew whether the ranks across from you were stiffened by a man with the ability to call down fire at will. It was a rather terrifying coin toss, as a small team of practitioners on a well-sighted spot were enough to turn the best-planned offensive into suicidal folly.

Roland remained unfazed by the picture I'd painted. He pretty much remained unfazed regardless of what you put in front of him. I wasn't at all sure this was a virtue. Steady nerves are critical on the battlefield, but the world is a terrible and shocking place, and past a certain point equanimity seems indistinguishable from idiocy. 'All of our reports say that the Dren have been massing their practitioners further south, preparing for their own offensive operations.'

'Our reports serve excellently as bathroom tissue. Beyond that, I've yet to be convinced of their value.'

One of the other officers, a captain, began to chuckle, but he turned it quickly into a nervous cough. Colonel Montgomery kept smiling, but to tell by his eyes he was starting to find my objections less than amusing. 'Headquarters has determined that the breakout should begin in sector three.'

Speechifying was never my forte – one on one I can generally figure out what I need to do to get someone moving in my direction, but pool enough of them together and the sheer mass of idiocy becomes immobile. It would have been better to have kept my mouth shut. But I was even worse at that than I was at oratory. 'Unfortunately, the Dren have some say in that decision as well – and by all evidence, they seem to be of the opinion that sector three would be of better use as an abattoir.'

Roland leaned back against the table and brought his fist up beneath his chin. At any given moment you could have frozen him in time and painted him into a portrait – *Hero Making The Hard Decisions*, this one would have been called. The pause lasted long enough for us all to appreciate it, and then he pushed himself up and came towards me at a rapid clip. I managed not to flinch.

'This man,' Roland said, slapping one hand onto my shoulder and staring at me with an intensity I found at once disturbing and enthralling, 'is the reason we're going to win the war.' He locked eyes with me for a moment, then turned about quickly to address the rest of the crowd. 'There is no finer man alive than the Rigun soldier, no truer patriot, no more honorable and dedicated warrior. And before us stands his very ideal!'

That I in no way agreed with this sentiment – neither in reference to me particularly nor as a broader commentary on the state of our population – did nothing to lessen the pride I felt at that moment. I stood up straighter, puffed out my chest, felt my heartbeat quicken.

'And it's because of men like you that the Empire will be victorious, whatever the numberless hordes the Dren throw against us, whatever the obstacles to overcome.' He turned his attention back on me, once again the lone holdout against his insanity, if the swell of enthusiastic faces surrounding me were any indication. 'You said the task before us is impossible – with men like you leading our forces, I have no doubt we can achieve it.'

The meeting broke with a hearty cheer of excitement. Never did a group of people sprint so enthusiastically towards their own demise. I didn't blame Roland for what he was – enough people tell you you're special, you can't help but come to believe it.

Things went pretty much the way I expected they would. The Dren cut us down with their usual brutal competence. Our men died in waves on the flat terrain, till the mounds of corpses themselves became our cover. After three hours of massacre came the order to retreat. I spent that night huddled around a bonfire with the skeletal remnants of my company, hoping the burn wounds running along most of my right arm didn't fester.

Above a certain position of prominence, the only reward for failure is promotion. And in fairness, the blame could be apportioned up and down the chain. Rather than do so, they just decided to call it a victory. The broadsheets wrote our stalled charge up as a heroic defense, and they promoted Roland from colonel to general.

I learned two things about Montgomery that day, two things that stuck with me throughout the remainder of the war and into the dark days beyond. The first was that his men would follow him off a cliff. The second was that he would lead them there.

II

By the time I left the Association headquarters the sun had clouded over like it was going to rain – it wasn't, but it looked like it, and the day was that much hotter for the hope. I threaded my way back through Low Town, south past the Earl, skirting the docks, stopping midway down a side street a few blocks from Kirentown. At my feet a homeless man with a cloth wrapped around the top half of his face begged alms in monotone.

'Hello, Eloway.' I dropped a coin into his tin cup.

'Hello, Warden,' he said, his spidery rambling replaced by a healthy tenor. 'Anyone around?'

A couple of corner boys lounged at the intersection. 'Nobody that matters.'

Eloway breathed a sigh of relief and pulled the stained cloth above his brow, revealing a pair of eyes that showed no immediate evidence of dysfunction. 'By the Lost One, it gets hot in there.'

'I don't understand why you still bother with this get up.'

'Force of habit, I suppose. Besides, you'd be amazed how much I hear sitting against alley walls – people tend to think the blindfold means I'm deaf as well.'

Eloway the Blind was not a beggar. He dressed like a beggar, looked like one even, a too-thin forty with bad skin and worse teeth. And he begged, a mewling patter that brought in more coin than a day of honest labor at the mills. But he was not a beggar, and in fact any reasonable audit of his finances would have placed him at the opposite end of the spectrum.

Eloway the Blind was the executive of the most efficient system of spies, plants and spotters operating anywhere within the city proper. The shiftless youth outside your window sent word to him on what you ate for breakfast, and the ten-penny whore you slummed with last night reported every nasty itch you asked her to scratch. His army was the dispossessed, the unwanted and unnoticed. Probably Black House could best him in the suburbs, though more than one underpaid serving boy cribbed their meager earnings selling scraps from their master's table. And of course his tendrils didn't reach outside of the capital into the countryside, or to foreign shores. But south of the Old City he knew everything there was to know, and if you needed to find a man or take a peek at his journal, Eloway was whom you spoke to.

Assuming you had the coin – though he asked for it, Eloway didn't run a charity.

'You got my cigarette?' he asked.

'Are you seriously trying to shake me down?'

Eloway tapped at his rags. 'Pockets kill the effect.'

'Śakra's cock, you think maybe you take this charade a little far?' But I rolled one up for him anyway.

He took it with a smile. 'What did Joachim Pretories want?'

Everything worth knowing, like I said. 'Trying to run me, Eloway?'

'What do you cost?'

'More than you could afford,' I said, though it wasn't true. 'I'm looking for a woman.'

'A clean one should run you a couple of argents, but this part of town you could get serviced for half that, if you ain't particular.'

'Name's Rhaine Montgomery, though she won't be using it. Early twenties, red hair, blue eyes. Top crust and trying to hide it. She overpaid for lodgings, and she's probably been took by half the clip men on whatever street she's holed up in.'

'Montgomery? As in Edwin Montgomery's daughter?'

Facility with names was a requirement of Eloway's position. 'Yeah.'

He ashed my cigarette on the ground next to him. 'I'm a patriot, Warden,' he said, impressively dignified given that his costume included a smattering of fresh dog shit. 'And not interested in causing the general any harm.'

'He's the one asked me to find her,' I said. 'Does that mean I get a discount?'

'I'm not that much of a patriot. When do you need it by?'

'What time is it?'

'Round two.'

'I'd like it before one-thirty.'

He chuckled and quoted a price. I quoted a lesser one. We reached an agreement, and I counted it out and handed it to him. One of the boys slipped over and took it, then ran off. 'Send word to the Earl?' he asked.

I nodded and he pulled his rag back over his eyes. As I left the cover of the alleyway a passing merchant looked Eloway over sadly and slipped an argent into his cup. Eloway's patter turned grateful, though I suspected beneath the blindfold he was winking.

12

It was no more temperate in the Earl than it was outside. But it was darker, and that was enough to pretend. I didn't bother to spark a lantern, finding my way to a chair in the corner and lighting a twist of vine. Between that and my general laziness, sleep came quickly enough.

I was awakened by Adeline standing over me. More accurately, I awakened with Adeline standing over me. For all I knew she'd been waiting silently for three-quarters of an hour, counting the seconds until some unrelated incident brought me up from sleep.

'Howdy darlin',' I began, blinking myself alert. 'How's the queen?' Adeline was wide-hipped and plain, and looking at her you wouldn't call her a pretty woman. But later on you'd remember her that way. Finding her was one of the few true pieces of luck Adolphus had ever received, and holding on to her evidence of greater wisdom than he sometimes displayed.

Her lips hinted at a smile, as if afraid to breach etiquette.

'Staying cool?' In keeping with the demeanor, her voice rarely rose above a murmur.

'Trying to.'

'I'll bring you some lemonade.'

'My angel.'

Despite the heat, Adeline didn't sweat, seemed barely even to breathe. It was difficult to square this passivity with the fact that she oversaw virtually everything that was required for the continued functioning of the Earl, as well as the needs of her husband and adopted son. 'I heard you had a talk with Wren.'

That was surprising – the boy was sullen in childhood, and even more loquacious youths tend to lose their taste for dialogue after entering adolescence. 'I know, he shouldn't be associating with such an unsavory element.'

'He said you caught him practicing the Art.'

'Is that what he was doing?'

'He said you told him you'll find him a teacher.'

'He's a chatty one, our Wren.'

'He won't sit on the shelf forever.'

'I know,' I said. 'I know.'

'So you're taking care of it.' Not a question, though phrased as such.

'I am.'

She nodded.

Talking to Adeline is like searching for meaning in the bottom of a tea cup, or the quivering in a line of fresh entrails. But near on fifteen years of practice had given me a feel for the hints which indicated movement beneath the waters. 'What else you got?'

'Adolphus.'

'He's a drag. What say the two of us ditch him and make for the coast, buy a little cottage and sleep the days away?'

She didn't laugh. 'I don't like his new friends.'

'Neither do I.'

'Then you'll speak to him?'

'He ain't Wren, Adeline.'

'He listens to you.'

'Not on this.'

She sighed unhappily, then disappeared, coming back after a few minutes with the promised glass of lemonade. Then she busied herself preparing for the evening trade, cleaning tables, sweeping the floor, activities that required illumination and thus made further repose impossible. I busied myself in the pages of a history tome I'd picked up a week earlier.

After a while a soot-faced boy came calling my name. I waved him over and he passed me a small slip of paper.

The Queen's Palace.

I set in into my pocket, and dug out a tarnished bit of silver. 'This is for you,' I said, 'for coming out here in the heat. Make sure Eloway keeps his greedy little hands off it.' The runner smiled and disappeared.

'Who was that?' Wren asked from behind me. One thing he hadn't lost since I'd fished him out the gutter was his preternatural capacity for quiet. He'd have been fierce at second-story work, though I supposed it was my job to keep him out of that sort of line.

'Your replacement. I need someone working for me I can rely on not to disappear all day.'

'Adolphus had me putting up fliers,' he said, his face red from excitement and not just the heat.

'Putting up fliers?'

'For the Association. For the big rally they're having next week. To remind the Throne of the sacrifices they made for the country, and to renew the bonds of fellowship too long allowed to remain fallow.'

He'd learned these last words that morning. I disliked hearing him parrot them. 'And where's the man himself?'

'They're having a meeting at the local chapter. They want to vote Adolphus chair.' He puffed his chest out, proud of the giant's accomplishments. Under different circumstances I would have found it rather touching. 'They say he was a hero, that he held the line at Aunis all by himself.'

'Did they now?'

'They said I couldn't stay. They said it was for veterans only.' This slight appeared not to have bothered him. 'They seem all right to me.'

There was no reason to be angry at Wren for following his father's orders. I found that I was, all the same. 'But then you don't know anything, so your opinion isn't worth as much as mine.'

It was a cheap shot, but it set him down a notch. 'I was just doing what Adolphus told me.'

'Adolphus is a grown man, and can make his own mistakes – you're a child who eats off my sufferance. So long as that continues, what I say gets the last ring in your ears.' I sipped through my lemonade, wishing it was liquor. 'You see Yancey before you decided to enlist?'

He nodded, no longer smiling. 'Said he's got a gig in Brennock, at the Pig and Fiddle.'

'He say when?'

'After eight.'

'If Adolphus is too busy playing soldier to take care of his responsibilities, then they fall on you. Go help Adeline with dinner. And don't ever make me wait on a message again.'

He gave me a pretty good eye-fuck on the way to the back, but he went. It seemed like today was my day to be the prick. A lot of days are like that, if we're being honest.

I took up a spot in the yard and re-lit the joint I'd fallen asleep over. When that wasn't enough I rolled another, and when that wasn't enough I figured nothing would be, and settled back to watch evening cross the cityscape.

13

I ate an early dinner then started off for Brennock. It was half a trek, and I broke up the monotony with a hit of breath when it felt appropriate, as it often did.

This section of the city was mostly industrial, cavernous mills and foundries with little nightlife to speak of. Yancey's having to play there was a sign of the blight that had overtaken his career, a sharp reversal from the decade of uninterrupted success his talent and drive had earned him.

While playing a private party a year back some noble had said something or done something that made Yancey decide to arrange his face into a different pattern – an understandable impulse, if self-defeating in the long run. He'd gotten out after five months, which was shorter than I had expected – putting a digit on a noble pays out the same as murdering a dockworker. Yancey wasn't soft, but the time he'd spent inside had done him no favors. His eyes were older and there was an occasional tremor to his vibrato. More than that, having gained a reputation for brutalizing members of the audience, his old fans weren't quite so enthused about having him round. He'd been forced into accepting gigs he'd have laughed off not long earlier, which was why I found myself in a shitty bar in an ugly part of the city, surrounded by a group of people who seemed distinctly unenthused to be consuming the poetic stylings of one Yancey the Rhymer.

Ironically his misfortune had been a boon for me – since being deprived of the opportunity to make money off his craft he'd had to put more work into his sideline: playing middleman for rich folks who wanted my services. I felt a little bad about it, but then we're all making our bread off someone's misery. Me more than most, I supposed.

Happily I'd come between sets, so I didn't need to watch him demonstrate his abilities to an unappreciative audience. He was at the counter dripping honey into the ear of a waitress two stone past pretty. She laughed and slapped at him playfully with a dishrag. Whatever else the Rhymer had lost, he could still string together a sentence.

'If it ain't the Duke himself.' He ticked his bare skull toward a side booth and turned back to the maid. 'Pour two beers for us, sugar – my man and I need to hash out some truth, and that always goes better well lubricated.'

The waitress went to get us our drinks, and I followed Yancey to the corner.

Yancey was a small man, with a coiled intensity that kept him constantly in motion. In the past he'd run to thin and wiry, biceps like pulled rope, but his time inside had bloated him and hemmed a ring of flesh around his midsection. Despite that his face seemed thinner and somehow paler, though his lineage was uncrossed Islander and his skin black as ink. He'd always been something of a coxcomb, his sense of style near as sharp as his ear, but lately that too had gone to pot, a casualty of his loss of income or interest.

My ass had barely scraped the wooden bench before he leaned in and tapped a finger against his nose. 'You got a toot for me?'

'Fresh out.'

'Pity.' Breath was a habit Yancey had taken to with unfortunate enthusiasm. 'So how you been?'

'I wouldn't mind getting rained on, like everyone else in the city. How 'bout you?'

'Nah, the heat don't bother me.'

'What's your secret?'

'I get my dick sucked a lot.'

'I didn't know that helped.'

'It helps with everything.' The server came by holding a pair of tankards in front of a pair of plump breasts. 'Something about these Vaalan girls,' he said after she left, sucking his teeth and falling silent – words failing him, for once.

'I'd prefer a woman I could share a carriage seat with.'

'More for me.'

'A lot more.'

Yancey laughed. 'Your boy said you wanted to speak to me on something.' His grin was wide. 'I remember when he came up to my waist, and wouldn't meet my eyes. Child's growing.'

'As it turns out, he's the purpose of the conversation.'

He motioned for me to continue. 'Your mouth ain't sewn shut.'

No one was listening, but I took a look around anyway. 'Wren has the gift.'

'Indeed.' He took a sip from his brew, white foam around his pink lips.

'I need someone who can give him the ins and outs of it, and who isn't affiliated with the Throne – someone as far off their map as you can get.'

'I'm no practitioner.'

'But somewhere, in your long list of acquaintances, I suspect you've a person who fits my description.'

The Islanders had fled their homeland a millennium back, taking to the seas as it disappeared beneath the waves, a catastrophe so inconceivable and distant it had long ago merged into myth. Centuries of living as half-wanted guests in foreign lands had given them an aversion to government that was virtually a racial trait. Their entire civilization flourished out of sight of the authorities. They had their own banking houses, their own religious practices – and their own magical traditions. After the war the Bureau of Magical Affairs had made it their business to bring the nation's practitioners under thumb, combing the disparate threads of the Art into a single weave – but the Bureau of Magical Affairs, like every other government organ, held small sway amongst the seafarers.

I imagined there were other avenues of the Art that the Throne had yet to strangle. Tarasaighn augurers drying herbs deep in the swamps of their homeland, heretics drawing otherworldly diagrams and whispering strange prayers – but I didn't know any of them. I knew the Rhymer, and I hoped he'd come through for me. He always had before.

Yancey drummed his fingers against the table, unconsciously and in perfect rhythm. After a moment he matched the beat with a nod. 'Yeah, I might know somebody – how far out you want to look?'

'Far as I can get.'

'There's a witch-woman, lives in the Isthmus. I've never had occasion to seek her services but word on high is she's legit – even the mobs toe her line, leave her little offerings and make sure not to cross her.'

'And the Throne remains blissfully ignorant of her activities?'

'Brother, her corner of Rigus, there ain't no Throne.'

'She got a name?'

'Mazzie. Mazzie of the Stained Bone. Ever hear it?'

'Muttered under the occasional breath. You think you could put us in touch?'

'I'll send someone around tonight – Mazzie keeps late hours. She gives the go ahead, I'll leave directions to her place for you tomorrow morning.'

'Stand-up, as always.'

Yancey was confident enough in his character not to be

particularly grateful for my validation. He went back to his drink. I realized suddenly we'd run out of things to talk about. I didn't remember that happening so much between us, back in the day. 'How's your mom?'

'She's all right. She asks about you some.'

That was a lie, though a kind one. I'd been close to Ma Dukes once, before my blindness and stupidity had put her son into danger some years back. Yancey had eventually forgiven me for my foolishness, but his mother wasn't so casual about the peril I'd brought down upon her seed.

I pulled a couple of ochres from out of my money pouch. 'I almost forgot – I owe you some coin for dropping my name to the Count of Brekenridge.'

'Yeah?' His eyes narrowed quizzically. 'You sure?'

'I'm sure,' I said, setting them next to his drink.

He looked at the coins for a long moment, then raked them off the table. 'Sweetness, bring me a bottle of something that bubbles,' he yelled over his shoulder, before turning back to face me. 'You sticking 'round to enjoy it?'

'I've got somewhere to be,' I said, standing. 'And I imagine our server will be a better companion – help keep you cool.'

His laughter was well bought at twice the price.

14

The Queen's Palace was not the second, nor fit for the first. A flophouse a few blocks from the docks, ugly even by the standards of an ugly trade. Its clientele consisted mostly of streetwalkers renting love nests by the hour, and addicts one short rung above abject destitution.

I knew it all right. Better than I'd like to admit, well enough that I didn't need to waste any time dancing with the clerk at the front desk. I plopped down an argent and tapped two fingers beside it, and my silver was replaced with the register. There wasn't a real name to be found, but one from three days prior was so obviously made up that I felt certain I had my quarry. I took note of the room number and nodded to the receptionist. He placed the faded tome back beneath the counter and went back to not seeing anything. I slipped upstairs.

The lock on her door was nothing of the sort, a bit of tin I could have opened with my fingernail, though for appearance's sake I slipped a thin spurt of metal out from my satchel and spent a few seconds teasing it open.

The door swung open on a small room, a largish closet really, barely big enough for a small bureau and a lumpy bed. She was sitting on this last, staring out at the alley below, but she turned when the hinges squeaked, pulling a small dagger from beneath the pillow. The hilt was burnished silver with a fire opal in the pommel, and she held it towards me, less a weapon than a talisman to ward away evil.

I closed the door after me. 'Whatever you're paying, it's too much.'

'What are you doing in my room?' she hissed, torn between fury and relief that I wasn't someone worse.

'This is your room? I thought for sure it was the High Chancellor's office.'

'Stay away from me,' she said, waving her blade about in an unbecoming moment of melodrama. 'I'll cut you if you come any closer.'

'I wouldn't. You'll need to pawn that thing in a day or two, and bloodstains will bring down the value.'

Her shoulders dropped six inches, and she set the knife back on her bed. 'What do you want?'

I took a seat on the edge of it. 'A hundred thousand ochres and a country estate – but at the moment I'll settle for you back up in Kor's Heights where you belong.'

'What made you think my answer would be any different than it was last night?'

'I'd hoped another day of futility might slake your thirst.'

She brought her spine into perfect vertical alignment. 'Then you didn't understand who you're dealing with.'

'Better than you'd think, maybe. I've had some experience with the Montgomery stubbornness.' A black stump of a candle flickered from the windowsill. It would be out soon, and the houseboy would gouge her for the replacement. 'How are you so sure your brother's death wasn't what it looked like? You say Roland was a hero, fine. A hero ain't a saint. So he sought the occasional

94

release of a woman, and didn't mind paying for it. There's not so much sin in that.'

Her face turned the color of her hair, but she managed to keep her voice even. 'My brother wasn't some . . . whoremonger.'

'You'd know that, at ten? Roland the sort of man to divulge bedroom peccadilloes to his little sister?'

'I knew my brother.'

'You didn't, not really – and anyway, you've spent the last twelve years turning him into a saint. You've dismissed the most likely possibility because you don't want it to be true, and you run around stirring up trouble because it's more exciting than going home and living your life.' The bed was the length of a coffin, and our faces nearly touched.

'So that's it then? Turn tail and head back to Daddy? Marry some callow noble, take up crochet and pump out children?'

'You won't find having your throat slit any more fulfilling.'

'I'm getting closer.'

'To an unmarked grave, maybe.'

She shook her head firmly. 'I paid a visit to the Veterans' Association this afternoon.'

'I'm sure they were pleased to see you.'

'You'd think so, wouldn't you? You'd think that Joachim Pretories would pay every courtesy to the sister of his dead commander, especially with Roland's picture papering the walls.'

'Thinking gets me into trouble. I avoid it whenever possible.'

'He told me I didn't have any business being there. He told me to go back home, and he told me it in a fashion I found rather aggressive.'

'Joachim Pretories is a bad man to antagonize.'

'Then you do think he was involved.'

'I don't think anything, I just told you that. But were I to break with habit, I'd tell you that whatever sins may or may not darken the man's conscience, he can't very well sit quiet while you knock about the city, all but accusing him of complicity in your brother's murder.'

'He's hiding something; I saw that in his eyes. If I work on him hard enough, it'll shake loose.'

'Joachim Pretories has been playing the game since before you started to bleed – ten years threading the narrows, and you think he'll break at a sharp word from you? Go home, Rhaine. You've had your adventure, gotten an eyeful of the slums you can chat up with your intimates. There's a surplus of warm bodies growing cold in Low Town – we don't need Kor's Heights to start exporting them.'

She bared her teeth in a fashion that made me think of a wolf, or at least an unfriendly dog. 'That's all you think of me? That my leaving home was . . . a whim?'

'I sure as hell hope so – if you planned things out this way, you're more a fool than I'd supposed.'

I was sure that would spark her, but it seemed to do the opposite. She looked down at her lap, then gave a little smile, the first I think I'd seen of it. She reminded me very much of Roland at that moment. 'Things haven't gone . . . as I'd anticipated.' Our legs brushed against each other. 'I suppose you must not think much of me.'

'I don't know what to think of you. You're a lot of things all at once. I'd like you to have time to figure out which of those to commit to.'

'What I am is someone who needs justice for her brother. I can see that leaving Father like I did seems the product of impulse. But my coming here was not. I've thought about it every day since Roland . . .'

'Yes.'

She didn't say anything for a while, which seemed very rare for her. In the quiet I caught a view of the little root of misery that had blossomed into perpetual belligerence. 'Roland's death emptied out Father completely. Even as a child I could see the change. He was a great man, once. But after we got the news . . .' she shrugged. 'He turned to his histories, and his garden, and he withered away quietly. I began to shout just to be heard. It was . . . difficult.' She turned hard, as if to pay me back for her unguarded moment. 'You couldn't understand.'

'I had a sister, once. A mother, father – the whole set.' It was hard not to hate them a little, these thin-skins from Kor's Heights, for whom a single death was an unimaginable tragedy. 'Bad things happen to us, Rhaine. The reasons don't matter. You carry it as best you can.'

'There wasn't a reason behind Roland's murder?'

'Knowing it won't make a difference.'

'When I know the reason, I'll know who's to be held responsible.'

'And?'

'And I'll bring him to justice.'

'Where?'

'What?'

'To what court will you bring them?'

'I don't understand.'

'Say that everything you think is true. Say that Roland's murder was the result of some elaborate conspiracy. Let's even go so far as to pretend that your amateur sleuthing is enough to sniff out the culprit, to find a trail twelve years fallow. Do you suppose the men who killed him are going to let you shout it from the rooftops?' I shook my head. 'They'll stretch you out right along with your brother.'

'The authorities . . .'

'Roland was all but an enemy of the state – you think Black House will be in any hurry to chase after his murderer?'

'My father is a powerful man. He's got plenty of friends in high places.'

'Your father sent me to hurry you on home – if you're relying on him for backing, your thinking is crooked as an alleyway.'

It was easier to get angry than to admit to folly. So she got angry. 'No one seems much interested in finding justice for my brother.'

'Meaning?'

'It means that rather than foil me at every turn, perhaps you should offer some help. Roland was your friend, after all.'

'I keep hearing that.'

'You were at his birthday party,' she said, almost an accusation.

A pause. 'I didn't think you remembered.'

'I remember everything about that night,' she said. 'It was the last time I saw him alive. He moved out of the house the next morning.'

I guess that argument with his father had been worse than I'd realized. 'Roland didn't have friends,' I said. 'He had followers. And if I was the latter, I'd sap you unconscious and drag you back home.'

'You'll need to, if you want to get me out of Low Town. I'll learn the truth or die looking for it. There's such a thing as justice.' But I wasn't sure if it was an assertion or a question.

'Truth is what the man holding the whip says it is, and justice what the strong do to the weak. You think otherwise because you've lived your life in a bubble made of money – and you ought to get back there as soon as you can, before the world disabuses you of your innocence in brutal fashion.'

She looked away from me for a while. When she looked back it was clear nothing I'd said had made a difference. 'Tell Father I'm going forward, with or without him, with or without you. My brother deserved better.'

'Most of us do,' I admitted. 'And few of us get it.'

But she wasn't listening – she'd gone back to staring out the window at the sordid landscape beneath us. I stood from the lumpy bed and moved to the exit, not exactly a trek. 'It cost me five argents to find you,' offering it as a parting shot. 'It wouldn't cost double to make sure no one ever finds you again.'

I took a last look at her as the door closed – I shouldn't have, but I did.

15

There's nothing half so foul as a body that's spent some time in the water, and I've seen enough of the world's unpleasantness to be something of an authority on the subject. The flesh takes on this viscous, wormy color between curdled cream and bone, and the eyes swell and bloat. After a day of immersion the skin starts to slough, peels right off the leg like a stocking, toenails and all. Plus the canal isn't exactly fresh water, so you can garnish that description with the stench common to anything that's been marinating in the main thoroughfare for the city's waste, ripe faeces and acrid urine. Vile as it was, our man hadn't been swimming long, and it was easy enough to make out his identity. I nodded at Crispin, and he nodded at the guard, and he tossed the sheet over the corpse.

It was four or five months after Roland's birthday party. I hadn't seen him since, but then I'd been busy. He'd been busy as well, as the rancid meat in front of me evidenced.

I lit a cigarette to drown out the smell. Crispin did the same. 'Did you know him?' my partner asked.

'Timory Half-hand,' I said, pointing to the appendage left dangling out from beneath the thin cloth with which he'd been inexpertly covered. It was malformed, three stubby sticks of flesh, a defect of birth rather than the product of accident or violence, nature being crueler than either. 'He moved dreamvine and the occasional clipped argent. Don't know why anyone would go to the trouble of killing him.'

'Yes, you do,' Crispin responded.

I nodded and we walked off.

'They're getting bolder,' Crispin said, threading his way around a beggar calling for alms against the alley wall. 'That's the third one this month.'

'Small fish, though. Unaffiliated with the syndicates, unprotected by any of the major powers.'

'They're flexing their muscles. Not even bothering to hide it. You see that broadsheet they posted last week? That the Hand of the Firstborn would wipe the poison dealers from the streets, make Rigus a paradise for the working man?'

'I had someone read it to me.'

We paused for a moment at an intersection, the crowd breaking around us like a swift-moving river. In a ditch next to us a street dog was happily consuming a fresh turd, deposited there by some member of the citizenry fussy enough to avoid doing their business in the street.

'And yet despite the death of young Timory,' Crispin began, 'we wait in vain for Low Town's promised rebirth.'

Barefoot in the sludge a boy stalked towards the mutt, a long wooden pole poised overhead. Once in range he struck the mongrel's back full force. It reared and snapped back at him, then ran off. The child laughed uproariously, eyes fixed on mine as if daring a reprimand.

'Looks pretty heavenly to me.'

I flicked my smoke into the gutter, and the urchin sprinted off.

'Thoughts?' Crispin asked.

'I could get breakfast.'

'It must be quite a burden, such depth of perception.'

'I muddle through,' I said, heading towards a nearby restaurant. We took a seat at a table. Crispin ordered steak and eggs and I did the same.

'After we finish up here,' he said, 'I think I'll pay a visit to the Veterans' Association, see if I can't shake anything loose.'

'Yes, Montgomery always struck me as a man likely to bend in the face of the wind.'

'A man was murdered. We find murderers.'

'Do we? When was the last time we were in Low Town, looking over the corpse of a petty criminal?'

'I imagine our boy had people. I imagine they'd be interested in bringing his killer to justice.'

'His mother disowned him when he popped out a cripple, and if he's got siblings they're too smart to admit it.' The server brought over two cups of coffee, black and lukewarm. 'Three Timorys a day find themselves dead in Low Town.'

'They aren't killed by armed rebels, advocating overthrow of the state.'

'Neither was this one, best as we know.'

'Best as we can prove.'

'As you like.' But I wasn't happy about it either, and couldn't stay silent. 'What do you care if the Association wants to cut up a few drug dealers? It saves us the trouble.'

'He'll move on to the syndicates soon enough. Word is, Roland's been making threats toward the Giroies.'

'You on their payroll?' That was a joke, of course, if not a particularly good one. Crispin was honest to a degree that I found quite tiring. Also, he was fabulously rich.

'I'd prefer if Rigus didn't descend into open warfare. Besides, you know as well as I do that Roland Montgomery doesn't give a damn about the mobs. Taking them on just serves to sharpen his blade. Once he's consolidated his position in Low Town, he'll start eyeing up the rest of the Empire.'

'Which makes this above our pay grade, you know that. Montgomery wants to take his shot, there are people out there who'll return it.'

'So we stand aside while Special Ops handles it? A knife in the dark or a few drops of Spite's Bloom in his liquor?'

'Them or one of the syndicates. I don't imagine they'll be pleased to watch Montgomery go after their livelihood indefinitely.'

'Just let the trash take care of their own?'

'There are some decent people in Special Ops.'

'No,' he said, 'there aren't.'

There were a lot of meanings in that last sentence, and I took a slow minute to work through them.

'You still thinking about trading up?' Crispin asked.

'I think about a lot of things.'

'You can't trust the Old Man,' he said. 'Whatever he's offering, it's not worth it.'

'Not to you.'

At the center there was something that we both knew but never voiced. Crispin was rich, and cultured, and powerful, and I was none of those things. Crispin could walk off the job and spend the rest of his life coursing hare or drinking tea or whatever the hell it is the rich do when they aren't bleeding the rest of us. He didn't need to put himself on the block to climb the ladder – he'd slipped out the womb and landed on the highest rung.

Crispin and I were a lot alike, but that was one thing we'd never share. He needed nothing, and I wanted everything.

The meal came and we ate it. Looking at the stringy gray meat we'd have been better off throwing it into the mud. But we didn't throw it into the mud, we ate it.

Crispin paid the bill. 'I'm going to visit Montgomery, see if he hasn't got anything to say. Feel like coming?'

'I've got better ways to waste time.'

'I'll see you later, then.'

We parted at the next intersection.

Black House looked the same then as it did now, but I saw it differently. The guard manning the front gave me a quick salute when I walked in, even though he was the same rank. I was a smart man to salute. Things were going my way – I was rising like a cork.

But still I wasn't there yet, and I hadn't had much cause to spend time on the second floor. So I went slow, making sure I remembered each turn, that I didn't get fumbled up by the fact that every hallway and office looked the same. I could have asked directions of course, but getting lost inside headquarters didn't exactly fit with the image I was trying to present.

His door was open, once I found it. His door was always open, he would often say.

'Agent, so lovely to see you again.' He gave a kindly little nod, as if flattered that I'd chosen to honor him with my attention. 'Have you given any thought to my offer?'

I took the proffered chair across from him. My hands instinctively reached for the pouch of tobacco inside my coat, and I forced them back down onto my lap. The Old Man allowed no one to smoke in his office – one of the prerogatives of owning the country.

'I've been kicking it around,' I said.

'And have you come to any conclusions?'

'I don't see what good martyring the man does us.'

'Better a dead saint than a live one.'

'I'm not sure you fully appreciate the esteem he's held in amongst his people. If they see our hand in it, we'll have problems that make the current slate look positively sunny by comparison. There's no point in extinguishing a fire while lighting a fuse.'

'I've made arrangements to ensure that their future conduct will be more . . . reasonable.'

'Those arrangements would be?'

His pink lips covered his smile. It returned brighter than ever, and I knew I was pushing too hard. 'Of no concern to you.'

'I'm just making sure of the big picture.'

'You don't need to be sure of it,' he said. 'I'm sure of it. You only need to be sure of your own tiny part. It would behoove you to remember that you aren't yet a member of Special Operations.'

'I've been an Agent of the Crown for the last two years,' I said. 'And served it loyally for a half decade before that,' I said. I wasn't really angry at the slight, but I felt it better to pretend.

He leaned back in his chair and settled his hands around the slight round of his belly. 'But you haven't served me.'

And therein lay the rub. Special Operations were the elite of Black House, a few dozen men that pulled the strings of Empire, faceless centurions making sure the foundations held together. That was power, real power, to get a peek at the machinery that whirred beneath the surface, bend it as you saw fit. That was power a slum kid from Low Town could only dream about. Had dreamt about, long nights sleeping in the gutter and swearing to get out of it.

Of course, like anything else worth having, it came at a price.

'Well?' the Old Man asked after a while, as if the answer was of no concern. 'What's it to be?'

16

I spent the first half hour of the next morning in bed, tracing the cracks in the ceiling. One upside to the drought was that it made the spiderweb fracturing of my home solely an aesthetic concern. When the weather broke I'd need to find someone to fix it, or spend the rainy season getting dripped on.

I put that out of my head and pulled on my shirt, then my pants, then my boots. Then I sat back down and removed them again, replacing them with the sweat-stained fabric I'd worn during my last meeting with Edwin Montgomery.

The plants in the general's garden had gone from wilted to dead since I'd last been there, victims of the unrelenting heat. After forty-five minutes in the sun I thought I might join them, lie down next to the withered rose bush and stop breathing. I had to bang at the door for a long time before a servant opened it, squarely built and about my age, but with a mane stained white as an octogenarian's.

'I'm here to see the general,' I said.

He closed the door without speaking, then opened it a few minutes later and waved me in.

Botha was waiting for me outside the general's study. His clothes were neatly pressed, and he seemed unaffected by the weather. I found myself disliking him more than was appropriate.

'I didn't imagine we'd be seeing you again, sir,' he said.

'Ain't it wonderful, at our age, that the world still finds ways to surprise us?'

'It is indeed. Unfortunately, the Master is even older, and I'm afraid not up for a similar shock.'

'I'll make sure not to set off any fireworks.'

He didn't find that amusing, but then I got the sense Botha was infrequently overcome with merriment. 'The general don't need to be worked up by a two-bit hustler.'

'When'd you get a look at my price sheet?'

Botha cracked a knuckle. It echoed like a shot through the stale air of the room. 'I'm not letting you in there.'

'It's called the chain of command, and it means you don't get to make that decision.'

'As far as you need be concerned, my word comes from the Firstborn himself.'

'I'm an atheist.'

Long fingers contracted into fists. His shoulders rolled forward. 'It's never too late to see the light.'

I wasn't sure how it would play out – I hadn't anticipated a tussle before my morning meeting, and Botha was not, best as I could tell, composed of pulled taffy. On the other hand, I was getting in to see his boss one way or the other, and I know a lot of others, and mostly they involve bladed weaponry.

A voice from inside called us off. A weak voice, a voice that wasn't about to do any singing. Still, I could hear it well enough, and so could Botha. He let his arms slip back to his sides, but his eyes never left mine, even when he opened the door for me to slide through.

Edwin Montgomery had not struck me, the last time I'd seen

him, as about to leap up from his desk and dance a quadrille – but neither had he seemed a man rapping weakly on the door of She Who Waits Behind All Things. Two days had pushed him distinctly in that direction, however. He was colored like a newborn larva, and wore a dirty robe open halfway down his sunken chest. What hair he'd last possessed seemed to have abandoned him in his hour of need. His breathing had ceased to be an unconscious reflex, each intake of air requiring the full measure of his strength.

I had squared Botha's attitude as general belligerence, but now I was starting to wonder if I'd mistaken it for the loyalty of a faithful servant. The general did not, indeed, appear to be in any condition for an interview. Looking at him I wanted to cut short our conversation and call for a doctor, though even our enlightened age has yet to develop a remedy for the passing of time. Nor was it lost on me that the news I was about to provide was unlikely to act as a tonic. But he needed to hear it – more importantly, I needed to tell it, clear myself of responsibility to the Montgomery family.

'Come in, come in,' he said, feebly. 'You'll have to excuse Botha. He can get a bit . . . overprotective.'

'I'm sure he's got your interests at heart.'

'He always did,' Montgomery said heavily, as if there was something more in it.

I took an unoffered seat. 'I appreciate you agreeing to see me again, General.'

His skull tilted down an eighth or so of an inch, then returned to its original position. 'Yes, of course.'

'I found Rhaine.'

'Yes,' he repeated.

'She's in Low Town, like you expected. In an inn called the Queen's Palace.'

'Is she?'

'I tried talking to her.'

'Yes.'

'But she wasn't interested in what I had to say.'

'No.'

'Honestly, sir, I'm not sure where to go from here. I can't force her to return.'

Two sentences seemed to stretch the limits of his focus. He'd aimed his gaze vaguely through the window at his dying gardens, though the dust and the morning glare obscured the view. 'I'm sure you did your best,' he said finally.

'Sir, perhaps now is the time to cash in a favor or two. Get in touch with someone from the Throne, Black House if you have to. I know you said you didn't want to draw yourself any attention, but Rhaine is in over her head. Alive and noisy is better than the alternative.'

A thread of spit trailed down from his upper lip. After a long moment he brushed it away and spoke. 'I'll do that.'

'If I was you, sir, I'd do it as soon as I could.' Trying to balance urgency with an appreciation for the fragility of the man's health.

'Yes,' he said, but he had gone back to looking out the window. 'Immediately.'

It was all I could do. It was what I did, at least, offering a farewell that he didn't answer and standing to leave.

'Wait,' he called me back, briefly returning to cognizance. 'A man . . . a man pays his debts.' Hands shaking violently, he managed to pull a purse from a drawer and dropped it on the desk. The string was loose, and I could see the yellow inside.

I answered quickly, before avarice could kick in. 'You don't owe me anything, General – I just wish I could do something else for you.'

Two days earlier he would have argued with me to take it. Now he just nodded vaguely and went back to staring out the window.

Botha was waiting by the front door, not quite smirking. 'Did you have a productive meeting, sir?'

'Aces, Botha. Aces.'

'I suppose this will be the last we'll be seeing you.'

I was seized with a sudden desire to squeeze my fingers around his throat, break his face into a pulp, go at him full-bore and see who ended up standing. 'I suppose you've supposed a lot of things that didn't turn out true, haven't you, Botha? A man like you, he's probably better off waiting for people to explain things to him, rather than go round supposing shit he don't know nothing about.'

For whatever reason this didn't seem to touch him – the inclination that had nearly brought us to blows a few minutes earlier had disappeared entirely. He smiled and dipped his head, the closest to servile I'd yet seen him manage, then opened the door out into the dead garden. I tried to catch the general's eyes through the window of his study, but the glare of the sun was too bright, and I had to turn away.

17

Back at the Earl I ditched the suit for my regular attire and slipped a long dirk into my belt. The unmade bed seemed more inviting than usual, but I forced myself to settle for a hard snarl of breath. The vapor was sweet and sickening as raw honey, and I let it expand into my cranium, pushing the general's decline, the whole Montgomery family, out of my thoughts. I had another meeting to attend this morning, and it was to take place in very different surroundings.

Suddenly the vial was empty. I tossed it aside and grabbed another one, then tripped myself out.

The Isthmus did not welcome trespassers, indeed, seemed to have been deliberately laid out to repel them. It runs southeast of the Beggar's Ramparts, along that corner of the docks which extends into the borders of Kirentown, though few enough heretics found themselves in the maze of narrow alleyways and unpaved side streets. Indeed, it was rare to see anyone whose skin tended north of ebony.

As such, it was one of the few sections of Rigus with which I was not intimately familiar, though in fairness, only a current resident could claim to be. The neighborhood was in a constant state of flux – no sooner was a shack erected, cheap wood with a thick cloth overhang, than it was torn down and replaced with another, or erased entirely. The Isthmus was a living outgrowth of an insular and dispossessed people, instinctively arranged to confuse and impede outsiders.

As a rule, the guard don't do their duty – but even on those rare occasions when the fancy strikes them, they don't do it here. To those unacquainted with the terrain, which was to say anyone not born and still living there, cutting through the gangways and tenements was a sure sentence of death.

I had memorized the directions Yancey had given me before coming – nothing says 'mug me' like standing around a street corner staring at a set of notes. But out of necessity, since the Isthmus is without street names or administrative markings of any kind, he was forced to rely on local landmarks as points of navigation – and since these were apt to be the victim of vandals or the Islanders' constant redevelopment schemes, my going was slow. It was a chancy thing, even early in the day. The thugs and sharps who lived and worked here were too small fish to have heard of my reputation as a man it was best not to try and rob, and my skin marked me as a potential target. So I stitched a scowl across my face and kept my hand on the hilt of my dagger, and while I didn't look in the eyes of any of the adolescent hyenas that lolled outside of every third domicile, neither did I look away.

And after a few false starts and wrong turns, I found myself in front of the house of Mazzie of the Stained Bone.

The high-class practitioners, the real Artists, Academy-trained and government recognized, could afford to do what they did any way they felt like doing it. Some preferred to keep up appearances – dark robes and grim prophecies, staining their beards white and letting them grow down to the floor. But for every one of those there were two you couldn't tell from a solid shopkeeper or banker, who went about their business without pretense or drama. The bottom feeders and base dwellers didn't have that luxury. They needed the public to know who they were and what they did, needed to advertise their services while warning off anyone that might want to do them harm.

Still, standing in the sun outside of Mazzie's hovel, I couldn't help but wonder if she wasn't laying it on a bit thick. The shack she inhabited was, in the broad-strokes, largely indistinguishable from those that surrounded it, but she'd gone to an elaborate effort to peacock it. Near every inch of the outside was festooned with the trappings of her profession, or at least those that the ignorant public was familiar with. Strange shapes and odd patterns had been drawn on the walls with discolored paint, labyrinthine squiggles without beginning or end, exotic figures just recognizable enough to be disturbing. Tufts of feathers added accent, ornamentation of bone and offal. These last let off quite a stench. I doubted any were more than decorative – a functioning Working is too expensive to keep hung outside to be rained on. Still, they fulfilled their purpose, which was to creep hell out of anyone looking at them. Outside of staking the corpse of a newborn outside her door, there was little Mazzie could possibly have done to more actively ward off guests.

The way I saw it, there were two possibilities. The first was that Mazzie was a fraud, and the elaborate show she put on was just that, her reputation earned by trickery and theater. This I more or less discounted – Yancey was no fool, and I doubted his recommendation would be so far off base. And besides, what little had made its way out from the slums of her activities hinted at more than parlor tricks and sleight of hand. The second possibility, considerably more disturbing, was that Mazzie of the Stained Bone was just what she seemed to be – a witch-woman, heir to millennia of folk-traditions and rituals, beliefs that had flourished out of reach of the rigid High Laws that constrained the Art within the Empire proper. Not exactly the sort of person to whom you wanted to entrust the education of your surrogate child.

But then again my options were distinctly limited. Since the founding of the Academy during the Great War, the government had tightened their control over the nation's practitioners, one more way to centralize and strengthen its rule. I knew by grim example that the Crown had no more rigid sense of ethics than the most twisted back alley conjurer. Nothing Mazzie could teach Wren would be any worse than what he'd learn from the authorities, and at least it would go down unleavened with hypocrisy.

I held my nose and snatched up my balls, then knocked loudly on the door.

'Enter,' said a voice from inside, and I did.

The interior was everything one would have expected from the front. Whatever other benefits it offered, Mazzie's profession had not made her a wealthy woman – or if it had, she'd put little of the coin into home furnishings. Her hovel was a single room with a curtain pulled against the back wall to provide some privacy for the sleeping area. One corner was taken up with a large iron stove, cooking away despite the heat. A shutter hole in the ceiling was open, leaking in a few strands of sunlight on the sole inhabitant.

Short and squat, black as soot and sin, Mazzie of the Stained Bone sat in a chair behind the table. The end of a fat cigar nested itself in her crooked teeth. She inspected me with a set of brown eyes rich as chocolate – in another woman they would have been called beautiful. Her stubbed nose flared as if to catch my scent, a wide hoop of ivory curling out from one nostril. She might have been thirty, or forty, or fifty. She might have been a hundred. She might never have been born.

'I'm the Warden. Yancey the Rhymer sent word I was coming.' I hoped this was true.

'I know who you are. Sit down,' she said, nodding at the chair opposite. 'Let's speak.'

I did as bidden. My stool was identical to the one Mazzie was

114

settled over, though her ample buttocks at least provided some cushion against the stiff wood.

'I'd offer you a cup of tea,' she began, 'but I don't think you'd like my blend.'

'I'm not here for tea.'

'What you here for then?'

I took out my tobacco pouch and started on a smoke. 'Shouldn't you know?'

'You give out a lot of samples, in your business?'

'Not so many.'

She rolled her thick cheroot to the end of her mouth. 'Guess we in similar lines.'

'Course, in my line, word gets out that I'm not reliable, that I ain't selling what I'm talking, my customers are apt to take it serious. Apt to come visit me some evening, pull my tongue through my throat.'

'I can see how that might happen.'

'So what's the verdict?' I sealed my smoke and caught the end between my teeth, then lit it with the stroke of a match. 'We in similar lines?'

She dropped a length of ash onto the dirt floor. 'We are indeed.'

'Somehow I thought we might be.' We sat puffing at each other, the difference in size between my thin spliff and the hogleg rooted in her mouth giving me a distinct feeling of inferiority. 'I've a boy needs training.'

She'd known already, either a tip from Yancey or from some other, more arcane source. 'No reason to bother old Mazzie. They got a school for that.'

'You registered with the Crown, Mazzie? They take a tax off your . . .' I waved my hand at the squalor, '. . . enterprise?'

'The Crown? I've lived under three of them, child – two back in Miradin, and the last twenty-five years under your Queen Bess,' she said, ticking royalty off on her broad fingers. 'Ain't none of them done nothing for Mazzie.'

'It seems neither of us are staunch monarchists, then.'

She scratched aimlessly at her chin. 'Never taken on no white child. No boy child neither.'

'I'll leave him in the sun awhile. Nothing to be done about the cock.'

'No light thing, taking on an apprentice.'

I pulled a purse from my pocket and dropped it onto the table, startling a fly enjoying an early afternoon repast. 'That even the scales?'

She stared at it evenly, as if to read gold through the leather. 'More to it than ochres and argents. You certain you know what you're asking?'

'Enlighten me.'

She weighed over the request like I'd asked for possession of her eldest son. Then she shrugged with something bordering on annoyance and started speaking. 'Take ten thousand babies, put them in a cage.'

'I'm not going to do that.'

'Watch them for ten years, maybe twelve. Watch them until the one half starts to bleed, and the other half starts to look at the first. One of those children, maybe one of those children, they'll start doing things the rest of them can't.'

'What do you do with the rejects?'

Mazzie was good at ignoring me. 'You take that child, you show her how to focus what she has. Teach her what you were taught, maybe give her books from people that learned something and wrote it down before they died. But it ain't like being a cobbler, first come the leather, then you hammer in the nails.' She shook her head. 'There's a reason they call it the Art – you got to have the feel, you understand?'

'I'm following along.'

'Everybody who does it, they've got a different way of doing it, depends on how their mind runs. Some folk like to build things, force a working onto a blade or a jewel or a clock. Some folk can listen to things that no one else hears but are always right about what they say. Some folk force the world into things that it isn't, coils of fire streaming from their fingers, cool the air till it's thick as ice. Some folk get caught looking up into the night when the moon's still fresh, wonder what's looking back at them.'

The conversation had turned a bit dark, in my estimation, though you wouldn't have known it from Mazzie's grin. 'They the ones that end up being trouble. They stop looking at you when they speak, have trouble remembering the two of you is human, and the things they've been looking at ain't. Back in Miradin we used to put the ones that forgot beneath a wall of stone, weigh it down till there wasn't nothing left. Here they burn them.' She shrugged. 'Not their fault, really – they just doing what comes natural. Everybody's got a knack.'

'What's your knack, Mazzie?'

She smiled but didn't answer. 'Point being, the road is crooked. Some of the paths end in a coffin. Some of the paths end in worse places. You'd best be sure of what you're asking from me, before you go ahead and ask it.'

'That was a nice speech,' I said. 'But you left something out of it.'

'Yeah?'

'That one child in the ten thousand, that girl who can do things the others can't – if you don't teach her to control what she has she'll burn her brain into mush, be left staring at the walls. I'm well aware of the dangers posed by the Art. If I had my way I'd reach inside the boy and strip the spark right from his soul, leave him just the same as the rest of us. Barring that, the least I can do is make sure he doesn't go mad before his fifteenth name day.'

'Seems like maybe you know more about this than you let on.'

I could have told her that the man who'd all but raised me had been the greatest practitioner in the Empire, and the girl I'd grown up beside had become perhaps the most evil. 'I've picked up a piece here and there.'

'How old is your boy?'

'Thirteen? Fourteen, maybe.'

'Awfully old to just be starting.'

117

'Then we ought not waste time.'

She never seemed to blink. I'm sure she did, sometimes, but try as I might I couldn't catch her. 'I'd need to give him a look first.'

'I didn't take this for a correspondence school.'

'What's his name?'

'Wren.'

'Tell Wren to come see me in four days' time. Tell him to wear this on his arm,' she said, pulling out a feathered charm from somewhere on her person and sliding it over. 'And folk won't bother him.'

'You got so much pull around here, Mazzie?'

She stretched back her lips. You might have called it a smile, if you were being careless. 'Enough.'

I put the charm into my satchel. 'I'll tell him.'

It was miserable in that fucking hut, our smoke and the fumes from her stove thickening the air. Still, I was seated, and so tired from the summer and the walk that I lingered despite the obvious conclusion of our conversation.

She looked at me cross-eyed over her cup of muddy tea. 'Death hangs around you thick as flies on shit.'

By the Lost One, it never fails – you can't spend five minutes with one of these two-copper soothsayers without getting an earful of dark augury and grim forewarning. 'I thought you said you don't give out samples. Sounds like you've been rolling the bones for me.'

'Don't need the bones to see what you are. Your victims swirl around you and scream in your ear, cursing at you day and night.'

'Funny – with all that noise I sleep like a baby.'

She smiled like she'd won a bet. 'No, you don't.'

'Maybe not, but I take a lot of uppers.' I tapped the purse on the table. 'You'll get another one of these every month. You teach him the basics – how to focus his mind, a few simple charms, not to bake his brain by drawing in too much. And leave out all the nonsense you do for the look-sees. He comes home chanting gibberish or trying to sacrifice any of our chickens and his mother will have my hide.'

She didn't say anything to that, not for a little while, just stared at me. Then she shoved the coin back over in my direction. 'I haven't promised you anything,' she said. 'You come back and see me after I've talked to the boy. I'll give you my decision then.'

I pocketed the money pouch and stood. 'I'm counting the hours.'

There were ways back to the Earl that didn't require me to swing past the Queen's Palace. I should have taken one. I wasn't planning on a visit – as far as I was concerned I was done with the Montgomerys. I'd told her father that. I'd been telling myself the same.

I could see the crowd about a block away, a small knot of people, growing fast. A handful of hoax had a loose cordon bottling up the mouth of the alley. At some point they'd figure out whose child they had lying under a sheet, and once they did the ice would be down here double-time, but it hadn't happened yet. The ranking officer was a fiend for the dice, in my pocket on top of what I spread around to his bosses, and I gave him a nod and he let me through without saying anything.

There was no reason to look. I knew what was under there, had known since I'd seen the herd, known since I'd left her room the night before. I looked anyway.

You think, being strangled, how bad could that be? Hold your breath for a while, the lights go dim. But it's not like that at all. Calloused hands around the soft of your neck, the beaming eyes of a man willing you to death, trying to scream and failing. The white rings around Rhaine's sky blues were punctured, blossoms of blood leaking in. A thick patch of her scarlet hair had been torn out, either in the struggle or afterward, as a trophy. Her nose was broken back into her face. Her throat was discolored, green and black.

I threw the sheet over her and moved to stand, but the heat, I say the heat, set me back on one knee. The guards turned away, embarrassed at my weakness and not wanting to cause offense. They knew who buttered their bread. I pulled myself back to my feet, managing to make it out of sight before reaching for the vial of breath I had in my satchel. I was very proud of my restraint.

18

There is a corner of every man's soul that would prefer him dead. That whispers poison in his ear in the still hours of the evening, puts spurs to his side when he stands atop a ledge. For the weak and the misbegotten, the suggestion alone proves sufficient, and the unfortunate runs himself a hot bath and adds his life-blood to it, or drinks a few pints of backyard whiskey and goes swimming in the canal. But most of us are too stubborn or cowardly to make a clean go of it, and this bit that hates us has to start thinking sly. Have another drink, it says, and maybe one more on top. Polish it off with a hit of breath, and ain't that man at the end of the bar been giving you the eye all night, all fucking night, and what's his problem exactly, and why don't you go over and ask?

After finding Rhaine's body I went back to the Earl, poured myself a tall draft and went to work wrestling that suicidal quarter of my consciousness into submission, or at least silence.

I had been aware of the youngest Montgomery's existence for

a grand total of three days, had spent perhaps forty minutes in her presence. In that time she had struck me as spoiled, self-indulgent and foolish, and her unfortunate outcome eminently predictable. The world is happy enough to distribute cruelties to the undeserving – best to save sympathy for those souls brought low through no fault of their own.

She had been nothing to me, not a lover, not a friend even. Contemptuous and acerbic even when she wasn't trying. A spoon-fed cunt from Kor's Heights that had gotten what she'd asked for.

I was alone in the bar, so I had to get up from my perch to refill my beer.

She had heart though, you had to give that to her. That last time I'd seen her she'd known what she was up against, seen the odds and stuck it out anyway. At first I'd thought her bravery petulance, the whole escapade a 'fuck you' to her old man. But I'd been wrong, it was more than that. You could call it rank sentimentality, and I did, but you couldn't dismiss it. She had wanted justice for her brother, and died looking for it.

And the fact that I'd known the truth, that I might have set her straight but hadn't – well, you couldn't very well pretend that didn't mean something.

I was empty again. A trip to the tap rectified the situation.

The general had heard the news by this point. It might kill him – the Lost One knew he hadn't been the picture of health that morning. If it didn't then he'd have the misfortune of adding a daughter to the son he'd buried. The Daevas were cruel, to repay his years of service with such misfortune.

Course the Daevas hadn't killed her – I knew where that honor rested.

But then again what I'd told Rhaine that first day was true: there's no such thing as justice, only revenge, and once you get it you realize how little it means. Edwin Montgomery's son rotted in the ground, and his daughter would soon join him. Giving them company wouldn't change that. I did the best I could for Rhaine while she was alive. It hadn't been enough, but there was no point compounding failure with catastrophe.

It made sense, when you looked at it like that. When you lined it up. The wise thing to do was forget it. Have a few drinks, then go upstairs and sleep them off. Wake up and have a few more. Repeat until it didn't seem necessary.

I am not a wise man. Clever, on occasion, but never wise.

Adolphus came in through the back, trying to take up less than his usual amount of space. 'You hear?'

'Yeah.' I pulled myself up from my seat, stretching my arms over my head, trying to shake loose three pints of booze.

'Where are you headed?'

'I'm gonna go pay a visit to the man who killed Rhaine Montgomery.'

'Who was that?'

'The same person who killed her brother, I suspect.'

19

The wooden platform outside of the Veterans' Association Headquarters was in use, a decent-sized crowd of onlookers watching a one-legged veteran howl his way through a stock speech. That is to say I assumed he was a veteran, though half the beggars in Low Town claim an honorable wound and a few coin on top of it, liars with bound legs spinning sob stories for fools. He looked the part at least, and he was making a fine go of it, rolling himself up to a good boil despite the heat.

'When the Throne called, we stood back to back, back to back against the enemies of our nation! When the blood roiled like the tides, when our brothers-in-arms fell like wheat at the harvest, still we kept faith, still we stood strong against the Dren menace!'

Some menace, an ocean and half a world away – you travel a thousand miles to kick a hornets' nest you ought not moan so over being stung. The rest of the crowd seemed to remember it differently, however, muttering along in agreement.

'Whatever was required of us, we gave! Gave without asking for compensation, gave till we had nothing left! We didn't do it for pay, and we didn't do it for medals! We did it so that our children would know a world without the fear of foreign enslavement. That they might grow up free and strong, proud subjects of the Rigun Empire!'

Oh, the children, the children, always with the children. Real bloodthirsty motherfuckers, our hypothetical progeny. More men have died on behalf of future generations than through disease, famine and drink.

'And after all our sacrifices, all our struggle – this is how the Crown thanks us! The Private's Silver is ours, brothers, ours by right of blood!'

Noble sentiments were all well and good, but it was money that drove my ex-comrades into a frenzy. We'd gained numbers since I'd come in, or at least we'd lost space, the beefy veteran behind me climbing my heels for a better view.

'Roland Montgomery had a dream – that those men who fought to save the country might have a hand in running it. Though he was taken from us—'

A voice yelled, 'Murdered by Black House!'

'Though he was taken from us,' the speaker continued smoothly, sharp enough not to slander the government outright though happy enough to inspire it, 'still we hold the faith! As we held it at Beneharnum, and at Sarlaut! As we held it at Aunis, and Darlaux, and Sulmne! As we hold it to this very day, firm in the face of any man who seeks to strip us of our rights and honors! Next week, brothers, I hope you'll join us on our march to the palace – to remind the Queen of what her people have done for her, and to demand just recompense for our efforts!'

The crowd erupted. I slipped away, running the gauntlet of back-slapping buffoons and teary-eyed nostalgics.

I found Hroudland standing stiff-necked near the entrance, his face beatific though he must have heard the sermon before. He was a true believer, it seemed, though I wouldn't have credited him as such. I filed the information away happily – zealots are easy to play.

Something of the speech had stayed with him, because he greeted me with a friendly smile despite my history of disrespect. 'Lieutenant,' he said.

'Hroudland. I need to see the commander.'

It took a moment for that to sink in. Hroudland was one of those rarest of military men, an individual whose rank had not outdistanced his talents and, as the main requirement of the middle ranks is attention to detail and a lack of imagination, he was having trouble dealing with this new development. 'The commander's busy.'

'I'm not here to waste his time.'

A longer moment still, then he nodded and walked me inside. I took a seat against the wall and watched him disappear through the back.

The entrance hall wasn't packed, but it was damn full for a weekday afternoon, dozens of men preparing for the march. The whole place was animated with an energy that hadn't been there the last time I'd come through, that probably hadn't been there for years, since before the Association had legitimized itself. The Crown's ill-considered attempt to decrease their rapidly expanding debt was bearing sour fruit, turning the apolitical into fanatics, reminding an untapped army of long-standing grievances. Still, they weren't sharpening knives or threatening to murder city officials, which I took to mean the news of Rhaine's murder was as yet unknown to them. Except, of course, for those members of the assemblage who had been detailed to kill her.

I sat mostly unnoticed in the corner, one more unkempt, middle-aged man in a small sea of them. One of my compatriots, a thuggish-looking sort with a head of white hair, kept staring over at me through crossed eyes, but he blinked away when I fixed my attention towards him. Instead I turned it on the portrait of Roland that stood above the fireplace. I didn't like it, I decided. The stern line of his face didn't match my memory of his upbeat grin, solid in the heat of battle or a crowded taproom.

Three-quarters of an hour sauntered past until an orderly waved me through the public area and into the hallway beyond. Inside I waited silently while a pair of guards removed my dagger and gave me a thorough once over. They'd upped security since yesterday, or else they just wanted to fuck with me. Afterward one of them escorted me to Pretories, knocking on the door and waiting for an affirmation before allowing me entry.

Joachim sat behind his desk, a thick bundle of papers evenly separated in front of him. 'I'm sorry to have kept you waiting, Lieutenant,' he said. 'As you can see, we've got a lot going on at the moment.' He pointed at the seat across from him, but I remained standing.

'Rhaine's dead.' I kept my voice flat, and low. It could have been accusing, or despondent.

'What?'

'Rhaine Montgomery is a corpse in the Low Town muck.'

Pretories gave a credible impression of being shocked: he slumped back into his chair, squeezed his forehead with one hand, and allowed an appropriate interval to pass without speaking. 'You're certain?'

'I saw her body.'

'By the Firstborn,' he said. 'I've failed him again.'

I took the seat he'd offered. 'I think we both know where the blame lies, Commander.'

If you were watching close enough, you could have seen a break in the façade, an angry crack in his false surface of regret. But then in fairness, I knew what I was looking for.

'Sons of bitches at Black House,' I spat out this last with sudden and honest venom, the first display of emotion I'd allowed myself. 'How long are we gonna let them do it? Roland wasn't enough – they had to send someone after his little sister too?' I slammed my fist down on Pretories' table, sending sheets of paper floating to the ground.

'Black House,' Pretories agreed after a moment. 'Sons of bitches.'

'It wasn't your fault, Commander,' I said, adopting his

mournful pose. 'It was mine. I was too slow in getting to her, and too slow in coming to you.'

'As you said, Lieutenant. We both know where the blame lies.'

'I've been no friend to the Association these last years, I know that, and I'm sorry. I was . . . I was afraid,' I said slowly, drawing it out. 'I have people to protect. You know I used to wear the gray. I'm in their books, a loose end they'd be happy to tie shut. I've got to be careful – I can't stretch my neck out.'

'And now?'

'Seeing Rhaine's body . . .' I shook my head bitterly. 'Same as her brother. Twelve years and nothing's changed – we're still nothing to them. They take everything we got and step on us if we make a noise. Someone needs to answer for her, for her and for Roland.' Strictly speaking, that last wasn't even a lie. 'I'm with you from now on, wherever it takes me.'

I wasn't sure how far Pretories was swallowing my sudden shift in allegiance. It didn't exactly fit with my reputation as a man whose sole concern was his own back. But of course, the less he trusted me the wiser he would be to fake it. Better to have me close, where he could keep an eye on me. 'With the Throne threatening our future, we need the support of every veteran we can muster. The march isn't for a couple of days, but of course there are ways to get involved before then. Check with one of the men at the front desk, they'll direct you as needed.'

That was the end of the conversation, but I stayed where I was.

After a moment, Joachim clarified his dismissal. 'If there's nothing else then, Lieutenant . . .'

'I'm afraid there is something else, Commander.' I swallowed hard and looked at my lap. If I had a cap I'd have taken it off my head and worried it between my hands. As it was I just tried to give that impression. 'There's something I should have told you the last time I was here. I should have told you, and I didn't, and I'm sorry.'

'Go on.'

'I've had to do things I'm not proud of since I left the service. I don't suppose that's a surprise for you to hear.'

'I'm aware of how you make your living, Lieutenant. And not in any position to judge.'

No, you bloody well aren't. 'But doing what I do, it means I hear things that not everyone else does. The word on the street is that the syndicates aren't happy with some of your recent developments. This march you've planned, it's got people riled. Wasn't so long ago the veterans marching in the streets meant blood in the gutters for anyone who got in their way.'

'We aren't in that line anymore – the Veterans' Association is one hundred percent legitimate, a duly registered organization advocating for the rights of its members.'

'Would the Courtland Savages agree?'

He waved that away. 'The Courtland Savages can do whatever the hell they want, so long as they do it in Courtland. They set up a shop around the block from us – I can't have them selling in front of the damn headquarters. Hroudland and his boys went over to talk to one of their higher-ups – there weren't any problems. They told me the issue was settled.'

'That's what they told you.'

'Spit it out, Lieutenant. Equivocation is unbecoming in an officer.'

'I'm not being coy with you, Commander – I don't have anything solid. Just whispers. Of course, whispers can turn concrete when you aren't looking.' I leaned across the table, like I was offering a secret. 'You know the Savages work for the Giroies.'

'What of it?'

'Memory serves, you and Roland put a fair number of Giroie boys in shallow graves.'

'Roland was my brother, and the greatest man I've ever met.' It rolled off his tongue smooth as chocolate. 'But he was misguided. The Association has no business going after the syndicates, however objectionable their activities may be. Our business is our people, making sure the government doesn't screw us any worse than it already has. Whatever . . . unpleasantness was between us and the Giroies was put aside long ago.'

'That shot you took at them, it knocked them back from the front ranks. They've been scrambling for footing ever since. I imagine that might be the sort of thing they'd remember.'

'It's been more than ten years since we were cross. Why start making trouble now?'

'Yeah, you're right. They seem like a nice bunch of people. I could send word their way – maybe they could come round for coffee and cake.'

Pretories was not a man for humor. 'I appreciate the warning,' he said slowly, 'and certainly hope you keep me abreast of any further developments. But beyond that . . .' He built his hands into a pyramid, elbows leaning against the table. 'Our organization is at the most critical point in its history since the death of Roland Montgomery. I can't afford to expend resources in ancillary theaters.'

'Of course. Do what you think is best.' I propped myself out of the seat. 'I'll keep my ears out, let you know what I hear. And if there's anything else, Commander, anything you need, make sure to contact me.'

He rose quickly and put one hand on my shoulder. 'It's good to have you back in the fold, Lieutenant. Remember: what we do, we do not just for us, but for those that have been taken – for Roland, and for Rhaine. The justice of the Firstborn is slow, but certain. Those responsible will get their due, have no fear on that.'

Something fierce brushed across my face. If Pretories had been watching me rather than pontificating, I think the game might have been up right there. 'You're damn right they will,' I said.

When I left the speaker was starting up again, on the dot for his one-thirty performance. I waited around for a few minutes to see if he'd ad-lib something, but it was hot as hell, and he didn't, and I split.

20

I'd been crapping blood for half a week when the lieutenant sent me to the wards.

This was a few months after Beneharnum, before I had met Roland, when I was still a private and had nothing more to think about than following the man in front of me. The front was still relatively fluid, the planes of Nestria not yet strangled by hundreds of lines of fortified trenches. The Dren had suffered some setbacks in the east, and were retreating a hundred-odd miles, tightening up their interior lines. We were marching forward to meet them.

It was my own fault, my own damn fault, and I'm not saying otherwise. But I'd never seen cherries before, let alone eaten one. And they looked ripe enough, a crimson flock weighing down their boughs. And we'd been walking through orchards for a solid afternoon, and I'd been three months on mealy biscuits and wormy meat – and I filled my stomach so high that a sharp sneeze would have coughed up a pit.

I paid for it soon enough, soon enough and hard, the tart flesh of the fruit turning to poison, sending me retching and sprinting for the bushes. After a few days it stopped. After a few more days it started again, worse this time, a lot worse. I couldn't keep down water, let alone hard tack. I ached all the time, but in a distant way, and I was having trouble with my eyes – if I focused on anything too long my legs started to shake and I needed to sit down. I couldn't sit down, of course, but I damn sure needed to.

So it was my own fault, like I said, but still the lieutenant didn't look happy when he said it. I'd just rejoined the ranks after my third shit of the day, rust-red water leaking out of my bowels, a fist of jagged metal in my insides.

'I think you need a rest, Private,' he said to me.

As usual Adolphus had taken the step behind me, and he slapped my back to show off my vitality. I did my best not to stagger from the blow. 'Come on now, Lieutenant,' Adolphus said nervously. 'He's not so bad as all that. He'll be all right once he gets a few hours' rest in him.'

This was an errant lie, obvious to anyone who spared a glance in my direction. In a week I'd lost a newborn's worth of body weight, and I wasn't a fat man to begin with. Tearing off my trousers during that last go round I'd felt the imprint of my ribcage pushing out against my skin.

'I'm fine, Lieutenant,' I said, holding my hands behind my back so he wouldn't see them shake. 'Just a case of the squirts. No reason to send me up. I can still handle a trench blade.'

The lieutenant was a decent fellow, good at his job and still possessed of some remnant of humanity despite the hell we'd all gone through – that was probably why the Firstborn decreed he'd die six weeks later, casualty of a Dren bowman, picked off during some meaningless skirmish that never made it into the history books. He knew what sending me up meant, had held off doing it in the vain hope I'd recover. Still, there was only so much he could overlook. 'You'll be fine, Private – a few days off your feet and you'll be right as rain.' But he didn't meet my eyes when he said it, and neither did anyone else as I grabbed my few belongings and got ready to head to the back of the lines.

No one but Adolphus, who squeezed my shoulder and told me that everything would be fine, that he'd stop by and see me later. I was just glad he didn't try and hug me. Adolphus was always something of a hugger, and in my injured state I wasn't sure I could take it.

It was a rest day. That was the way we moved – two days on and one day off. We weren't exactly sprinting through Nestria. On the march our baggage train extended miles and miles behind the infantry, artillery and equipment sharing road with the material indulgences of the officers and a sub-army of merchants, whores and servants keen to fill the needs of the largest horde of men the region had ever seen. It took me a solid hour to reach the wards from my post, though admittedly my pace was slowed by my stomach's insistence that I leave a memento behind every bush and tree.

Our battlefield hospice met, perhaps even exceeded, the high standards of competency that reigned throughout the Allied military machine. A canvas tent stretched over thick wooden poles, a hundred-odd collapsible beds – the whole thing small enough to be packed into a few mule-drawn wagons. The operation was overseen by a handful of drunkards and dolts with perhaps six months of medical training between them. In theory it was meant to serve as a triage station – the lightly wounded patched up and returned to the lines, the severely injured stabilized and sent to recuperate further afield. In practice, few survived to go home.

Two men sat at a table underneath the awning, playing cards and drinking from an unlabeled bottle. They were out of uniform, and dirtier than doctors should be. My arrival in their midst was not the cause of any great commotion – a solid minute passed before either thought to react.

'Name and rank,' one asked finally.

I gave it to him.

'What you want?'

One would think that was a fair bit obvious, but I didn't have the energy for sarcasm. 'Lieutenant says I'm on rest.'

'Yeah?' Not exactly brimming with interest.

It was too much effort to answer.

'What's wrong with you?' he asked finally, grudgingly.

'Got the shits.'

'You been eating cherries?'

I nodded.

He swatted away a fly and shot his comrade a look. They shared a laugh. 'You dumb fucking infantrymen. Don't you know they ain't ripe yet?'

I wanted to set my hand into his unwashed hair and pull his face down into the wood, watch his nose come apart in my hands. See how much help his partner did him then. As it was I could barely stand, couldn't talk, and even thinking about sudden motion sent unhappy waves through my stomach. So I just nodded again.

He pulled over a ledger and pointed at an empty spot. 'Sign here,' he said, 'or make your mark.'

I barely managed the former.

He closed the ledger and set it aside. 'Grab a bed. We'll bring some soup by later.' He slapped a high card down against the table. His partner let loose a pretty good stream of invective, for a civilian. After a few seconds of forgetting I existed the first turned back up to me, vaguely annoyed to discover I'd yet to follow his order. 'Either you'll ride it out or you'll die,' he said, by his tone not strongly invested in the outcome.

That was about the way I figured it too. If it was the former, I promised myself the good doctor and I would have another chat, under different circumstances.

We'd been marching for an odd week, and there hadn't been a real battle for twice that, but still a good half of the beds were in use. Boys down with the flux, or having fallen prey to any of the various rotting maladies courtesy of the mass of whores that traveled with us, an army only slightly smaller than our own. Most of the patients looked near dead, too weak to scatter the bands of flies that flocked over wounds and open orifices. Some of them I felt certain were so, the corpses yet to be removed by a less than compulsively diligent staff.

I scanned around for a cot that looked cleaner than the rest, but they were pretty uniformly vile, so I dropped myself onto one in the back corner. The beds were composed of the same material as my armor, rough and callous as a camp follower. The bugs had gotten to it just the same, perforating ochre-sized holes in the boiled leather, their attentions as effective as a crossbow bolt. A line of nits marched in admirable formation up the strut and toward the burlap sack serving duty as my pillow.

The orderly came by, a Nestrian, native to the country, one of that proud race whose freedoms I had killed to protect. 'Liquor?' he asked in mangled Rigun, and tilted a glass jug of yellow liquid towards me, the rim stained by what I hoped was only dirt.

I shook my head.

He shrugged and downed my ration. I turned myself towards the wall and passed into a fitful sleep.

My dreams were bitter and clouded, and they hung thick as smoke, staying with me even when I lurched up from bed and sprawled my way to the nearest outhouse. Contra the doctor's promise, no one came by with any soup.

I was ripped firmly back to consciousness by screams and cannon fire. Night had fallen. The only illumination in the tent was provided by a heavy lantern set on a pole in the center. Its light didn't reach me, but towards the front I could make out the frantic movements of the staff, broken out of their lethargy by an unexpected rash of casualties.

They'd attacked at supper, making us pay for our hubris, for thinking we could stroll toward the Republic without forward pickets and scouts clearing the way. They hit us that night all across the front, the entire retreat revealed to be a feint, our optimism premature and quickly ended. The Dren were proving better than us when it came to grand strategy.

The Dren were proving better than us when it came to virtually everything.

The rest are scraps of images out of order, dealt from a shuffled deck, my illness and their own nightmarish quality breaking chronology.

A limbless boy, nubs of flesh waggling at me, begging for someone to kill him, the doctors too busy or foolish to oblige him.

A blood-spattered saw next to stacks of arms and legs set atop each other like children's blocks, so high that the nurse has to stretch to add another.

The two doctors who'd signed me in, the younger white as the bone he'd been cutting, slack-jawed at the horror, the elder trying to slap him back to consciousness, three sharp retorts without effect.

Then doubling up on beds by the end of the night, waking from a stupor to find a corpse beside me, too weak to roll him off my slab.

A man across the aisle pulling at my shirt, pleading for something, his voice stolen by a sucking chest wound. Getting more animated as he slips away, his pleas violent and unanswerable, having to near break his hand to get him off.

The orderly stripping the bodies, rifling pockets, picking off wedding rings and prayer medals. He sees me looking and brings a dirty finger to a guilty smile.

The screams, an untidy hymn of misery, voices dropping away from the chorus, silenced forever.

Many other things also, things that kept me up late into the night, that keep me up today.

The next morning I hobbled my way back to lines, and when the lieutenant came out to inspect us he slid his eyes over my shaky salute like I belonged there, and I thanked Melatus and every one of his siblings for it.

A day or two after, I managed to start keeping down water, and a few days after that I could eat solid food. I have never swallowed another cherry, and feel confident I will die in that same state.

The Association orator could talk about honor, he could talk about pride in country and the nobility of sacrifice. As far as I'm concerned, war is shitting out your insides while boys die in the dark around you. Everything else is storybook fantasy, and you can leave it there.

21

Wren was out back, hunched up in the thin line of shade provided by the wall. His spindly legs straddled an empty beer crate, and he was flipping a knife into the ground.

I reached down and picked it up. Double-edged, four solid inches – standard issue during the war, though I'd long lost track of mine. Another gift from Adolphus, or his Association chums. 'Say thank you.'

My back was against the sun, and he squinted up at me. 'For what?'

'For providing you with a roof, and food while you sit beneath it.'

'Thanks,' he said, but I didn't think he really meant it.

'Thank me again.'

'I think once was enough.'

'I got you a tutor.'

Wren was not prone to strong displays of emotion. Frankly, it was one of the things I liked about him. But still I was expecting something more than nothing, which was pretty much what I got. 'Yeah?'

'She's an Islander, supposed to know her craft. Name of Mazzie.'

'Mazzie of the Stained Bone?' he asked, suddenly wary.

'You've got your first meeting with her in four days.'

'The veterans are having a big rally, getting ready for their march. I told Adolphus I'd come along and help out.'

'When I first picked you up, you couldn't pass an apple cart without knocking it over – now you're happy playing regimental mascot.'

'He's going to give a speech.'

I hadn't expected that. 'A speech?'

Wren nodded.

'I've heard that man stutter through his name. What's it on?'

'The war.'

'It's over. We won. Sorry to spoil it.' The glare reflected off everything, off the windows and the ground and the clouds. I envied Wren his cover. 'You been bugging me about this for years – don't tell me your feet have gone cold all of a sudden.'

He ran his hand through an ungainly mess of hair. 'I've . . . heard things about Mazzie.'

'Yeah.'

'Those things weren't nice.' It was as close as the boy would get to admitting he was nervous.

'You like it here?'

'Well enough.'

'You think you'd prefer a spot in the Academy, locked up for the next ten years, brainwashed till you walk in lockstep?'

'No.'

'Then we've got a limited slate of options. Whatever else Mazzie is, she's not working for the Crown, and that's the most important thing. Listen to what she has to say, follow her directions, and don't offer no lip – but keep your ears open and your eyes up. She does anything that seems off, don't be slow telling me.'

'And?'

I tossed the knife into the dust. 'And I'll handle it.'

I guess that was enough for him, 'cause he nodded and went back to his game. Like I said, Wren wasn't big on histrionics.

My room was hot as an oven, stagnant even with the windows open. I'd have given ten ochres for a fresh breeze, had there been someone to accept the offer. I stripped off my shirt and tried to catch a few hours of sleep, but between the day and the breath I wasn't having much luck. I pinched a spread of dreamvine across a layer of tobacco and puffed it into the sour air. When it was out I rolled another. It wasn't quite slumber I fell into, more a state of pleasant catatonia, but I was happy enough to have found it just the same. Time slumped against itself. It was late afternoon when a rumbling from the floor below brought me up from my stupor. After a few wasted minutes trying to recover it I put my shirt back on and descended to the kitchen.

Adolphus was down to his skivvies, restocking supplies we didn't need, a happy pretext by which to cause a great deal of commotion.

'You can stop. I'm here.'

He turned a scowl on me. Above it his one eye leered angrily. Normally he bowed to etiquette with a stretch of cloth over his empty socket, but today he hadn't. It's not such an easy thing to argue with a man while you're staring at the inside of his head, and I'd come off second best on more than one conversation because of it. I think he planned it that way – Adolphus was better at guile than he liked to let on. 'Gotta get ready for tonight.'

'Yeah, I'm sure we'll have a run on sherry. You gonna tell me what's wrong, or I am going to have to guess?'

He grunted but kept to his work.

'You miss your mother. You lost your half of the bar at dice. You've fallen in love with a dancing boy and want to run off to the Free Cities. Stop me if I'm close.'

143

He set a half-keg of cider on the ground, then turned to me. 'Wren says you're sending him to see some darkie witch-woman.'

'You got the broad strokes down.'

'Since when do you make that kind of decision without me?'

'You're a tough man to get a finger on these days, Adolphus, what with all this running about pretending that you're still a soldier.'

'I've got a right to know what's going on with him.'

'And now you do.'

'You're gonna send him down to the Isthmus, let some hag teach him to read the future in a pig's entrails?'

'It's Mazzie's lack of qualifications you object to? I knew a First Sorcerer once, but he's dead. Course, if you've got a suggestion, you're welcome to throw it into the ring.'

'I don't see what the point is. He'll grow into it.'

'It's not a pair of trousers – either we teach him to handle it or we wait until it burns out his mind. And while we're on the subject of Wren's future, what are you doing trying to turn him into a drummer boy?'

A back the length of a half-pike rose and fell. 'He likes it.'

'He'd like it if you spiked his tea with ouroboros root, but we're not going to fucking do it. It's our job to make sure he does what's smart, not what he enjoys.'

'Isn't like I took him to a recruitment center.'

'You're setting a bad example. He's a boy – he likes blood and loud noises and the naked threat of force. There's no need to encourage him.'

'That wasn't all it was.'

'I shortened it for the sake of brevity. Since you've got me going, I don't like him hanging around with the crew of miscreants you've decided to make your new best friends.'

'You deal with worse people.'

'I'm a drug dealer, so that's not much of a recommendation.' I discovered my pouch of dreamvine was still in my pocket. I thought about rolling up a spliff but thought better of it. Then

I thought better of that and went ahead and started on it. 'Your man Joachim Pretories, Roland Montgomery's successor, the Private Soldier's best friend. How much you think he's worth?'

Adolphus's eye got shifty. 'I never thought about it.'

I pinched shut the paper and lit it with a match. 'I got time.'

'I guess he gets a stipend. The dues they collect go to the wounded, and to the widows and children.'

'Every penny, I'm sure, but you haven't answered my question. What is Joachim Pretories worth?'

'I dunno. I'm not his banker.'

'He can lay hand on twenty thousand ochres, or I'm a nun.'

'Bullshit. Joachim Pretories is an honest man.'

'A unique specimen, then – we ought to frame him and mount him on the wall.'

'You jape like a monkey, but I've yet to hear any evidence.'

'Close your eyes tight enough, you'll miss the sunrise. Pretories is no different than the head of any other mob. He's got his base, and he's got his muscle.'

'The Association isn't a syndicate,' he growled, close enough to savage to be a warning, for all that I didn't heed it.

'How many men you think Roussel's killed since he mustered out? I bet it's more than he ever did in uniform.'

'You're no saint yourself.'

'And I recognize my own.'

'If you hate them so much, why'd you throw in with them?'

I ashed the joint onto the floor. 'You heard about that, huh?'

'I did.' And he didn't seem happy about it.

'I'm in an ugly line of work, Adolphus. I have to spend time with a lot of ugly people.'

'This is some . . . some scheme of yours?' he asked, horrified and bewildered, like I'd spat on a statue of the Firstborn.

'Not at all. I woke up this morning and remembered how much I loved soldiering, and the joy that would stir in my breast to find myself once again in the ranks.'

'I don't want to know about it,' he said, waving his hand as

145

if to ward me away, fat jiggling around the white of his undershirt.

'That fits well with my plan of not telling you.' But I continued just the same. 'These men aren't who you think they are – tell me you're not so desperate to relive your youth that you've blinded yourself to that fact.'

'Not everyone's as crooked as you.'

'Sure they are – they just go through more effort to hide it.'

There was a lot of nastiness floating around the bar, and with evening falling I had an errand that excused my quick absence. Upstairs I pulled a long black trunk from below my bed. Inside was a cache of weapons I don't generally need for day-to-day work. I put a knife in my sleeve and in my boot. Then I tied a trench blade to my belt, the short, wide-edged cutting swords that had been universal on both sides during the war. They weren't enough for what was coming, but they were all I had.

22

Evening is an undignified time to perspire, but that's mostly what I did on the walk over to Estroun. Weeks of drought had turned the Andel into something that could only kindly be described as a stream, a brackish trickle of water winding its way to the docks. A girl about Wren's age stood silently in the dry riverbed, watching me cross the bridge. She wore a cotton dress and had a bruise running the length of her face. In one hand she held an empty bucket. After a moment her eyes narrowed, and she spat into the current and walked off. I knew how she felt.

The Eighth Daeva Tavern took up most of the block, three towering stories and a rooftop deck that had the best view of the city north of the Aerie. To walk into it was to be whisked into a chaotic and licentious skein, a citadel of, if not debauchery, at the very least excess. It was a popular hangout for a curiously broad range of the population – bravos blowing a week's worth of thuggery on one memorable evening, slumming nobles from the Heights dipping their toes into the city's underbelly. All and sundry were welcome, so long as you had the coin and kept the peace. Aiding the first were a dozen barmen on every floor who passed out dreamvine as easy as whiskey, along with an impressive selection of gaming tables and an equally inspiring stable of whores. Ensuring the second a hand-picked squad of bouncers swept the premises regularly, unmissably large gentlemen in handsome attire loose enough to throw a punch without rupturing a seam. These were supplemented by a subtler detail, a sprinkling of wiry boys sipping watered-down beer and keeping keen eyes on the proceedings. You could do all the business you wanted in Estroun outside of the Eighth Daeva, so long as you kicked up your percentage to the man who owned it, but the bar itself was inviolate. Such was the implicit guarantee that inspired so diverse a swath of the population to revelry, a promise backed by the full faith and credit of the Swell Man.

The heat had done nothing to diminish the crowd, twenty or thirty people bottle-necked outside. I slipped to the front and took up a spot by the doorman, a brawny Vaalan with sad eyes that missed nothing. As a rule, weapons were not allowed in the Eighth Daeva, but I'm not part of the normal trade, so he glossed over my armaments. 'Hello, Warden.'

'How's the day, Koos?'

He reviewed the foremost applicant, a silken courtesan a few years past prime, then waved her in without enthusiasm. 'I'm not one to complain. Not about the weather, or the stink. Or the Crown, or the plague, or my pay.'

'You're not one to complain,' I agreed.

'No sir, I am not. Boss is on the floor somewhere – you shouldn't have trouble catching up with him.'

'Hold solid, Koos.'

'I'm a rock, Warden.'

I don't particularly like Swell's joint. Humanity is tiring enough one-to-one – I never saw what was so recreational about culling a bunch and dumping them into an enclosed area. And the Daeva was too deliberately a place to see and be seen, and I wasn't much for the spotlight – a side effect of my business dealings, I suppose. Still, it was hard not to be impressed by the sheer jubilant cacophony. From one flight up I could hear a band banging out a tune, the roof shaking in unison. Down at sea level things were a bit calmer, gallants staking their claim on the whores and the not far from it, the unloved or out of pocket drawn up despairingly against the walls.

It was a good night in the Daeva. It was always a good night in the Daeva, and Reginald Tibbs, the Swell Man, worked hard to make sure of it. He had any number of other interests, varied and lucrative, but the Daeva was his mistress. Koos had told me he was on the floor, but I hadn't needed the report. Tibbs was always on the floor, glad-handing patrons, buying drinks, laughing and chatting. He'd well earned his nickname. I caught the sway of his stovepipe in the midst of a bulge of handsome women and rich men, hanging on the wit he saw fit to dribble.

Everything about Tibbs was over-large, garish and vulgar, from the royal purple of his top hat to his canary yellow boots, bright with silver trim. A waxed mustache curlicued up to striking green eyes, countered by a forking beard that stretched down nearly to his stomach. The rest of his outfit was as expensive as it was tasteless, perfectly tailored and contrasting violently in color. He had a walk that kept pace with the sprint of lesser men, his towering midsection held in place by a pair of stork-like legs. A performance, to be sure, but one with a purpose – while your eyes trailed the dazzle, a steel trap marked you, jotted down your net worth to the copper, memorized any detail that might one day be of use. I liked Tibbs more than I distrusted him, and I checked my purse after every meeting.

He saw me and cut short his conversation, forging ahead at a step his bodyguards were hard pressed to match. He took my hand with two of his and nearly pumped it out of its socket. It was the same greeting he gave to everyone, but I liked to think he meant it more with me. 'If it isn't the Warden himself, slipped out from his caverns beneath Low Town to pay a call on his old friend.'

'Long time, Tibbs.'

'Too long, Warden, too long.' He had a voice like a slick of lamp oil. 'Not a day goes past that I don't lament your long absence. Don't I say that every day, Nissim, that I wished the Warden would manage us a visit?'

Nissim was the suitably sized Islander at his shoulder. He always seemed to be on the verge of speaking but never quite got there, and today was no exception. Tibbs answered his own question in the affirmative. 'Every day I say it!'

'I bet that's tiring.'

'You're here now, and I suppose it's up to me to make sure you come back! What's your pleasure? Try your luck at dice?' He blew on his closed hands and threw a set of imaginary bones. 'No? Who am I asking – the Warden makes his own luck! How about a shot to warm the belly? Not that you need it on a night like this – I tell you, I'm on my third pair of silk underwear!' He laughed again, and slapped me on the back hard enough to loosen teeth.

'Actually, I was hoping you might have time for a private chat.'

'It breaks my heart to think this is not a social call.'

'I'll let you stand me a whiskey, if that would keep it beating.'

Tibbs's smile was as wide as his teeth were crooked. 'Best done in the back, I suppose.' He was leading me in that direction when a man filtered out from the crowd and whispered something in his ear. Tibbs towered over him, as he did most people, and had to bend nearly double to facilitate conversation. A few sentences passed between them, eclipsed by the din of the bar. After a moment he straightened up and nodded. 'It seems I have one small piece of business to deal with before we begin.'

'Lead on,' I said, following him behind the counter and through a small door offering access to the catacombs below.

The basement was hard stone, nothing smooth or elegant about it. Rows of liquor bottles on iron racks, crates of the same in the corner. We went through another door into another room, more or less indistinguishable from the first – except that in the center of it a man lay bound across a small table. A crew of heavies stood over him, professionals, impersonally waiting to execute the word from high.

Tibbs doffed his hat and held it to his chest, looking on sadly. 'Charlus, Charlus, Charlus.' Melancholy grew with repetition.

Charlus's eyes flickered up, then back down to the ground. 'Hello Mr Tibbs,' he said.

Charlus was a Tarasaighn in his early twenties, thin and dirty, all elbows and knees. I wondered why Koos had let him into the place, looking like he did. I didn't think I'd ever seen him before, but then I don't have the head space to keep track of every purse-cutter in the city, what with most of it filled by narcotics and regret.

Tibbs squatted down level, eye-to-eye with the captive. 'This is the second time, Charlus.'

Charlus nodded, an awkward motion given his position. 'I know, Mr Tibbs. I'm sorry.'

Tibbs shook his head with a sense of disappointed wonder. 'The second time, Charlus.'

'I know, Mr Tibbs. Like I said, I'm sorry.' He seemed to mean it.

'No one works the bar, Charlus. I run a reputable establishment. The highborn come here because they know they won't be bothered.'

'I know, Mr Tibbs.'

'Didn't I give you a goose last Midwinter, to take home to your woman?'

'It was New Year's,' Charlie answered sorrowfully. 'And we greatly appreciated it.'

Tibbs nodded, standing. 'So it was,' he said. He curled his mustaches, then pronounced a sentence. 'Two fingers – the little ones.'

'Thank you, Mr Tibbs! Thank you,' Charlus said, choking with gratitude.

Tibbs ducked back down and wagged a digit in the face of his victim. 'This is the last time I go light on you – any more trouble and it's the chop.' He snapped his right hand against the wrist of his left.

The top of Charlus's head shook back and forth in the negative. 'Never again, Mr Tibbs, I promise.'

'Give your woman my compliments,' he said, again assuming his full height. He nodded towards the next room and I followed him into it, Nissim and the rest remaining.

'The Firstborn bless you, Mr Tibbs!' Charlie yelled at our backs. 'Bless you and keep you safe!'

Tibbs's quarters were modest, given his tendency towards the rococo and the fact that he probably cleared ten thousand ochres per annum. Small bordering on cramped – a crumbling desk, a coat rack and a bar. A heavy safe was sunk into the corner, cash on hand to defray his operating costs, a fortune for the average citizen.

'That boy'll come to a bad end,' Tibbs said, pouring two glasses of whiskey and taking a seat behind the desk.

I followed him to roost. 'At least you'll know you tried,' I said, not sure if I was kidding.

Tibbs nodded thoughtfully, then focused his attention on the matter at hand. 'If it was up to me, I'd settle into my high-back and we could toss words around all night. But I know you, Warden, and much as it bleeds my soul, you are not the sort for aimless jabbering. So,' he set the whiskey into my hand, and clinked my glass, 'let's get to it.'

A sharp crack interrupted us, a scream following immediately on its heels. Again the same. I took a sip of the liquor. It tasted like the sunset, and I told Tibbs so.

'A luxury I allow myself. Imported from Kinterre – you people can't distill a decent batch to save your life, if you don't mind me saying.'

I didn't. 'I need to know the time and location of the next shipment of Giroie choke,' I said.

'I don't move wyrm.'

'And I don't have a seat on the royal council, but I know where the palace is.' I could hear Charlus whimpering through the walls. You don't need your pinky fingers, strictly speaking, to pick a pocket, but their absence certainly wouldn't help.

'What are you getting involved with the Giroies for? You know the son is running it these days, and he doesn't have enough wit to fill a sock.'

'He should be about at my speed then.'

'It's not like the old days. The Islanders run the docks now, them and the heretics. Been a long time since the Tarasaighns held monopoly on contraband.'

'Come on, Tibbs, the senior Giroie wouldn't so much as shake a Kiren's hand – no way in hell Junior started cashing his chips with the foreign born. The Giroies still work through you swamp dwellers. You aren't really gonna look me in the eyes and tell me that you don't have a few friends amongst your countrymen?'

'A few, I suppose,' Tibbs said, with no great enthusiasm. 'Of course, it's a substantial favor you're asking.'

'It'd have to be, to make a dent in what you owe.'

'You did me a solid, back in the day.' He sucked at his teeth and reached out with a hard gaze. 'Back in the day.'

'Years and years ago – so I suppose it's been accruing interest.'

He smirked. 'I could put someone on it. Not like the Giroies run a tight ship.'

It'd be a foundering one soon enough, but there wasn't any need to spread that around. The Swell Man topped me off from his decanter, then took the same liberty with his own glass. 'What are you up to, Warden?'

'Treading water. You know how it goes.'

'Sounds to me like you're making a play. It's been a long time since the Giroies have been top-shelf, and their head's a fool – but he's got a fair share of men beneath him.'

'How many is a share?'

'More than zero, which means they dwarf your own reserves.'

'I never had much in the way of a formal education,' I said. 'Arithmetic makes my head fuzzy.'

'You know your business, Warden, I won't say otherwise. Been running that little kingdom of yours for a while now – though having been there, I'm not at all sure it's worth the effort.'

'A man gets accustomed to his surroundings.'

He took off his top hat and set it on the table. Without it he seemed distinctly diminished. His hair had turned silver since I'd seen it last, and in the bad light he didn't look like a man who'd live forever. 'You know, I can remember when you still wore the gray. I bet there aren't so many men who can say that.'

'My acquaintances tend not to live so long. Read into that what you will.'

'I'm still alive, Warden.'

'You are indeed.'

'Thirty years I've held my territory.'

'Long time.'

'Seen a lot of people end up sleeping in the harbor.'

'I don't doubt it.'

'After you left Black House, I remember thinking you'd be one of those unfortunates.'

'Never too late to dream.'

'All that trouble with Mad Edward's mob—'

'Poor Edward. Put his faith in the wrong people.'

'You seemed like a fellow sprinting towards a bad end.'

'More of a marathon – same destination, though.'

'But eventually things settled down, and I figured I'd been wrong.'

'Don't take it to heart – I was wrong once, too.'

'You've played it smart. Kept your grip tight, never made yourself a nuisance to anyone big enough to scratch you.'

'You're gonna make me blush, you don't cut this short.'

'Now I'm thinking I was right after all. You're tough, Warden, damn tough, and too contrary to go smooth. I think maybe you just haven't found anybody to put you down yet – but I think maybe you're still looking.'

'That was a hell of a sermon. Too late for you to join the priesthood? I think you missed your calling.'

He snickered. 'Not enough the hypocrite.'

I thought it polite not to argue.

'This information, whatever you want it for – it won't be good, not for you, not for anybody.' He rolled the brim of his cup up to his lip, then rolled it back down to his desk, empty. 'If I was your friend, I wouldn't give this to you.'

'But we aren't friends, Tibbs. You're just a guy I do business with.'

After a moment he nodded sadly and flipped the hat back on his head with one smooth motion. 'How could we be otherwise, since you never come to visit? I'll send a man around tomorrow with what you need to know.'

23

I walked into the Hen and Harpy early the next morning. It took up the first floor of a red-brick building in a quiet corner of the Old City. It was not a particularly nice restaurant – the décor and menu had remained unchanged since the plague. But then it didn't need to recoup its costs. It needed to advertise that the Giroie family had money and age, and it did that effectively. The kitchen was closed, but a man sat at the bar, pouring coffee into a porcelain mug. He was dressed like a maître d', but beneath his coat could be seen the outline of a knife.

'I'd like to speak with Artur.'

He took a long look at my frayed shirt. 'And who would you be?'

'I'd be the Warden.'

He took another look at my frayed shirt. He was having trouble squaring it with my name, though what exactly he expected from the attire of a slum kingpin, I wasn't sure. 'Is Mr Giroie expecting you?'

'Not unless he can see the future.'

'So then you're hoping he has a break in his schedule?'

'Praying for it.'

Humor confused him, and it was a while before he answered. 'I'll have to send up and see if he's available.'

I nodded and set down to wait. The concierge detailed a serving boy, then returned to his seat and his coffee, sipping slowly, pinky extended. When Senior had run the joint the bottom floor of the Hen was guarded night and day by thugs in bad suits, big guts and bigger arms, split even between friendly and threatening. I hadn't liked them, but I'd liked them more than their replacement, a silk-clad twit who'd simper while slitting your throat. After a couple of minutes a firm set Rouender with no pretensions of belonging in the service industry took me up to the top floor.

If you followed the Giroie line back far enough, you'd find a man. A real fierce motherfucker, two-fisted and vicious, the kind you wouldn't want to meet in a dark alley, or a lit one, or anywhere else for that matter. Savvy enough to catch the angles others missed, with the balls to take advantage of them. A man who'd carved an empire at the edge of a blade, who'd locked onto it with both hands and held it against all comers. Who'd inscribed his name deeply enough into his territory that it had become an inheritance. You could have seen traces of this man in Artur's father – not the full allotment, but something of his progenitor's savagery and cunning, rough patches beneath the polish.

Not so Junior – in him the blood had finally gone false, watered away to nothing. As far as he was concerned the family business was just that – he'd have been as comfortable running a merchant consortium or a winery. Had he been cognizant of his own weakness, he might have been OK, content to hold on to what his ancestors had earned, hopefully pass it down to a son who was hewn a little closer to his forebears. But Artur was a snake who thought himself a lion, and the Giroie family wouldn't last him. It had genteeled itself out of existence.

He was still high on his recent success, having swallowed up some unaffiliated street gangs a few weeks back. I doubted he'd have long to enjoy it. There were plenty of players out there larger than the Giroies, and it didn't do to draw their attention just to add a few blocks of territory. But then, Junior had a hard time seeing past his next meal. I'd known him for years – he used to hang around the restaurant, his father's lieutenants bringing him candy and paying him compliments, a spoiled child who'd become a callow youth.

His office was altogether too elegantly outfitted for a man who, bottom line, made his living off choke and leashed whores. He was sitting at a table about the length of a coffin, and didn't bother to get up as I came in. The top of it was one smooth sheet of translucent crystal, because who doesn't want to be staring at another man's thighs while conducting business?

'Warden,' he began happily. 'A pleasant surprise.' Artur was the wrong sort of pretty for his industry. Muscled but soft, with blond hair trailing to his shoulders and an outfit that seemed cut from a courtesan's bed sheet.

'Appreciate you making the time.'

'A pleasure, a pleasure. How's business going?'

'A glorious string of uninterrupted successes. Yourself?'

'It goes very well,' he said. The sunlight came in through the windows and off his teeth. 'Very well indeed.'

'Good to hear.'

'Can I get you something? Whiskey? Cigar?'

It was nine-thirty in the morning, but offering gifts reminded Artur that he was rich, so every meeting was my birthday. I shook my head just the same. 'I'm solid.' I took a deliberate look at the surrounding opulence. 'Been some changes since I sat here last.'

'Change comes for all of us, Warden – either we embrace it, or we let it swallow us.'

I'd make sure to polish up that pearl of wisdom and set it

somewhere safe. 'That's what happened to the James Street Boys? They got eaten up by the future?'

He smiled, coy as a ten-ochre whore. 'You heard about that?'

'Word spreads.'

'An ugly sort of business, really. If it were up to me, these sorts of things wouldn't be necessary. Business could be conducted honestly, with all sharing in the profit. But,' he sighed dramatically, 'we do not live in such a world.'

'Your world, maybe – mine's nothing but spun sugar and sunsets.'

'You'll have to invite me over sometime.' He leaned back in his chair and folded his hands. 'I'm sure you didn't make the walk up here just to listen to me ruminate.' Though that wouldn't stop him. 'What is it that brings you to the Hen before noon?'

'Call it a sense of neighbourliness.'

That crossed his eyes. 'I was unaware our homes abutted.'

'All the world is my home, Artur, and every man my neighbor.'

His laugh was too close to a giggle for my tastes. 'Speak on, citizen of the world.'

'I hear you've been having trouble with the Association.'

He looked faintly quizzical. 'No, not really.'

'You won't be able to say that much longer.'

His desk was covered with a wide variety of bric-a-brac, paperweights and gilded timepieces, useless but expensive gadgetry from the Free Cities that chimed when you tapped them. He picked one of the assemblage, a miniature pikeman, and began to wind its key. 'What kind of trouble?'

'The kind of trouble an organization subsisting of narcotics distribution would have with an organization once sworn to eradicate it.'

Artur grimaced, unhappy to be reminded he didn't operate a cotton concern. He set the toy back onto the desk. It marched forward a few inches in awkward lockstep, then tumbled over. 'The family has many and varied interests, most strictly legal. I wouldn't at all describe us in the terms you used.'

'I'd assumed both of us were too busy for hair splitting, but if I'm the only one who's got things to do today . . .'

'We haven't been in conflict with the veterans for over ten years, since Roland Montgomery was killed.'

'I hope you enjoyed the break.'

'You're saying they're going to move on us?'

'Haven't they already? You think Pretories doesn't know who pulls the Savages' strings?'

'The Savages are not affiliated with the Giroie family,' Artur said. 'Like any other wholesale operator, we have a wide variety of customers. Whatever activities they engage in after our transactions are finalized is no concern of ours, I can assure you.'

'A neat distinction, one I doubt the other syndicates will make. The street respects winners, Giroie – and not yesterday's winners, either.'

'You don't need to tell me my business,' he said with a pinched-lemon face. 'Where's your information coming from? Is it reliable?'

'You don't need to tell me my business either, Artur. I wouldn't have wasted the walk if I didn't think what I had to say was on the level.'

He tapped nervously at the glass shelf. 'No offense, Warden – I know your sources are well placed. But the Association has kept themselves out of our business for over a decade, and we've done the same. Pretories has never shown any willingness to renew our conflict, and I don't see why that would change now.'

'You hear about this march they've got planned?'

'Of course.'

'Next week he'll have fifty thousand men underneath his banner. Numbers like that, might be he gets to thinking about settling old scores.'

'Might be,' he responded, unconvinced but nervous.

I boosted myself to my feet. 'Do whatever you want, Artur – this was a courtesy.'

Artur stood as well. 'Don't misunderstand – I appreciate the information. You've always been a loyal friend of the family.'

I'd never been anything of the sort, but there was no reason to point that out. 'I'm near enough to Association territory to warrant keeping an ear out. They finish with you, might be they set sights on me next.'

'I doubt it will come to anything,' Junior said, back straight, doing his best to seem like a person of importance. 'But if they make a play, we'll answer it.'

Downstairs the maître d' and Artur's guard sat together at a table, drinking coffee and playing chess. They played ugly, trading pieces at random and without any sense of deeper strategy. The guard had mate in three, but he didn't see it. I watched their game for a moment, wondering if either would be alive at the end of mine. But it was too hot for speculation, let alone sympathy, and I headed on out.

24

Twelve hours later I stood in front of a beaten-down mansion, ancient and decaying, a monument to the time a half-century past when the docks were prime real estate and not the city's dumping ground. The late summer sun had dipped below the skyline but its residue offered some succor against the coming night. On the ramparts above me the usual line of stone gargoyles gave silent warning, half-animal figures with broken appendages and fractured leers, the population within slow to scare and quick to vandalize. The rest of the abode had gone in the same direction, product of the passive indifference and bored maliciousness of a generation of squatters. You wouldn't have thought anything to look at it, unless you spent a few minutes watching the stream of passers-by cross the street rather than walk past.

The Bruised Fruit Mob owned a stretch of territory along the boundary between the Isthmus and Kirentown, an area so impoverished as to blur racial animosity, skin color rubbed away by the abject misery of circumstance. They bore close resemblance to a lot of other Islander gangs, smuggling goods through their section of the docks and hiring out as muscle to anyone foolish enough to take them. They had no real ties to anyone who mattered, and their activities were of the kind that tended to make a lot of noise, which in the long run is poor strategy for a criminal organization. For the moment, though, they punched above their weight, making up in sheer savagery what they lacked in resources and sanity.

A bravo lounged outside the entrance, charcoal-skinned, a curved short sword swinging from each hip. Though my visits were frequent and nothing but beneficial to his clan, still he bared back his teeth when he saw me, unable to conceive of any other greeting. I paid it little mind, shouldering him aside and descending through the door into hell.

The founder of the Bruised Fruit Mob had fancied himself an artist, as well as a thug and killer, and he'd compulsively tattooed his dreams throughout the interior in vibrant and garish colors. His initial creations were distinctly light-hearted, smiling clouds blowing gusts of wind across dancing children, an anthropomorphic sun smoking a joint and winking. As his craving for wyrm had festered, he'd painted over his visions with things far darker – horned figures engaged in ill-defined blasphemies, abortions mouthing their hatred at the world. He'd died a year or so back – choke will do that to you – and his masterpiece had begun to degrade, the results of his different periods blurring together into an infernal overlap of pigment.

The building itself had been unsafe for habitation since before its current crop of occupants had turned their teeth from the nipple. Rotting walls leaned against each other, standing solely from force of habit. The smell of decay was heavy and omnipresent, pulped wood and mildew, rainwater seeping through ceilings and into the foundations. Given the size of the structure, one would have supposed it reasonably simple to confine refuse, and for that matter bodily waste, to a specific wing or floor. One would be disappointed. Trash of all kinds lay strewn about, and the stink of urine emanated from stains on the walls.

There were five or six thugs hanging out in the hallway, passing thick spliffs of dreamvine back and forth, and laughing in a not altogether friendly fashion. They cut the chatter short when they saw me. Despite the extravagant, labyrinthine layout of their headquarters, large enough to accommodate every member of the gang and his extended family besides, the antechamber was always packed. A close-knit crew of lunatics were the Bruised Fruit Mob. This batch managed a slightly more genial greeting than their confederate outside, mumbling my name and nodding me through a wooden door painted to resemble the back of a throat.

Inside the main room was the man and his heavy, strung over a collection of furniture that had been the subject of frequent outbursts of aggression. The muscle perched precariously on a stool too small for him, sharpening a knife that would have been a sword in a normal man's hands. It didn't need sharpening, but he was sharpening it anyway. I could never remember his name; it was enough to know his purpose.

Adisu the Damned was stretched out on a couch, scraping his grin with a toothpick. He was young, a few years over twenty – they seemed always to be getting younger, these vice-lords and corner kingpins, though maybe that was just me getting older. Truth told he didn't look like much – a runt of a man with bad skin and a shaved head, and eyes that were too big for their frame.

But looks can deceive. Adisu was, in fact, as hard a man as you'd ever meet, greedy and fierce, and apt to forget you were the same. He needed constant watching, else he'd try and make a play on you – it wasn't enough that he got his end, he wanted yours as well. You needed to make sure he kept firm in his head that you were not a fellow with whom to fuck, but politely, without any outright challenge.

Because the other thing about Adisu was that he was shithouse crazy – you could see it in the way his eyes never quite settled on anything, and in the nervous movement of his hands. It wasn't a put-on, he wasn't mad-dogging to keep an edge on his people

– there was something wrong with him, something broke. So even if you played everything perfect you still weren't home free, 'cause at some point whatever was inside his skull would tell him to jump, it was only a question of time. I'd seen him do it once, beat a runner to death with a frying pan he'd pulled up off the fire – one minute we're laughing and passing around a blunt, the next Adisu's smashing bits of brain out of the poor kid's nose. Afterward he'd said it was because the boy was stealing, but that was nonsense. There wasn't a reason, not a real one.

The whole mob was mad for ouroboros root, they kept a simmer pot of it going on the table day and night, and it filled the air with a thin soup of hallucinogens. 'Hello, Warden,' Adisu said, leaning over the table and fanning back the fumes. 'What can I do for you?'

I shook my head. 'Close, but no ring.'

'All right then. What can you do for me?'

'Depends. How you feel about money?'

The half of his grin that was pure gold gleamed in the candle-light. 'I'm for its acquisition.'

'And the Giroies? Where do you stand on them?'

He laughed. The muscle laughed too. The muscle was well trained. 'We love all them yellow-haired white boys. Sticky as honey, the batch of us.'

'That's a pity.'

'Is it?'

I nodded. ''Cause I happen to know where their next shipment of wyrm is getting dropped, and if you weren't sweethearts, you might be able to lay your hands on a quarter-stone of uncut choke.'

The muscle stopped sharpening his knife. Adisu stretched back against the couch, stroking a tuft of padding that stuck out through the torn leather. 'Now that you mention it,' he said, 'I fucking hate the Giroies.'

'Tomorrow night, around one, a skiff will dock at the tip of the Sugarland Pier. Some men will get off it. Other men will meet them.' Or at least that was what had been written on the sealed note Tibbs's man had brought by the Earl that afternoon, brought it and waited while I read it, then watched as I held it over a candle.

'Yeah?'

'That's the plan at least. Of course, sometimes plans have a way of not working out.'

'Security?'

'I doubt it's being escorted by nuns, but last I checked you don't run a monastery.' I'd been doing my best not to take in any of the frying root, but a fellow can only go so long without breathing. I could feel it buzzing at the base of my brain stem, and my tongue felt slow and swollen. A pair of fornicating demons on the back wall stopped their lovemaking to turn and leer at me. Above them an intricately detailed portrait of the Lost One wept tears of blood that trickled down the walls.

'Where's your end in this?' Adisu asked.

'Say a third of what you get from selling off the stash.'

'Say a fourth.'

I nodded ascent. I didn't so much care about the money – for my purposes the only thing that mattered was that there wouldn't be any Giroies left to talk up who'd hit them. But then the Bruised Fruit Mob had a well settled 'no survivors' policy, and I didn't think I needed to voice my concern.

'The Giroies . . .' Adisu began. 'They probably wouldn't be happy if they found out a crew of inks made off with their stash.'

'Why, you thinking of telling them?'

Adisu rested his chin against his hands, weighing his options silently. A silhouette of my mother on the back wall reached out her hands to me, sympathetic and disappointed. I blinked her away. 'What you think, Zaga?' Adisu asked.

The muscle let the sword fall from his hand, its weight wedging the tip into the floorboards. 'Set up,' he said, beady eyes snarling in a skull the size of a coconut.

'But on whom?' Adisu reached over and pulled his man's weapon out of the wood. 'You know Warden here used to be an agent?

High up in it too, from what I hear. Made sure the Dren didn't swoop over the bay and pillage the city. Protect the country and shit.' He made a mocking little salute. 'He still thinks like that, like we was pieces on a board. He wants us to play the hammer on some poor set of motherfuckers.'

'We gonna do it?' the muscle asked.

'Hell yeah, we gonna do it. 'Cause the Warden, he makes sure the angles meet. We just little fish, ain't nothing he wants to concern himself with. If the take ain't square or if the Giroies are waiting for us . . .' He gestured with the blade. 'There's gonna be trouble, trouble our man don't need. And he's too smart to make trouble for himself.'

Adisu the Damned would be dead in six months – no one could hold to his narcotic regimen indefinitely, and he ran his boys too hard, and he was too fond of close-in work. But none of that changed the fact that he was half a genius, sharp as the steel he was holding.

'One o'clock, Sugarland Pier,' I reminded him.

'I'll make a note of it,' Adisu said, bright-eyed and smiling.

I pushed myself up from the chair, unsteady from the smoke but trying to hide it. False, horrifying things swarmed the walls like crabs overflowing a barrel. The first man I'd ever killed waved hello to me, a boy really, grinning at me beneath a caved-in skull, pink oozing out the hole I'd made. Soon he was joined by a host of others, slit throats and burned bodies, corpses barely remembered, all standing abreast, laughing silently and gesturing for me to join them.

'What you got against the Giroies?' Adisu asked, breaking me out of hallucination.

'Absolutely nothing,' I said honestly, then fell on out.

25

I was finishing off a pot of coffee the next morning when they came for me, a pair of them, the collars of their gray-blue dusters upturned despite the heat. Not big men, but big enough, short blades at their sides, hard in the right places. I was the only person in the joint but they took a few seconds before coming over. First thing an agent learns is you never hustle, not unless it's time to snap the trap shut.

I'd been wondering how long it would take before the ice decided to pay me a call. I would have figured I'd have time for a few more moves before they made theirs, but this was fine. Actually this was good – it meant they were keeping an eye on Pretories.

I didn't know either of them, but then I'd been out of the Crown's service eight years, and recruitment continued apace. They seemed to know me, however, and while one smiled and took a seat, the other stayed standing, eyes hard, hands ready to make sure I went easy.

'You busy?' the friendly one asked. His face was fat and freckled, like a jolly uncle. The rest of him told you this impression was a lie.

'Never too busy for the Crown.'

'That's good to hear. You'd be shocked to discover how many of your neighbors feel otherwise.'

'Spare the details, please. I've got a weak heart.'

'I don't suppose your sense of duty would extend to a trip to Black House?'

'What kind of patriot would I be otherwise?' I asked, standing. They walked me to the small carriage waiting outside, opened the door for me even. Then they took seats across from me, smiling and unsmiling, respectively. I wondered if they ever switched roles. It gets boring being yourself all the time.

Black House is the center point of the Empire, where the decisions get made – we just keep the palace around so tourists have something to look at. From inside its soot-colored walls a few hundred uniformed men work diligently to fetter the hands and bind the eyes of some millions of their fellows. I don't like going there, and not just because the last few times I'd arrived in cuffs. A life like mine, most lives really, you're better off not looking back – my years in Black House belonged to a different epoch, a distant and best-forgotten age.

Still, if I had to pay a visit, it was nice not to have a sentence of death hanging over my head. We stopped in front of the entrance, a footman arriving swiftly to help us alight. Then the gray-clad pair escorted me down the front hallway and into the back, up a flight of stairs and through the door of a corner office where I had the first legitimate shock of the day.

'Hello, Warden,' Guiscard said. 'Grab yourself a seat. There are some things I'd like to run past you.'

It had been three years since I'd seen him, but time is a malleable thing and well more than that had passed on his end. He'd been a pretty little peacock when I'd known him, eye candy for the heiresses and perfumed fairies at court, but he wasn't any longer. There was a gauntness to his face that accentuated the beak-like turn of his nose. His hair was still a striking shade of white-blond, but it had receded over his temples and he'd trimmed what remained to stubble, a far cry from the curls he'd once sported. His uniform was spotless but faded – it seemed his coxcombry had gone the way of his hair.

Or maybe he just didn't have the time to keep up a fashionable exterior. The fact that he had men to order about had tipped me, but the five-pointed star on his lapel confirmed it – Guiscard was a member of Special Operations. The last I'd seen him, when he'd treasoned me out to the Old Man, he was still slumming it with the rest of the freeze, chasing down murderers and rapists. Now he was a member of the elite, and stopping crime beneath him. His new duties tended towards spy craft, counter-intelligence, preemptive assassination – that wide variety of unsavory activities that ensure those in power remain so.

I guess selling my secrets had earned him the seat. I didn't blame him. The Firstborn knew I'd done worse to get there.

'Nice digs,' I said.

'Thanks.'

'Normally when I get called down here, it's to see the chief. I'm feeling a little unloved.'

'Don't take it too hard. The Old Man's delegated me to look in on you. He's not as young as he used to be.'

'He was never young.'

'No, I suppose he wasn't.' Guiscard waved again at the chair. 'Have a seat.'

'I'll stand.'

The agents stirred behind me. 'You really gonna buck at the offer of a chair?'

'You really gonna muscle me into one?'

'Yeah.'

I sat. I'd been expecting to be doing this with the Old Man, but the fact that Guiscard was point would make the whole thing easier. I wondered how much he knew of Black House's past history with the Association, and about Roland's murder in particular. Less than he supposed, I was sure. The Old Man didn't like anyone to know anything. Better to have a subordinate ruin an operation through ignorance than weaken his own position internally.

Guiscard nodded at the two agents. They closed the door on their way out, and the rumble of the building dulled away.

'Word is you and Joachim Pretories have been having a lot of meetings.'

'That the word?'

'That you've thrown your hand in with the Association.'

'What do you think?'

'You never struck me as a man inclined toward nostalgia.'

'You'd be wrong there. I still have the rocking horsey I got for my fifth name day.'

'Nor someone apt to end up on the losing side of things.'

'You're definitely wrong there.'

'So that's it then? You and the commander, arm-in-arm?'

'I dunno about any of that. Maybe I just felt like paying a call on a fellow veteran. Talk about old times, relive our youths.'

'Whatever you may think, Joachim Pretories isn't a man to be trusted.'

I laughed.

'You disagree?'

'No, not at all – it's just funny to be on the other side of this conversation.'

'Then why would you set yourself up as his pawn?'

I had to play this tight. Black House needed to think they were running me, and not the other way around. 'I'm a small-timer these days, Agent – I job with whoever offers it.'

'And you aren't overly concerned with who your patron is?'

'I used to work here, didn't I?'

'Fair point,' he admitted.

The Guiscard I knew had been brash, youth and high status inclining him towards playing the bull. But he'd picked up a trick or two since then. Best to let a man come to you, not to force it. You don't need to force it if you've got the leverage, and Black House always had the leverage.

'So you called me in here because you were worried I was hanging with a rough crowd. I'm touched. I'll make a point to mend my ways in the future.'

'That wasn't exactly what we were hoping.'

'Subtlety makes my head hurt.'

'You say you've got the commander's ear. Maybe you could stick around, let us know what falls into yours.'

'I don't know – I really took that warning you gave me about Pretories to heart.'

'It would be in the interests of the Crown.'

'I'm not that interested in your interests.'

He shrugged, then threaded his fingers through one another. 'How's the Earl?'

'It runs. Come by sometime – I'll spit in a glass of ale for you.'

'How's Adolphus? And the boy?'

I smiled unpleasantly. 'Let me give you a lesson in making threats, Guiscard – start small, 'cause you can't go backwards. It don't mean anything to tell a man with a slit throat that you're gonna break his kneecaps. Threatening my people . . . that's as heavy as it gets. So now, when I tell you to go fuck yourself, you got no cards left to play. You'll just have to sit there like an impotent faggot, moaning at my impertinence.'

'There's no reason this needs to turn sour. Believe it or not, I didn't call you in to muscle you. I'm hoping the two of us can help each other out.'

'You offered me help on something once before, I remember – what was it again?' I snapped my fingers theatrically. 'Yes, of course – you promised to help find the man who murdered our ex-partner, then you turned around and sold me to the Old Man.'

'Look, Warden. You sat where I'm sitting once, and you had the same conversation we're about to have. This is Black House. We own the city. We own the country. We own the sea and the skies. If there's a place you go to when you die, we own that too. We spin the shuttlecock of your fate – the woof can go easy, or it can go hard.'

I fished out my tobacco pouch from my pocket. The heat had dried it out, and the tab I rolled was awkward because of it. 'I used to give that speech better.'

'How did people respond?'

'Depended on who I gave it to.'

'How are you going to respond?'

'Say it goes easy.' I lit my cigarette. 'What would that look like?'

Guiscard opened a drawer in his desk and pulled out an ashtray, then set it in front of me. 'We aren't entirely without resources, nor are we unwilling to compensate associates for their assistance.'

'What kind of assistance?'

'Let's begin with what you know.'

'I know lots of things, Guiscard. We start in that direction and we'll be here all day.'

'Confine yourself to the recent goings-on of the Veterans' Association.'

'They've got a march coming up.'

'So far I'm not blown out of my seat.'

'And before fifty thousand men charge the palace, Pretories is gonna detail a few of them to burn out a syndicate.'

That didn't quite blow him out of his seat either, but he leaned back in it at least, mulling things over before responding. 'To what end?'

'I'm not privy to his innermost thoughts. I suspect this thing with the Private's Silver has him unsettled. Makes him look weak, like he can't take care of his people. So while he's got the numbers he figures he'll use them, remind everybody that the Association isn't to be taken lightly, and neither is their leader.'

'Who's the target?'

'He wouldn't tell me outright, but I suspect the Giroies. They're big enough to win him some merit but small enough to swallow without choking. And there's still a lot of bad blood between the two, after what happened last time.'

'Last time,' he repeated thoughtfully. 'Going after a

syndicate – that was more in his predecessor's line, if I remember my history.'

'I guess he's feeling sentimental.'

Guiscard cleared his throat obtrusively. 'This is all a bit . . . difficult to believe.'

'That's the nice thing about being omniscient – you can wait around for life to prove you right. Then you get to laugh at the people who didn't believe you.'

'What does Joachim want you for?'

'I'm reasonably well informed as to underworld gossip. He hoped I'd spread the scuttlebutt one further.'

Guiscard cleared his throat again. It seemed to have replaced his sneer as the go-to in his arsenal of mannerisms. 'Your suspicions aren't exactly rock solid.'

'I asked him to sign a confession, but for some reason he proved leery.'

'So you got nothing.'

'Today I got nothing.' I leaned forward and pressed my tab out into the ashtray. 'In a week I'll be the smartest motherfucker alive, and you'll marvel at my intuition.'

He shrugged affably, then gestured toward the door. 'I guess I'll see you next week then.'

I whistled walking home, though the sun parched my throat and my head buzzed for a shot of breath. The dominos were falling in line. Soon it would be time to tip another one over.

26

I spent the rest of the day looking after various aspects of my business that had gone to seed while I'd been sprinting about the city like some addled knight errant. It was a slow month, uncomfortably so. The weather had sapped the recreational instincts of my clients, and the bartenders and short dealers who copped from me were mostly still flush. Something about hundred-degree heat made people less interested in hopping themselves up on breath. Most of my top-end trade, the Kor's Heights boys and budding merchant princes, were spending high summer on their country plantations, so that avenue had dried up as well. It was an unprofitable afternoon, and it left me in something of a mood.

The messenger came by while I was eating my way through the mutton stew Adeline had made for dinner. It was too fucking hot to be eating mutton stew, and frankly I was happy for the interruption.

I have urgent information, urgent and valuable. I repeat, urgent and valuable. Find yourself at my domicile with all conceivable haste, and bring along twenty ochre as a down payment.

Signed,
Iomhair Gilchrist, Factor

Beneath that, as if suspecting that his promise alone would be insufficient to move me, he had written:

I know who killed Rhaine Montgomery.

As it happened, so did I. All the same, I figured seeing what Iomhair had to tell me was worth the walk. I finished off my mutton, smoked a cigarette, and went upstairs to get twenty ochre. Actually giving it to him was, of course, a last resort, and not one I imagined I'd need. Most likely I'd lie or beat out whatever Gilchrist had or thought he had, but on the off-chance the man had grown a spine since last we spoke, I figured it couldn't hurt to have a back-up.

The evening was the rare balmy dollop, still sticky as ball sweat but a fair improvement over the afternoon. I glided through streets empty of traffic, enjoying the constitutional and trying not to fixate on the destination. Iomhair's house was as unprepossessing as ever. Someone had scratched 'cunt' across his run of new paint, presumably the same wag responsible for the original, though I imagined it was a popular sentiment.

Habit being what it was I didn't bother to knock, but for once the door was locked. 'Gilchrist,' I yelled. 'Open the fuck up.'

No answer – nothing spoken, at least. But from inside I heard a bustle of motion, and muted mutterings, and I wondered if perhaps Gilchrist hadn't been exaggerating when he'd demanded my haste.

I sprinted around the side of the building in time to see a man climbing out of Iomhair's side window. There wasn't enough light to make out any detail, but I figured he was unlikely to be a clandestine lover so I upped my speed and launched myself at him. He still had one leg hanging from the frame, an awkward position to be in when someone sets their shoulder into your chest. I heard something pop on the way down, probably his ankle, but it didn't slow him. We tumbled through the dust, nothing pretty or skillful about it. He got his hands around my throat but I broke free, reared up and hammered his chin into the dirt. A few more of those and he went limp, and I pulled him to his feet and set him up against the wall.

In the pause I recognized him, the white-haired mope I'd seen hanging around the last time I'd gone to visit Pretories. It took his mind a long moment to square itself from the beating he'd taken, then his eyes fixed on my face and gleamed with recognition. 'What are you doing here?'

I hesitated in answering, trying to think up something smart. It's a good thing I'm not all that clever because the silence was interrupted by a noise from the alley behind me, and I grabbed my man and swung him around. It was instinct – I can't pretend I knew what the sound was, but on some dim level I realized it was better to have my captive between me and it.

There was another sound then, one I did recognize – the *thwack* of a released bowstring. Concurrent with this, or nearly so, was the grunt of my human shield, and the sight of a quarrel head poking out from his chest.

At that distance there was a fair chance the bolt would have passed through its target with enough force to do me as well. I didn't take time to enjoy my luck. Leaving the mug to drop where he was I dove back through the window, an awkward motion, desperate and ungainly, my shin banging against the frame. Once inside I ducked down below the window, taking care not to present a target. A taper on the desk provided the only light, and I searched for something to knock it over with. My hands settled on a heavy ledger, and I sent it spinning at the candle. Given the debris there was a better than average chance the falling spark would set the place off like a tinderbox.

But it didn't, and I stayed crouched down in the dark, my trench blade in one hand, a throwing knife in the other. If whoever was out there decided to rush me I figured they'd do it then, and I'd be set to meet them. If it was just the one guy it might end in my favor. It probably wasn't just the one guy, I conceded.

Five minutes passed. If they were waiting me out, they were doing a good job. Another five. Nobody's that patient, not after killing a man. Whoever had fired that bolt was gone. I waited ten more to be sure, then sheathed my weapons, closed the window and started searching for the candle.

It was a while before I found it, rolled beneath a pile of half-decade-old broadsheets. I lit it with a match from my belt and surveyed the room. It was still a cluttered mess, uneaten food on the bookshelves and rotting paperwork on the floor. It was chaos when I'd been there last – it was chaos now. Whatever struggles had taken place in the last half hour had left little enough mark on the terrain. Little enough except the body on the floor, of course.

To be absolutely honest, I would not have bet my stake of the Earl on the continued vitality of Iomhair Gilchrist – still, I'd been hoping he'd stick around a little longer, for purely mercenary reasons.

Wish in one hand and shit in the other, as they say. The corpse at my feet seemed definitive proof as to which was the more effective means of filling a palm. Iron Stomach had been no great beauty in life, and death hadn't done him any favors. His fat face was swelled like an over-ripe melon, his mustache a thin line of silver amidst the bloated red. He'd swallowed most of the rag they'd stuffed into his mouth to keep him quiet, and two wide handprints were bruised into his neck. Had they been made by the same pair that had done Rhaine? Somehow I didn't doubt it.

Not that I'd needed confirmation, but I had it. Joachim Pretories had killed Rhaine's adviser, just as he'd killed Rhaine herself. I left the corpse where it was, undid the front door and slipped out into the night. On principle, I didn't like leaving the body there to rot, but I couldn't very well call attention to my presence by contacting the authorities. Besides, the way things were going, he'd have plenty of company.

27

I slept poorly.

The dinner trade had been sparse and languid, a thin squad of losers out-drinking the coin in their purses. Violent though – twice Adolphus had been forced to leave his perch behind the bar and express to our patrons the necessity of tranquility in fashion both sanguinary and ironic. At the end of the night Adeline had soaked blood out of her mop. Hadn't been the first time, wouldn't be the last.

I'd spent the evening alternating shots of liquor and snorts of breath, and trying to convince myself that the death of Iomhair Gilchrist wouldn't lead directly to my own. It had been dark in the alleyway – too dark, I hoped, to make out faces. The fact that the bowman had mistaken his own for me was proof enough of that. If he had recognized me, though, the whole thing was fucked sideways. Pretories less than half-trusted me as it was – if he heard I'd been freelancing he'd put me down, no sense leaving me around to make trouble. It would be the smart move and, despite his missteps, I didn't think Joachim a fool.

Practically speaking, of course, it didn't matter. I was in it to the hilt. That's the thing about sprinting downhill – you run it out or you tumble.

Around one o'clock I'd climbed up to the roof, angled my feet off the balcony and rolled a spliff. Somewhere out in the darkness men were dying because of me. They weren't very good men, I supposed – the thugs and bully-boys Artur Giroie the Second had hired to watch his shipment of poison. But then I wasn't a very good man either, and perhaps shouldn't be so casual with the lives of my confederates in immorality.

It was a long time before I'd gone to bed, and as I mentioned, I hadn't had much success once I'd gotten there.

My morning schedule was light. Apparently Wren's was as well, because I'd been up for a solid hour before he made an appearance, and I'm no early riser.

He came in finally from the back, yawning and shirtless, thin as gristle, skin stretched over bone. 'Anything left for me?'

I forked a last morsel of egg into my mouth. 'You're a resourceful child. I'm confident you'll find something.'

He scowled unhappily, then took a seat at my table.

I pulled out the armband Mazzie had given me and passed it over to him. 'Wear this when you go to your appointment – make sure the local element knows you've been marked.'

Wren eyed it with discomfort bordering on disgust, like I'd dropped a turd onto the table. Then he stuffed it into his back pocket and muttered something.

'What was that?'

'I don't see the point.'

'I thought I clarified it during our last conversation.'

'I don't need any help. I can figure out what I need to on my own.'

'You can't, but that wasn't what I meant. If you don't go see Mazzie tomorrow I'm going to hang you out the window by your fucking ankles. That firm up your schedule?'

The threat left him silent for a whole five seconds. Then he wiped his nose with a dirty hand and continued, 'Adolphus has a speech tomorrow.'

'That didn't interest me the first time I heard it.'

'It's a big deal. There might be five thousand men watching him.'

'So you can ask one of them how it went.'

'It's important to him. He's a hero, you know.'

'Is he? I hadn't heard.'

'He held the line at Aunis. Killed twenty men single-handed.'

'That what makes a man a hero? Killing a lot of people?'

'It does if they're Dren.'

'You meet a lot of Dren in Low Town?'

He shook his head.

'You ever watch a man burn to death? You ever smell a man char?'

He swallowed hard, but kept his eyes on mine.

'You won't ever look at a chop steak again the same way, I can guarantee you that much.'

Now he did look away, craning his neck to avoid my gaze.

'Wouldn't be so quick to talk about glory neither, I'd reckon.' I sipped my coffee and turned to look out the window. 'Keep that sloppy cunt mouth of yours shut around me from now on, or I'll close it myself.'

There was a long pause, and I thought he might take the advice. But there was still too much of the savage in him to swallow my abuse without spitting some back out. 'I think you're jealous.'

I laughed. 'You nailed it. They didn't pin enough tin to my chest, and I've never forgiven them for it.'

'I'm going to Adolphus's speech.'

'You trying to make me cross? 'Cause I'm halfway there already.'

'You don't tell me what to do.'

'Don't I?' I asked, and by then my humour had quite turned. My hands were around his shoulders, and I was

185

pulling him out of his seat when I was interrupted by a noise at my side.

'What's going on here?' Adeline's voice is perpetually pitched midway to hectoring, but this time I think she really meant it.

'Just talking,' I said, letting go of Wren's shoulders.

Her eyes thinned to slits, a dash in the series of conjoined circles that composed her body and face. 'I know about your kind of talking.' She turned to Wren. 'Chores, now.'

He shot hate at me for a second, then slithered off. 'You'll be at Mazzie's,' I called to his back. 'Don't fucking think otherwise.'

I sat back down. Adeline remained standing beside me, but given her height we were about level.

'What was that about?' she asked.

'Just impressing upon our boy the importance of a strong education.'

'You've been "impressing" things on him a lot lately.'

'Was that a joke? How droll. I thought you'd be on my side with this. Weren't you the one bugging me to get him a teacher? I get him one and my return is nothing but hassle.'

'He's scared,' she said evenly. 'You could see that if you weren't up to your ears in whatever mess you're making.'

'The world is a scary place – the sooner he learns to fear it the better off he'll be.'

'Is that why you put bruises on him? To teach him some caution?'

'Mostly it's just because he gets on my fucking nerves.'

I was trying to goad her, but it didn't have that effect. 'Your nose is bleeding,' she said finally.

I put two fingers against my upper lip. She was not wrong – I hadn't realized I'd been hitting the breath so hard.

'Did you bump it against something?'

I'd rolled a cigarette for after breakfast, and figured this was a solid time to start on it. 'You know me. Clumsy as an ox.'

'What the hell is going on?'

'I don't know what you mean.'

'Agents coming by the Earl? You and Adolphus huffing at each other? What con are you running, and where is it gonna leave us? The last time you pulled something it almost got Wren killed, do you remember that? What trouble are you bringing down on us now?'

'You want me gone? Is that what this is? All you gotta do is ask. Course, you might find things ain't so easy out from beneath my coattails. Not like the Earl is some great moneymaker. How much have I sunk into this place over the years, bridge loans during the dry seasons? It must be nice, drifting so far above it, hands clean as buttermilk and a conscience to match. I imagine it's quite an embarrassment having someone like me in your house, a common criminal.' Smoke streamed through ruptured nostrils. 'But you take my coin, don't you, Adeline – and you ask my favor, when you need it.'

She recoiled into silence. Her mouth shuttered up and down, silently weathering the blow.

Nothing like striking a saint to buff your self-image. It was time to get going, ten or fifteen minutes past time. By now Artur Giroie would be aware that his shipment had been smashed and his boys killed. He'd be angry, and he'd be looking for a direction to aim that anger. I figured I might be of some service to him.

'You have a nice morning,' I told Adeline, yet to recover from my abuse. 'I gotta ride a man off a cliff.'

28

When I came in Artur's tantrum was trailing off, his muttered profanities the light mist left by the storm that had just leveled the room. One of his crystal paperweights was lodged in the wood paneling beside the door. The painted canvas above his desk had been stripped from the wall, a rent down the middle defacing the dull pastoral scene. Junior stood next to the line of windows overlooking the neighborhood he owned, or pretended to. His hair was mussed.

I righted the visitor's chair and set myself into it, untying my tobacco purse and shaking out a sheave.

Blind fury takes its toll on a man. Junior sat down after I did, but it was a while before he stopped breathing heavy. I was kind enough to wait before beginning.

'Rough morning?'

He had taken a spiced cigarette from an ivory box on the table, but was having trouble getting it started, a mass grave of used matches lining the glass. I lit mine with a quick pass, then leaned over and did the same for him.

He took a stuttering drag and blew clove and tar into the air. 'Someone hit a shipment of ours last night. Killed the guard to a man, made off with the merchandise.'

'That's not very friendly.'

He slammed a fist down against his desk, setting what bric-a-brac had survived his conniption rumbling. 'A hundred ochre gone. Would have made five times that on the street.' He ran a hand through his long, blond locks. 'Not to mention the loss of my guards.'

'Not to mention.'

'It's the veterans, isn't it? First the Savages, now this.'

'Could be.'

He folded his arms and ducked his head down into them. 'I'm going to tear Pretories a new hole. Then I'm going to pull his intestines out of it.'

'Sounds painful.'

'Thinks he can fuck with the Giroies, he's gonna learn clear otherwise.'

'Blessed are the teachers.'

'Him and all his men. They got no idea what's coming for them.'

'Make the Dren look like milkmaids.'

He'd been too lost in revenge fantasies to hear me, but this last seemed to have broken through. 'You find this humorous?'

'It's all we've left, in these times of tragedy.'

'Easy for you to take things light. I've got responsibilities. The entire family waits at my word, and falls if I fall.'

'The burden of leadership,' I agreed.

His face bloated scarlet. 'When I get my hands on that son of a bitch . . .'

As keen as I was to hear the remainder of Giroie's hypothetical torments, the day was getting long. 'It's too early to start picking your targets, Artur, let alone getting flushed. You don't even know who it was for a certainty.'

'Don't be daft – you yourself said they were coming after me, in that very seat, not three days ago!'

'I was passing on a rumor, not handing you testament from the Firstborn.'

'I didn't think you the sort to go soft in the belly when things got hot,' he snorted, some portion of his faded ardour quick to return and happy to find a new target.

'Is that what I'm doing? Going soft?'

'Damn it, Warden! A few days ago you're a perfect oracle, now you sit there like a half-wit, spouting stale lines and repeating my words back to me!'

I didn't answer. A droplet of sweat had crawled down from his forehead, languishing on the tip of his nose. He brushed at it and looked away.

A quarter inch had burnt off my smoke before I started again. 'If my presence here is a nuisance, I'll shuffle off directly.'

He mumbled something that wasn't quite an apology. 'I suppose there are any number of players that would be interested in acquiring my merchandise.'

The toy pikeman lay on its side. I picked it up and wound it, then left it to pace across the desk. 'Any number,' I agreed.

'Perhaps . . .' He seemed almost to be searching for permission. 'Perhaps it would be wise to make further inquiry, before committing my forces.'

'Makes sense. And anyway, even if it was the vets – maybe you're better off letting it go. They're well supplied with muscle, and they won't be slow to press the advantage.'

'What's that supposed to mean?'

'What did you say to me last time I was here? That the family is a business, like any other? No profit in blood. Write it off and move on. So your rep takes a hit, so what? Nobody ever comes out of a war in the black.'

'Is that what you think?' His glance would have withered a daisy. 'Is that what they think? That I'm weak? That my name is dust? That the Giroies can't even look after their own interests?'

'Nobody's saying nothing, Artur. Even your father didn't go up against the Association lightly.'

He cocked his head, as if catching something. 'Even my father?'

'I just meant—'

'I know what you meant,' he snapped. 'You presume too far, Warden.'

I studiously avoided smiling. 'My apologies, of course. No offense was intended.'

'Accepted,' he said after a moment, nodding slowly, his thoughts of blood. 'Too many think as you do – that the Junior is not the Senior, that the Giroies have slipped, that we aren't to be reckoned with. I assure you,' he said, snapping his attention back to me, hands folded on the table, back straight, a portrait of composure surrounded by the possessions he'd destroyed. 'These delusions will swiftly be proven false.'

I picked an ashtray up from off the carpet, set it on the desk, then stumped my cigarette into it. 'No doubt.'

29

Adisu was a long time coming. Another man would have intended the delay an insult, meant to indicate how little water I drew in their eyes. As it was, I figured he'd probably just forgotten – punctuality was not a strong point of the Bruised Fruit Mob. It can be hard to keep track of the minute hand when you spend most of the day wrapped up in a blanket of high-grade hallucinogens.

Dizzie's was an ugly restaurant with an odd layout, no bathroom and a very noticeable stable of vermin. But it was located in a section of Offbend that no one ever went to, and the servers knew when to leave you alone. I sat on the small verandah and watched my coffee cool. It was slow going. I wasn't sure that the kettle had been any hotter than the porch.

Between the weather and the exertions of the last few days, I wasn't paying much attention to my surroundings and didn't notice Adisu till he dropped down on the bench across from me.

He'd come accompanied by his bodyguard and a thick layer of body odour.

'Adisu,' I said.

'Warden,' he returned, but he didn't look at me while he said it. His eyes were blood red circles around little black dots. An angry sheen of cankers had erupted across his forehead and beneath the patchy growth of his beard. Below the table his foot tapped an uneven rhythm. He hadn't slept the night before, probably hadn't slept since last I'd seen him, spending the intervening hours binging on breath and savoring the violence I'd set him to. He was coming down now, feeling antsy and jagged, and easy to provoke. It did not bode well for the remainder of our conversation.

The waitress was dowdy, middle-aged, and frightened. She approached our table in tiny steps, like a rabbit crossing an open field, wary of predators.

Her arrival sparked Adisu to life. 'How you doing, darling?' he said, turning his gaze on her full bore. He was making an attempt at being friendly, but between the outsized leer and the clear madness in his eyes, his attention seemed to have the opposite effect.

'I'm fine,' she managed.

'Just fine, huh? Nothing better than that?'

She shrugged.

'You know, any day you wake up, that could be your last day, you hear? You got this little flame, but all it takes is a stiff wind, you know? A stiff wind and . . .' He brought his hand up in front of the Muscle's face and snapped his fingers. The Muscle didn't react. Part of being the Muscle was not getting rattled when Adisu started acting a little crazy. 'And you gone, you know? Just like that. You gotta take every minute like it's on loan, you dig?'

'I'll . . . I'll try and do that,' she said. I had no doubt that at this moment the poor woman was very conscious of the fragility of her existence.

Adisu smiled and nodded his head up and down for an

uninterrupted five seconds, like he'd gotten lost midway through the motion and couldn't stop. 'You got steak and eggs?' he asked finally.

'Sure.'

'I'd like an order of steak and eggs.'

'You want those eggs scrambled, or fried?'

'Bring me both,' he said. 'And some grits. And potatoes. And a cup of coffee. And some milk. Is your milk fresh?' He didn't wait for her to respond. 'And some cornbread. Plus some bacon – burnt to hell, you understand me? Not the steak, though – I like my steak just this side of raw.' He snapped his attention over to the Muscle. 'What you want, Zaga?'

'Coffee,' he said.

'That's it?' Adisu asked, incredulous and with an odd sense of concern. 'That's all you gonna eat? Breakfast is important, man, you gotta fill yourself up, we got shit to do. Have some eggs or something at least.'

It was past noon, but amongst the social conventions ignored by Adisu the Damned was the notion that breakfast ought to be consumed at a specific hour of the day.

Zaga shook his head. 'Coffee,' he said again.

Adisu shrugged and turned back to the waitress. 'You gotta leave people to make their own decisions, at the end of the day, you know what I mean?'

She nodded in frantic agreement. I imagined there was very little she wouldn't have agreed with at that point, if it meant a speedier end to the conversation.

'You're a smart woman,' Adisu said. 'But you ought to chop off those bangs, sweetness. They ain't doing you no favors.'

The waitress put her hand to her forehead, opened her eyes wide as an ochre. I found myself agreeing with Adisu. He had a keen aesthetic, for a man whose pit-stains ran from underarm to crotch. Now more humiliated than frightened, our server took off back to the kitchen at high speed.

I had never seen Adisu by daylight before, it occurred to me then. His madness had been less apparent, or at least less objectionable, in his natural habitat, amidst his decaying mansion and a gang of almost equally cracked confederates. Out in public, contrasted against the civilian world of working stiffs and passing pedestrians, it stood in stark relief. It began to occur to me that perhaps I'd picked the wrong root-breathing lunatic to do my dirty work.

'Everything go all right?'

In the ten-second interval between speaking to the waitress and my spitting a question, Adisu had delved pretty deeply into the confines of his skull. His lips moved up and down in noticeable but silent conversation. He managed to stall his inner monologue long enough to answer me. 'What did you say?'

'Did everything go all right,' I repeated, 'with that thing I asked you to do.'

'Oh. Yeah, it went fine. Everything like you said. Dominoes falling into place and whatnot.'

'That's great.'

'Yeah,' he agreed, though he didn't seem particularly excited by it.

'So then you've got my cut.' It was a statement, though in truth by that point I was far from certain about anything regarding Adisu the Damned.

'Your cut,' he repeated, as if unfamiliar with the term. 'Actually, there's something I need to tell you about your cut.'

'Which is?'

'I'm not going to give it to you.'

The Muscle puffed up his shoulders till they were about level with the top of his skull. I sipped at my coffee in the least threatening fashion possible.

'I want you to understand, Warden, it's not like I just decided to con you out of the deal.'

'Of course.'

'That's not the way I do business – ruin a good connect just to pick up something on the short end. What kind of sense does that make?'

'No kind at all.'

'I'm not the sort to quibble over a couple of copper.'

'Wouldn't have thought it of you.'

'Thank you,' Adisu said. He seemed genuinely touched. 'Like I said, I was planning on bringing you your cut. I even had a little package for you, didn't I, Zaga?'

The Muscle spat out onto the street, which I guess could have been taken as confirmation.

Adisu nodded vigorously. 'Twenty-five ochre, one-fourth of what I figure we'll clear off the wyrm. And that's a generous estimate! The way prices have bottomed out lately, that might even be north of what I owed you. But then, I'm not the sort to quibble over a couple of copper.'

'You said that already.'

'When did I say that?'

'About thirty seconds ago.'

Adisu spent something like that length of time trying to recollect it. 'Right, yeah – what I meant was, it's not about me turning coat on you, just so I could have your ends. I had every intention of paying you, honest I did. But then I got to thinking.'

'A dangerous recreation.'

'I figured the Warden, what's he doing stirring up the Giroies? He got a nice little operation, he ain't the sort to bring trouble back his way just to make a few ochre. Wouldn't be . . .' He turned abruptly to his second. 'What's that word I'm looking for, means you don't do nothing gonna come back and bite your ass?'

The Muscle shook his head. The Muscle did not know the word Adisu was looking for. As far as I could tell, the Muscle had about a hundred-word vocabulary, consisting exclusively of monosyllables.

Adisu snapped his fingers and started to grin. 'Prudent – that's what I was trying to say. You a prudent motherfucker.'

'Thank you.'

'Too prudent to be stirring up trouble – unless . . .' Adisu leaned his face into mine, teeth yellow as beaten gold, breath like he'd been scavenging road kill. 'He wants the trouble! He don't care about the money at all.'

'Tell you what – if it'll break this conversation short, you can keep my part of the deal. That settle you down?'

'I just told you man – it ain't about your cut. I don't give a shit about twenty-five ochre. Twenty-five ochre don't mean nothing to me. I'd scatter twenty-five ochre in the mud outside my house, just to see the bums pick around for it. So don't fucking bring up your cut again, all right? I find that shit insulting.' And indeed, he seemed genuinely wounded.

'Sorry,' I said.

He weighed over my apology for a moment. 'It's all right,' he said. 'So anyway, I started doing some digging, made a point of keeping my ears open. Word comes out that the Giroie are awful riled up about the bodies we made. Ain't no surprise there, I mean who likes having their men made into corpses?'

His pause extended onward. Eventually it occurred to me that the question had not been intended rhetorically. 'No one.'

Adisu nodded happily, like he was pleased with my progress. 'Exactly, don't no one like it, not one bit. But here's the interesting thing – the Giroies, they're not looking in our direction, says the scuttlebutt. They looking at the vets. Don't that seem strange to you?'

'I'm too old to be surprised.'

'Not me, man! It's a crazy world we're living on. You got to take the time to recognize what's in front of your face, dig? Otherwise what's the point?'

It's an odd fact about lunatics and junkies, but every one I'd ever met is just dying to share their life wisdom. I started rolling up a cigarette while I waited for Adisu to continue.

'You shouldn't smoke, man,' he said. 'Bad for your health.'

'Thanks.'

'Don't mention it. Anyway, I don't mind telling you, Warden, figuring out your puzzle, it made me feel awful good about myself. Awful smart, you dig? Made me want to start crowing, let the whole world see how slick I am, that I can follow along with a real heavyweight like yourself.'

'I hope you restrained yourself.'

'I have,' Adisu nodded emphatically. 'So far. But you know me, Warden, I get bored easily. If something don't come by to hold my attention, I might have to start making the rounds, bragging about my genius.'

'And what exactly would it take to keep you occupied?'

'We can start with what I was gonna give you. Twenty-five ochre – when you've got it, I mean I know you aren't carrying it on you, don't worry. I'm a reasonable man. And if I was you, I wouldn't be thinking of this as no one-time thing – 'cause I've got to be honest, my attention span, it's not exactly limitless.'

'I hadn't noticed.'

He shrugged apologetically. 'Nobody's perfect. Point being, if I don't see a regular supply of coin coming my way, say once a month till forever, well – I can't make no guarantee as to whom I might take it into my mind to chat with.'

'I imagine the Giroies might take offense to finding out you murdered some of their men.'

'The Giroies don't scare me so much. I figure they won't be so quick to come into the Isthmus looking for us, not when they've got you as an easy scapegoat.'

I finished up my cigarette, sparked it and put it to my lips. 'You've come out of this pretty well,' I said, doing my best to affect a reasonable tone. 'Seventy-five ochre worth of wyrm, should catch you a couple hundred if you move it smart. Now that's found money, and you didn't have to work much for it. You said I was a prudent man – why don't you take a lesson from me. Walk away with what you've got.'

He'd been staring at the wall behind me during my speech. He continued a while afterward, then blinked twice and turned back to me. 'Sorry, what?'

'I said that you'd be better off without making an enemy of a friend.'

'We aren't friends.'

A bit of my own medicine. I drank it down with the dregs of my coffee. 'We're friends in the sense that I'm not actively seeking your demise, Adisu. By my standards, that makes us damn near bosom brothers.'

'Bosom brothers,' he repeated, enunciating each syllable with peculiar intensity. 'Bosom brothers.' He seemed quite taken with the term, and it took a moment to free himself from its grip on his mind. 'Were you breastfed?' he asked.

'One more time?'

'Were you breastfed? Did you suckle your mother's titties?'

'You know, Adisu,' I said, making a show of thinking about it, 'I can't rightly remember.'

'Right, course,' he laughed. 'Me neither. But Moms, I mean back when she was around, she told me I wasn't. You got any siblings, Warden?'

I found I wasn't particularly interested in sharing the specifics of my upbringing with Adisu. 'We're getting off topic.'

'I'm the youngest of eleven. Nine brothers, two sisters. Moms said that by the time she got to me there just wasn't nothing left. Said she used to mix up some goat's milk with water, soak a rag in it and put it in my mouth.' He shook his head sadly. 'Ain't right, you know? A little child, having to live on that. Sometimes I think: maybe, if I'd had what the rest got, I'd have turned out different than I did. Been taller, maybe. Used to make me angry, back when I was a kid, thinking what I could have been. On the other hand, though, it learned me something early on that most people don't figure out till later.'

'And what was that?'

'There ain't but so much milk to go around.'

As I'd mentioned, being cracked as an outhouse rodent didn't stop Adisu from being right about most things. I'm not sure what exactly that says about the world. Nothing good, I don't imagine.

'All right,' Adisu said, standing abruptly. The Muscle seemed caught off guard as well, because it took him a moment to do the same. 'I said what I got to say. Twenty-five ochre by the day after tomorrow, or my gums start flapping with the wind.

Whatever cakes you got baking, you sure as hell don't need my crazy ass sticking a finger in the dough.' He was back in good humour, smiling at me affectionately. 'You be well. I'll see you soon.'

The Muscle waited a second, then gave a sort of half-shrug and disappeared after him.

I finished off my cigarette and started on another, running over the last ten minutes. They didn't look any better through the smoke. I had too much to worry about to add Adisu's madness to the mix. And while the Bruised Fruit Mob were hardly considered reliable, there was enough truth in his story to get me killed by any number of people.

Of course, there were other ways to fix the situation than the one he'd presented.

The waitress came back to our table. On her shoulder was a tray. On the tray was enough food to feed a family of eight. 'Where'd your friends go?' she asked.

'Weren't never here,' I said.

She dropped her burden onto the table, rattling the plates and sending coffee spilling. 'Well, who the hell is gonna pay for all this?'

'He is,' I said, pulling an argent out of my pocket. 'He just doesn't know it yet.'

30

The man at the front desk of Black House was not inclined towards letting me wander the halls unaccompanied.

A day had passed since my meeting with Adisu, a day spent avoiding the sun and Adeline, holed up in my room burning through a half-ochre worth of dreamvine. In the city outside the seeds of my plot were beginning to sprout, soon to flower into chaos and violence. They'd require cultivation, but at that exact moment all they needed was a little bit of time. I went to bed early, and woke up the same, heading out to visit Guiscard before breakfast. I'd thought a lot about what I was going to say to him, but I'll admit I hadn't foreseen the possibility that said dialogue would never take place.

Back when I'd worked in Black House the desk was occupied by an agent. I suppose there had been some sort of a change in policy, because their new doorman was nothing but that, a functionary with gray eyes and a soul to match. I didn't blame him not letting me in. Keeping out the riff-raff was chief amongst his duties, and I certainly looked the part. I did, however, blame him for being snide, narrow of mind, and less capable of independent thought than a marching ant. 'I'm sorry,' he said, not sounding like it. 'But without an appointment there's really nothing I can do.'

'Just send someone up to tell him I'm here.'

'There's no one here but me – and if I go upstairs to give him a message, there would be no one left to watch the desk.'

'I'll stay here and watch it.'

'I don't . . .' The introduction of an alternative confused him. 'I don't think that would work.'

'Perhaps we could rig up some sort of machine which would pass the note along to him. Something with rigs and pulleys.'

'I'm not very mechanically inclined,' he admitted.

'How about carrier pigeons? Do you have any of those?'

He shrugged helplessly. He'd been well trained for his position. Mostly, organizations do not reward solving problems – they reward not fucking up, and the easiest way not to fuck up is to do nothing. But true inertia is a difficult state to reach, and after a few moments of silence an idea seemed to come to him. It was a rare thing, no doubt. It took him a while to recognize it, and longer still to give it voice. 'Maybe if you told me what business you have with Agent Guiscard?'

How to answer that one? That Agent Guiscard had forced me to act a double agent, setting up the downfall of a rebellious entity conceivably bent on the destruction of the Crown? Or that the above was false, that I was in fact engineering a conflict between Black House and the Association, and Agent Guiscard the unwitting instrument of my revenge? 'I'm afraid he wouldn't want me to divulge the specifics.'

I heard the door open behind me and I tensed up slightly. There were still people walking the halls who remembered when I'd done the same, and I imagined they'd be quick to greet my return with violence.

Turned out I didn't need to worry. 'Agent Guiscard,' the doorman said.

'Hello, Brunsford.'

Guiscard pulled up next to me. 'What are you doing here?' he asked, but before I could answer he shook his head. 'Nevermind – best discuss it in my office.'

'One moment,' I said, turning back to Brunsford. 'If you knew he was out, then why did we have to go through all of this?'

Brunsford shrugged, having difficulty seeing the connection. 'You didn't ask.'

In a sense, I envied him. Few people are so well suited to their duties. I thanked him, then followed Guiscard upstairs.

He took a seat, and I joined him. 'How much do you like me?' I asked.

'I'm sorry?'

'Am I just some ten-copper trollop whom you pick up and use at your convenience? Or is what we have between us real?'

'This is a rather tedious introduction to whatever you're here for.'

'Let me summate.' I leaned back in my chair and propped my legs up onto his desk. 'I need you to crush a bug for me.'

He narrowed his eyes, stiffened one arm and pushed my boots back to the ground. 'What kind of bug?'

'Islander, early twenties, savagely insane. Goes by Adisu the Damned.'

'Never heard of him.'

'When I had your job, Guiscard, I knew the name of every criminal who could command a blade from Grenmont to the docks.'

'You don't have my job anymore.'

'And I still know the name of every criminal who can command a blade from Grenmont to the docks.'

'This Adisu – what exactly has he done to you?'

'At this exact moment, he hasn't done anything. But if we wait around till tomorrow, he'll make sure I'm not here to answer that question a second time.'

'I'm sure you've done something to deserve it.'

'We've all done something to deserve it.'

'And what exactly would you like to have happen to your unfortunate adversary?'

'The world would be a finer place without him crawling on its surface, but so long as he's out of my way, I don't really mind. The bay or the dungeon, your preference.'

'I can't just disappear a fellow without reason.'

'In fact you can – that's basically the point of being in Black House. You can pretty much do anything you want to anyone, and they can't do anything back to you.'

'All right,' he said. 'Say I could do it. Why would I?'

'In exchange for the kindnesses I'm doing you.'

'Awful presumptuous of you, thinking to cash in a chit you haven't earned yet.'

'Meaning?'

'Meaning for all your big talk about having Joachim Pretories' ear, so far you've given me nothing more solid than broken wind.'

'I don't imagine I'll be of any more help to you dead,' I answered. 'Try to think a few moves ahead, Guiscard. The Association and the Giroies will be at war soon enough. You'll be happy to have me around when they do.'

'So you've said – I'm still not sure I understand why Pretories would want to stir up violence against the Giroies.'

'Same reason any leader goes to war – to divert attention from their own failures. Better to get everyone focusing on an enemy than have them mull over his inability to keep their pensions inviolate.'

'It doesn't make any sense.'

'The world rarely does,' I said. 'You need to look past how you think things should work, and pay attention to how things actually do.'

'Regardless,' he said after a brief moment of thought, 'I'm an Agent of the Crown, tasked with upholding the law and enforcing justice. Neither of those activities are served by what you're asking.'

'You never hit a suspect? Never set a man up for a fall he didn't know was coming? Your past so lily white as all that?'

'There's a difference between bending the rules and bringing the full force of Black House to bear on a private struggle between two . . .' he sputtered for a moment, trying to find a term to sufficiently convey his contempt, '. . . degenerate fucking drug dealers.'

'You wound me. Like I said last time – I used to fill your seat. This pretense of decency is unnecessary.'

'You'll forgive me if I don't take your career advice too closely, given that you were stripped of your rank.'

'It's a funny thing about my fall – it didn't come about because of a moral lapse. Quite the opposite, in fact. And having come to ethics late in life, and to my own detriment, let me offer up a warning. Don't risk it – you gave up the luxury of being a decent human being when they added the star to your collar. Things with the Association are going south fast. You need someone on the inside, who can give you a heads up beforehand. What's that measured against the life of a handful of slum dwellers, and criminals at that?'

I'd decided to have Guiscard remove Adisu for three reasons. The first was that I didn't trust the Islander to keep his mouth shut. The second was, as a point of principle, I prefer not to let a man bend me backwards. Even if no one else ever finds out about it, you'll still know it happened. Finally, I liked the idea of having Guiscard act as my cat's-paw. It suited my sense of vanity. Moreover, it put some dirt on him, shifted the fundamental balance of our relationship. Guiscard would do violence to another man on my behalf, would lower himself into the muck along with me. Nothing binds two people like a shared sin.

He stroked the bridge of his long nose, closed his eyes, in short, made quite a show of contemplation. 'I'll need something to hang on him,' he said finally.

'There'll be enough narcotics stashed away to keep half the city high through Midwinter.' I thought about the Bruised

Fruit Mob's headquarters, its stagnant smell and subterranean depths. 'If you look hard enough, you'll probably find a decomposing corpse or two, but the drugs alone should merit a ten-year stretch. Also, they'll resist arrest.'

'They sound like lovely folk. Where will I find them?'

I gave him directions. 'It needs to happen tonight, or early tomorrow. And it needs to be a clean sweep, make sure none of them are around to plague me later.'

'I know my business,' he said. 'You just keep yourself close to Pretories. I want to know everything you know, and I want to know it as soon as you do.'

I ticked a salute over a smug smile, happy to have played a part in Guiscard's continuing education. My own enlightenment had come at a far higher cost – for me, and for a lot of other people.

31

I'd been waiting a solid hour when he came in, my back against the wall of a quiet cafe in the Old City, drinking wine by candlelight. I didn't mind. Everyone had to wait to see the man. Not that his tardiness was meant as a slight – such vanity was beneath Roland Montgomery. But he was remaking the world, and that was a serious undertaking, one that left little time for social engagements.

He looked apologetic at least, flanked by men who would have died for him happily during the war, now – it didn't make a difference. They eyed my ice gray unhappily, even threateningly. Black House had replaced the Dren in the affections of the men of the Association. What with my time in the ranks I was worse than the average freeze even, a turncoat, a traitor.

His bodyguards took seats at the counter, and Roland dropped himself across from me without affectation. 'Lieutenant.'

'Sir. I hope you don't mind, I ordered a drink.'

'Not at all.' He took a moment to inspect me. 'It's been a long time. Longer than I'd have liked.'

The war had changed everyone. From the scatter-eyed, stammering beggars on the docks, pawning tarnished medals and rattling their alms cups, to the young-old men from Kor's Heights sitting alone at garden parties, sleeves pinned over stumps, flinching when champagne was uncorked. Those unlucky enough to need to work for a living took what they could find of it, back-to-back shifts at the mills, trading one line for another. Or they joined the thick squads of bullyboys selling service to the syndicates, peddling their hard-won practice to organizations more grateful than the Crown, or at least more remunerative.

It had changed all of us, but it hadn't changed Roland. His eyes were bright as they'd ever been, fever-bright, and he still spoke like he was trying to overawe artillery.

I didn't like it. The war was the war – I'd spent five years trying to get the hell away from it, I didn't need it being dragged back onto home soil. Not everyone felt like that, of course. It had given a lot of empty men a purpose, and hollowed out a lot of men for whatever purpose they might have had. Spend a few years bunk-mates with She Who Waits Behind All Things, you find it hard to forget her. Whatever else you do starts to seem awful silly, writing out receipts in a general store somewhere, planting lines of potatoes in neat little rows. Roland's men were like that – there was nothing in their eyes except what he gave them.

'I'm still not used to seeing you in your new uniform. Congratulations, once again. It's quite an honor, being made an Agent of the Crown at such a young age.'

'I'm not so sure your boys would agree.'

He flashed his entourage a quick smile. 'They're a mite protective.'

The serving girl came by to take an order. Roland asked for a glass of what I was drinking, and when she came back he gave her a smile that won a convert for life. The other patrons, quiet, well civilized, their lives bound up inextricably with the establishment, their interests as far from Roland's as you could get, took sidelong glances and thought up kindnesses they could do him.

'You've been making a lot of waves, over in my neck of the woods,' I said.

'Would that be Black House, or Low Town?'

'It would be both.'

'Those are two very different places.' Roland was too gracious to crow, but you could see he thought he'd scored a point.

'They are indeed.'

'Does it ever get confusing?'

'I could ask you the same question.'

'Oh?'

'Kor's Heights is a lovely neighborhood. I'd think a fellow who grew up there wouldn't be in such a hurry to burn it down.'

'Not burn it down, Lieutenant, not at all. I only work to ensure its bounty is more equitably shared.'

'And your father?' The news had come out a few weeks back – General Edwin Montgomery had officially retired from public life, preferring a dignified solitude to the hustle and bustle of politics. A comfortable fiction cloaking the reality that it was quite impossible to put him in charge of the Empire while his son seemed to be doing his best to destroy it.

For a moment, though a very brief one, regret showed through Roland's assurance. It left quickly, as I said. 'Filial piety is an important virtue. But it pales beside loyalty to one's nation, and countrymen.' He waved his hand in front of his face, as if batting away a fly. 'I've made my choice – I've got no regrets.'

'What was that choice, exactly?'

He had an answer prepared for this very occasion, and was pleased to share it. 'Shepherding tomorrow's arrival.'

'A morning Timory Half-hand won't be around to see.'

'Who?'

'One of the vice-peddlers your boys strung up.'

'There's a saying about omelettes that I think would be appropriate here.'

'About eggs, not skulls.'

He shrugged. There wasn't much difference to him. 'I would think you of all people would understand the importance of what we're doing. Growing up where you did, coming from what you came from.'

'You spend a lot of time in the slums?'

'Haven't had the pleasure.'

'You ought to head down to the Isthmus one day, or take a stroll through the bleaker sections of Kirentown. They got these rows of tenements there, walls no thicker than the width of your hand, foundations held together with plaster that's mostly rain-water. Thousands of people crammed in like rats. To look at them, you'd think they couldn't stand. You'd think they'd have to collapse beneath their own weight.'

'But?'

'But they do stand, General – and do you know why?'

'Enlighten me,' he said, and he even seemed to mean it.

'Because they lean against each other. Any one of them, alone, would collapse in a stiff wind. But together? Together they're solid enough to live in.'

'Who'd want to?'

'It beats the alternatives. The thing is, the balance is precarious. If you were to knock out a wall, move around a strut or two – the whole structure might tumble.'

'I hadn't known you were such a poet, Lieutenant.'

'Your shot at the Giroies is having consequences you don't see. The Tarasaighns are getting antsy, figuring maybe they ought to make a move on what the Rouenders still hold. The heretics watch them squad up and start worrying where their hammer is gonna fall. Across the city, knives are being sharpened and targets staked out.'

'The rest of the syndicates can enjoy their temporary good fortune – I assure you, it won't last. The Old Man and his ilk might be content allowing half of Rigus to be run by racketeers, but I'm afraid I'm not.'

'Wipe them all away, will you?'

'They'll make a decent start.'

'What comes then? Revolution?'

'The revolution came. It came when hundreds of thousands of men stirred themselves from their villages, from their boroughs and sleeping hamlets, and traveled across the Thirteen Lands to bring death to strangers. You say I'm shaking the foundations, but you're wrong – they're already broken. I'm just the first one willing to admit it.'

'That's very eloquent. And yet the crown still sits atop Bess's head, and the guards still swear her fealty.'

'For how long? Soldiers sick of fighting go back to the provinces and find every acre of their farm entailed and the rent past due. They move to the cities, pack whatever family they have into a room the size of a kitchen cabinet. They wake up before dawn and toil till dusk for two copper an hour, maybe lose a hand if they're tired or careless, and on their way home they pass a plump tick in a velvet coat, growing fatter on their labor.'

'One thing I've learned in my time – ain't nothing so bad it can't get worse.'

'You aren't one for easy answers. I respect that, but the situation is untenable. We bring it down ourselves, or we let it fall on our heads.'

'Things have always been fucked – you just recently came round to noticing it. The poor have always been poor, and weak, and apt to get beat upon. The powerful have always aimed to get more so, and never cared much how it happens. Your line isn't anything I haven't heard before – I could find a dozen drunks at any Low Town dive who could spin it better.'

He laughed. He was the sort of person who could laugh at his own expense. It was one of the many things I liked about him. 'I'm sure you could. But said drunk wouldn't have a hundred thousand men at his command.'

'And you do?'

'I will.'

'What comes afterward? When you've set fire to everything,

when the Old Man swings from a scaffold and the crown is broke in two – what will you build in the ashes?'

He looked at me silently for a moment, the question so obvious it barely merited answer. 'A better world.'

I had harbored vague hopes that this first part of our conversation would go differently. Perhaps hopes were too strong – delusions might be a better term. Roland Montgomery had never second-guessed himself on anything in his life, and wasn't likely to start now.

'You've set yourself quite a task,' I said.

'Like in the war – conquer, or die.'

'Of course, you didn't win the war all on your own.'

'What are you saying?'

'There are men in Black House less averse to change than its leader.'

'Then why aren't they sitting here?'

'Because their lives are worth more to them than mine is.'

He weighed that for a moment, then nodded. 'Go on.'

'The men I'm talking about can't let it be known that they're talking.'

'It wouldn't play strongly to the affections of my constituency either,' he said. 'Of course, if they aren't willing to show their faces, it seems unlikely we can reach effective union.'

'They sent me out here to gauge your interest. Make sure that you're committed to the task at hand, that you won't flinch when the moment comes to strike.'

'And?'

'It's clear that you're prepared to do anything to reach your aims.'

There were depths to that, if Roland had cared to look. But he didn't – his eyes were on the future, on his grand plans and grander ambitions.

'I'll contact you soon, with the details of a meet,' I said.

'Where?'

'It can't be your territory, because my people can't be seen with you. And it can't be ours for the same reason. I'm thinking

Low Town. I'll set up security, some of my old friends from the neighborhood, uninvolved with either side and not particularly interested in politics.'

He mulled that over for a while, then stood and smiled. 'I'm glad to have you with us, Lieutenant.' He put a firm hand on my shoulder. 'A light awaits us at the end of the struggle.'

He nodded at his guard and they fell in behind him, sparing a second to toss final snarls of disapproval. I stayed a while afterward, finishing the wine, then calling for something stronger.

32

The Square of Benevolence was a cobblestone space that stretched out from the Chapel of Prachetas, the unofficial barrier between the Old City and the beginnings of the ghetto. On a brisk fall afternoon it was the best spot in Rigus, lined with quiet cafes where a man could grab a drink and watch the world rot around him. In the height of summer, crowded with a division of ex-soldiers, it was stifling. Sun reflected off the red bricks, sweat stench off the multitudes. Despite the heat there was a festive atmosphere, concessionaires doing a good business in fried honey-bread and chilled tea. No doubt the pickpockets were doing better, though this last wasn't a game for amateurs. The men who'd filed their way into the plaza had been killers, once. It wouldn't take much for them turn so again.

From Black House I'd headed over to Association Headquarters, hoping for a few minutes with Pretories. They'd sent me over here, told me he was helping set up for the rally. I didn't see him, but I did catch a glimpse of Hroudland and his crew stationed near the back, and headed over in their direction.

When Rabbit saw me he broke out of his conversation and took my hand between his calloused palms. 'Nice to see you again, Lieutenant.'

'Any day with you in it is a good one, Rabbit.'

He seemed happy to see me. But then he seemed pretty happy, period. 'Gotta say, Lieutenant, I was surprised when I heard you'd signed up with us.'

'Fucking shocked,' Roussel said. He was chewing on a stalk of straw like it had done him evil.

'I like to keep people on their toes.'

'Don't make no sense to me,' said Roussel. There was a rosy bloom to his cheeks, either from the heat or his barely suppressed homicidal rage.

'Ignorance is a lamentable condition,' I replied.

He grunted and went back to milling grain between his sneer.

'What can we do for you?' Hroudland asked, splitting the difference in attitude between his two subordinates.

'I need to whisper to the man.'

'Tell me what it is – I'll take it to him.'

'Won't cut it. I need a face-to-face.'

'The commander's got a lot going on at the moment, what with the speeches about to start.'

'I got a bum leg. You think we can skip the song and dance?'

'How'd you get gimped, Lieutenant?' Rabbit piped in.

'Fell out of bed with Roussel's mother.'

'Mom's dead,' Roussel answered, without much in the way of emotion.

'I hope she lived long enough to see her son make good.'

The back and forth had given Hroudland enough time to make the decision we both knew he was going to. 'Fall in,' he said, 'but this better not be a waste of his time.'

'I am an awful boring person, so no guarantees.'

The commander sat alone in a back corner of one of the surrounding establishments, beneath a covered awning on a raised patio. A few solid men stood guard at the entrance. Hroudland knocked off to talk to them, leaving me alone with his superior.

'Good morning, Lieutenant,' Joachim said. 'What's got you all the way out here?'

'You're gonna get hit,' I answered.

His eyes were dark and sad. You could have dropped a live snake in his lap and they wouldn't so much have flickered. 'You live long enough and that'll happen.'

'You live a little longer, you learn to try and dodge it.'

He nodded vague agreement, then waved at a spot next to him. I slid into it. 'Can I dodge this one?'

'Maybe. If you're quick.'

'And who's looking to add my scalp to their collection?'

'A whole bunch of folk, I imagine, though the only party I can say with certainty works out of a restaurant in the Old City.'

'The Giroies?'

'Got it in one.'

'I'm starting to feel like I've had this conversation already.'

'Last time I was passing on a rumor. This time I'm tipping you tomorrow's broadsheet.'

'I didn't realize you were a soothsayer.'

'Nothing soothing about it.'

'I'd think puns beneath you.'

'There's very little that's beneath me, Commander.'

That didn't seem to encourage him. 'Look, Lieutenant,' he began slowly, laying it out for me. 'We went through this. The Giroies and the Association have been quits for ten years. Until I see proof otherwise, I'm not going to do anything to stir the waters.'

'You think I enjoy these go-rounds so much that I'd come up here if I wasn't sure what I was talking about?'

'Nobody's right all the time.'

I drew myself up from the chair. 'Enjoy the speeches.'

'Sit down,' he said, a command.

I didn't follow it, but I stopped moving.

'Sit down,' he repeated, softer, and this time I took the

suggestion. Pretories drummed his fingers against the table, considering. A waiter came over, poured out some water, then left. The square below us was filling up rapidly, near packed, the dull roar steadily forcing our own conversation to be conducted at a volume inappropriate to its substance.

'What's your source on this?' he asked finally.

'A little bird alighted on my shoulder.'

'That's not good enough, not for this. I need specifics.'

'You know everyone I know?'

'Try me.'

'Scratch is his street name. Half-Islander, freelance muscle.' I knew three separate people who fit this general description, and I didn't imagine any of them would be easy to find. 'He tells me the Giroies have been adding men to the rolls, double quick.'

'Why would he tell you that?'

'Either because we're best friends, or because I pay a premium for relevant gossip.'

'And what does your man say is coming down the pike?'

'You must have outposts apart from headquarters.'

'Of course.'

'Double their guard.'

He cracked one finger against another, then shook his head. 'We're stretched to capacity as it is, preparing for the march.'

I waved a hand at the crowd. 'Five thousand men here, you telling me you can't detail anyone to stand outside of your joints and look tough?'

'There's a difference between paying dues and strapping on steel. These men are my constituency. I work for them, not the other way around.'

It was nice to know Pretories was back on his heels. 'Conscript someone then. It worked for the Crown, didn't it?'

'Volunteers are more reliable.'

'Numbers matter, when you're going to war.'

'We're at war now? I don't remember receiving a declaration.'

'I'll make sure and register a complaint with the relevant authorities. You'll be a corpse by then, but at least it'll comfort your kin.'

He swiped his tongue across his teeth. I must really have been getting to him. 'The Giroies,' he began finally. 'They're serious?'

'Well, they're not the Dren,' I responded. 'But you don't have to be to stick metal in meat.'

I stood up for a second time, and for a second time the commander stopped me. 'Aren't you sticking around?'

'I was five years in the service. I don't need a monologue to remind me of it.'

'Just thought it might interest you, what with your friend being our first speaker.'

'What?'

Pretories nodded to the stage. A half-dozen men sat behind a podium, awaiting their chance to speak. Stationed at the far left, notable by virtue of being twice the size of any of the others, Adolphus shuffled his feet nervously.

What I got for not paying Wren proper attention. I pointed myself back at Pretories for the parting shot. 'I get it, Commander, you don't quite trust me. That's fine, I'm not quite a trustworthy person. But I'm right about this – the Giroies are coming. Prepare yourself today, or lament your lack of faith tomorrow.'

Pretories was a tough one to read, and I wasn't sure which way he'd go. For my purposes it didn't really matter. 'I'll take it under consideration,' he said.

I padded off the verandah, past Roussel's sneer and Rabbit's corpse-grin, down into the sea of flesh surrounding us. Once engulfed it was hard to make out the stage. I angled myself as best I could and started toward it, brushing my way through the throng. The role of master of ceremonies was played by the same speaker I'd ignored the last time I'd been at headquarters, and his loquaciousness gave me time to elbow my way to the front. I had a pretty decent view of the podium by the time Adolphus stepped up to it.

He was sweating more than the heat strictly demanded, but

other than that he looked good, for an ugly man deep into middle age. He uncreased a sheet of paper and set it against the podium, hands fumbling. His mouth opened and closed in a reasonable imitation of speech, but I couldn't make anything out.

'Talk louder!' someone yelled from the audience.

'Some of you know me,' he began again, shouting.

Laughter rippled through the crowd. My best friend blushed uncomfortably, and I joined him.

'Some of you know me,' he said a third time, striking an appropriate middle ground.

'The Hero of Aunis!' a voice amended, most likely a plant.

He shook his head. 'Sergeant Adolphus Gustav, of the First Capital Infantry – that's good enough for me.'

A rumble of agreement from the audience.

'Good enough for any man,' he ad-libbed, and the mass cheered, and he was off.

I wouldn't have thought Adolphus much of a public speaker, but he did all right. The wound helped, and his size – everyone looking up at him knew that this was a man who had fought for the Empire, fought hard and suffered for it.

But there was more than that. He believed what he was saying, and it came through. No paid herald mouthing another man's words. He spoke slowly and simply, and after a few sentences he stopped looking at his notes. He knew the story well enough, after all. A boy from the provinces who'd never been ten miles from his village, who'd signed up to serve his country and found himself holding a pike in a foreign land. Who'd done his duty and been called a hero for it. Who didn't resent his loss, who was just happy to have been able to come back home when so many others hadn't. Who'd never asked for anything more than his due, but who owed it to the fallen to demand what was due to them.

It was a good speech. Most of it was even true.

'Will we let them turn their backs on our brothers, dead in a foreign land? Their families, desperate for a few crusts of bread?'

The chorus answered in the negative.

'Is it time to remind them of our sacrifice?'

Enthusiastic agreement.

'The day after tomorrow, I'm going over the top – and I hope to the Firstborn you'll all be coming with me!'

Five thousand men screamed their support, threw their fists in the air, climbed over each other in excitement. One kept silent, and in the tumult that followed, he forced himself out from the ranks and made his way home.

33

Back at the Earl I opened every window and propped the door. In the alley outside the corpse of a mule was starting to rot, and flies were trickling in with the stench. Apart from their fetid buzzing it was a quiet afternoon, languid even. Wren was at Mazzie's, or damn well should have been. Adeline was running errands. I took a seat at the bar and set to rectify my sobriety with workmanlike diligence.

I'd more or less accomplished my task by the time Adolphus came through the door, chest out and whistling. He dropped himself at my table with a grunt, his uneven grin wide enough to swallow a calf. Half of me was happy to see him so, and half of me wanted to bust my glass against his melon.

I wasn't shocked to find my lesser nature winning out. 'That was quite a speech.'

'You were there?'

'Joachim . . .' I corrected myself. 'The commander and I had business.'

A glancing blow, insufficient to snuff out his good humor. Maybe there was some part of him hoping I'd changed my mind about the whole thing, decided to support the vets honestly. Adolphus always was a desperate optimist. 'What did you think?'

'The war sounds like lots of fun. I'm sorry I missed it.'

'That wasn't funny.'

'Maybe I'm losing my touch.' I pulled out a vial of breath and held it to my nose.

'You been going at that awful hard lately.'

Fifteen seconds went by, then I brought it back to my side. 'I've got a thing or two on my mind.'

'That help?'

'Doesn't hurt.'

He chewed over his cud lips but didn't say anything. 'Too bad the boy couldn't see it. Then again, I suppose it's time he started his learning.'

It was an olive branch, but I wasn't in the mood to take it. 'That what we think now? Time to start his learning?'

'I'll bring him along next time,' he said. An aside, but meant to be noticed.

'What does that mean, next time?'

'The commander asked me to speak again tomorrow. Wants me to help rally some of the other Low Town vets. Even asked me to take a spot in the front line for the march.'

I took a last snoot, then put the bottle back into my satchel. 'Sakra's cock, Adolphus, when are you gonna give this up?'

He squared his shoulders. 'When the Crown holds to their obligations.'

'When the Firstborn comes to claim us, you mean? I'd bring a book.'

'We're owed,' he said, his voice gravel and not easily dismissed.

'Come off it, Adolphus. A ten percent tax on your pension won't break your back. This has nothing to do with money. It's more fun for you to play hero than it is to tend bar.'

I'd struck a nerve. His eye narrowed. 'You think so little of me?'

'This isn't a game. What's the Crown going to do when they see the Association making trouble?'

'We got the right to peaceful assembly.'

'You got every right in the world, till they decide to start taking them from you.'

'We're not the sort to melt in the rain – the Dren discovered that. Black House wants trouble, they'll learn the same.'

'That was what Roland Montgomery thought,' I said. 'It'll get you what it got him.'

'General Montgomery was assassinated while fighting for the rights of his country and his men. I'd be proud to fall the same way.' Hours spouting rhetoric were affecting his judgment. 'There's such a thing as right and wrong.'

'No, Adolphus – there's just alive and dead. The war should have taught you that.'

'Maybe we learned different things.'

'Maybe you don't remember your lessons.'

'Quit telling me what I believe!' he bellowed suddenly, bull chest straining his shirt, face red. He gave himself a moment to deflate before continuing, but it didn't seem to help. 'You know what I think?'

'Waiting to hear it.'

'I think you don't like to see me being cheered for. I think you got used to me being your lapdog, watching your back while you play the big man.'

'That's what you think? That your celebrity offends my ego?'

'Fifteen years carrying your water. Fifteen years being your second. I guess it's natural you'd get jealous, try and work your way in with the commander.'

It was strange to discover this vein of rancor amidst such well-trammeled territory, like finding a torture chamber hidden in the kitchen closet. How many other conversations had this echoed through, I wondered? 'It's not like that,' I said feebly, knowing there was nothing I could say that would close a wound so long festered. 'What I got going with Joachim . . . it ain't about you.'

But he didn't seem to be listening. 'I strike out on my own, and you do everything you can to strangle it.'

'Make sure your jaunt doesn't carry you off a cliff.'

He shook his head, then fell into silence. Mulling over swallowed insults, arguments that I didn't remember but that had taken purchase in my best friend's soul. Strange, what a man carries with him, that you don't see.

The breath buzzed around my skull, muting my semi-constant headache. I started rolling up a tab. 'Bitterness is the prerogative of middle age – have at it. But you've got a family, a real one. You want to leave Adeline a widow? Wren half an orphan?'

'What kind of father would I be to the boy if I didn't stand up for myself? If I didn't stand up for the memory of the fallen?'

'You want to pretend piss is whiskey, that's on you. But don't go filling my glass. You're doing this for yourself. Same with the war. It's only after the killing's done that anyone starts to think up a reason for it.'

'You talk about the war like it was nothing, like we just wasted our time.'

'Masturbation is a waste of time. The war was a cancer.'

'We were defending our homeland.'

'My homeland is Low Town, and no one who's ever seen it would think it worth the corpse of a single infantryman. The Dren didn't have anything to do with me, with us. We died so rich men could get richer.'

'I'm not talking about the brass. I'm not talking about the nobles, or the Crown – I'm talking about *us*. Whatever poison you've got in your stomach, I won't hear you badmouth the ranks.'

'Take a boy out from his home, out from everything that makes him what he is. Give him a weapon, soak him in blood – that sound like a recipe for sainthood to you?'

'That's all you've got for the men you fought with? Who fought for you? Makes me sick to hear you talk like that, to think I got passed over for a man who doesn't care about his brothers.'

'That rankle so? That you never got your second bar?'

'I was a better soldier than you.'

'You were a better soldier than me,' I agreed. 'You weren't ever a better killer.'

Adolphus's sneer sat uneasily on his wide face. 'And you're proud of that?'

'No, I'm not, but that's all it was. Don't let the way they dressed it up make you forget. It was murder, plain and simple. That we did a lot of it doesn't make it any better.'

'That's not true!' he said. Our conversation had enlivened him enough that the twist of his bull neck sent droplets of sweat into my hair. 'We did what was called of us. War ain't pretty, but I've got nothing I'm ashamed of.'

I stuck my cigarette into a grimace. 'You weren't ashamed at Zwollen?'

That shut him up so quick I almost felt bad about saying it. He shoved his hands in his pockets and looked away.

'We weren't heroes, my friend,' I said. 'At best we were victims.'

He shrugged his shoulders, unwilling to concede the point but unable to counter it either.

That was the end of the conversation, and since Adolphus looked pretty stable where he was, it was left to me to split out. I didn't mind – it was hot as hell in there anyway. It wasn't till I was out the door and the sun was beating on my head that I realized I didn't have anywhere to go.

34

One before you go over?' Roland Montgomery asked, blue eyes sparkling.

We were in his quarters, a half mile outside the walls of Zwollen. It was a canvas tent about ten square feet, a slit on one side opening it to the elements – standard issue to any soldier above the rank of private, the only addition a make-shift desk. He could have billeted himself somewhere, four walls and a roof, but he hadn't.

I threw back the moonshine. It tasted like someone ran up and kicked me in the gut, but it was sure as shit safer than the water I'd been drinking.

'I know you're busy with your preparations, Lieutenant. I won't keep you long.'

'Yes, sir, of course.'

This whole thing was a formality, and as a rule I am not a big fan of those. We were going at them tonight – that was the word from up on high. Every member of the Allied forces had known it since noon, which meant that the Dren had known since twelve-thirty. If the spies littered amongst the camp followers had been slow to spill the news, the artillery barrage that had been going on the last two hours had most assuredly tipped them. Surprise was out – we'd be doing this the hard way: a picked squad with siege ladders, hoping to buy enough time with their flesh for the second wave to win through. Any private lucky enough to survive received extra pay, and whoever was fool enough to lead them was virtually guaranteed a promotion. I'd set my cap a few grades higher than lieutenant, though it's hard now to remember why. Regardless, when they'd gathered us together and asked for a sacrifice, I'd raised my hand and gallantly offered up the men of 'A' company.

'I'm not going to waste your time with any grand oratories. You aren't a rookie and neither am I. We both know this operation has been a clusterfuck since day one. If my predecessor had done his duty instead of drinking himself to death we'd have been inside two months ago. If the brass had seen fit to back us up with a half-dozen competent practitioners we'd have been inside six weeks ago, and if the rain hadn't collapsed our mines we'd have been inside this morning. But I don't control the Army, Lieutenant, nor the weather. The only thing I have to call on is the strength of my right arm and the men under my command, and the first won't be enough for tonight's business. I won't ask you to do it for the Queen, or for Rigus – Śakra knows you've done enough for both of them, and been ill-rewarded for your services. I'm asking you to do it for me, and I take care of my own.'

'Yes, sir.' I tossed it out from my chest. 'We'll take it, sir.'

He nodded, and rested his hand on my shoulder. 'I don't doubt it.'

I fell out of his tent and into the rain. Back at the front I arrayed my company before me, armed and armoured, water beating down on the head of a hundred-plus fierce, tired, hungry souls – veterans to a man, six months, a year, the solid three that I'd suffered.

'I ain't gonna start with no speech,' I said, and unlike Roland, I meant it. 'You know the reward for making it inside. You know what it'll take to get there. There are twenty ladders in front of us, and two men to a team. I need thirty-nine men. If you want in, step up.'

Adolphus was first off the mark, but there were a fair number close behind, and once it had all shaken out I didn't need to conscript anyone. They were good men. They were as good as you could be, under the circumstances. Whatever that meant.

'The rest of you will be attached to "B" company, and we all know what a bunch of pussies they are.' There was a general rumble of forced laughter. 'I'm counting on you to give them some backbone. We'll do our part, but I want you coming in full-bore.'

The sane two-thirds of my company strayed into the background. Those of us who remained checked our equipment one final time. The frugal ones drained whatever they'd saved of their daily allotment of liquor. The delusional ones said their prayers, mumbling introduction to She Who Waits Behind All Things.

It's the interim that kills you. I'd met a few fellows who could bear it without strain, but I was never one of them. My throat was parched as salt, and it was an act of will to keep my hand off my canteen. It's a narrow line, rationing water. Your instinct is to drink until your belly bloats, but once the action starts a full stomach means wet trousers, and you lose something of your authority with piss-stains on your pants. Though what with the rain, I didn't imagine anyone would have noticed.

A sudden blast of red sparks lit up the night, the flare our signal to begin. I grabbed my end of the ladder and Adolphus did his, and then there was no time for my legs to remember they weren't working, just three hundred yards at a dead sprint, or as dead as one can make with fifty pounds of wood on your shoulder. The terrain was mud broken up with corpses, every step a struggle. It was too dark for the enemy to see us, let alone get a decent bead, but they fired off quarrels anyway. I could hear them landing in the sediment around us, thicker than the drizzle, and it occurred to me that a lucky shot will kill you same as a good one. These were intermittently joined by bright beams of light, corridors of heat tearing through the falling rain, illuminating the surroundings then disappearing. The Dren practitioners hadn't gotten any less deadly since Beneharnum, but they couldn't see in the dark any more than the bowmen. At least, I hoped they couldn't. You never knew exactly what to expect, where the Art was concerned.

The moat was a trash-strewn ditch, the run-off knee-deep and mostly sewage to judge by the smell. Littering the bottom were sharpened caltrops, the tainted water ensuring an injury would end with infection. A man on the ladder team next to mine set his foot against one and collapsed in a heap. He let out a scream that gave away our position, but there wasn't time to do anything about it. I plunged forward, hoping to Maletus I didn't meet the same fate.

The Scarred One took pity on me, in so far at least as I made it through without injury. A few feet before the battlements I set the bottom of the ladder in the dirt, and after a second Adolphus sent the rest hurtling up against the stone. I unsheathed a knife and shoved it between my teeth, then clambered up the rungs before my partner could do the same.

Cannon fire from the battlements above us flared in the night, but I kept my eyes on the wall and climbed as quick as I could. If there was anyone looking down I was dead, an easy shot with a crossbow or a barrel of burning pitch. That last was the worst, heated tallow eating through your clothes and sticking to your skin, maiming anyone who survived, a long life begging coin and frightening children. Course, if I was lucky the fall alone would kill me – a happy thought indeed.

On the top rung I discovered the motherfucking ladder was short. I was still a good two feet from the rim of the battlements, but at that point there was no going back. Hoping to Śakra Adolphus had those bovine arms of his firm on the bottom struts, I braced myself and leapt for the summit. My fingers found purchase on the stone, but it was an agonizing moment before I could swing my legs up.

It took a second for me to get my bearings. I'd been so certain the run over would kill me I hadn't bothered to give much thought to what I'd do if I made it to the top. Happily the Dren nearest to me seemed as surprised as I was, hesitating to do the obvious and run me through with the pig sticker he'd been issued for that exact purpose. I got over my shock quicker than he did his, pulled my knife from my teeth and slipped it between his ribs. He moved at the last second, turning a lethal strike into a glancing blow, but it unmanned him enough for me to get him by the shoulders and trip him over the side.

A trio of guards from down the line were coming to their comrade's aid, too slow for salvation but in plenty of time for revenge. I pulled a grenade loose from my bandolier and struck the flashpoint against the floor, setting the fuse to light, then tossed it underhand and dropped to the ground. A deafening caterwaul and a wave of flesh. I pushed myself up as quick as I could, every second lost a desperate one. A thread of entrails was caught in my hair and I brushed it off negligently, one more horror I didn't have time to process. If I gave them a chance to fall on me I was good as buried, audacity was all I had. I pulled my trench blade from its sheath and took a running leap into the sea of men swelling up the stairwell from the courtyard below.

The Great War was the largest conflict in human history. Millions of men killing each other across the breadth of the Thirteen Lands. You get enough people together and all kinds of wacky shit starts to happen – it's just a function of the numbers. I once saw a man take an entire Dren platoon all on his lonely, screaming like Maletus and swinging a flamberge one-handed. Walked half of them back tame as sheep, fifteen-odd soldiers with their eyes down. I wouldn't have believed it if I hadn't seen it, but I did and it happened. A shell got him a few days later, but he was the toast of the division in the interim.

Point being what happened was just luck, random and blind – any stray bolt could have done me, and there must have been a hundred thousand soldiers as hard as me, or harder. But that night, I didn't run into any of them. That night, couldn't no one touch me.

I moved on that part of the brain that is below the conscious mind, which is remembered only impersonally, as if watching the actions of a third party. The edge of my blade surged forward of its own volition, and what it touched dissipated like water. In the narrow confines of the staircase numbers didn't count for anything, it was one-to-one. The Dren in front of me held his spear above his head, lips trembling, and I sheared my blade straight through the shaft and into bone. The next one got a boot in his chest hard enough to crack a few ribs, and he fell from the steps, carrying one of his mates with him.

I was mad with the sheer joy of it. I'd have laughed if I'd had the breath.

The last two broke and ran – one I caught while he was turning but the other took off at a good sprint and I didn't bother to chase after him. At the distant edges of my mind I realized we'd broken through, could see my men running past me, down the other sets of steps and into the city proper. The hand on my shoulder was Adolphus's, a wound on his arm that bore looking into but a smile on his face just the same. He laughed and I laughed with him. After a few moments there was an explosion off to the right, the space I'd carved giving our sappers time to demolish the main gate. Reinforcements would be on their way, but it wouldn't matter – whatever strength had allowed the besieged to hold out against the full might of the Rigun Empire was utterly spent. Immediate survival was now the sole concern.

For a few blissful moments I stood there, watching as, I assumed at the time, the rest of my company chased after the fleeing Dren – and I felt like I was supposed to feel. Like a man who had done his duty, right as the falling rain.

Then the screams started, distinct from the noise of battle by the presence of feminine voices, and I realized, neither for the first time nor the last, that I was a fool.

The soldiers streaming past me weren't under my command

but I shrieked at them anyway – halt, form a line, retreat, anything I could think of. No one listened. Victory can unmake an army just the same as defeat. Two months camped in front of those walls, freezing and wet, while the people inside lobbed explosives down on our heads – I guess we'd worked up something of a grudge.

In the middle of the street a man barely old enough to shave held a woman against the ground. She struggled desperately, screaming for help, and he slapped her silent, then went back to struggling with her petticoat. Adolphus roared over and tore him off, nearly ripping the boy's arm out of its socket. In his pre-coital excitement he seemed barely to notice, laughing as he pulled his pants on. 'All right, all right – officers first. No need to get rough, there's plenty of wool to go around.' He ran off into the night, the streets full of prey.

His victim stared up at us, certain that we were next. I remember that look better than anything else about that night, the fear in her eyes and the hate behind it. After a long moment she got to her feet and sprinted off into an alleyway.

In the distance a line of fires were spreading, the product of an upturned candle or deliberate vandalism. My friends and comrades continued their triumphant rush into the city proper. I'd given up trying to stop them. In the light of the burning metropolis they seemed faceless, interchangeable. If you weren't up to it, the next man in line certainly would be – so why not be up to it? The herd don't have no code. I'd learned that a long time ago. I wasn't sure why it still surprised me.

I looked up at Adolphus. He looked back down at me. We fell off into a side street. After about a hundred yards we stopped in front of a house, decently built but nothing special, residence of a shopkeeper or minor merchant. Adolphus put a foot in the middle of the door and it splintered away to nothing.

The burgher standing behind the entrance held a carving knife forgotten in one hand, eyes saucer wide, any will to fight lost at the sight of the giant. Behind him stood his wife and daughter, meat-faced and wide-hipped, almost indistinguishable, clutching each other with terrified ferocity. Adolphus grabbed the man's wrist, firmly but not cruelly. Steel clanged to the ground. I slipped past my partner and took a seat at a kitchen table that dominated the room. Private Gustav took the one across from me. 'Food,' I said in my pidgin Dren. 'Drink.'

The matron sobbed piteously, a tune her progeny soon took up. I repeated my request to the old man, and after a moment he shook himself out of his shock and headed to the larder. Adolphus stared off at the wall with sad, dull eyes.

We spent the rest of the night like that, our host bringing us dark beer and what sundries were left in his pantry, the mother and daughter never letting go of each other, convinced at any moment we would break our repast and ravish them. Between the two of us we finished off half a keg, trying to get drunk enough to forget what was going on around us without passing so deeply into inebriation as to allow the old man a chance to slit our throats. It was a difficult task we set ourselves, and we didn't quite meet it.

In the darkness outside, terrible things happened.

The pillage lasted three days, after which the men gradually formed back into that shape that distinguishes an army from a band of marauders. I daresay there were some men in my company who spent those days like Adolphus and I did; I daresay there weren't many. I would have received a promotion for my role in the assault, but the second afternoon I got drunk and broke the jaw of a man who turned out to be my captain, and it was all Roland could do to keep me from being busted down in rank, or flogged.

35

I spent the evening in an apartment I own in Offbend. It's
an ugly apartment, in an ugly building, in an ugly
borough in an ugly city. I could keep going. The neighbors
do their best to live up to the surroundings, spiteful folk with
bad skin and crossed eyes, but they didn't know nobody and
they never saw nothing. That was more or less the sole virtue
of the dwelling, and it was worth the few coin a month I dropped
on it.

Back at the Earl I changed clothes and undid the latch on the
hidden shelf in my bureau, swapping a few vials from the professional stash into my personal. I noted sourly that it had been a
lot more crowded a few days earlier.

A letter waited on my night table, a block 'M' sealed in wax
on the back. I opened it and watched a leaf of paper flutter to
the ground. The text was neat, ink pressed into muslin.

Lieutenant,

No doubt you've heard of my recent misfortune. Its arrival is to be laid at my feet, and mine alone – you owe me nothing. Indeed, it is I and my family who are in your debt, and while your refusal to accept payment does you credit, your services merit reward. Please take the enclosed as just recompense, and as a mark of esteem from an old man.

General Edwin Montgomery, (Ret.)

Recent misfortune. The general was a hard man, but then he'd have to be, having lost one already. And what could you expect? Tear stains in the margins, like a virgin's love letter? I picked up the fallen slip of paper. It was a promissory note to be drawn at one of the city's oldest banking establishments, the sort with ivy growing up stone walls, a sign too small to notice and a million ochres in the basement. It felt light in my palm. It had enough zeroes on it to weigh down a corpse. I tore it into slivers, then dropped the slivers into the trash.

The ball was already rolling; I'd be wise not to step in front of it. And besides, the general didn't know what I owed him – if he did, he wouldn't have been so quick to offer coin, or his esteem. I undid the cap on a vial of breath and let the pink vapor filter through a nostril. Rhaine Montgomery would get her due.

I folded the letter back up, then stopped and reopened it. The wax sigil had been reheated, ably, subtly, but noticeably, if you knew what to look for. I hadn't been the first person to read the general's missive, though I had a pretty good idea who was.

At some point while I was upstairs Wren had taken a spot at a front table. He was gouging out pieces of the wood with the tip of his dagger, and he didn't react when I took the seat next to him.

'I know the furnishings aren't exactly in prime condition, but that's not a reason to deteriorate them further.'

He didn't answer, and he didn't stop.

'How'd your lesson go?'

He grunted.

'I don't speak surly adolescent. You'll need to translate.'

'It was fine,' he said, sharp as the tip of his blade.

I put my hand on the hilt and settled it against the table. Then I put my face next to his, close enough to smell his breath. 'You don't feel like chatting, that's fine, I'm in no mood for a confessional. But I'm going to see Mazzie later on today to start paying for the rest of your education, and I'd like to make sure I'm not getting cheated.'

I held him firmly in place for a long moment, then let go and reclined back into my seat. 'She's all right,' he said after a while. 'So far at least. We didn't do much. She made tea, and we talked some. She told me I need to learn to make my mind hollow. It didn't make much sense to me.'

That sounded about right. I didn't suppose he'd be initiated into the higher mysteries on his first day. I picked up a splinter from Wren's whittling and picked at my teeth. 'It don't need to make sense to you. She's your teacher, it just needs to make sense to her. But like I said, you keep your head swiveling. Anything happens that don't feel right to you, you let me know.'

He wasn't in the mood to agree with me about anything, so in place of a nod he went back to picking out bits of the table. I left him to it long enough to get comfortable, then dropped the weight.

'You aiming to take a spot with the ice?'

'No,' he said, confused.

'Then why you been reading my mail?'

He left the knife sticking upright in the wood and opened his mouth to lie.

'You drip a false syllable and I'm gonna beat you blue,' I said, but my heart wasn't in it, and it didn't draw more from him than a shrug.

'It seemed interesting.'

'This what you learned beneath my roof? To gnaw at the hand that feeds you?'

A childhood spent picking pockets and running scams had mostly inured Wren to the effects of guilt. No doubt he'd earned a more physical manifestation of my displeasure, but it was awful hot to be getting hot.

'What did you do for General Montgomery?' Wren asked after it became clear there wouldn't be immediate consequences for his misbehavior.

'Very little of value, as it turned out.'

'It have anything to do with that woman who came in here last week?'

By the Firstborn, he was smart. You had to sprint to keep ahead of him. 'Yeah.'

'How'd it turn out?'

'Not particularly well.'

'This General Montgomery,' he began again, after a pause. 'He Roland's father?'

'Not anymore.'

'Adolphus says Roland was a legend. Says he gave his life trying to better his men's.'

'Death makes a fellow popular.' My headache wasn't going anywhere. I thought about rolling a spliff, but it was gonna be a long day, and I'd do better if I kept my edge.

'You knew him?'

'Yeah, I knew him.'

'What was he like?'

A man like any other. A Daeva, straight from Chinvat. A mad dog in the street, best put down, and fast. 'Depends on where you sat.'

'And where did you sit?'

'He was my superior, for a while, back during the war. After . . .' I flicked my toothpick onto the ground. 'We were at cross-purposes.'

'But you were a soldier, like Adolphus – Roland was fighting for you.'

My hopes of reaching mid-morning without losing my temper were starting to seem increasingly vain. Wren had perfected the ability to make me want to hurt him. 'Let me explain to you how it is, boy – I wouldn't think I'd need to, you growing up how you did. But you're young, and still stupid, so I'll tell you. There are men who walk in front, and men who stand behind them. The man behind, he's always got a reason why he has to be where he is. Roland was better than most of them – at least he believed his line – but at the end of the day, it's still the men up front catching the arrows.'

'The veterans seem to think he was more than that.'

'He had a good patter, like I said.'

'That's all there is?'

'The Dren you hate so much – what do you think they marched for? You think their commanders told them they were the horde, make ready to swoop down on civilization and burn it to its embers? They got the same speech we did – glory, honor, justice. It comes down to where you're sitting, like I said.'

'None of it means anything?'

'Not enough to die over.'

'Then why are you doing this?'

'Doing what?'

His eyes were hard and cold, harder and colder than a fourteen-year-old's had any right to be. 'You've got wheels spinning,' he said. 'You been spinning them all week.'

'I spin wheels for a living.'

'So you'll see yellow out of what you got going with the veterans?'

Nothing like having the tables turned on you by a boy still holding his cherry. 'It's not all about coin.'

'What's it about then?'

I didn't answer.

'Glory? Honor?' He smiled savagely. 'Justice?'

I was saved by a knock from outside, a solid banging that seemed nearly an attempt to break the door down.

Wren went back to playing with his blade. 'For a man who doesn't stick his neck out for anything, you stick your neck out a lot.'

The thumping continued. 'Warden, you in there?'

'Yeah,' I answered, but my eyes didn't leave the boy.

'It's Hroudland. Commander needs to see you.'

'One fucking second!' I shouted back, then leaned my face against Wren's. 'Next time you touch my property you can expect the conversation to be a good deal less pleasant,' I said, then rose and opened the door.

Hroudland and a couple of veterans stood outside, and they didn't seem cheery. 'Hello, boys – you miss me?'

36

Pretories was in a small cafe across from the burned-out wreckage of a building. He sat at a booth by the window, sipping from a mug too small for his hands. Three of his boys kept him wedged in respectfully, five if you counted by width. Each was engaged in impressive displays of fury, cracking knuckles, eyeballing passers-by, making quiet threats at no one in particular. By contrast Joachim seemed but faintly ruffled, blowing softly over his coffee.

This one would be a tight play, no room for error. The vial of breath swung heavy in my pocket, and I let it stay there. These Association types weren't so liberated as my usual crowd.

'I'm sorry, Commander,' I said.

He swallowed my courtesy with a nod. 'We had four boys in there, when they hit it.'

'Like I said, I'm sorry.'

There was an uncanny stillness to Joachim that made you

jittery by reflection, made your beard itch and your brow sweat. 'Let's hear it,' he said finally.

'Not sure I follow.'

'You warned me, told me what was coming. I gave you the brush-off. You're entitled to crow.'

I took the seat across from him. 'I take no pleasure in the death of your men.' Though I wouldn't lose any sleep over it either – petty thugs with ten years of Joachim's dirty work beneath their belts.

That was the last thing anyone said for a while. I watched tufts of white smoke leak out from the hole in the other side of the street. The boys watched me. Pretories didn't seem to watch anything.

Without warning he brought his fist down against the table. The crockery rattled, and so did the personnel. He waited till both settled before continuing. 'I don't need this shit right now.'

'I don't imagine.'

'Tomorrow is the biggest day in the history of our organization. Fifty thousand men marching in step, the largest contingent of veterans since the end of the war, taking our demands straight to the palace.'

'Heavy.'

'And now some . . . fading crime lord wants to go a round with us, bring up dirt that's been buried for a decade.'

'I admit – the timing is suspicious.'

His eyes rolled up to meet mine. 'What does that mean?'

I took a deliberate look around the table. 'Perhaps we'd best continue this in private.'

'I don't know what you're used to, Lieutenant, but these men are my brothers. There are no secrets between us.'

The goons sat up straighter.

'Word is the Giroies get their backing from a man on the top floor of Black House.'

'Boys, secure the perimeter.'

The goons trickled out the booth, hurt and petulant.

Joachim waited until they were gone before continuing. 'That's impossible,' he said, and perhaps he wasn't quite straight as a quarterstaff.

'Why?'

'Black House has no reason to come after us – we're a legitimate organization.'

'Stirring up trouble with the council and the Crown. You think the Old Man is above taking sides on a political matter, you need to take another walk around the block. And besides, the Association might have put their revolutionary activities behind them, but Black House has a long memory. They're not adverse to stepping on you for past misdeeds.'

'I'm well aware of our history with Black House.' He curled his lip up like he'd smelt something sour, and if he wasn't quite fidgeting, it was close enough to see I'd gotten to him. 'But we've reached an . . . equilibrium, at least, since Roland's death. They've no reason to declare war on us.'

'They didn't – you did, when you decided on your march. Whatever unspoken accord you think you have with the Old Man, I can assure you, it lasts only until he thinks you're making trouble for him – or till he sees an open shot at your throat.'

'So he spurs up trouble with the Giroies to . . .'

'Turn your flanks. They figure they'll distract you with an old enmity.'

He seemed to realize the balance between us had shifted, and came on strong, trying to reassert his authority. 'This is all very interesting, Lieutenant. I'm wondering why you didn't think to mention it before?'

'All I had were rumors, underworld gossip.'

'And now?'

'I did some digging since yesterday. There are still a few men in Black House willing to chat, so long as I'm buying the drinks, and the drinks cost ten ochre a pop.'

'Whispers from underworld contacts and ex-colleagues – this is a far way from hard evidence.'

'Fits though, doesn't it?'

His silence was confirmation enough. There was another long

pause, but this one I didn't think was planned. Even for a man as unflappable as the commander, things were moving pretty quickly. He slunk down over his drink. 'Years pulling ourselves out of Roland's hole, years spent sitting on anything that touched on our old activities. Building our rolls, making contacts at court. Winning a place at the table for the men who'd fought for and earned it. This morning I wake up to the news that our station was bombed, four of our brothers murdered, and we're back where we fucking started.'

I set one finger on the rim of the milk pot, then pushed it over. A puddle settled onto the table, seeping into the cloth and trickling slowly to the floor.

Pretories watched it drip, then looked up at me.

'You gonna cry over it?'

He didn't answer, but his eyes were angrier than I'd ever seen them.

'Let this go unanswered and what do you think you'll get for an encore? The Giroies need a rap on the nose, or they'll keep coming,' I pointed out.

'And if Black House is pulling their strings?'

'All to the good. They learn their lesson, but it don't look like you taught it to them.'

'The Old Man can't lose a pawn and not retaliate.'

'You think he'll send flowers to the funeral?'

'He's not a man to cross lightly.'

'If you wanted to keep to the status quo, you shouldn't be marching on the palace. As it is, you got two options – let yourself look like you can't back your play . . .'

'Or?'

'Show them you ain't the one to fuck with. Push back hard enough and the Old Man will eat the loss – he's got no interest in starting a full-scale war.'

'What's to stop him from coming at us another way?'

'Tomorrow's problems can be dealt with tomorrow. Today's problem is that the Giroies are making mince out of our people, and unless you want that to continue, you need to make a move.'

Salvation, a line for a drowning man – who wouldn't grab it? Just make sure he doesn't learn you're the one who tipped him overboard. Joachim wasn't the sort to go off half-cocked. He didn't say anything for a while, a long while, his eyes blank as a catatonic's. 'What do you recommend?'

'Something loud. It needs to carry.'

A minute more passed. Then the weave of his mouth curled upwards. 'Thank you for the information, Lieutenant. We'll speak again soon.'

I knew a dismissal when I heard it. Joachim remained where he was, finishing off his coffee. A serving boy ran over and blotted up the spilled milk. There'd be blood to join it, soon enough.

37

Guiscard's hounds came in a scant twenty minutes after Joachim's had deposited me back at the Earl, and this time weren't neither of them playing nice. I'd figured they might stop by, so in the interim I'd divested myself of any legally questionable arms or substances, but they took a good long time making sure. They stopped before my pants were around my ankles, a fact for which I was grateful.

'I keep a shiv in my asshole.'

The friendly one hit me in the stomach hard enough to make me a ball on the floor. The unfriendly one kicked me in the head. That was why he was the unfriendly one.

They pulled me to my feet. I fell back down. They pulled me up again, and held me steady. I blinked the light away, wished I could do the same with the blood.

'That was my best shirt,' I said, the red bloom adding contrast to the sweat stains.

The friendly one looked ready to give me another, but the

unfriendly one waved him off, cuffed me and led me out the door. I was thinking maybe I needed to switch their tags. The ride over was pretty similar to its predecessor, except that this time no one smiled, and every bump in the road splintered through my skull.

Black House seemed much the way it had last time, though I was brought through it at a rapid clip so there wasn't much opportunity for inspection. A few minutes and I was back in Guiscard's windowed office, with a forced seat in an uncomfortable chair.

He'd worn since I'd seen him last, which was a good sign that my work hadn't been entirely in vain. My eyes had mostly swelled shut, and it hurt when I breathed, so I did my best not to.

'You've dropped the ball, Warden. You were supposed to keep me apprised of the situation. I wake up today to find out there's a smoking crater where an Association bureau used to be, and three bodies smoldering in the rubble.'

'Four bodies,' I said. 'Don't short the count.'

A floorboard creaked behind me, and then my jaw struck against my chest. The unfriendly one, I figured. Six inches down he'd have snapped my neck, but he knew what he was doing. The correct method by which to hit a seated man was something you learnt coming up through the Black House ranks.

'I'd have figured, after some of the things I've done for you lately, the least you'd do is keep me abreast of current events.'

'In what fashion have I been remiss?'

'What do you know about the Association hitting a shipment of the Giroies?'

'I know they hit it.'

'Then why didn't I know that?'

'I figured you'd get word eventually.'

This time Guiscard didn't delegate. He'd never have the raw talent of his subordinates, but it was a credible effort just the same. At that point though I hurt too much to feel anything else, and that gives a man a certain audacity. 'Forgive me for crediting you with the wit to smell smoke.'

'The house is on fire, is it?'

'The whole city, soon enough.'

'Because of Giroie?'

I shook my head sadly. 'You can't really be as slow as you act.'

Behind me I could hear my escort positioning himself for another blow.

'Slip the cuffs,' Guiscard said, 'then split.'

There was a pause, but with my head settled like it was I couldn't figure what occurred during it. After a moment one of the dogs unbound my hands. I settled them together, pride keeping me from checking my injuries.

'Keep out of trouble,' the friendly one said on his way out.

The door closed. 'Got a cigarette?' I asked.

'I quit.'

I smiled through loosened teeth. 'You ain't gonna pretend you don't have a hold out stashed somewhere?'

He sighed grudgingly, then opened a drawer and passed over a small leather pouch.

'You ask them to work me over?'

He didn't answer.

'Just left it up to their discretion? You gotta be careful with that – they get enthusiastic and suddenly there's no one left to interview.' My fingers shook, and I made a mess of the tab. But Guiscard was off on his own, and he didn't notice. They'd been kind enough to leave a book of matches in my pocket, and I struck one and used it.

The sound seemed to bring Guiscard back to the immediate. 'Have you spoken to Pretories?'

'You ought to know the answer to that, if you're a quarter competent.'

'What did he say?'

'What do you think he said? He's going to pay a visit to the Giroies, and . . .' I brought my thumb against the table, like I was squashing a nit.

'You holding something back from me, Warden? I wouldn't

recommend it. The Old Man wants this situation with the vets taken care of, and he doesn't care how it happens. If you're thinking about running a double-blind on me, then you've been huffing too much breath.'

'I've certainly been doing the latter.'

Guiscard ran his fingers up the bridge of his nose and between his eyes. 'I don't buy it. It isn't in anyone's interest to start trouble, least of all Pretories.'

'Why? Because he's in your pocket?'

I'd been holding that one back for a while, and it was a spot of light to see it land. He didn't roll with it well either – I mean, I'd done a better job with the tap he gave me. Though I've had more practice being hit. 'How the hell do you know that?'

'You think there are things you know that I don't?'

The silence spread too long, and he came on hard to compensate for it. Foolish – anyone could see we'd swapped chairs. 'Then you should know it doesn't line up. Pretories banks our checks. Has for ten years. He keeps the Association on the straight, makes sure none of his wilder members get to thinking any of their old master's heresies, and we let him play the big man.'

'And the rally?'

'A sideshow – lets his boys blow off some steam.'

'Is that what it is?'

'We got a good arrangement going.'

'You can't buy a whore, Guiscard. Only rent one.'

'Oversubtle, for a thug.'

'Should I break it down for you further? Pretories' interests aren't your interests. They were for a while, now they ain't.'

He grated one line of perfect teeth against the other. 'There's nothing for him here. He knows what happens if he goes against the Crown.'

'Your problem is that you're a reasonable man, and you think everyone else is likewise.'

'People tend to act to their own benefit.'

'You'd be shocked at how little that's true.'

He opened up a few inches of his collar. 'I hold no illusions about Pretories – if he'd betray his own people, he'd fold on us. But doing so wouldn't get him anything. He's been marching to our beat too long to go back to calling his own tunes.'

'Yesterday, yesterday – yesterday y'all baked apple dumplings and played rat-in-a-hole. Today he's murdering drug dealers in the streets, and tomorrow he marches on the palace with fifty thousand men. Wait around a week, he'll be gang-raping your daughter and shitting in your kitchen.' I huffed smoke and dropped my trump. 'Maybe it's time we brought in the Old Man.'

No one likes being reminded they're mid-list in the pecking order. 'That won't be necessary.'

'It's a lovely office, but we both know where the strings get pulled. A change in policy needs to be signed off on from upstairs.'

'I am upstairs.'

'We gonna argue semantics?'

'I told you once before – I run this show.'

'Then you'd best go ahead and fucking run it,' I answered.

That was that. He made with the contemplation, but I knew he'd bend in the breeze. It was a dull minute. My cigarette was mostly ash before he thought to pass over a tray.

'You want a handkerchief?'

I shook my head, regretting it immediately. 'I'd rather bleed on your desk.'

He snorted and started to twist himself a smoke.

'So you've taken care of my little problem?' I asked.

'As of this morning there are a half-dozen Islanders rotting in cells in jail – and three taking up slabs in the morgue. I'm told Adisu is one of the latter.'

'You're a prince amongst men.'

Guiscard didn't answer, just sat there puffing away at the cigarette he'd rolled. I could have told him you never really quit, you just take a break while things are going easy. 'You ever think about Crispin?' he asked suddenly.

'I try not to.'

255

'I guess he could have sat here, if he'd wanted to.'

'Yup.'

'I guess he didn't want to.'

'Don't let yourself get too down,' I said, standing. 'It ended well for me.'

By the time I was outside my punch-drunk had worn off, and the orchestra in my head had gone from background noise to overture. Bile climbed up my throat, and it was only through sheer will that I forced it tumbling back. I must have been quite a sight – passers-by watched in horror, though none offered help.

38

Back at the Earl I sipped through a few ounces of liquor and passed out. When I woke the pain was worse, but the swelling had faded and I could see enough out of my right eye to be blinded by the afternoon light. It was late, and my day wasn't over. A half-vial of breath reminded me of my duties. I palmed another into my satchel in case I got forgetful. Then I put a blade into my boot and slipped downstairs. The Earl was empty. Adolphus was off preparing for the evening rally, and Wren was probably with him. I had no idea where Adeline had disappeared to, but I was happy she'd done so – the longer I could put off explaining why my face looked like a mass of uncooked meat the happier I'd be.

Walking through the Isthmus I was conscious of the fading hour, and that my injuries were an appeal to the worst instincts of the native element. But the heat hadn't abated with the sun, and the air was thick as a smoker's cough, and the cock-a-walks were largely absent, drinking in darkened juke-joints or trying to sleep through to night. I found my way to Mazzie's without any trouble, and this time even managed to reach the entryway without faltering my step.

She sat in the same position, down to the length of ash on her cigar. Even the oven working in the corner remained as it had been, the same pots bubbling rank on top of it. She waved at the open chair, but waited a while before starting.

'What happened to your jaw?'

'A brick wall hit me.'

'And your eye?'

'I couldn't let the jaw go unanswered.' I crinkled a trail of dreamvine in the hollow of a wrapper, then added a twist of tobacco for cover. 'So. You set your eyes on him.'

She bobbed the ebony sphere of her skull. 'Did at that.'

'What's the verdict?'

'He's got talent. Should have long started his learning, but he's got talent all the same.'

'Then you'll take him on?'

She motioned with her shoulders in a fashion that indicated nothing one way or the other. 'I figured, after your introduction, he must be kin to you.'

'Ain't got no kin.'

'How'd you meet him?'

'Let me think now – ah yes, the Duke of Courland introduced us over high tea. We needed a fifth for whist, and our Wren's a deft hand at cards.'

'He says he was a street child, and he begged you for a job.'

I lit my spliff off one of the colored candles dripping wax onto the table. 'That might have been it, now that you remind me.'

'So it was his idea, coming in under your roof?'

'Damn sure wasn't mine.'

There was something intoxicating about Mazzie that held your attention and wouldn't let go. Every feature seemed amplified, overstated – her smile a slant that cut across the width of her face, nose broad as a bullock's, eyes strong as rubbing alcohol. 'Awful kind of you, putting up an orphan.'

'I got a twenty-four karat heart. Market keeps going up on gold, I'm gonna cut it out and sell it.'

'That's what they say about the Warden. That he's sweet as cane sugar and soft as sunshine.'

'You gonna circle all night, or you gonna throw?'

'What you want with the boy?' she asked, all in the back of her throat, syllables hard against each other.

I didn't answer for a moment, holding in a chestful of violet smoke. 'Questioning my motives, Mazzie?'

'Just curious. Do you take in every stray child you meet, or just the ones of use?'

'I've drowned puppies done more for me than that child.'

'A homeless boy with the art – that's pure flake. Course he's smart, but you needn't have known that at the time. They're not all smart – one of the crews back in Miradin, they had a boy with a fair-strength spark, and a face beat in by his mother when he wasn't but three. Couldn't talk nothing, couldn't barely think more than that, but he could light a fire without a match, anywhere you pointed, any size.' She took a long draw off her cheroot, then pulled the exhaust in through her nostrils, each wide as a copper piece. 'Kept him on a collar, made him eat off the floor.'

'You've got the nicest friends.'

'Your boy's got too much steel for that, of course. And he's got power too, waiting to be kindled but there just the same. He gets to bucking, he'll break you straight in two.'

'What's it to you, Mazzie? The color of my ochre don't change with my reasons.'

'Won't have no part in turning a child into a weapon.'

'Mazzie of the Stained Bone, witch-woman of the Isthmus. Thrown out of Miradin for blasphemies unspeakable. The things that are darker than night whisper secrets in her ear, and the High Laws no more than chicken scratch. Don't make any bargains you can't keep, or she'll snatch up your firstborn and leave a straw doll beneath the pillow. Didn't figure you for a soft stomach.'

'No more surprising than discovering the king of Low Town takes stragglers in beneath his roof.'

'Everything they say about you true?'

'Enough of it,' she acknowledged. 'Besides, it's not about what I heard. I saw what you were from the first foot you stepped inside my house.'

'It's the spirits, then? They let you know the sort of man I am?'

She didn't answer.

'The spirits got a line on tomorrow's racket numbers?'

She puffed silently at her cigar, eyes never leaving mine.

'They never do, do they?' The dreamvine was bright and potent, and I was enjoying the whole thing more than I should have.

'You think you can live the kind of life you've lived, do the kind of things you do, and not have it leave any trace?' she asked.

'Is your own history so uncheckered that you can afford to pass judgment on mine? What would I see, if I had your gift? What does the mirror tell you, Mazzie, when you look into it?'

There was nothing light or friendly in her smile, nothing of a smile at all really. Nothing but the form of the thing, her teeth crooked and white. 'Don't have one.'

The spreading silence gave me time to recollect how much pain I was in, slowly but surely bleeding past the dreamvine. I'd need something stronger, and soon. The sunlight percolating in through the hole in the roof was fading fast, evening soon to plant itself on a city that was near boiling. The stove popped suddenly, a wet spot on a log flaring to life, but Mazzie didn't jump, didn't so much as move.

'I figured you was coming by today. Decided to take your advice from last time, break out the shakers, give them a roll,' she said.

I leaned back in the stool and opened my arms wide. 'Take your shot.'

'You build a maze around you, and dare fools to walk through it.'

'A fool don't need any help taking a tumble.'

'No merit in pushing them.'

'I think of it as a public service.'

'Corpses stand at your shoulder, and they wave at brothers ahead. The fuse is running fast, and when it sparks it'll level more than you thinking, more than you plan. The blood you avenge will be repaid a dozen-fold, a hundred, repaid in rivers and torrents. You ain't careful you'll drown beneath it, die with it choking your throat and filling your lungs.'

'You finished?'

'Just about.'

Suddenly it didn't seem so funny, didn't seem funny at all, and I wanted to give her a shot straight on that false grin. 'If that's the best you got then your gift ain't worth a tarnished copper. You see dead men in my past because I've put a string of bodies in the ground, and dead men in my future because I've got a list of motherfuckers waiting to join them. I don't need your bones to know there's trouble brewing – I've been arranging its arrival all week.'

'The bones, they say one more thing – they say you running around in the dark, that the things you think true are false. They say the more you struggle, the tighter the bonds.'

I swallowed that with the last of my joint, then dropped the butt to the floor. 'The boy needs training or he'll end up mad, or worse. If you've got any of the ethics you affect, you won't leave him twisting in the wind. Far as the rest goes, you don't know nothing about me, not where I been nor where I'm headed.' I kicked over my stool and walked to the door. Her cackling followed me out into the street.

Between the beating, and the dreamvine, and the day, and my life, I wasn't in top shape. If they'd have been smarter they could have probably snatched me up with my back turned, and that would have been the end of it, or near enough. But a few blocks out from Mazzie's I caught sight of someone tailing me, and if I didn't put the whole thing together I was at least sharp enough to smell a threat.

Not that there was much I could do to head it off. I was still deep in the Isthmus, miles away from a friendly face. I was too tired to run and anyway I didn't know the geography enough to chance it. The best I could do was put myself in a position to meet them head on. An alley led off the road I was on, dead-ending after about twenty yards. I followed it, put my back against the wall, pulled the knife from my boot, and waited for the end.

It wasn't long coming. Adisu rounded the corner, the Muscle with him, both the worse for wear. A bandage was rolled around Zaga's arm, saturated with crimson, though it only had the effect of emphasizing the width of his bicep. Adisu himself had an ugly scar marring a face not noted for its beauty. It was turning a color that suggested medical attention was in order.

He didn't appear worried about it, though. In fact, he seemed positively giddy. 'You seem surprised to see me.'

He was not wrong. I had a pretty long list of folk I'd like to have seen returned from the dead. Adisu the Damned was not on it. 'Looks like you boys have been through some trouble.'

'You could say that. A squad of boys from Black House came by and paid us a visit. Maybe you heard about that. Maybe you even heard they put me down,' he laughed. 'Probably the ice figure one Islander is as good as another.'

As someone familiar with their thought process, I could confirm that this was exactly how the ice figured. No doubt Guiscard had believed himself honest when he'd told me that Adisu would no longer be a problem. No doubt whatever heavy had told Guiscard that Adisu would no longer be a problem had believed himself honest as well.

'I'm sure glad to hear you survived it,' I said.

'No, Warden, I don't think you are.'

'You're not suggesting I had anything to do with your misfortune?'

'Who the hell else would it be? I pay my taxes to the guard, same as everyone. And there isn't anything I'm into that would get the ice looking my way. Nothing except you. I didn't realize you still had pull with your old people.'

'It took some talking,' I admitted.

'You look like you've had almost as rough a day as me,' Adisu said.

'It was a long morning.'

'Who been beating on you?'

'Black House, believe it or not.'

Adisu laughed. 'You know something, Warden, I think you're the most hated man I've ever met.'

'It's a talent,' I agreed.

'I'm glad they left something of you for us to play with. I'll tell you honestly, I was pretty worried I wouldn't get this chance. The ice only left the two of us, and I wasn't about to head out your way, not with that tame giant you keep behind the bar. But then I remembered you'd been frequenting old Mazzie's. I figure we'd wait around for a while, see if you'd show. It was a long shot, no question. I certainly didn't think we'd nab you so quick. I guess I must have done something to please the Firstborn.'

'More likely I did something to piss him off.'

'Works out the same either way,' he said. 'I've been thinking about how I'm gonna kill you for the last ten hours, since I saw the ice break my cousin's face into the ground. I've got all sorts of ideas.'

I flourished the knife in my hands, but it was mostly for show. I was as weak as a newborn kitten. After the tuning-up Guiscard and his boys had given me, I didn't imagine I'd give a credible account of myself. Still, you never know. Maybe Adisu would decide to sprint forward and impale himself on my blade. I figured I'd at least give him the option. 'You smell like you rolled in shit,' I said. 'And I find your grandiosity immensely tiring.'

He took the criticism with equanimity. 'I'll work on that,' he said, and seemed even to mean it. Then he nodded at the Muscle. 'Don't rough him up too bad,' Adisu said. 'We've got all night for that.'

Zaga pulled a length of chain from his back pocket and came towards me, whirling the metal above his head in a steady loop. It was meant to fix my attention, so I ignored it, let it bounce down off my forehead and above my eye. It hurt like a motherfucker, hurt through what I'd already suffered, but it left me ready for Zaga's follow up. He came in behind the lash and he met the edge of my knife, left off with a chunk of flesh missing from the hand he'd stretched out to grab me.

Adisu laughed and clapped twice 'That was a nice move, Warden.'

Zaga seemed less enthused. This time he made no attempt at subtlety, just bull-rushed me back against the wall, pinning down my arms. I leaned into him, brought my mouth to where his neck met his shoulder, tore a chunk of flesh from it, tasted blood. He screamed and dropped me and scuttled backwards.

Our struggle seemed no longer to amuse Adisu. 'Can't you do a fucking thing I ask you?' he said to his man, angrily. A knife appeared in his hands, and he started to circle around to my right.

He needn't have bothered. The wounds I'd given Zaga had done more to enrage than slow him, and his bear hug had left me faint and short of breath. I wouldn't last another pass. Black dots clouded my vision, like I'd been staring too long into a fire.

I guess that was why I missed her entrance, didn't realize she was there till she spoke. I guess the others were pretty taken with the action in front of them, because they seemed as surprised as I was. 'What you boys doing out here, with the sun so bright and your souls so dark?'

Mazzie leaned against the walls of a tenement. I'd only seen her sitting, and by candlelight, and she was shorter and uglier than I'd thought, bad skin and fat legs. Her calico dress was faded, and stuck to her flesh with sweat. But her words had been accompanied by a gust of wind, the first breeze in a fortnight. A cold one, too cold – it set the spine shivering, unsettled the mind.

Adisu felt it. A moment before he'd been as eager as a virgin in a whorehouse, but you could see him start to wither. 'I got no quarrel with you, Auntie. This is between me and the man here.'

'Little bird, little bird,' Mazzie continued. 'What you doing so far from home?'

'This is my home,' Adisu said, then gestured at me. 'I'm dealing with a trespasser.'

'This is *my* home, little bird. Your nest done burned. And your wings never quite grew like they should have. Why is that?'

'He wasn't breastfed,' I said, but no one seemed to hear. I'd become a sideshow at my own execution.

'You got no call to be here, witch,' Adisu said. 'Get going, before I set a man on you.'

It might have been a trick of the light but Mazzie's eyes seemed black as ink, as a tomb, as the void. She spoke in the singsong she always used, with the same gentle lilt, but it was as threatening as cold steel. 'I see it now, little bird. Poor, poor thing. Broken from the beginning, broken right from the egg. The things been done to you, you never had no kind of chance.'

'I'm warning you, keep that fucking mouth shut!'

'When he used to sneak into your room at night, the things he did. It comes back to you, don't it? When you go under, when sleep comes. You can snort breath all you want, but you gotta drop down sometime. And he's waiting when it does, isn't he? Waiting for you, just like when you was a child.'

'Shut her up,' Adisu said to the muscle, his voice cracking.

'Any hand you touch me with is gonna rot off before dusk,' Mazzie answered, though she kept the sloe pools of her eyes on Adisu. 'By tomorrow it'll be in your other arm, then your legs and your ears and your tongue and your cock. By the full moon you'll be wagging stumps at passers-by, and hoping they drop coin in your cup.'

Zaga looked at Mazzie for a long while. Then he took a small but distinct step backwards.

'He set the crack in your mind, didn't he? And it only gets wider, little bird, wider and darker. One day it'll swallow you up, swallow you right up and there won't be nothing left. You'll do it yourself, I think, hoping it'll get you free of him. But I've seen what comes next, little bird – and I'm sad to say it, but he'll be waiting for you there too.'

The slim hold Adisu had maintained on sanity was slipping

fast. 'I couldn't do nothing to stop it,' he said, almost pleading. 'I wasn't but four or five.'

The cheroot sparked to life. Zaga jumped about a foot and a half. 'You fade away now, little bird,' Mazzie said. 'This is no place for you anymore.'

The mad are capable of depths of passion unknown to the sane, and during our association I'd seen most every emotion played in extremity across Adisu's face. Fury, joy, despair. But I'd never seen fear. Now that was all there was, emanating out like a stench, enveloping the man he'd brought with him. He turned and broke without even glancing at me, so utterly had he forgotten his revenge in the terror of the moment. Zaga was close on his heels.

That was the last I ever saw of Adisu. They found him floating off the docks a week or so later. He'd been in there long enough that determining the cause of death was no longer possible, or so I was told. I figured he'd topped himself, but it didn't seem at all impossible to imagine it was reparations from one of his boys, or payback from a competitor. Let's just say there were a lot of dry eyes in Rigus, the day Adisu the Damned was pulled out of the harbor.

Mazzie watched them disappear, puffing her smoke, eyes gradually returning to their customary cocoa. 'How you holding up, Warden?' she asked.

'Peachy keen,' I said, then tumbled forward into the muck.

39

The first thing I saw on waking was a thick circlet of flies hovering above my head, tumbling over each other in excitement at the upcoming feast. It was a few moments before I had the strength to brush them away. Their buzzing seemed to intensify, as if angered to discover I wasn't yet dead. I could empathize with their disappointment.

I was lying on a bed. It was lumpy and hard, but it wasn't a shallow grave, so I didn't have much cause to complain. Mazzie was in the opposite corner of the shack, hovering over her stove, spooning one of the pots. If she noticed I'd revived, she didn't make any point of congratulating me on it. For my part, I was happy for the silence to go on indefinitely.

Only death goes on forever. After a while whatever task Mazzie had set herself seemed complete. She filled a brass cup from one of the kettles, then brought it over to me.

'First thing to be said – if it was just a question of you being made a corpse, I wouldn't have bothered to walk outside my house.'

'All right.'

'I don't want you thinking that you matter to me.'

'Not for a moment.'

'But you were right when you said there's something special in that boy. And you were right when you said it'll ruin him if he doesn't get help. I don't just mean with the Art. He's got wildness in him, and if it ain't shaped he'll get himself knifed in an alley even if I keep him from burning out his brain. He needs someone to look out for him, and the Firstborn seems to have decided that would be you.'

'I understand,' I said, and I did.

She nodded and shoved the cup into my hands. 'Drink this.'

It was mostly cheap whiskey leavened with honey. What wasn't cheap whiskey leavened with honey was the foulest rot I'd ever tasted.

'Don't you puke on my sheets,' she said.

I managed to follow her directive, but it took some doing. 'Is this going to fix me up?'

'There's no kind of medicine to fix your type of broken.'

I wasn't in any position to argue with that. All the same I finished the rest of what was in my cup.

'The drink will speed up your healing. In an hour, you'll look like hell but won't feel like it. In five, you won't look like it. Least,' she smiled nastily, 'not because of the bruising.'

'I'm grateful,' I said.

'You don't need to be grateful – it's like I said, I'm not doing it for you. I'm doing it for the boy.'

'I'll make sure he sends his thanks along as well.' I slumped back into the bed. The thing I'd drunk felt worse in my stomach than it had going down, as if the substance itself conspired to ensure its release by tearing its way out through my intestinal tract.

'You can stay here another quarter hour,' Mazzie said, dropping herself into the chair with a sigh. 'Then you have to leave.'

'You got another appointment?'

'No.'

After a few minutes the bubbling in my gut leavened out near as quick as it had come. A dull, warm glow fell over me. 'The stuff you were saying before,' I said. 'About what was coming for me.'

'Yeah?'

'All that true?'

'Yeah.'

'I guess there's nothing I can do to head it off?'

'All sorts of things you could do,' she said. 'You could go down to the docks, book the first passage to the Free Cities. You could go to the man you fixing to do wrong to, tell him what you're going to do, see how he treats you. You could stuff your pockets with rocks and go swimming in the bay.' She tapped the ash off her cheroot. 'But you're not going to do any of those things, so why ask? The future isn't set in stone – it's you that can't bring himself to change.'

I spent a few more of Mazzie's promised fifteen minutes thinking about that. Then I pushed myself to my feet. 'I'll take my leave of you then, Mazzie of the Stained Bone. With appreciation for the hospitality, and hopes I won't need to avail myself of it again for a while.'

'Suit yourself,' she said. 'Send the boy around early part of next week, if you're still alive by then.'

That last was an open bet, and not one I'd have wanted to give odds on.

40

By the time I made it to Low Town I was walking on a foot of cushioned air. Whatever the other merits of Mazzie's concoction, it was the best anodyne I'd encountered in a long life of experimentation. I couldn't feel anything. Not pain from my injuries, not fear at what was coming, not guilt at why I'd set it into motion. I was quits with the world. I could almost forgive the sun for shining.

My good humor scuffed some when I walked into the Earl and found Adeline at one of the tables, drinking a cup of tea and half-scowling. I figured I'd need something to buttress my well-being, and took it out the ale tap before sitting down across from her.

'I'd hoped to avoid this conversation,' I said.

'We live in the same building. We were bound to run into each other sooner or later.'

'The way things are going, I thought someone might off me before we had the chance.'

'Sorry to disappoint you.'

'That's all right.' I took a long draw off the ale.

'Where you been?'

'I paid a visit to Wren's new governess, wanted to make sure she was still up to the task.'

'Is she the reason your face looks like an open sore?'

'Actually, Mazzie's just about the only person I've met today that didn't hit me.'

'I haven't hit you.'

My beer was nut brown, and sweet as lost youth. 'But you're making ready to.'

'I'm not wasting any more time yelling – it just makes it easier for you to feel bad about yourself.'

Not quite the hardest shot I'd taken, but on a lot of other days, it would have been. 'Damn noble of you,' I said, because I had to say something.

'I don't need to know what you're doing.'

'That's good. It would take too long to explain, and I only half understand it anyway.'

'But maybe you could let me know why you're doing it.'

'Different reasons.'

'She was pretty, that girl. And she seemed like she needed help.'

'It's not just the girl.'

'No?'

'I owe something to her father.'

'To her brother, you mean?'

'To all three of them, I suppose.'

'So this scheme you've got going, it's going to fix the things you made wrong?'

I didn't answer.

'Somehow I thought not.' She shook a grimace side to side. 'Do you so love corpses?'

'What do you know about corpses, Adeline? I've seen more dead men than you've seen live ones. The plague, the war, what I done after.' She'd overstepped, and I was happy to take her to task for it. Easier to be angry than it was to be anything else. 'Made my fair share, too. A few more won't tip the balance.'

'You think you're the only person who ever done anything they wish they hadn't? It's vanity, that's all it is.'

'We have to pay for the mistakes we've made.'

'You can't let yesterday poison tomorrow.'

At some point while I'd been busy talking, someone had run through and finished off all the ale in my tankard. I went and decanted a second. It seemed only fair, though Adeline's hectoring look followed me as I came back to the table.

'I wish you'd just figure out whether or not you're going to kill yourself. These half measures are exhausting.'

'Good to see you keep chilly, despite the heat.'

'You want to wallow, you can do it without my help.' But she was kinder than her words, and after a silent moment she offered just that. 'We're responsible for what comes to us. If you want things to go different, it's on you to make sure they do.'

There was too much wisdom there to bear looking at. I was glad I didn't have to. 'You're wasting your time. We're past the midway point of this one – it's too late to do anything.'

She threw her hands up, finally exasperated. 'Of course it's too late to do anything. You only get to thinking when it's too late to do anything. Then you drink, and lament the world's cruelty.'

Mazzie's elixir, proof against fist, boot and chain, proved nothing against five minutes conversation with Adeline. Which is to say my headache had returned with something of a vengeance. I finished the rest of my beer in unhappy silence.

'It'll be done tomorrow,' I said. 'One way or the other.'

'It won't be done until you're dead,' she answered sadly, and to the wall, and I couldn't think of a response.

I put my empty tankard on top of the counter, and grabbed a bottle from beneath it. The stairs to my room were more numerous than I'd remembered, but I managed them. The clothes went into the corner, the cork came out of the rotgut, sleep came deep and dreamless.

41

In general I rely on Adolphus and our patrons as my first line of nocturnal defense. Most nights, anyone wanting to make trouble for me would have to slip past the giant and a crew of gentlemen who, if they weren't strongly inclined to lose their lives in defense of mine, at least enjoyed a little tussle for its own sake, especially against boys from outside the neighborhood.

But the bar was closed and I was drunk, and so I didn't make anything out until they were almost up the stairs. I rolled off the bed and grabbed the dirk I keep stuck in the floorboards beneath it.

Three solid knocks at the door that I didn't answer, then a pause and three solid more.

'Who is it?'

'Hroudland. Let me in.'

Fuck fuck fuck. 'Now's not a good time. I'll see you at the rally.' I tiptoed towards the window but knew it wasn't an option.

The drop was two stories, and these were competent men – they'd have someone down there waiting to finish me if the fall didn't.

'Tomorrow won't do. The commander needs to see you. Now. Open up.'

They say a trapped wolf will gnaw off his paw and escape three-legged, take bleeding to death in the woods over being a skin above a fireplace. I can't swear to it, not being a country sort myself. One thing I can own, however, is that a man is not a wolf. Face-to-face with the end, your average soul does not struggle – doesn't kick and scream, doesn't throw himself at his attacker. He makes peace with She Who Waits Behind All Things, takes her hand quietly, without fuss.

I pulled on my pants. I pulled on my shirt. I pulled my socks on, and my shoes. I unbarred the door.

Hroudland hustled in, Rabbit, Roussel and three others coming after him. I'd never had so many people in my room before. It was cramped. 'You bring enough men?' I said, trying to keep it casual.

'Things are afoot.'

'What kind of things?'

'The commander will break it down for you.'

'All right. Give me a minute to gear up.'

Hroudland shook his head. 'We'll sort you out at headquarters.'

And that was that. I nodded feeble acquiescence, my tongue thick in my throat.

Out of the Earl and they surrounded me, three ahead and three behind. I wondered what I'd done to tip them, where I'd run off the track. I'm not as smart as I think I am. I hoped they'd make it quick. A look over at Roussel and his vacant smile and I figured they probably wouldn't.

No one said anything, but then they didn't have to. That they hadn't done me in my bedroom suggested the commander wanted a word, likely punctuated with a scream or two. Belatedly I realized that my facial swelling was gone – whatever Mazzie had given me had worked wonders. I savored what I felt confident would be my last few minutes without pain. Outside the temperature had nodded off a few degrees, and the stars were very bright. Under different circumstances, it would have been a pleasant walk. Rabbit whistled tunelessly. Pedestrians hurried away at our approach.

A pair of guards stationed outside of the main doors stiffened up when they saw us. It was late enough in the evening that there wasn't much traffic, but still I was surprised to be going in through the front. I wondered how I'd go out, doubled into a pauper's grave or chopped up fine and dumped in the harbor.

The main room was empty, and quiet. A dim row of torches illuminated the path ahead. Roland stared down at me from the wall. He seemed displeased. We continued past him, toward the cells reserved for the inner members of the organization. Hroudland put his hand on the door latch, then turned and nodded, the signal for his men to fall on me. 'Here we go.'

I held my breath.

The back room was a bustle of motion, well-lit and hectic. A line of newly sharpened trench blades had been laid out on a long wooden table, along with a selection of similarly purposed tools, curved daggers and single-headed axes. A half-dozen veterans I knew by sight but not name were arming themselves, slipping sharp things into their belts, checking the sights on their crossbows, preparing themselves for violence. My escort broke around me, and started to do the same.

'I'm to see the commander,' Hroudland said, then gestured at the table. 'Take what you want. We're out in ten.'

I counted about four of these before realizing I wasn't dead. Business continued as usual in the meantime, the men readying themselves for tonight's escapade, the exact nature of which was still unclear. Rabbit broke me out of my stupor, synching the straps on his leather armor. 'You want a suit?'

I shook my head. 'What exactly is going on?'

Rabbit just smiled and went back to what he was doing. Made no damn sense asking him anyway – Rabbit was the tip of the quarrel, the last man alive involved in making decisions. 'Guess it's been a while for you, eh?' he asked.

'It's a nice break from my knitting.'

'You still remember how to use one of these?' Roussel asked, leaning against a wall, his palms resting on a matched pair of swords swaying from his hips.

'The sharp end points away from you, right?'

Rabbit laughed. Roussel spat on the floor. It was his floor, but I guess that hadn't occurred to him.

There wasn't anything to do but go along with it and thank the Lost One for the opportunity. I buckled a trench blade onto my hip. Trailing down off the wall were bandoliers of black-powder grenades. I hadn't seen one since the war – they weren't easy to come by, even for people used to getting hardware. I took one off the wall and ran my fingers along the rough canvas, then looped it over my shoulder.

The back door opened and Hroudland came out with Joachim. The commander looked happy, damn near elated. 'Hope we didn't disturb your sleep,' he said, too polite to smirk outright.

'I never sleep.'

I don't think I'd ever heard him laugh – I really was fucked.

'Don't you have a rally to attend?' I asked.

'I'll be heading there directly.'

'And where exactly will I be heading?'

Pretories patted me on the shoulder. 'Something loud, I believe you said. Send Giroie a message.' He nodded at the weaponry, and the men taking it. 'I hope you don't mind running it over to him.'

'Nice to know about this kind of business beforehand.'

He was enjoying off-footing me. 'First thing a soldier learns – adapt to survive.'

That was one of the many things I hadn't liked about the army, but I kept my mouth horizontal. Now wasn't the time to show teeth, not surrounded by a dozen hardened killers. The fact that I was here at all meant that Pretories questioned my loyalty – to raise an objection, even to look insufficiently enthusiastic, would seal my fate. Better to have a hand in bringing Artur Giroie to heel than replace him as a target.

Hroudland motioned for the men to approach, and they spread into a semi-circle radiating out around the commander. 'All right, boys,' Joachim began. His voice was low by nature, and no one would ever accuse him of being a great speaker. But then oration was more in Roland's line – strategy and execution were the two areas in which Pretories had made his name. 'Today we put four of our brothers into the ground. Tonight we make damn sure they don't get lonely. The Giroie family has been owed for ten years. It's a long time to let a debt lapse – let's make up for our poor etiquette.'

Measured rumbles of agreement. Dress it up with whatever rhetoric you want, we were on a mission of murder. And these weren't soldiers anymore; they were bully-boys, no different than you'd find working the ranks of a syndicate. Professionals don't get excited at the prospect of killing – it's what distinguishes them from those in the amateur ranks.

Pretories whispered a few more words to Hroudland, who nodded and turned to face us. 'Transport is outside.' His voice was the standard-issue bellow. I hadn't heard it since I'd left the ranks, and I hadn't missed it.

I followed the line through a hallway and into the alley behind. A crumbling transport wagon was waiting for us, the kind used to carry supplies to restaurants and businesses. It was big, slow-moving and ugly, and there wasn't any reason to look at it. This time of night there would be hundreds of identical craft navigating the city. Our expedition had been well planned.

We piled into the back, grabbing seats along two small wooden benches. Chance or cruel fate dictated my spot next to Roussel, who at this point was a walking armoury, having added a crossbow and two sets of bombs to the trench blades he'd held earlier.

'You looking a little shaky, Lieutenant,' he said, voice like a choirboy.

'I appreciate the concern.'

The driver cracked the reins and we crawled forward.

'This is the real thing,' Roussel continued, pushing his leer into mine. 'Not like running your mouth with the giant to prop you up.'

'No?'

'Men are gonna die tonight,' he said. 'Die ugly. Die bleeding. You ready for that?'

'I've killed more men than you've fucked, Roussel. Near as many, at least.'

Rabbit laughed and put his hand on his confederate's shoulder. 'Lieutenant knows his business. He's a solid one, you'll see,' he said, giving me an approving wink. It was nice to know I had his confidence.

Roussel felt differently. 'You don't see the smart ones when there's trouble – you ever notice that, Rabbit? When red gets spilled, you can't never find them.'

'Shut the hell up, the three of you,' Hroudland said from his perch at the front. 'Keep your head on the mission.'

I suspected Roussel was hating me with his eyes, though it was too dark to be sure.

Half an hour later I watched the Hen and Harpy pass through the back flaps of the canvas tarp. It was closed and shuttered – I halfway hoped it was empty too, that Artur had given his men the night off and joined them in taking it. You can hope for anything – water in the desert, a fire in the night – but you can't drink it and it won't ward off a chill. Pretories had been too long an officer to be ignorant of the value of current intelligence. No doubt he'd had the joint cased before he'd sent us, no doubt he knew for a certainty there were people here worth killing. They'd pulled me in last minute to fuck with me, but this operation had been planned as competently as any Dren raid.

Our cart pulled to a stop in front of a side street leading to the back door. Hroudland struck a match, inspected us briefly in the dim light. 'Everyone clear on their role?'

A chorus of low grunts, a synchronized bobbing of heads.

'You're with me,' Roussel said, a threat if ever I heard one.

Hroudland tossed over a look like he expected me to object, but I nodded, and he shrugged. The men piled out the back in a line, and when it was my turn I followed them.

The lane was narrow, and we were near as crowded outside as

we had been in the carriage. 'Don't be thinking of going faggot on us,' Roussel whispered.

'You look awful good in leather,' I returned, but my heart wasn't in it.

There's rarely any great competition to be the first one through the door, but they had that down as well. The biggest of the group, a Vaalan with an egg-shaped head and a matching two-handed mace set the latter into the door. It quivered but didn't break. He ripped his weapon free, carrying with it enough of the frame to offer entry, an opportunity he was quick to take.

There were eight men in before me, so I only caught the aftermath, two corpses on the floor, line cooks to judge by their white uniforms, part of the legitimate business of which Artur was so proud. Their killers hadn't waited around, sprinting out through the three separate doors that led deeper into the complex.

Rabbit and Roussel broke down a hallway and I followed after them, up a flight of stairs and into another room. Four men were playing cards around a table, piles of small change glittering on the wood. Cheap toughs in expensive suits, bleary-eyed from liquor and bonhomie. They were as unprepared for what was coming as a newborn fresh from the womb.

The quickest of them shot up from his perch. 'Who the fuck—' he began but didn't finish, cut off by the cleaver Rabbit put into his skull. By some curious reflex he stayed standing for a solid five count, eyes crossed at the piece of metal split between them, brain leaking down the bridge of his nose. Roussel was a bare second behind his partner, a trench blade in each hand, falling on two of them with all the enthusiasm of an amateur rhythm section. By the time he was finished there was blood on his shirt and in his hair, a spray painted across his wild eyes.

The last one was dead and knew it, his movements confused and uncoordinated. He tripped backward coming out of his chair, watching oblivion stalk towards him with quivering eyes and quivering mouth. Roussel wasn't quite playing, but neither was he in any great hurry, a smile on his face and a bulge in his pants.

I wanted to look away but didn't. The thug finally thought to scream, then the steel dropped downward and he went silent.

I'd remained in the doorway, my trench blade limp at my side. It was not lost on me that my own life might well depend on the enthusiasm I mustered for the proceedings, but all the same I was having trouble forcing it. An hour ago I'd been sleeping off a drunk, now I was expected to play the savage. The transition was proving a little much for me to handle.

'You'll miss all the action if you're not careful, Lieutenant,' Rabbit said, near to beaming, his grin wide as the moon, dwarfing even his usual expression of good humor.

'Told you he was talk,' Roussel said, but it was leavened by the joy of his recent kill.

Rabbit slapped me on the shoulder – no harm, no harm – then sprinted ahead like a child on Midwinter morning. A few yards down, the hallway forked. Rabbit and Roussel exchanged glances, passing something between them.

'Commander says you're to paint your sword,' Rabbit said, half-apologetic.

'What color?'

'He'll get it wet,' Roussel answered, 'or I'll wet it for him.'

Rabbit nodded, then gave me a thumbs-up sign and sprinted off to the right. Roussel and I headed left, down a corridor ending in front of a pair of doors. Roussel pointed at one, eyes brooking no disobedience, then set his foot against the opposite. It was a flimsy thing and it splintered without trouble, and Roussel was off, bringing his particular brand of succor to another set of waiting souls. Mine wasn't locked, the latch turning smoothly. Roussel's probably hadn't been locked either, but he was having too much fun for that to stop him.

A pair waited for me, too well dressed to be help, but absent the dull violence of the men in the last room. Part of the organization, but not muscle. Cousins of Artur, maybe, or acquaintances, spoiled boys from Kor's Heights, lives spent sucking at a silver spoon gilded by the suffering of the less fortunate. If I'd known them I'd have hated them, I didn't doubt that for an eye blink.

They carried thin dueling blades with jeweled hilts, never unsheathed in anger. Between the screams and the percussive clamor of black-powder bombs they must have known what was coming, but just the same they seemed utterly unprepared to resist. One of them fumbled for his weapon, catching the cross guard against his petticoat. The other let his eyes drop to the ground, waiting to be murdered.

A man is not a wolf, as I've previously noted. At least these punks weren't, and then again, neither was I.

'Fuck. Off,' I said, two distinct sentences.

It took them a moment to go along with it. One nodded and grabbed the other, and they both disappeared through a back door. Maybe they'd make it down a side staircase and out into the street, if they were quick and lucky. Maybe they'd run into one of my compatriots and get turned into gristle. I'd done what I could do. I rolled a grenade off my bandolier and into the center of the room, slipping into the hallway before it detonated.

No civilian building is meant to withstand the sort of punishment the Hen and Harpy was enjoying – I was lucky my explosives didn't bring the whole third story crashing down on us. The smoke took a while to dissipate, and when it did it left nothing but ruin, the furniture and decorations splintered into oblivion, a fair-sized segment of the wall scattered across the floor.

'You need to blow the room?' Roussel asked, coming up behind me in the corridor. I leaned away to let him pass, and he took a step into the wreckage.

'Yeah, I did,' I said, and whistled my trench blade across his throat. A jet of red spurted forward, but credit where it's due, the bastard was so vicious he still made a play for me. His eyes wavered but stayed focused, even with most of his life fluid spilling out on the floor. He sputtered something through the hole in his neck, and tried to raise his weapon above his head. But it was a futile effort, and after a moment he pitched forward, knees first, then the rest of him.

I'd been looking for an opportunity to put Roussel down for

a while, half because he was too loose to leave around to muck things up, half just on general principle. And with what I'd done I didn't have another option – once the smoke cleared he would see the rubble wasn't painted pink, and half the point of the night's errand was to see me off someone. And he was too stupid to try and con, certain to resort to steel if he thought I was making a move.

And that's the way it is, I guess. There's no blessing so pure it doesn't bring harm to someone. The reprieve I'd offered two strangers meant death for Roussel. Though if I was being honest about it, I felt no more slitting his throat than I would have stepping on a cockroach – less really, 'cause with the cockroach I'd have needed to clean my boots.

At least no one could accuse me of half-measures – I'd wet my trench blade, as instructed.

I popped the cork on another grenade and dropped it on the corpse, then sprinted back down the passageway. It went off behind me, splattering Roussel's insides against the walls, swathes of red flesh and white bone. A loud crack and the top floor caved in on top of him, a half-dozen tons of brick and wood. It was quite a cenotaph. More than he warranted, were I to be frank.

Out the way I'd come and I felt the building weakening around me. A black-powder bomb doesn't make nothing like the damage of an artillery shell or a battle hex, but you drop enough of them and they'll do the trick. It was clear I wasn't the only one who'd decided the obstructions to his path would best be leveled by heavy ordnance. Things went on like this and there wouldn't be enough left of the Hen and Harpy to shade a vagrant from the sun.

Most of the other vets were waiting in the alley, and after a moment the rest came charging out as well. One or two were bloodied, none seriously. Security hadn't been that at all – men waiting around to die would be more accurate. Artur had thrown a glancing blow, and figured the veterans to do the same, chew at their edges, hit a safe house or execute a few low-level players. That had been his mistake – Pretories wasn't a crime lord, didn't

284

abide by their customs and codes. The commander learned something from five years dancing with the Dren, though the Daevas knew most of the rest of the higher-ups hadn't. In truth it was as precisely executed a mission as you could ask for, a decapitating strike that lasted all of ten minutes, with barely a casualty taken.

Barely.

'Where's Roussel?' Rabbit asked once we were back in the wagon and pulling away, the excitement of the evening momentarily blinding him to his partner's absence.

I shook my head. 'They got him.'

'Bullshit,' he said, and he wasn't smiling anymore. 'Not Roussel.'

'Anybody can get it, Rabbit – you been doing this long enough to know that.'

'Where's the body?' Hroudland asked.

'I had to clear the room.' I tapped at the empty rack on my bandolier. 'There was nothing to carry out.'

'You were supposed to have his back.'

'What the hell do you want from me? Roussel was a berserker – once he smelled blood he wanted to make more. I couldn't keep up with him.'

'Son of a bitch.' Rabbit's hands began to shake, clenched but wavering. 'Son of a bitch!' He turned his square shoulders and slammed a fist into the side of the wagon. Even short a man the confines were tight, and the vet sitting next to him had to scramble to avoid being struck.

'Cool off,' said the oversized Vaalan who'd taken the door down. He was sitting across from Rabbit, flexing his hands around the hilt of his mace. 'Roussel knew the risks – getting crazy won't do nothing to bring him back.'

The rest of the wagon echoed agreement. I got the sense that even amongst this pack of killers, Roussel was little loved. And there wasn't any reason to think things had gone any way except how I'd said it.

Rabbit was gassed to hell, sweating and snorting like a stallion.

Hroudland was looking at me in a fashion I didn't care for, but he was at least savvy enough to see that now wasn't the time for further violence. After a moment he leaned over and whispered something in his subordinate's ear, and whatever it was it seemed to work. The madness gradually drained out of Rabbit's eyes, replaced with a broad smile. Not his normal friendly idiocy, but something tainted and deadly as a rusty nail. 'We made them pay for it, though. By the Scarred One, we made them pay for it.' He pulled something from a pouch on his back, then tossed it to the wagon floor.

At my feet were Artur's blond tresses, now stained with red, a fair bit of waxy scalp attached.

'A class act, Rabbit,' I said, turning away. 'Don't ever let anyone tell you otherwise.'

42

Back at the Earl I stepped right past our ale tap and pulled a bottle of liquor from below the counter, then found myself a spot in the corner and went to it. I knew what I was in for when I set things rolling, I told myself after the first shot. After about the third I even started to believe it. At some point I discovered the vial of breath in my pocket was empty, though I didn't remember using it.

By the time Adolphus and Wren came in, thrilled with the progress of the evening, I was the sort of drunk no man should get. The sort of drunk where you don't notice mistakes, where you get to enjoying making them.

'If it isn't the Hero of Aunis, and his faithful sidekick.'

They'd missed me in the dark, had already crossed to the bar. Adolphus stopped smiling, but Wren's grin seemed slapped on, cheeks flushed red. Probably Adolphus had given him a nip or two in the bustle and the excitement, Adolphus or one of our ex-comrades.

I stood up from my seat, slow enough to keep my legs steady, then ambled over to meet them. 'Late night, I see.'

Adolphus muttered something under his breath.

'Me too, as it turns out. Noble service to the corps, the both of us. Though I imagine mine had a different tenor.'

'Adolphus was a hit. He left everyone in tears,' Wren piped in, happily drunk or actively trying to aggravate me.

'Just like the Dren!' The words swelled together incomprehensibly.

'Best you go to bed now,' Adolphus answered, his bad eye refusing to meet my gaze, and his good one.

'Spare a few moments for a drink with an old veteran, down on his luck.' I reached behind the counter and slopped some liquor into fresh cups. 'You wouldn't want to leave a man behind.'

Adolphus didn't like where this was going, but he went along with it anyway. After a moment Wren took his cue as well, hands small and stiff around the mug.

'What should we drink to?'

'It's your show,' the giant grumbled.

'Indeed it is.' I angled my tumbler above my head. 'To the men of the First Capital Infantry, as slippery a batch of motherfuckers as ever planted a knife in a man's back.' I rolled back the rim of the cup.

Wren downed his own, then raised a mocking hand to his forehead.

I cuffed it away. 'Don't ever fucking salute me,' I said. 'Don't ever fucking salute anyone.'

'Boy, bed,' Adolphus ordered, and this time I didn't contradict him. Wren slunk off to the back room, then put an ear to the door, if I know anything about anything.

'You ought to be more careful with your words – you can only coast on that liquor but so long.'

I poured whiskey into my cup, then into my throat. 'I'll stand by them.'

'You're drunk.'

'But right just the same.'

'I won't listen to you badmouth the men we died with. I'm proud to count myself a member of the Fightin' First.'

'You been telling Wren that?'

'There are worse things than being a soldier.'

'I will see that child in the ground before I see him in uniform.' I took a long swig straight from the bottle, cutting out the middleman. 'I'll put him there myself.'

'Because your current employment is so praiseworthy?'

'Damn right. I kill a man now at least I know it's in my interest, not 'cause he's wearing different colored leather.'

'Why do you insist upon pissing on everything we were?'

'Because I remember it accurately – I'm not puffing myself up to impress a child.'

Adolphus wasn't looking for a fight, but neither was he one to run from it. He finally took his drink, knocking it back in one smooth motion. Then he set his cup on the bar and turned towards me, his hands conspicuously unoccupied. 'Watch yourself.'

I caught the bright sheen of metal pinned to his ill-fitting dress coat, and felt fury like bile well up from my throat. 'What'd they strike that medal from? Platinum? Gold? Horseshit?'

'I already warned you once.'

'Hero of Aunis – that's a hell of a title. What did you do to get a title like that?'

The look on his face would have made a wise man run. Even most stupid ones for that matter.

'Funny thing is,' I continued, 'I was at Aunis, and I don't remember no heroes. Just a turn-color coward who left his best friend to die.'

I won't blame it on the drink, though I was drunk enough that I barely saw it coming – had I been sober as a churchman, it wouldn't have mattered. Adolphus was just about the best man with his fists I'd ever seen, truly skilled, not just big. On the credit side of the account the booze meant that I barely felt the blow. I was standing and then I was lying down, but what came between was as abrupt as a thunderclap.

I lay there awhile, in no great hurry to stand. I'd have stayed there all night, really, if decorum had allowed it. My nose was broke, one more tick on a long tally. I didn't suppose it would make me any uglier. 'Big man,' I said, pulling myself up finally. 'Tough as a boot nail with an old drunk.'

He'd used all his anger up on my face, seemed more stung by the blow than I was. 'I'm . . .' He stuttered over this opening for a while, his mouth flapping in apology.

'For the punch? Or because I was right about why you threw it?'

He didn't answer.

'Stay the fuck away from tomorrow's march, unless you want to join Roland in martyrdom.'

I had the presence of mind to grab the bottle on my way out. I left it in a ditch off Pritt Street and kept walking, and given that I was a third full with liquor, making it all the way to Offbend displayed extraordinary fortitude. I didn't suppose I'd get a medal for it, though.

43

It was raining. It had been raining since the beginning of time, so there was no reason to expect it to stop now.

It rose ankle deep on a good day, but most days weren't, and it settled up around your knees. It soaked through your clothes, of course. Through your greatcoat, through your shirt. Through your backpack and anything you had in there. Through your pants, and your underwear. You'd think at some point you'd get used to wearing wet underwear but you'd be wrong, you never do.

It rained every moment of the day, whatever you were doing. It rained when you were on watch, when you tried to roll a cigarette, when you tried to smoke it. When you slept, when you shat and pissed. It rained during mealtime, a garnish on whatever you ate. Bully-beef with rainwater. Worm-ridden grain with rainwater. Our liquor ration was mostly water, but we drank that with rainwater too.

The rain was bad. The mud was worse. Mud doesn't really

describe it. Women step over puddles of mud in the street, children make mud pies and throw mud balls at each other. Mud doesn't swallow whole men, full-grown adults with five stones of equipment. Our mud did though. A member of our battalion swore up and down that he'd once excavated an entire supply wagon, a team of mules and a driver. I wasn't there to see it, but I wouldn't bet against it either.

A distant third, after the rain and the mud, were the Dren. Sure, now and again they'd murder a few of us, but we did the same to them, and their occasional forays at least broke up the monotonous struggle against the elements. You could slit a Dren's throat and at least feel you'd accomplished something – good luck taking aim at a raincloud.

It was the fourth year of the war. From Beneharnum we had moved hundreds of miles inland, slowly and fitfully, marching over the bodies of our comrades, every inch won with a pint of blood. When we had first found ourselves in Dren territory nine months back, it had seemed that things might be coming to an endgame. Unfortunately it turned out the only thing more ferocious than a Dren fighting to take another country was a Dren fighting to keep his own, and progress had long since slowed to a crawl.

Little else could be said of our general situation with any certainty. Accurate information was more or less impossible to stumble across. You could read the broadsheets, but they were all lies, censored away to nothing by the anxious pen of the commandants. The headline of every issue trumpeted victory and the small print foretold of similar success in the immediate future. Victory when we advanced, victory when we held steady, victory when we retreated. Victory at every point on the map.

If this was victory, you could fucking keep it. We'd stalled out, and the Dren were getting ready to respond. All month there had been signs. Our raiders had captured men from companies we'd never heard of, and intelligence reported vast goods being stock-piled in the trenches in front of us, shells and quarrels, spare blades and bandages.

I was the head of a company of a hundred and fifty men. A hundred and fifty on paper, maybe half that in reality, the rest sick, missing or deserted. Most were the first two. Everyone wanted to run off, of course, or at least I sure as hell did. But there was nowhere to go – we were hundreds of miles from the coast and even if you somehow made it, you couldn't very well swim to Rigus. Desertion was the act of the broken and desperate, practically speaking little different from suicide. They hung absentees, rotting corpses strung from rotting ropes, gallows behind the lines instilling martial spirit in the living.

It was shortly before the theoretical dawn, though the permanent overcast and the dense layer of fog rendered morning indistinguishable from afternoon, and evening only barely distinct from day. I was huddled beneath my greatcoat in the support trench fifty yards back from the front line, propped up on a couple of crates, keeping my legs elevated out of the run-off. Every so often I'd nod asleep and wake up a moment later hell-deep in slush. Finally I dragged myself up and went to check on my number two, currently taking his time on watch.

Adolphus had weathered his time as well as any of us, which is to say he was a broken shell of a man. I couldn't remember the last time I'd seen him smile. Not that there was much to smile about – despondency was appropriate to the situation. He'd wrapped his body around a half-pike and a wool blanket around his body, and all three were caked in mud. He didn't stir at my approach, which didn't exactly instill confidence as to his abilities as a sentinel.

''Lo, Sergeant.'

He didn't answer.

'Adolphus.'

He raised his head up slowly, but his eyes wouldn't stick on me, slick as the weather. 'Hey.'

I let his lack of proper military etiquette slide. 'Quiet night, I guess.'

'I guess.'

'Nothing to report?'

'Nothing to report.'

It was a half-hour before the watch would change. 'Why don't you head back, try and scare up some grub.'

He nodded, but it took him a long time to stand. 'I guess they're gonna hit us today,' he said, passing me the pike.

'You never know. Maybe they've all gone pacifist.'

He didn't laugh, but then again it wasn't funny. Thirty minutes later I gave a very surprised private a spear and went to get breakfast.

There was no breakfast. Our supply wagon had been hit by artillery, or gotten lost trying to find us, or the commandant sold it on the black market and pocketed the change. I'd meant to save something from dinner the night before, a cracked biscuit or a few mouthfuls of salted meat. I hadn't though. A line of very glum men sat on the barest nub of an incline, trying to light cigarettes beneath wet greatcoats and parceling out what remained of their liquor ration. The silver on my collar precluded my joining them, so I went back to check on the line.

Four years of being ground beneath a millstone meant that virtually the entire company consisted of replacement soldiers – besides Adolphus and I, there were barely a half dozen men remaining who could remember our defeat at Beneharnum, and the terrible days after. Still, under our circumstances, it didn't take long to turn a recruit into a veteran – anyone left standing after a month was hard as burnt steel. I toured the main trench, nodding at men distilled away to gristle and teeth, watched them sharpening knives and cribbing smokes. Mostly they knew their business, but here and there I made a few adjustments, repositioning guards and sending the weakest-looking back behind lines – though we all looked pretty damn weak, and the support trench wouldn't hold long if our defenses were breached. Some of them asked for extra bolts or more grenades, and I promised I'd get them as soon as I could. Some of them just wanted to grumble, and I'd listen for a while, then slap a hand on their shoulder and keep walking.

We were as solid as we could be, without supplies, without

reinforcements, without there being any reason for us to be there. I figured we'd hold a diversionary attack, but anything more serious and we'd burst like a swollen corpse. Nothing to be done about it. I'd been sending runners to the back lines for two straight days, damn near begging for support and receiving increasingly curt responses. We were on our own. If Maletus was with us, the weight of the Dren thrust would fall elsewhere. But the Scarred One keeps his own counsel, and I didn't imagine the lives of a handful of infantry figured much into them.

We'd carved the main trench through a low hillock, and if you managed to angle yourself right, there was an overhang that sort of kept the rain off. It was as good as you were going to get, at least. Beneath it I found a wooden bucket buried in the mud, and I flipped it over and sat on it.

To exist without awareness, that was what you aimed at. Memories worn to irrelevance, the future equally insubstantial. Obey orders and don't think beyond them. Don't think about your sweetheart back home all alone, don't think about her pink thighs, or how lonely she must be getting. Don't think about fresh fruit, or a seasoned chunk of pork, or a strong dark ale. Don't think about blue skies, or the sun.

Don't think about the men in the trenches ahead of you, skin like leather, eyes dark as coal. Don't think about the friend you put in the ground yesterday – maybe not a friend, but acquaintance at least, and in the ground for certain. Don't think about whether today was your day, don't think about how many times you'd gotten lucky, whether that luck would hold.

The crack of cannon brought me to. The worst thing about artillery is there's nothing you can do against it – the whistle of the shot gives you a few seconds' head start, but if you moved you were as likely to run into it as escape the blast area. Best to hunker down, stay where you are. If the ball had your name on it, then you were good and fucked. Might as well meet She Who Waits Behind All Things with your dignity intact, seeing as your body wouldn't be.

At first I figured it was a quick burst to unsettle us. The Dren loved that sort of thing – fire a few shots over to make sure you weren't getting too comfortable. But the initial barrage was followed by another, and another. Two solid hours I spent curled up beneath that overhang, wave after wave of munitions rolling over me. Long gone were the days when artillery was a passing concern – the Dren had gotten scalpel sharp with theirs. They could drop a shell into an outhouse hole six inches round and half a mile distant. They were working against the environment though, like all of us. The one upside to the terrain meant that anything short of a direct hit did nothing more than toss mud into the air. Sometimes the artillery would stop for a minute, or two, or five – the Dren hoping to lure us out prematurely, then make us into scrap when they turned the fire back on.

It had been off for a while when it finally struck me that this was the real thing, that they'd be hitting us soon. I ducked out of cover and sent the alarm as best I could, signaling down both ends of the line to form up. It got to our bugler, who sounded off on his horn, though after the last two hours I doubt many could hear it.

Most of the company were already at the front, and those who had survived the cannon prepped themselves for what was coming. The rest joined us soon enough, slipping in from the support trench. I caught Adolphus's ungainly bulk drop awkwardly into the mud and waved him over. Even the most haggard son of a bitch gets a shot of energy in the moments before a fight, but just the same he looked lost, battered. I hadn't the time to worry about it, figured he'd snap awake at the smell of blood. A peek over the precipice showed lines of gray men emerging from the gray mist. I dropped back down and gave the all clear for free fire, and our bowmen, perched inside narrow barricades set above the lines, started sending bolts into the gloom. A trickle of screams made their way in our direction, gratifying if meaningless – our missilists alone wouldn't be enough, not nearly, not even if they'd had enough bolts. This wasn't no diversion – the Dren were playing for keeps.

The first one came over, a husky motherfucker with mud up

to his hips, leaping down from the edge. He bounced his sword off mine but didn't stop moving, heading down the line, trying to carry the trench by sheer momentum. I hoped one of our boys would set a hand-axe in his brow, spent too long hoping and missed his follow-up – there was a movement at the edge of my vision, and then I was lying face up in the muck, breathless and waiting to die.

He was big, naked from the waist up, and cooked out of his fucking skull. Word was the Dren passed out breath to their commandos, some sort of mass-produced junk. It was a source of great wonder for us, how they were able to get their hands on narcotics, given that our own commissary usually couldn't provide us with bread. The man towering over me must have been saving up his rations. The veins in his neck pulsed, and the whites of his eyes had swallowed their irises. He carried a self-made mace in both hands, a fence post with a whittled handle and a half-dozen long nails hammered through the business end.

A spearhead peeked out suddenly from beneath his breast, a flap of skin carried along the end – one of my boys looking after his commander. The Dren failed to notice he'd just been murdered, whirling around with such force that he tore the half-pike out of its wielder's hands, the butt passing over me. He didn't scream, I remember – he must have been really far gone. I lifted myself out of the muck and started putting my sword into his head, and after the third or fourth time he finally caught up to the reality of the situation, and dropped to the ground.

I was gonna say something to the man who'd saved me but he'd already moved on, and I decided it would be best to repay the good turn. I caught a flash of Adolphus's bulk off to the side of me, uncharacteristically hard pressed. I had a curved knife near the size of my trench blade swinging from my hip, and I unsheathed it and planted it into his attacker, through the sternum and up into his heart.

In the storybooks people are always recognizing each other on the battlefield, even find time to say a few words of challenge. But in my experience a mêlée consists of little knots of soldiers backstabbing each other, watching for any opportunity to overwhelm a straggler. The best men in the unit were wiry bastards with roving eyes, wild dogs on the watch for weak prey. In a ditch Adolphus's size was a quasi-virtue at best, too big for subtlety and an easy target for any man with a crossbow – he did his best work above ground, where he had room to maneuver. Even still he seemed at half speed, as if slow to waken to the seriousness of our situation.

'Get your fucking head together!' I screamed, the limit of my wise counsel, events making further discussion impractical. There were fresh targets a plenty, all keen for our little corner of heaven. One of these seemed to have turned his ankle coming down, and he struggled to right himself. I was behind him, and made sure that he didn't. Never even saw it coming, the lucky bastard.

Taking a trench is a tricky business – send too many men at once and they'll get bogged down by sheer weight of numbers. Send too few and you risk the enemy defeating them in detail. You have to time your waves right, assault in pulses of movement, breaking the line then clearing out resistance. The Dren had it down to a science, to a fucking science – the very moment you thought things were starting to swing your way, another pack of gray-clad troopers dropped into your home. In theory, the spell-slingers should be raining down fire on anyone making their way to our lines, but I sincerely doubted they'd stuck through the artillery barrage. Either way they didn't seem to be proving much of an impediment to the enemy's flow.

At some point I'd picked up a hatchet, and I tangled it in the defenses of a sharp-looking officer, hook-nosed and stern-eyed. In another life he might have been a priest, banging a pulpit till his voice gave out. In this one he fell for a feint and I buried the axe in his chest. It stuck when I tried to pull it out, and a spray of blood got in my eyes and my mouth, and so I said fuck it and left it where it was.

The trenches consisted of wide rectangles traversed by narrow, crooked lanes, the layout dispersing us so that a lucky artillery shell wouldn't wipe out half the platoon. It also made it damn near impossible to get much of a sense of the ebb and flow of the battle. Still, I was pretty sure we weren't winning. Corpses lay thick on the ground, more of them than us, but still too damn many of us. There was pressure moving on our right – they'd cleared out a section of the line and were bottling us up. I could feel the survivors getting antsy, losing heart.

'Keep it solid, boys,' I yelled. 'We'll have back-up here in a moment!' A lie as sure as any I'd ever told, but there was nothing else but to believe it.

The next wave hit us, hit us hard, and I could feel the line waver. Trying to follow the arc of the battle I very nearly lost my place in the thick of it, trading blows with a young Dren whose skill belied his age before the chaos pulled us apart. By the time it was over we were down to a skeleton crew, and I knew there was no way in hell we were going to last another attack.

Calloway was a decent sort, been with us eighteen months or so. Nothing particularly special about him – not to me, I mean, though I'm sure his mother thought differently. He was a hell of a scrounger, he could dig up a bottle of wine from ground that had been picked clear by rats and men alike, and he wasn't slow to share. I guess I'd say I liked him, though truth be told after four years as an officer I didn't think in those terms. Anyway, he'd shouldered his burden as long as we'd asked him to, and as my gaze roamed over the men who remained, I didn't spend any particular time checking after him. He stood bent over his weapon, exhausted and near broke like the rest of us, and then his half-pike was in the mud and he was off.

Not a man alive wants to be the weakest link, but curiously, no one gives much of a shit about being the second. Which is to say that once the initial grunt loses his water and breaks out, it's open season and there's not much can be done about it. The men of 'A' company, veterans of a dozen major battles and hundreds of minor engagements, turned tail with every ounce of energy they had left. I did my best to rally them, yelling threats and exhortations, but I was never much of a speaker and no one was in the mood to listen anyway. At one point I was pulling a fleeing man off a ladder, and then I wasn't doing much of anything.

Later, as the frantic events of the day congealed into something resembling a narrative, I would recognize the gap as being the product of a black-powder bomb detonating a few yards off. But that was later. At that moment I was gone, snuffed out like a candle.

Time passed.

My eyes offered two distinctly separate views of reality, and it took a while to reconcile them. I was lying face up, and the mud was a greedy thing, ever hungry. By the time I'd managed to right myself our collapse was all but complete. A pair of Dren, the first scouts from the next wave or slow stragglers from the last, landed feet first in our ditch, and they didn't seem in no mood to parlay.

It wasn't the first time I'd found myself lost on the battlefield, my odds slipping from bad to nil. Always before an immutable presence had my back, shoulders like a bear and a blade keen as winter.

He's dead, I thought, and it cut through even the immediate haze of the fight, his corpse buried amongst the mounds of surrounding bodies, vacant eyes open at the sky, food for the rats. When I caught him out of the corner of my eye, despite everything, I almost laughed with joy. It took a moment to put together why his back was turned, climbing up the trench ladder.

'Adolphus!' I screamed.

He was halfway out but he turned back to look at me, looked right at me, saw me looking back at him.

Then he was gone, up over the side, and I was alone.

When I got my focus back where it belonged it was damn near too late. Only a desperate sideways leap saved me from the full force of the attack, and even so it cut through my armor and ate out a solid few ounces of flesh. The world swayed around me, tilting like the deck of a ship. I threw myself at the one who'd injured me. Sometimes you get lucky with that – a man gets too quick to thinking he's got you. This one didn't though – he gave a step, knowing time was on his side. His comrade sidled to my left, streaked with mud from the neck down, but clear-eyed and ready. They knew what they were doing, and I was tired and wounded. I'd played out this scenario on the other end enough times to know where it was leading.

It was chance that saved me, blind random luck. One tried for a cut to my head and we caught our blades against each other, and his fractured straight down the middle. Dren steel was tough as the men who wielded it, but mass produce a half-million of anything and I guess you'll come up short a few times.

For a singular second we both recoiled, shocked at the development, then I split his neck down into the spine. Too far down, an amateur's mistake. He collapsed and carried my weapon with him, and I had to wedge my foot against his chest and pull with both hands to get it free. If his second had reacted quick enough he'd have had vengeance right there, but the sudden shift of equilibrium was too much, and he hesitated until I could turn my full attention on him. He wasn't bad, but he wasn't good either, and I managed to mop him up after another half minute.

Everyone was dead, dying, or gone, the strange vagaries of combat aligning to ensure a moment of surreal tranquility. If you could ignore the screams of the wounded that is, and I'd had long practice at that. Our defenses had collapsed completely – the next wave of Dren would be able to occupy the position without drawing a blade, and from what little I could tell things were even worse to our right. The scaffolding was well used and sturdy. It had held for the rest of the platoon. It would hold for me.

I don't know why I stayed. Wasn't any sense of duty, Šakra knows. I was an ant, and no ant suffers under delusions of their own importance. The battle was lost, me sticking around wasn't going to salvage anything. Wasn't pride neither – I'd run before when it had made sense, I'd do it again without any regrets.

I guess I'd say I was just tired. Tired of the whole thing – the weather and the rats, the blood and the shit, death all the time, death everywhere. Maybe the runners had been braver than me. Four years I'd been doing this. Can you imagine? Four fucking years.

The pause lasted only a moment. Then a squad of them came out from the defile to my right, and the window slammed shut, and I readied myself for the end.

The transport trench was too cramped to allow them to swarm me, and I wedged myself into it. The hilt of my trench blade was slippery with mud, or maybe brain, I wasn't sure. The last of my black-powder grenades was in my other hand – worse came to worst I figured I could set it off and take a few with me. They were thinking the same thing I guess, because they were slow to get moving.

But not too slow. One went off, rashly as it turned out, tripping over the outstretched hand of a corpse, stumbling toward me headfirst. A quick chop creased his brain pan, but it didn't do anything to slow his momentum and I had to scramble backwards to keep from falling. A second followed close on the first, and we struggled awkwardly in the narrow, and then he was dying at my feet. After that they got hesitant. A few words in clipped gutter Dren that I couldn't make out and they fell back. Grabbing a missilist, I assumed – no point in losing anyone else.

Dimly I realized that they were taking longer than they should have, that if they were out of black powder they could have just stripped one off the dozens of surrounding corpses. In different circumstances I might have wondered about it. As it was the observation itself represented the absolute apex of what I was then capable – drawing conclusions was as far beyond me as the sky is to a fish.

A soldier came into view, blue trim faint beneath the layer of mud. I blinked away the dust in my eyes and looked again. Still blue trim. My first thought was that I'd gone crazy – no way there were any of us left. I realized belatedly that he was saying something to me, screaming it, and I struggled to make out what it was.

'Bess,' I yelled back finally, dragging the day's password from some hidden corner of my mind.

He bobbed over to me, the mud barely covering his parade-ground polish. 'We thought they'd taken this sector.' Silver clustered on his lapel, but he was young. By Prachetas he was young, too young and too excited to have been at this long.

'What are you . . .' I stammered. 'How did you . . .'

'Make it through the mud? Some new trick of the sorcerers,' he said. 'Real hush-hush. They didn't tell anybody it was coming – firms up the terrain into something you can move over. Marched two companies right around their flanks. Broke their sides while you boys held them.' The rest of his unit started spreading into our trench. Their uniforms were fresh blue, and they went about their business with a purpose. 'Buck up, soldier!' The officer slapped me on the back. 'You'll get the Star of Maletus for this – I'll put you in myself. What's your name?'

He stood next to a pile of corpses nearly as high as his knees. Behind him a Dren bled out from his gut, frothy pink bubbling out his lips. He begged for water with the rain falling on his face, until one of our reinforcements finished him off.

'Adolphus,' I said. 'Sergeant Adolphus Gustav.'

'Gustav, huh? Hell of a fight, soldier. Hell of a fight. Why don't you fall back? We'll take care of the clean up. Get yourself some rest – the Firstborn knows you've earned it.'

Whatever had carried me through the day was gone, even the memory of it, and I was so tired I would have collapsed right there, used the nearest body as a pillow. But the boy officer helped hoist me up, and I managed to make it back to the support trench, and from there the next half mile to headquarters.

It was some kind of victory. The flower of 'A' company lay dead on the field. The survivors were only barely that – I doubted two in three would ever see service again, so utterly had three months at Aunis wrecked their bodies and snapped their minds. Then I altered my assessment. The Empire needed men. The remnants would be scraped together and thrust into action soon enough.

I found my best friend huddled with the scattered remains of a dozen platoons – refugees from the madness of the battlefield, one spot of blasted earth as good as any other. His eyes took up most of his head. They'd passed out hot rum, but his hands shook terribly, and he couldn't bring the cup to his mouth. He stared up at me without a glimmer of recognition, mute and uncomprehending. I commandeered a greatcoat from the nearest corpse and wrapped him up in it.

No man is all one thing or another, an undiluted well-spring of bravery or a broke-down craven. I don't know what a hero is, but I've met a lot of cowards, and Adolphus isn't one of them. Nine days out of ten he was the furthest thing from it, cold as tempered steel and savage as the frost. But that day . . .

That day he wasn't.

I figured whoever they gave the Star of Maletus to was pretty well guaranteed a free ticket back to Rigus, and I was pretty sure Adolphus could use it more than I could. That was part of it. But most of it was that I didn't want a fucking medal, didn't want any part of legitimizing what they'd done. What I'd done. Corpses and corpses and corpses, and they pin something shiny to your lapel and you puff out your chest and tell them it was an honor. Even now I think about it and my fists clench and I start gnashing my teeth.

Of course, it didn't end up mattering. It was two weeks before the announcement came down that Adolphus was to receive the Star. A week before he'd taken a bolt in the eye during a routine patrol, and that was the end of his military career, invalided home.

We hadn't spoken of it since. There hadn't ever been a reason. There wasn't a reason for it that night either, beyond the common instinct to spark fire with those things we've decided we love.

44

I spent that night in the apartment in Offbend, the same as I had the evening before. As a rule I don't do that, and morning had barely broken through the windows when I was reminded why.

Footfalls up the stairs pulled me awake, loud with an even rhythm, four or five men moving with purpose. I figured whoever was coming could kill me as well in bed as out, and I pulled the covers up around my ears.

A little while later I was on the floor, somewhat the worse for wear. The three men standing over me came from that branch of law enforcement that swell knuckles on jaws. Though insistent I dress they took my attempts to stand with great umbrage, and were quick to display their displeasure. Their leader waited in the doorway, just out of sight, though I was pretty sure I recognized the outline.

They let me get my pants on before he came into the arc of the light, which was kind of them. I hadn't thought there was

305

enough left of me to be scared, but as it turned out my reserves are somewhat deeper than I'd realized.

Crowley was an ugly man, had always been so. He was squat and hard and walked like something whittled from oak. His eyes were shellfish slits through which the world filtered. As a point of pride, the freeze keep their uniforms spotless, unblemished sheets of ice gray, but Crowley's was wrinkled and scuffed. The mystical gem carried by every agent, the Crown's Eye, was a small blob of silver swallowed by the fat of his neck.

But you didn't look at that – you looked at the scar that ran down the length of his face, that split his mouth into two deformed halves, curled his lips like a scrap of paper thrown on a fire. It was an old scar, but it would never heal. It had become his distinguishing characteristic, the quality marked by any observer, over and above his innate unsightliness. In that sense I thought I'd done him a favor, that night three years past when I'd carved out the discolored line from his flesh – though I didn't imagine he saw it that way.

How does a man forget about a man who wants to kill him, especially a man who's tried? Volume, in short – there were a lot of people who could match Crowley's loathing of me. Maybe not quite – my ex-colleague had a real flair for hatred. But still, if I went around worrying about everyone who wished me in the ground, I'd never find time to add anyone new to the list.

'Hello, Crowley.'

He didn't answer.

'All smiles, I see.'

Again, nothing. Crowley didn't seem to see me. 'I'm to take you to Black House,' he said, but dully, as if repeating something he didn't quite understand. If there was one thing to be said for Crowley, and there might not have been, it was that he was predictable. Predictable in his fury, predictable in his swift recourse to savagery. The man I'd known wouldn't have been able to keep a smirk off his face, or his hands off mine. I guess I'd cut him deeper than I'd intended – deeper than I'd realized at the time, at least.

They didn't bother to chain me, which seemed to speak well for the prospect of my immediate survival. True to form, none of my neighbors had reacted to the commotion. The occasional arrival of the frost, followed by the permanent disappearance of whomever they visited, was an infrequent but not overly noteworthy occurrence.

Clouds gathered. It was still hot as the inside of a boot, but a drape had been pulled across the sun and a storm rumbled in the distance. You couldn't feel it yet, but you could hear it.

The walk seemed longer than distance strictly merited. My friend at the front desk made a point of not saying anything, and we ascended to the upper levels unhindered, up a blank stairwell and down a featureless hallway. Black House is egalitarian in its contempt for aesthetics and comfort. The top man worked out of an office the equal of a mid-level counting clerk, and went home to a modest two-bedroom. Money didn't mean anything to him, and recognition even less, an active hindrance to the control he worked to effect over every inch of the Empire, and as far beyond as he could push it.

He was of average height, a uniform moustache over an undistinguished mouth. Neither fat, nor thin. A characterless suit, a face you thought you might have seen before but weren't certain. He had long fingers on soft hands, and his eyes were the blue of a newborn's blanket. Try to pin him in a memory and you'd come up short, a hole in the canvas leaving a vague impression of good humor and easy senescence, both of which were absolutely false.

It went without saying, the heat did not affect him.

'Welcome back,' he began. 'It's been far too long.'

Even before my disgrace, when the Old Man was my patron and not my enemy, he still made my skin crawl. There was something hollow about him, obvious enough if you looked, though most didn't. At the time I'd been willing to ignore it, willing even to pretend I didn't see it.

But I was young back then, and stupid. Now I'm only the latter. I figured if he was going to get nasty I'd be strapped into a chair in the basement, and not for the first time. Just the same I calculated the distance between us, tried to figure out if I could get my hands around the Old Man's neck before Crowley could move on me, and whether my death grip would be enough to bring to an end a life that had stretched out far too long. I took a casual look around for some more effective tool to enforce my malice, but as usual the only object marring the clean perfection of his desk was a dish of hard candy. Cherry, by the color.

He chased away thoughts of murder-suicide with a friendly wave to my escort. 'Thank you, Crowley, that'll be all. And be so kind as to send in a cup of tea on your way out – that's a good fellow.'

I was certain this would have elicited a response from my old colleague, given the precariousness of his temper and the relish with which he took offense. But Crowley obeyed without comment, and indeed, a moment later a starched suit came in with a chipped tea set. The Old Man added a spoonful of sugar into his mug, then a few more. 'I suppose you know why I've called you here.'

'Enlighten me.'

'We've decided it's time for the Veterans' Association to experience a change of leadership.' His smile took on a nasty edge. 'The more things change, as they say.'

'And here I was thinking you and Joachim were thick as lice.'

'Time moves, my boy. Pretories has . . . overstepped.' He shook his head sadly. 'I wouldn't have thought him for an idealist, not after all the coin that's flowed through his pockets. But then, the years can do strange things. A man starts seeing gray in his hair, gets to thinking about his legacy. All this trouble and fuss with the pensions, stirring up resentment against Throne and Crown – and then this bother with the Giroies on top of it.' He clicked his tongue. 'I'm afraid our Pretories won't be around much longer. Guiscard says you've been a help to him these last few days, and I wouldn't want you getting caught in the crossfire.'

'I didn't realize you cared.'

'Do you imagine your continued survival is an oversight? If I wanted you dead, the rats would chew your nipples before nightfall.' The threat was offered in the same tone with which you'd greet an acquaintance.

'Your good graces didn't stop Crowley from trying to off me last time.'

'I assumed you capable of handling it without my assistance. In fact, I was surprised to find my deputy still up and breathing, at the conclusion of events.'

'Sorry to let you down.'

'Not at all,' he said. 'It was what I would have done. You know he's never been the same, after that night – that last little bit of savagery that made him so . . . uniquely skilled for his position, it went away when you marked him. Really, I have to applaud you. Anyone can kill, but to break a man? To reach inside him and make him something else? That takes talent.'

I didn't say thank you. But then, I'd been badly raised.

The Old Man never seemed to be in a hurry – he could saunter out from a burning building. There was a long period during which neither of us spoke, during which any outside observer would think the two of us friends, or at least amiable associates. When he judged it had spooled out long enough he started again. 'Strange, isn't it, that Joachim would make a stink after so long in my pocket.'

'Life is strange sometimes.'

It was the sort of petty banality that appealed to him. 'Yes, indeed it is.' He pushed the dish of candy at me. I pushed it back. 'Out of character, one might even say.'

'You think you know a man.'

'And what in the world would have inspired the lesser Giroie to go on the offensive?'

'Who knows why anyone does anything?'

He nodded sagely, as if I'd passed along some bit of profundity. 'Indeed. As a particular, I've been racking my brain to discover what exactly determined your willingness to play the tattle.'

'Didn't have a choice in the matter.'

'Our little Guiscard frightened you so, did he?'

'Terrified.'

'I'm sure.' He took a sip of his tea and made a face, then added another lump of sugar. 'So none of this had anything to do with the unfortunate demise of the youngest Montgomery?'

If I hadn't already been sweating, I would have started. 'Who?'

'Have it your way.'

Another long pause. He raised his cup to his mouth, pinky finger elaborately extended, but his late summer eyes never left my own. 'Do you know what the most important requirement of my position is?'

'A dazzling smile?'

'Facility with numbers.' He set the cup down on the table. 'People don't like numbers – they like people, and they get confused when the first becomes the second. But I don't get confused. For a while, I thought you were the sort who didn't get confused either. But of course, that wasn't true at all – you're as bad with sums as anyone I've ever met.' He lifted a thumb from out a fist. 'There was Iomhair – no great loss, we might agree, but a tick mark just the same. The five Giroie boys guarding that wyrm shipment. Artur's retaliation took the lives of four men – veterans, like yourself. They're still pulling bodies out of the Hen and Harpy, so it's too early for an exact count, but let's say a dozen for ease.' He'd been tallying them on his fingers, sharp flutters of movement, but this last addition overran his count and he tossed up his hands as if to acknowledge it. 'That's twenty-two souls, and we haven't seen the end of it yet. Twenty-two men. Not sprung from the earth, I wouldn't imagine, but bred in the regular way. Mothers and fathers. Siblings. Wives and children, perhaps. A strange sort of debt, don't you think, which needs to be repaid two dozen times over?'

I scratched at the back of my neck. 'That was a really long monologue.'

He snickered and folded his hands, clearing the ledger. 'Doesn't matter now, not really. The line has been crossed. Whatever his motivations, Pretories' usefulness has ended. Of course, if this was all revenge for Rhaine Montgomery, I'm surprised you let a conspirator remain unpunished – knowing your, shall we say, rather savage sense of justice.'

It didn't do to admit ignorance in front of the Old Man, but it slipped out before I could say anything. 'What are you talking about? Pretories didn't want Rhaine throwing mud on him, weakening his position before the big march. He arranged to have a man kill her.'

He looked at me strangely. 'There's a reason Joachim Pretories couldn't achieve his position honestly. He's too weak a reed to do what's needed, not without long consultation. It was the same when we took care of Roland – you can't imagine how long he dragged his feet before acquiescing in our designs. I'm not sure he'd have gone along with it at all, if I hadn't had help persuading him.'

A pit was opening up beneath my chair, a dawning sense of horror at my own extraordinary foolishness.

Something of this must have shown in my face. 'You never put it together, did you? The identity of our silent partner?' I'd heard the Old Man laugh before, but always as part of his façade, as a tactic to lull the unwary into the delusion that he was human. But I'm not sure, before that moment, I'd ever heard an honest expression of levity cross his lips. A line of goose pimples ran up my arm.

'You're lying,' but even as I said it I knew it was off – the Old Man didn't lie. He never told the truth either, but he didn't lie. You bluff with a weak hand, and the head of Black House held four aces and hid two extra up his sleeve.

'I assure you, I very much am not. At the time of Roland's death, his father was a hair from being High Chancellor. Even I couldn't kill the scion of such an esteemed house without fear of repercussions. Happily, the general appreciated the necessity of curbing his son's misbehavior. He was my back channel to Pretories, him and that Vaalan who laps after him.'

Pieces began to slip into place, pieces I'd overlooked or ignored. The fight I'd overheard the night of Roland's birthday party. The

311

general's palpable misery the second time I'd been to see him, as if he already knew that Rhaine was dead.

The Old Man began to laugh again, laugh until his blue eyes swelled with tears. 'Oh my dear boy,' he started between chortles. 'My dear stupid, stupid child. You set all this in motion, and you never even knew? Rather than risk having anyone learn of his filicide, Montgomery sent his daughter to join his son.' He set one palm against the table to steady himself and raised his other against his brow. 'You aren't the architect of this stratagem – you're the mark.'

45

I started hitting crowds at Broad Street, a good half-mile from the epicenter. I didn't know what count Pretories had been hoping for when he'd put this shindig together, but whatever it had been he'd blown through it. There were contingents of veterans from throughout the Empire, from every corner of the Three Kingdoms: Tarasaighns from Kinterre in brightly colored outfits, piss drunk despite the hour; lines of Ashers with clipped black hair and clipped black eyes, eternally solemn, taking no part in the festivities; Islanders strolling in full naval regalia, red velvet coats and gilded thread, grinning in the heat. Groups had been piling into the city all week, setting up makeshift shelters at the march site. They milled about happily near their lean-tos, swapping lies about the war, buying food from passing vendors, catching up on regimental gossip.

Joachim's logistical abilities hadn't faded – it was a masterpiece of planning, executed with extraordinary precision. I'd say military precision, but having been in the service I know that to be an oxymoron. Everything so far was legal as sea salt. The Throne couldn't refuse permission for a march by the men who had guaranteed its survival. What they could do, and indeed had done, was surround the protesters by a cordon of hard-looking men in dark brown uniforms, carrying thick-headed clubs of the same color. Not city boys either, the hoax were too smart to let themselves get pulled into this mess. Levies from the provinces if I had to guess, bumpkins culled from the fields and brought south. Fifteen years earlier they'd have been called out to fight the Dren. They were the nephews and sons of the men they would soon be attacking, though it would have been too much to ask of them to realize it.

It was a vast host, too thick a chunk of humanity to comfortably force down. I hadn't seen its like since the war itself. Reminded me of the war in a lot of ways, looking at the faces of men soon to die and knowing nothing can be done to stop it. At least during the war everyone was aware of the possibility of imminent demise. But the atmosphere at the march was anything but tense, self-righteous certainty buttressed by the joyous folly of the crowd. They'd have thought me mad if I'd tried to tell them what I knew, or taken me for a provocateur and lynched me from the nearest pole. Nobody likes being told they're walking in the wrong direction, even if the trail ends at a cliff.

I struggled my way through the tightening mass, conscious of the hour's steady beat. Closer to the front progress choked to a standstill, and I started throwing elbows and getting them back in return. The storm rumbled from a few blocks over, but from where I stood the sun was bright as it had been the last week. Too bright, you had to squint against it. Sometimes that's how close it is, the line between the two.

There was a barrier separating the organizers from the mob. I saw Adolphus on the other side of it, not for the first time grateful that he was closer to two men than one. I hopped over the obstruction, ignoring the dirty looks of the unwashed. The press of people loosened enough that I could make out the face standing at Adolphus's side. They were smiling to each other and talking, but they cut that shit short at my approach.

For a moment the ties that bound me to the giant, ties that were strong enough to have induced me to risk my life in getting him to safety, strained. I looked at Wren, then back at his guardian savagely. 'Are you out of your fucking mind?'

Dimly Adolphus must have realized he'd overstepped, or perhaps our last interaction was still wearing on him, because he didn't answer.

'Not enough risking your own fool life, you gotta drag the boy in as well?'

'I can take care of myself,' Wren piped in, doing his best approximation of an adult. 'I'm man enough.'

I cuffed him against the side of the head, hard enough to set him to his knees. 'No, you ain't. Not nearly. Get home, now.'

He peered up at me, then over at Adolphus, who seemed strangely apathetic, paralyzed by my arrival. After a moment he dragged himself off the ground, then slipped out from the crowd, shaken and pale.

I felt great about myself. Adolphus still refused to look straight at me, his one eye fluttering off at the margins. 'We'd best follow his example. Right now.'

He ejected a thimble of spit from his square jaw. 'I'm not talking about this with you again. I made my decision. It's settled.' A drop of rain splattered against his pockmarked nose.

'Today ends badly.'

'Never pegged you for a prophet.'

'I got the inside line.'

'From whom?'

'The head of Black House.'

Adolphus shot a quick look around, concerned that my

intemperate announcement might have made its way to the men surrounding us. 'Keep your voice down.'

'There's no time for subtlety – the Old Man's gonna make his move, and make it soon, and when he does blood's gonna water the dust.'

He had enough respect for me not to call it a bluff, which I appreciated. But still it took him a while to process it, time we didn't have, my heart beating near through my chest. Adolphus wasn't stupid, but he was slow – sudden shifts of direction were not his strong suit. Finally he reached a decision. 'Even if that's the case – especially if that's the case – I'm not going anywhere. These are my people. I'll stand with them.'

'Wren's your people. Adeline's your people.' I set my palm against his chest and shoved him, playing the frantic, though it wasn't hard to fake it. His bulk barely wavered, but at least it got his attention. 'I'm your fucking people.'

He didn't have anything to say to that, but then he didn't have to. Stalemate would kill us both – I needed to shock him into movement.

'Pretories is a Black House plant,' I said, loud enough to make sure our neighbors heard it.

A thunderclap echoed in the distance, and not the distant distance either. Adolphus took a quick look around, checking the audience for signs of threat, then hissed under his breath. 'Don't be tossing that kind of shit around.'

'He's been working for the Throne since he let Roland Montgomery get killed.'

'That's bullshit. You got no cause to talk like that.' But his voice fluttered.

'Pretories bit the Old Man's gold and didn't taste the lead.'

'How do you know this?' Adolphus asked, though I bet he could have made a solid guess.

'Because I was the one behind it – it was my way into Special Ops. I thought Roland was crazy, or maybe I didn't – it doesn't matter now. I did it, and Joachim was in on it, and he hasn't gotten any better in the last twelve years. This . . .' I waved my hand at the mob that was beginning to show signs of movement. 'It's a pageant, a way for the veterans to loose some fury off aimlessly. Except it isn't – the Old Man thinks Pretories has got too big and plans to put him down, and when he does things are going to get bad, real bad, bad for everyone here, understand? It's too late for these people, but it's not too late for us.'

His mouth hung open, condemnation or confusion, I never did find out. There was an explosion from somewhere in the back, and an uninterrupted half hour of screaming began.

I'd been expecting its arrival. The Old Man hadn't bothered to divulge specifics of his set-up, but the easiest way to do anything is backwards. Who was to say there wasn't an extreme contingent of the Association discontent with Joachim's policy of non-violence? Who was to say they hadn't brought in explosives, set them off at the outskirts as an exercise in nihilistic radicalism? No one, not after today.

The crowd was as unprepared as a virgin, and in the immediate aftermath reacted with stunned confusion – but stampede was in the air as certain as the storm. The guards semi-circled ahead of us, however, were not surprised, not at all – if one had a grim turn of mind, one might even imagine they'd known about it beforehand. They didn't march forward so much as surge, a coiled spring unwound, wading into the front ranks and swinging their big, knobbed clubs.

Pretories had filled the first rank with war heroes, men like Adolphus, thinking their status would be certain proof against violence. He'd reckoned without the Old Man's savagery – a curious error given their history. Two men holding a banner aloft found themselves the first casualties, their message inked over with blood. An amputee stumbled backward over his crutches trying to escape, a line of medals pinned across his chest. Having lost a leg for his country, he had perhaps thought he'd earned the right not to be beaten to death by men in its employ. It never pays to underestimate ingratitude.

Truth was even the Association's muscle, Rabbit and Hroudland, the men who'd taken care of Giroie, hadn't come prepared for a fight. The switch between civilization and barbarism isn't a finger snap, even the most savage of motherfuckers needs a few minutes to get going. The line of marchers stretched well back into the horizon. Most of them couldn't see what was going on, but those who did started moving backwards.

Pretories did his best to rally them, grabbing up a standard and waving it in the breeze. Last-minute heroics weren't really his line, but he did all right. More than that, if I'm being honest. He moved with courage, and certainty. Roland himself couldn't have done any better.

One of his boys, one I hadn't ever thought to pay attention to, one who looked pretty much like the rest, lifted his hand up to his commander's neck. There was a bright line of scarlet. The colors dropped into the dust. Pretories followed.

It was a quick few seconds, easy to miss. I doubted many saw it. That was how the Old Man got to be so old, you see – he always has a piece behind you. I wondered who'd get me, when the time came. I wouldn't see it coming, of that I was sure.

Considering the trouble I'd gone through to see it happen, the death of Joachim Pretories provided me little pleasure. Watching his men trample his corpse in the dirt trying to escape, it was hard to hate him. All things considered, I'd met worse men. But then again, I'd killed better ones, so there wasn't no point in getting sentimental.

With the loss of their leader any semblance of order collapsed completely. We were at life and death, and everyone realized it. Accordingly the knee-high barrier separating us from the thickest part of the throng stopped doing that, proving no impediment to the movement of fifty thousand angry, frightened men. The march had become a rout – I was a drop in a sea of flesh, and could do nothing but paddle with the current.

Adolphus had it easier – even the most scattered fellow will avoid running into a brick wall if he can help it. But I'm not much bigger than average, and the surge carried me along. Like any great body of people it moved without purpose or direction, mankind in the aggregate no brighter than in detail. The explosion had sent the men in the back sprinting forward, and the barbarity of the guards had sent the men in the front sprinting back. Adolphus and I made for the flanks accordingly, but it was like wading a swollen river. A river that's screaming at you and shoving fingers into your eyes.

An errant blow from a passer-by sent me to my knees, my head spinning, the sheer press of men near to crushing me. An ugly way to go, and I managed to regain my footing with a few sharp hooks. By the time I got my head up Adolphus was gone, swept onward by the tide. Or perhaps he just hadn't cared to wait – I got the sense that my well-being was not his foremost concern.

Chaos like that, there isn't anything that distinguishes one man from another – survival comes down to drunken chance. I was in the front when it started, and I knew it was coming, so I had a better shot than most, but not much of one.

A packed squad of guardsmen hammered their way toward us, and the crowd surged backward like a wounded animal. I broke forward, figuring to take my chances against one fool with a weapon than ten thousand unarmed. A uniformed scab took a swing at me, and I ducked beneath it and took his legs out from under him. I wanted to stay there and beat on him a little, but there wasn't time. I was off and sprinting as quick as I could muster.

Off the main boulevard I took my first full breath, lungs expanding into bruised bone and injured flesh. I wasn't sure how long it had lasted, the mad press of bodies. Not as long as it had felt like, that was damn sure. The wind was scattering sparks of fire further into the city, and things were getting bad fast. Worse, I guess I should say. Still I turned to watch, climbed a few feet up the wall of the alley, finding footholds in parched ivy. I'd set the fuse – it seemed only right to stay till the end.

For once the Old Man had overreached. Most of the people in the crowd hadn't seen violence in fifteen years, but that's not never. Enough of it was coming back to them to make the comparatively tiny number of guards distinctly insufficient. The Ashers, ever prepared for combat, had formed into a tight square and were edging their way to safety, distinct by their outfits and discipline. Mostly the guards were smart enough to stay away from them, but occasionally one got too close and found himself pulled under, executed efficiently though not painlessly by men who'd made violence a religion.

They were the only knot of organization to be seen, but in chaotic remnants here and there once dangerous men recalled their powers. The guards were armed, and made savage by youth, but their opponents had earned degrees in brutality at the definitive institute in history. A Vaalan the size of an ox snapped a guard over his knee, back breaking like a rotten tree branch. Further down the line a pair of Islanders had isolated one unfortunate, had him against the ground and were beating him to death with something akin to glee. Joachim had stipulated that no one was to carry a weapon, the better to head off this exact scenario – but amidst the tens of thousands some remnant had come with blade or bronzed knuckle. What had begun as blind flight was rapidly hardening into a battle, and I felt an incongruous moment of enthusiasm for my brothers-in-arms.

But the outcome was a foregone conclusion. Another explosion ricocheted through the crowd, then another and another, pops like fireworks, each signaling death, and whatever had braced the spirit of the mob was carried away by fear.

The drizzle had turned into a downpour, but it wasn't doing anything to stem the spread of the flames. The second wave of explosions had dirtied the air, rendering further observation of the proceedings futile. The city was ripe as a tinderbox, the ground so dry a dropped cigarette would burn cobblestone. There was a burst of heat as the windows of a house a block over erupted, and I dropped from my perch and started off.

The smoke was in my eyes and in my throat and in my lungs, and I coughed my way through the alleys trying to get away from it. I wasn't the only one hoping to make an escape – I passed a steady stream of veterans breaking out in any and every direction, so long as it was away, away, away. I was of the same desperate strain of mind, so it was a hell of a surprise to make a U-turn in a cul-de-sac and find myself face to face with a pair of old friends.

'If it isn't the lieutenant,' Hroudland said, and for once Rabbit didn't smile.

'Thank the Firstborn you two survived! Where's the commander?'

'Commander's dead,' Hroudland said.

'Heavens!' I exclaimed. By that point I was pretty sure talking wasn't going to square us.

'What happened to Roussel, Lieutenant?' Hroudland asked.

'I might have killed him,' I admitted, giving up the charade. 'And I might have enjoyed it.'

Rabbit nodded, unsurprised. 'As I will this.'

My interview with the Old Man had left me unarmed, and there hadn't been time to make good the lack. Rabbit held a thin stiletto in his off hand, but he let it drop blade-first to the ground and gestured at me to come forward. I'd never had any great desire to engage the man in fisticuffs, but it didn't do to show him that. I went in strong as I could, feinting a body shot and trying for an eye-level straight – but he just grinned that grin that I'd come to loathe and dipped his head, and I broke two knuckles off his cranium.

It was a short fight, and the rest of it went the same way. What little I landed might as well not have, and every one of Rabbit's short, sharp punches found purchase on my own flesh. Soon I was on the ground and he was kicking me in the ribs, the beating somewhat superfluous given what I'd already suffered. Another moment of fun and he dropped down on top of me, pinned his knees against my shoulders and wrapped his fingers around my throat.

The smoke was thick as marmalade, and it seeped into my brain. The margins of my vision folded inward, narrowing on an impossibly wide grin, teeth as big as chess pieces, running together into eternity.

A palm reached out of the fog and wrapped itself around Rabbit's skull, pulling it towards the wall and dragging the rest of his body along with it. The passageway was ruined brick, but all the same Rabbit's bald head created a sizable indentation. He slumped slowly to the ground, leaving a streak of blood in his wake.

The hand attaches to an arm attaches to a body, and it's Adolphus's, and I am saved.

There are men who wouldn't have hesitated then, but there aren't many, and Hroudland wasn't one of them. His jaw quivered and he held his knife loose in his hand. Adolphus slapped it away casually, the blade skittering off into the dirt. A second backhand rebounded Hroudland off the well, stunned him insensible, left him open for the finale. While I'm aware that it is not literally possible for a punch to knock a man's head off, somehow that's the only description that fits.

I lay motionless as my best friend approached me, wondering if perhaps he'd set his boot against my chest and make a clean go of everyone who'd fucked him. Instead he bent down and lifted me to my feet like I was a child.

'Let's go home,' he said, and that's what we did.

46

It only took Roland a moment to see he was going to die. We were in a small safe house I had set up in Low Town. That much I had held to. But the men who sat at the table with me were, even at a glance, not the sort of people who would be sponsoring an internal *coup d'état*, even had there been such a faction within Black House. They were, very distinctly, the sort of people the Old Man keeps around to do evil things. I guess he kept me around for the same reason, though of a subtler kind.

You can learn everything you need to know about a person by how they react to their death, though of course you can't do anything with the information afterward. Not that I had any doubts about Roland's courage. He stopped short, just past the doorway. For a brief moment you could see him thinking about making a run for it, see it in the sudden tensing of his hands. But I'd put two men on the entrance he'd come through, and he must have realized there was no point.

He looked at me, then closed his eyes for a long moment. When he opened them he was smiling, and he strode towards us at a brisk pace and with no evident trace of concern. He took the seat I'd left for him. It was at the head of the table, as was well warranted.

'This is it, then?' he asked.

I nodded.

'I suppose I should have seen it coming.'

I shrugged.

'But then, your story sounded plausible. And with support from Black House I could have moved up my timetable by a year, maybe two. It was worth taking the shot.'

A lack of caution was always Roland's weakness. I'd realized that the day I'd met him, been confident he'd fall into the snare. 'No one with anything to lose wants you to win. You overstate the base of your support.'

'Clearly,' he deadpanned.

I stopped a chuckle. This was not really the time for levity, though you wouldn't have been able to tell it from Roland's demeanour. A bottle of whiskey sat on the table. It had been full when I'd set it there a half-hour prior. It wasn't any longer. I poured the man a few fingers and passed it over.

He nodded thanks and knocked it down. 'If you kill me,' he said, after savoring the bite for a moment, 'the country will go up in flames – my men won't stand for it.'

'If you live the country will go up in flames anyway. And I'm sorry to say so, but you're wrong. The Association will mourn your death – but they will do so without violence. We've taken steps to make sure of that.'

'Joachim?' It was perhaps the first time in his life that Roland had even lost his composure. Certainly it was the first time I had ever seen it. He set his hands on the table, looked at them for a while without saying anything. I felt a sudden and very vivid pang of regret for revealing his best friend's betrayal, somehow felt worse about it than my own. 'I wouldn't have thought it of him,' he said.

I wouldn't have thought it either, still had trouble believing it was true. But the Old Man had as much as confirmed it.

'Was it money?' Roland asked, mainly to himself. 'The thought of taking over?'

Both, probably. Pretories came from that brand of nobility without two coppers to rub against each other. And no one likes looking over another man's shoulder indefinitely. Though it could have been simple self-preservation – Joachim was no fool. Maybe he'd simply looked over the path Roland was marking out and seen the same thing I did, blood and ultimate failure. 'I'm really not sure,' I said. 'I didn't handle that side of it.'

'Why did you do it?'

'I tried talking you down.'

'That's hardly an excuse.'

'It wasn't meant to be – I gave you my reasons the last time we spoke. All the death we've seen, all the bodies, five long years of it – and you'd see us dive back in again? Commit your veterans against the Crown, plunge the Empire into civil war?'

'Better to die a free man than live as a slave.'

'I can see you've never been a slave. It's a funny thing about the downtrodden – they don't want to burn the city to the ground, they want to own it.'

'Then your actions are at that ideal intersection of morality and self-interest?'

'I don't apologize for my ambitions, any more than you do yours.'

'But mine were very grand,' he said. 'And yours are small, and petty.'

'You can tell a great man by the bodies he leaves in his wake.'

'Nothing important was ever accomplished without sacrifice.'

I let the argument rest on that one. It had been foolish to get into it with him, you were never going to convince anyone of the necessity of their murder.

'Is there anything you'd like me to do?' I asked. 'For your family, your people?'

He took a moment considering, then shook his head. 'I have no regrets.'

'Saints and fools say that. And you're no saint.'

He laughed and poured himself another shot of liquor. 'My name will echo on,' he said, downing it. 'There's nothing more that a man can ask.'

You could ask for a long life spent in comfort, a wife to hold your hand as you passed, children to walk on ahead. But Roland wouldn't get any of these things, and there was no point rubbing his nose in it.

One of the agents I'd posted outside slipped in, shutting the door behind him and approaching us quietly. I knew him a little, better than the other two thugs the Old Man had given me, both of whom I was sure had orders to do to me what we were about to do to Roland, if I had any signs of getting second thoughts.

I poured Roland another shot. When he reached out to take it I gave the man behind him a nod.

It was very quick – that was the least I could do. The Agent brought a blade across his throat, one quick movement. Blood sprayed onto the table, though I was far enough away to avoid the spill. Roland's eyes seemed locked on mine. After a few seconds the light went out of them.

'Wrap up the body,' I said, getting up from the table. 'Dump it where I showed you. And for the love of the Firstborn, don't let anyone see you.'

The investigation would be brief and perfunctory. Roland's corpse was found outside a whorehouse in a part of Low Town that even I avoided, a part where a man could die easily and for no particular reason. The sordid quality of his demise did little to blemish his reputation. The Association had a mass funeral, beat their breasts and rent their clothes, called for investigations into Roland's murder, demanded a raise in the pension fund. What they didn't call for was open violence. Joachim Pretories kept up his end.

And the Old Man kept his. In exchange for my act of betrayal, I was made a member of Special Operations, fast-tracked into the halls of power. In a year I was the Old Man's second-in-command, practically speaking one of the five or ten most powerful people in the Empire. In three I was back in Low Town, dealing breath to meet my ends.

You grow up reading stories, and you start to think your life is one. Every punchline has a set-up; every action a motive. But that's horseshit – we're all just stumbling about blind. You do something and decide why you did it afterward. Roland was mad – beautiful, and noble, but mad as well, mad as only a man with a dream can be. I was no dreamer. Roland's life had taught him that anything is possible. Mine had taught me that you hold on to what you have with both hands.

At least that's what I tell myself, when I think about it late at night and early in the morning. I never quite manage to believe it, though.

47

Edwin Montgomery's door was unlocked. Not a good sign – it meant they knew I was coming, and weren't concerned.

Back at the Earl I'd armed up, huffed pixie's breath until I couldn't feel my teeth, and headed out. The city was straight bedlam – I hadn't seen anything like it for thirty years, since the worst days of the plague. The effects of what would come to be known as the Veterans' Riot were felt far beyond where the fighting had taken place. Anyone lucky enough to have a barred door was huddled behind it. Gray storm clouds, swollen by the smoke, hovered just out of reach, pissing down on me with every step.

Whatever was coming, I wasn't in any shape to see it through. The breath carried me along like a scrap of trash in the wind, but that wouldn't last. When it was gone I wouldn't have enough left in me to stand. But delay was a non-starter. Twelve years this had dragged on – it would end today, one way or the other.

Botha was in the drawing room. He'd stripped down to his undershirt and was shouldering the grand piano into the corner. He'd done the same with the rest of the furniture, the tea table set against the wall, a Kiren rug rolled on top of it. He saw me but didn't stop what he was doing until the room was clear of obstructions. Then he picked up a wrapped parcel from amidst the clutter, held it against his shoulder and waited for me to begin.

I obliged him. 'Expecting company?'

'The last three days – I figured we'd see you after I did for Gilchrist.'

'What was he going to tell me?'

'I assume he was going to tell you that I stopped by the night before Rhaine died, got him to put us in touch. Don't think too badly of him – he didn't know what I intended.'

'I guess he paid for it, either way.'

'He did indeed.'

'Did you miss with that bolt?' I asked. 'Or did you just prefer your backup silent?'

He shrugged, head bobbling on broad shoulders. 'I guess I wasn't so careful as I could have been.'

'Who was he?'

'Pretories' man. I went to see the commander about Rhaine, make sure he understood what needed to be done. Commander insisted on detailing one of his thugs to follow along after me.'

'The commander's dead, you know.'

'Pretories never meant nothing to me – I only follow one commander,' he said proudly. 'Only ever did.'

'You willing to die for him?'

'Willing to kill.'

'You certain that's how this ends?'

'It's how it always has.'

'For me too.'

He smiled and pulled his weapon out from the bundle, an heirloom flamberge, two-handed with a wavy blade, treated metal glittering.

'You did her yourself, didn't you Botha?' I asked, watching him wrap his hands around the pommel.

'Pretories said he'd send a man, but I waved him off – the mistress was a stupid whore,' the Vaalan said blankly. 'She got what was coming.'

'Like her brother?'

'Roland was worse.' Botha spat a wad of gunk on the floor. It was distinctly unbutler-like behavior, but I supposed we were past that. 'Never appreciated what he had, spent his whole life trying to screw the man who gave it to him.'

'I was worried you might end up being one of those people I have to murder because they're standing in the way – and I sometimes feel bad about that afterward. It's kind of you to make this personal.'

'My weapon is half a millennium old,' Botha said, holding it so the light scintillated off the edge. 'It's been bathed in the blood of far better men than you.'

'It'll fetch four ochre at a Pritt Street pawnshop,' I said, pulling my trench blade from my belt. 'And I'll spend the money on drugs.'

Botha wasn't big on chatter, nor one to cower at a cruel word. He widened his stance slightly, then motioned me to come forward.

I let the throwing knife ease out of the cuff of my shirt and into my palm, then brought my hand up casually – but either he saw what I was going for or he was stone-cold, because the square bulk of his body shifted downward, and the throw went high.

Not for the first time I wished I was as tough as I talked.

But it was too late for second-guessing, and I double-timed an advance, his reach being an advantage I knew I could only compensate for with speed. He knew the same thing and back-pedalled, meeting my advance with a swing of his weapon that I barely dodged.

Botha was stronger than me, and his earlier endeavours had given him a wide field to play with. The mismatch between our weapons meant that I couldn't risk a straight parry, had to duck

331

and flit out of his reach. But the downside to swinging a weapon four feet in length is that you have to keep swinging it, and that takes a lot out of a fellow, a lot out and quick. On the other hand he had not spent the last two days getting the shit kicked out of him, and thus had more by way of reserves.

All the same it wasn't long before the both of us were feeling our exertions, the steady tango slowing to an uneven rhythm, punctuated by moments of pause. 'Getting tired?' I asked. 'Feeling out of breath? Ain't as easy as strangling a girl to death, is it?'

He sneered and made a fancy little play, feigning retreat then swiveling forward. I about half fell for it, not so far as to make myself cadaverous, but enough to get a chunk of flesh nicked out of my stomach.

I made like it didn't hurt, made like I didn't notice it, that part of my body which was no longer there. 'Was it the money, Botha? Did you think with his children dead, the general would make you his heir?'

'Never gave a shit about money,' Botha said, his chest heaving, the tip of his sword following me as I circled around him.

I pulled my second knife from my belt. 'Course not, you just wanted the pat on the head. What's the matter, Daddy didn't love you enough? You figured the general was a good substitute?'

I managed to survive this next exchange without losing any more flesh, but it was close. Botha held his flamberge down by his side, ready for the killing stroke.

'Don't matter how many of his kids you murder,' I said, hoping to push him into it. 'You won't ever be his kin.'

He screamed in rage and brought his weapon up to halve me. I took a knee, felt the force of his swing sweep over the top of my skull, brought the knife in my left hand down into the bridge of his foot. He screamed again, in pain this time, and I rolled out of his reach.

It was over, though he was slow to realize it. I played it careful, circling him slowly, watching the hole I'd made flood crimson onto the floorboards. After a moment his eyes started to get that dull look that arrives when the head isn't getting its requisite amount of ichor. I feinted forward and he went in with everything he had – but his movements were sluggish, and it was easy to dodge. He lacked the strength to halt the force of his stroke, and I countered with my own, taking his arm off at the elbow. The stump doused me with blood. His severed fist stayed clenched on the hilt of his weapon, along with its still functioning twin. Botha watched me like he couldn't quite believe what was happening, open-mouthed, life draining out of his injured limb.

Ain't right to play with a dying man, don't matter who he is. Botha's end wasn't long in coming, nor any more painful than it had to be.

I pulled my trench blade out of his skull, cleaned it against the Kiren rug and looped it into my belt. Then I fell backward onto the grand piano, its cacophony echoing around me. The injury Botha had done me was ugly but not fatal. Added to everything else I'd suffered, however, I found I was having a hard time with it. I propped one fist firm against the wound and forced myself into the next room.

The general looked close enough to the end to make this whole errand seem awfully superfluous. He had remained at his desk despite the fighting, and he wouldn't quite look at me.

I gave him a sharp salute with the hand that wasn't holding in my intestines. It was a bit melodramatic, but I blame it on the blood loss.

He shriveled into his seat.

'Forgive me for coming unannounced, General, and in such inappropriate attire.'

It took him a long time to answer. 'I suppose Botha is lying dead in the parlor?'

'I wouldn't expect to have your bed turned down.'

'You're here to kill me as well?'

'Something like that.'

'That suit you, murdering an old man?'

My legs were starting to buckle. I set my hand on the desk to steady myself. 'After the last few days? A few more drops of blood won't make any kind of difference.'

He met my eyes finally, and under different circumstances I might have admired his coolness. 'Best get to it, then.'

'We've got time,' I said, though it wasn't true. My wound needed looking at, and the general – well, the general didn't have long to go either. 'When you first sent for me, did you know about my part in Roland's end?'

'You did what you had to,' he turned his withered head back down to the desk. 'My son was mad – the war drove him mad. He'd have set the whole country to flame.'

'That slips us both off the hook pretty easy, doesn't it? Was I ever supposed to bring Rhaine home? Or did you just need a patsy to flush her out of hiding?'

'I had hoped it wouldn't be necessary. I had hoped she'd listen to reason.'

'I don't think you did. I think you hoped I'd take care of Rhaine for you – that I'd get worried she might find out the truth, arrange an accident on her behalf. When I didn't, you had Botha call on Pretories, make sure the commander saw things the same way you did.'

'It wasn't like that,' he said. 'I hadn't planned it out that way, it just happened.' I wasn't sure if I believed him – it was hard to tell, old and weak as he was, hard to read anything on a face so close to a corpse. 'Joachim would have killed her anyway, after he found out she was sniffing around. Once she left for Low Town, there was nothing I could do.'

'You could have come clean. Told her what happened. She'd have hated you, but she'd still be alive.'

He gave a slow smile, if you could call something so bitter a smile. 'You could have done the same.'

The rain tapped on the windows – a pleasant, even pattern, and my pulse slowed to meet it. My legs suggested I stop standing on them, curl right up on the carpet like a collie. A short nap, or a long one, or the last one. 'Tell me about Roland.'

'I would have been a very good High Chancellor,' Montgomery answered after a moment, though not to me particularly. 'I could have helped our boys. Could have seen to it that they got what they deserved. I could have done great things.'

Strangely, I didn't doubt any of that. 'If only your son had fallen in line.'

'It was all a game to him,' Montgomery hissed, still furious at Roland's misbehavior after twelve years and a definitive revenge. 'He just did it to spite me.'

'And one day the Old Man came to you, and he whispered things in your ear – reasonable things, quiet things, things you wanted to hear.'

'He said there was still a chance to right the situation – for me to become Chancellor, for the Empire to avoid the horror my son seemed destined to inflict upon it. He asked me to contact Joachim, to see if we could squeeze Roland out before things went too far. He said it still might be possible to save Roland from his own folly.'

'Did you believe him?'

'I don't know,' Montgomery said, and seemed to mean it.

'I'm not one to be surprised at the things men do. And I guess I can understand Roland – at least, I'm not in a position to judge. But I'd figure where you are now, the next generation would be all that mattered.'

'Get on with it.'

'Was she worth so little, that you'd strangle the root for a few months of peace?'

It's easy to make a man a villain in your head, a creature undiluted by decency, as alien to you as night is to day. I'd done that on the way over, been doing it since the Old Man had tipped me to the general's play. It was harder to hate him now – an almost corpse, preceded into the next world by everyone he'd ever loved. And I knew something of the way choices can start to carry their own weight, carry you further than you'd thought, further than you ever wanted to go.

'You've no regrets?' he asked finally.

'A few here and there. But regret's not enough – you have to pay for it.'

This seemed to spark something in him, some dying ember. His mutter became a shout, or the closest he could muster. 'Have you paid for it, Lieutenant? Have you paid? You couldn't save Rhaine, so you set the city awash in blood. I see the smoke from outside my window! How many did you kill for a girl you barely knew? You stand here and lecture me on morality, as if your hands weren't red to the elbow! As if you had no role in leading Roland to the slaughter!'

'I wasn't his father.' I pulled the locket he had given me that first day from my back pocket and sent it spinning across the desk. 'Nor hers.'

That was enough. He opened the necklace with trembling hands, spent a while staring at Rhaine's face.

I took a knife from my belt and flicked it into the wood. 'Do it.'

He raised his eyes up to mine. 'They'll cover it up, won't they?'

I nodded. 'They'll cover it up.'

They did. General Edward Montgomery died of a heart attack, unable to stand the loss of his second child. A few days later they laid him in the family crypt, there to spend eternity beside the bodies of his murdered kin.

48

I t's a sure thing, Warden. You know I wouldn't steer you wrong.'

It was late afternoon, a week or so after the march. I was sitting at a table outside our front door, trying to move as little as possible, which demands more effort than you'd think. The rain had been coming down more or less constantly since it had started. Walking soaked a man to the skin in half a minute, and the streets had turned from dust to quagmire. It almost made one miss the heat – almost. The storm was finally showing signs of easing, but it hadn't yet, and I was happy for the overhang that kept me from its reach. I'd been mixing whiskey with water since noon, and started doing away with the water not long after.

'Ten ochres will get you a hundred in a month, month and a half at the outset. How's that for a return?'

Tully the Hook was a choke head. If he had other characteristics I don't remember them. He'd swung by a few minutes earlier, the storm nothing against the chance to fill his lungs with wyrm on my copper.

'Now sure, I could take care of it myself, but then I figured, why not bring the Warden in on this one? There's a man, I said, there's a man what knows his business. There's a man what knows an opportunity when he sees it, and if this ain't an opportunity, I'll eat my hat!'

He'd have eaten a turd wrapped in broken glass if he thought it would get him a pipeful of stem. On principle alone, I ought to have injured him – clearly my reputation was weak beer if a mutt like Tully thought he could waste my time and not risk violence. But every part of me still hurt – walking downstairs left me winded and bitter. I had a vial of breath in my pocket, the same one that had been there for four days, but for some damn fool reason I wouldn't let myself use it.

'The whole city's off-balance – now's the time to make a move. These Islander folks, all they need is a little push. They'll do the lifting, dig?'

I took another swig of the whiskey, then set my head on the table. It was not soft. 'Tully, you say one more word I'm going to kill you and leave your body in an alley. You know I'll do it.'

There was a sputtering sound of disagreement, but it didn't harden into speech. Maybe my name still hung together after all. Time passed. Half drunk with my eyes closed I wasn't sure how much.

The muffled fall of steps alerted me to Tully's return. Dumb motherfucker couldn't figure when to make an exit. I pulled a knife out from my boot and slammed it in the table, brought my face up after it, trying to think of something threatening to say.

Wren stared back at me, little impressed. 'That's a nice knife.'

'I . . . thought you were . . .'

'Tully flitted out the back.'

I nodded uncomfortably, then waved at the opposite bench. Wren set himself into it but didn't speak. The blade went back in my boot.

We stared at each other for a while. It wasn't exactly riveting entertainment. The sky was a patchwork fabric of sunlight streaming through the clouds. My whiskey was almost gone. A long pull from the bottle and I lost my last reason for sticking around.

'Rain's letting up,' I said.

'Looks that way.'

'I gotta run a thing over to a guy. Fancy a stroll?'

After a moment he nodded, and I pulled myself wearily to my feet, and we started off.

Walking pulled at the spot of stomach that I didn't have anymore, and reminded me of the dozen other injuries I'd sustained the past week. I was too old to survive many more of these. I was surprised I'd survived this one, truth be told. Wren eased himself down to my pace. It was a while before I mustered the courage to say anything.

'How're the lessons going?'

'All right.'

'Mazzie doing right by you?'

'She hasn't cut me up and made me into a stew, if that's what you're asking.'

'Yet,' I said. 'She hasn't cut you up and made you into a stew, yet.'

He didn't laugh. The welt on his face was faded but noticeable. I didn't like looking at it, but wouldn't let myself look away.

'You learn to do anything beside spin colors?'

'Learning to move things without touching them.'

'I imagine that might be useful.'

The mud pulled at my boots – I had to tug them loose with every step. Despite the break in the weather, we were the only ones on the streets, hobbling down boulevards a dozen stout men could pass abreast. As we edged toward Offbend we started to pass the first signs of the riot, burned-out shells of houses, charred staircases ascending into nothingness, stone cellar skeletons of quaint A-frames. It had taken fifteen years, but the war had come to Rigus. I hoped this was its parting shot, and not the introductory rampage of a successor.

'I needed you gone,' I said finally. 'Things were set to get bad – there wasn't any time to do it soft. You stuck around any longer, you wouldn't be here now.'

'I know,' he said.

'As for the rest . . . It could have been handled better.'

We stopped in front of a bar. I walked in, then I walked out. My bag was light a few things that had been in it, my purse correspondingly heavier. We started back towards the docks.

'Adolphus says Pretories was a traitor, says he was working for Black House,' Wren began.

'Yeah?'

'Says he had Roland killed so he could take over the veterans.'

'He went along with it, at least.'

'Why'd he do it?'

I'd been mulling that question over for a while now, ever since I'd watched him die, in fact. I wish we'd had the chance to talk it over, foolish as that sounded. The usual lust for power and money? Was he tired of running the master's water? Or had he an inkling that Roland was cracked, that someone needed to step in? No sin in refusing to follow a man off a cliff, though there is one in tripping him. 'We don't always know why we do things,' I said.

'What happens to the Association now?'

'Same as always. Things don't really change.' Though I wasn't quite sure I believed that. The riots had been a rare black eye for the Old Man. Blame the violence on some renegade offshoot of the Association all you want – at the end of the day, a fair portion of the city was in ashes, and that's not something that the head of national security is supposed to let happen. I doubted he'd intended it to go quite as it had. Maybe he was losing his touch. It was a disturbing thought, the Old Man growing old. Like the weakening of the tides, the stilling of the wind.

'How about you and Adolphus?'

We'd yet to speak more than pleasantries, muttered greetings when we passed in the stairwell. I was having trouble meeting his eyes, or he was mine. 'I don't have an answer to everything.'

The sun took advantage of its short window to glare off every bit of scrap metal and glass, but it did nothing to ease our passage through six inches of sludge. Outside the front door of a one-room shack a child played naked in a puddle, burbling happily, youth and grime obscuring the sex. Its mother appeared from the egress and shrieked incomprehensibly, dragged her seed out of the muck and started on a beating. I averted my eyes – I'd learned my lesson on family quarrels.

'How much of it did you set up?' Wren asked.

'Less than I thought at the time.'

'Was it worth it?'

I considered that for a while before answering. 'Probably not.'

We hooked a right off Light Street and down a narrow alley, cobblestone, thank the Firstborn. It curved its way through a row of tenements, taking us away from the main streets.

'This isn't the way back to the Earl,' Wren said.

'You got something to do?'

After a hundred yards the road narrowed till we had to walk in file, Wren sprinting on ahead, me pulling myself after as best I could. The defile ended at a little plateau that hovered above a corner of the harbor, a few dozen square feet of dirt and sand cropped into a low hill that rose out of the bay. The water was dark and choppy, blurring at the horizon with the clouds above it. In the jetty below the remains of a handful of skiffs lay dashed against the rocks, casualties of the storm.

'Did they at least get what was coming to them?' Wren asked.

'Who?'

'The guilty.'

He looked so small at that moment, so damn young. There was a scrub tree growing up out of the rocks, and I leaned against it and rolled up a cigarette. It was burnt down to a nub before I answered. 'Not all of them.'

That didn't seem to satisfy him. It didn't satisfy me either, but it was all I had to offer. Another few minutes watching the roiling ocean, and I led us back home.

For the first book I had a lot of time to muck about with compliments and in-jokes, but the hour is growing very late, so no one gets anything more than a shout out. Sorry, I'm pushing a deadline as it is.

Business-wise: Chris and Oliver.

As for family: Mom and Dad. Teddy and Jeanette, Ben, Rachel and Jason. My Grandmother. The Mottolas, with particular attention to Uncle John and his set. All of them, really, and apologies I keep missing Thanksgiving. Next one for sure!

And the friends: Bobby, Mike, Pete, Elliot, Sam. Rusty for military advice. Lisa. Will and John. Alex, with apologies that he didn't get repped better the first time around. You're twelve foot tall and piss like a fire hose, all right? Tommy/Bosley. The Eleftherious, and the Roots. The strangers, now friends, that let me sleep on their couches/floors/beds.

I'm sure I'm forgetting somebody, and my apologies to that person/people.

Discover Daniel Polansky's masterful debut

THE
STRAIGHT
RAZOR CURE

I

In the opening days of the Great War, on the battlefields of Apres and Ives, I acquired the ability to abandon slumber with the flutter of an eyelid. It was a necessary adaptation, as heavy sleepers were likely to come to greeted by a Dren commando with a trench blade. It's a vestige of my past I'd rather lose, all things considered. Rare is the situation that requires the full range of one's perceptions, and in general the world is improved by being only dimly visible.

Case in point – my room was the sort of place best viewed half asleep or in a drunken stupor. Late autumn light filtered through my dusty window and made the interior, already only a few small steps from squalor, look still less prepossessing. Even by my standards the place was a dump, and my standards are low. A worn dresser and a chipped table set were the only furnishings that accompanied the bed, and a veneer of grime covered the floor and walls. I passed water in the bedpan and threw the waste into the alley below.

Low Town was in full stream, the streets echoing with the screech of fish hags advertising the day's catch to porters carrying crates north into the Old City. At the market a few blocks east merchants sold underweight goods to middlemen for clipped copper, while down Light Street guttersnipes kept drawn-dagger eyes out for an unwary vendor or a blue-blood too far from home. In the corners and the alleys the working boys kept up the same cries as the fish hags, though they spoke lower and charged more. Worn streetwalkers pulling the early shift waved tepid come-ons at passersby, hoping to pad their faded charms into one more day's worth of liquor or choke. The dangerous men were mostly still asleep, their blades sheathed next to the bed. The really dangerous men had been up for hours, and their quills and ledgers were getting hard use.

I grabbed a hand mirror off the floor and held it at arm's length. Under the best of circumstances, perfumed and manicured, I am an ugly man. A lumpen nose dripped below overlarge eyes, a mouth like a knife wound set off-center. Enhancing my natural charms are an accumulation of scars that would shame a masochist, an off-color line running up my cheek from where an artillery shard had come a few inches from laying me out, the torn flesh of my left ear testifying to a street brawl where I'd taken second place.

A vial of pixie's breath winked good morning from the worn wood of my table. I uncorked it and took a whiff. Cloyingly sweet vapors filled my nostrils, followed closely by a familiar buzzing in my ears. I shook the bottle – half empty, it had gone quick. I pulled on my shirt and boots, then grabbed my satchel from beneath the bed and walked downstairs to greet the late morn.

The Staggering Earl was quiet this time of day, and absent a crowd the main room was dominated by the mammoth figure behind the bar, Adolphus the Grand, co-owner and publican. Despite his height – he was a full head taller than my own six feet – his cask-like torso was so wide as to give the impression of corpulence, though a closer examination would reveal the balance of his bulk as muscle. Adolphus had been an ugly man before a Dren bolt claimed his left eye, but the black cloth he wore across the socket and the scar that tore down his pockmarked cheek hadn't improved things. Between that and his slow stare he seemed a thug and a dullard, and though he was neither of those things this impression tended to keep folk civil in his presence.

He was cleaning the bar and pontificating on the injustices of the day to one of our more sober patrons. It was a popular pastime. I sidled over and took the cleanest seat.

Adolphus was too dedicated to solving the problems of the nation to allow common courtesy to intrude on his monologue, so by way of greeting he offered me a perfunctory nod. 'And no doubt you'd agree with me, having seen what a failure his lordship has been as High Chancellor. Let him go back to stringing up rebels as Executor of the Throne's Justice – at least that was a task he was fit for.'

'I'm not really sure what you're talking about, Adolphus. Everyone knows our leaders are as wise as they are honest. Now is it too late for a plate of eggs?'

He turned his head towards the kitchen and growled, 'Woman! Eggs!' Aside completed, he circled back towards his captive drunk.

'Five years I gave the Crown, five years and my eye.' Adolphus liked to slip his injury into casual conversation, apparently operating under the impression that it was inconspicuous. 'Five years neck deep in shit and filth, five years while the bankers and nobles back home got rich on my blood. A half ochre a month ain't much for five years of that, but it's mine and I'll be damned if I let 'em forget it.' He dropped his rag on the counter and pointed a sausage-sized finger at me in hopes of encouragement. 'It's your half ochre too, my friend. You're awfully quiet for a man forgotten by Queen and country.'

What was there to say? The High Chancellor would do what he wished, and the rantings of a one-eyed ex-pikeman were unlikely to do much to persuade him. I grunted noncommittally. Adeline, as quiet and small as her husband was the opposite, came out of the kitchen and offered me a plate with a tiny smile. I took the first and returned the second. Adolphus kept up his rambling but I ignored him and turned to the eggs. We'd been friends for a decade and a half because I forgave him his garrulousness and he forgave me my taciturnity.

The breath was kicking in. I could feel my nerves getting steadier, my eyesight sharper. I shoveled the baked black bread into my mouth and considered the day's work. I needed to visit my man in the customs office – he'd promised me clean passes a fortnight past but had yet to make good. Beyond that there were the usual rounds to the distributors who bought from me, shady bartenders and small-time dealers, pimps and pushers. Come evening I needed to stop by a party up towards Kor's Heights – I had told Yancey the Rhymer I'd check in before his evening set.

Back on the main stage the drunk found a chance to interrupt Adolphus's torrent of quasi-coherent civic slander. 'You hear anything about the little one?'

The giant and I exchanged unhappy glances. 'The hoax are useless,' Adolphus said, and went back to cleaning. Three days earlier the child of a dock worker had gone missing from an alley outside her house. Since then 'Little Tara' had become something of a cause célèbre for the people of Low Town. The fishermen's guild had put out a reward, the Church of Prachetas had offered a service in her honor, even the guard had set aside their lethargy for a few hours to bang on doors and look down wells. Nothing had been found, and seventy-two hours was a long time for a child to stay lost in the most crowded square mile in the Empire. Śakra willing, the girl was fine, but I wouldn't bet my unpaid half ochre on it.

The reminder of the child provoked the minor miracle of shutting Adolphus's mouth. I finished my breakfast in silence, then pushed my plate aside and rose to my feet. 'Hold any messages – I'll be back after dark.'

Adolphus waved me out.

I exited into the chaos of Low Town at midday and began my walk east towards the docks. Leaning against the wall a block past the Earl, rolling a cigarette and glowering, I spotted all five and a half feet of Kid Mac, pimp and bravo extraordinaire. His dark eyes stared out over faded dueling scars, and as always his clothes were uniformly perfect, from the wide brim of his hat to the silver handle of his rapier. He strung himself up against the bricks with an expression that combined the threat of violence with a rather profound indolence.

In the years since he had come to the neighborhood, Mac had managed to carve out a small territory by virtue of his skill with a blade and the unreserved dedication of his whores, who to a woman were as enamored of him as a mother is her firstborn. I often thought that Mac had the easiest job in Low Town, seeming to consist mostly of ensuring that his streetwalkers didn't kill each other in competition for his attentions, but you wouldn't know it from the scowl etched across his face. We'd been friendly ever since he'd set up shop, passing each other information and the occasional favor.

'Mac.'

'Warden.' He offered me his cigarette.

I lit it with a match from my belt. 'How're the girls?'

He shook some tobacco from his pouch and started on another smoke. 'That lost child has them worked up worse than a clutch of hens. Red Annie kept everyone up half the night weeping, till Euphemia went after her with a switch.'

'They're a sensitive bunch.' I reached into my purse and surreptitiously handed him his shipment. 'Any word on Eddie the Quim?' I asked, referring to a rival of his who had been chased out of Low Town earlier in the week.

'He works a stone's throw from headquarters and doesn't think he needs to pay off the hoax? Eddie's too stupid to live. He won't see the other side of winter – I'd go an argent on it.' Mac finished rolling his cigarette with one hand and slipped the package into his back pocket with the other.

'I wouldn't take it,' I said.

Mac tucked the tab loosely into his sneer. We watched the ebb of traffic from our post. 'You get those passes yet?' he asked.

'Going to see my man today. Should have something for you soon.'

He grunted what might have been assent and I turned to leave. 'You oughta know that Harelip's boys have been peddling east of the canal.' He took a drag and exhaled perfect circles of smoke, one following the other into the clement sky. 'The girls have seen his crew off and on for the last week or so.'

'I heard. Stay slick, Mac.'

He went back to looking menacing.

I spent the rest of the afternoon dropping off product and running errands. My customs officer finally came through with the passes, though at the rate his addiction to pixie's breath was progressing, it might well be the last favor he'd be able to do for me.

It was early evening by the time I was finished, and I stopped off at my favorite street stand for a pot of beef in chili sauce. I still needed to see Yancey before his set – he was performing for some toffee-nosed aristocrats near the Old City, and it would be a walk. I was cutting through an alleyway to save time when I saw something that clipped my progress so abruptly that I nearly toppled over.

The Rhymer would have to wait. Ahead of me was the body of a child, contorted horribly and wrapped in a sheet soaked through with blood.

It seemed I had found Little Tara.

I tossed my dinner into a sewer grate. Suddenly I didn't have much of an appetite.

2

I burned a few seconds taking stock of the situation. The rats of Low Town are an immodest bunch, so the fact that her body was intact suggested that she hadn't been left out long. I crouched down and set a palm on her tiny chest – cold. She'd been dead for some time before being dumped here. Up close I could see the indignities her tormentor had inflicted more clearly, and I shuddered and withdrew, noticing as I did so a strange smell, not the sickly sweet scent of decayed flesh but one abrasive and alchemical, harsh against the back of my throat.

Retreating from the alley to the main street, I flagged down a pair of street urchins idling beneath an awning nearby. Among the lower classes my name carries some small weight, and they presented themselves as if they expected me to draft them into a scheme of some kind, and were excited at the opportunity. I gave the duller-looking of the two a copper and told him to find a guardsman. When he was around the corner I turned to the one who remained.

I keep half the Low Town guard in whores and watered-down beer, so they wouldn't be a problem. But a murder of this sort would demand the attention of an agent, and whomever they sent might be foolish enough to think me a suspect. I needed to get rid of my merchandise.

The boy stared up at me with brown eyes deep-set against pale skin. Like most street children he was a mutt, features of the three Rigun peoples intermixed with any number of foreign races. Even by the standards of the dispossessed he was painfully thin, the rags he wore as clothing insufficient to hide the bony protrusions of his shoulder blades and elbows.

'You know who I am?'

'You're the Warden.'

'You know the Staggering Earl?'

He nodded, his dark eyes wide but unclouded. I thrust my bag towards him.

'Take this there and give it to the cyclops behind the bar. Tell him I said he owes you an argent.'

He reached for it and I dug my fingers in the crook of his neck. 'I know every whore, pickpocket, junkie and street tough in Low Town, and I've marked your face. If my package ain't waiting for me I'm going to come looking for you. Understand?' I tightened my grip.

He didn't flinch. 'I ain't bent.' His voice surprised me with its cool confidence. I had picked the right urchin.

'Off with you then.' I released the bag and he sprinted around the corner.

I went back into the alley and smoked a cigarette while I waited for the hoax to show up. They were longer than I thought they'd be, given the gravity of the situation. It's disturbing to discover your low opinion of law enforcement is still unduly appreciative. Two burned tabs later the first boy returned, a pair of guardsmen in tow.

I knew them vaguely. One was fresh, new to the force six months, but the second I'd been paying off for years. We'd see how much good that would do if things curdled. 'Hello, Wendell.'

I held out my hand. 'Good to see you again, even under these circumstances.'

Wendell shook it vigorously. 'You as well,' he said. 'I had hoped the boy was lying.'

There wasn't much to say to that. Wendell knelt beside the body, his chain coat dragging in the mud. Behind him his younger counterpart was turning the shade of white that prefaces vomiting. Wendell shouted a reproach over his shoulder. 'None of that. You're a damn guardsman – show some spine.' He turned back to the corpse, unsure of his next move. 'Guess I should call for an agent then,' he half asked me.

'Guess so.'

'Run back to headquarters,' Wendell ordered his subordinate, 'and tell them to send for a chill. Tell them to send for two.'

The guard enforce the customs and laws of the city – when they aren't paid to look the other way – but investigating crime is more or less beyond them. If a murderer isn't standing over the corpse with a bloody knife they're not of much use. When there's a crime that matters to someone who counts, an Agent of the Crown is sent, officially deputized to carry out the Throne's Justice. The frost, the cold, the snowmen or the gray devils, call them what you want but bow your head when they pass and answer prompt if they ask you something, 'cause the chill ain't the guard, and the only thing more dangerous than an incompetent constabulary is a competent one. Normally, a dumped body in Low Town doesn't warrant their attention – a fact that does wonders for the murder rate – but this wasn't a drunk drowned in a puddle, or a knifed junkie. They'd send an agent for this.

After a few minutes, a small squad of guardsmen arrived on the scene. A pair of them began cordoning off the area. The remainder stood around looking important. They weren't doing a great job of it, but I didn't have the heart to tell them.

Bored of waiting, or wanting to impress his importance upon the newcomers, Wendell decided to take a stab at police work. 'Probably some heretic,' he said, scratching at his double chins.

'Passing through the docks on the way to Kirentown, saw the girl and . . .' He gestured sharply.

'Yeah, I hear there's a lot of that going around.'

His partner chimed in, baby face spouting poison, choked-back bile heavy on his breath. 'Or an Islander. You know how they are.'

Wendell nodded sagely. He did indeed know how they were.

I'd heard that in some of the newer mental wards they set the mad and congenitally stupid to rote tasks, having them sew buttons onto mounds of fabric, the futile labor working as a salve to their broken minds. I wonder sometimes whether the guard is not an extension of this therapy on a far grander scale, an elaborate social program meant to give the low-functioning an illusion of purpose.

But it wouldn't do to spoil it for the inmates. This burst of insight seemed to exhaust Wendell and his second, and they lapsed into silence.

The autumn eve chased the last shreds of daylight across the skyline. The sounds of honest commerce, as much as such a thing exists in Low Town, were replaced with a jittery quiet. In the surrounding tenements someone had a fire going, and the wood smoke almost covered up the state of the body. I rolled a cigarette to block out the rest.

You could sense their arrival before you could see them, the packed Low Town masses scuttling out from their path like flotsam brushed aside by a flood. A few seconds more and you made them out apart from the movement of the crowd. The freeze prided themselves on the uniformity of their costumes, each an interchangeable member of the small army that controlled the city and most of the nation. An ice-gray duster, its upturned collar leading to a matching wide-brimmed hat. A silver-hilted short sword hanging at the belt, both an aesthetic marvel and a perfect instrument of violence. A dusky jewel trapped in a silver frame dangling from the throat – the Crown's Eye, official symbol of their authority. Every inch the personification of order, a clenched fist in a velvet glove.

For all that I would never speak it aloud, for all that it shamed me even to think it, I couldn't lie – I missed that fucking outfit.

Crispin recognized me from about a block away, and his face hardened but his step didn't slow. Five years hadn't done much to alter his appearance. The same highborn face stared at me beneath the fold of his hat, the same upright carriage bore mute witness to a youth spent in the tutelage of dance masters and teachers of etiquette. His brown hair had retreated from its former prominence, but the curve of his nose still trumpeted the long history of his blood to anyone who cared to look. I knew he regretted me being here, just as I regretted him being called.

The other one I didn't recognize – he must have been new. Like Crispin he had the Rouender nose, long and arrogant, but his hair was so blond as to be nearly white. Apart from the platinum mane he seemed the archetypal agent, his blue eyes inquisitorial without being discerning, the body beneath his uniform hard enough to convince you of his menace, assuming you didn't know what to look for.

They stopped at the entrance to the alleyway. Crispin's gaze darted across the scene, resting briefly on the covered corpse before settling on Wendell, who stood stiffly at attention, doing his best impression of a law enforcement official. 'Guardsman,' Crispin said, nodding sharply. The second agent, still unnamed, offered not even that, his arms firmly crossed and something like a smirk on his face. Sufficient attention paid to protocol, Crispin turned towards me. 'You found her?'

'Forty minutes ago, but she'd been here a while before that. She was dumped here after he finished with her.'

Crispin paced a slow circle around the scene. A wooden door led into an abandoned building halfway down the alley. He paused and put his hand against it. 'You think he came through here?'

'Not necessarily. The body was small enough to be concealed – a small crate, maybe an empty cask of ale. At dusk, this street doesn't get much traffic. You could dump it and keep walking.'

'Syndicate business?'

'You know better than that. An unblemished child goes for

five hundred ochre in the pens of Bukhirra. No slaver would be foolish enough to ruin their profit, and if they were they'd know a better way to dispose of the corpse.'

This was too much deference shown to a stranger in a tattered coat for Crispin's second. He sauntered over, flushed with the arrogance that comes from having one's hereditary sense of superiority cemented by the acquisition of public office. 'Who is this man? What was he doing when he found the body?' He sneered at me. I had to admit he knew how to sneer. For all its ubiquity it isn't an expression that just anyone can master.

But I didn't respond to it, and he turned to Wendell. 'Where are his effects? What was the result of your search?'

'Well, sir,' Wendell started, his Low Town accent thickening. 'Seeing as how he called in the body, we figured . . . that's to say . . .' He wiped his nose with the back of his fat hand and coughed out a response. 'He hasn't been searched, sir.'

'Is this what passes for an investigation among the guard? A suspect is found standing beside a murdered child and you converse cordially with him over the corpse? Do your job and search this man!'

Wendell's dull face blushed. He shrugged apologetically and moved to pat me down.

'That won't be necessary, Agent Guiscard,' Crispin interrupted. 'This man is . . . an old associate. He is above suspicion.'

'Only in this matter I assure you. Agent Guiscard, is it? By all means, Agent Guiscard, search me. You can never be too careful. Who's to say I didn't kidnap the child, rape and torture her, dump her body, wait an hour, then call the guard?' Guiscard's face turned a dull shade of red, a strange contrast to his hair. 'Quite a prodigy, aren't we? I guess that set of smarts came standard with your pedigree.' Guiscard balled his fist. I swelled out my grin.

Crispin cut between the two of us and began barking orders. 'None of that. There's work to be done. Agent Guiscard, return to Black House and tell them to send a scryer; if you double-step it there might still be time for him to pick up something. The rest of you set up a perimeter. There's going to be half a hundred citizens here in ten minutes and I don't want them mucking up the crime scene. And for the love of Śakra, one of you find this poor child's parents.'

Guiscard glared at me ineffectually, then stomped off. I shook some leaf out of my pouch and started to roll a smoke. 'New partner's quite a handful. Whose nephew is he?'

Crispin gave a half-smile. 'The Earl of Grenwick's.'

'Good to see nothing's changed.'

'He's not as bad as he looks. You were pushing him.'

'He was easy to push.'

'So were you, once.'

He was probably right about that. Age had mellowed me, or at least I liked to think so. I offered the cigarette to my ex-partner.

'I quit – it was ruining my wind.'

I wedged it between my lips. The years of friendship stretched out awkwardly between us.

'If you discover something, you'll come to me. You won't do anything yourself,' Crispin said, somewhere between an inquiry and a demand.

'I don't solve crimes, Crispin, because I'm not an agent.' I struck a match against the wall and lit my smoke. 'You made sure of that.'

'You made sure of that. I just watched while you fell.'

This had gone on too long. 'There was an odor on the corpse. It might be gone by now but it's worth checking.' I couldn't bring myself to wish him luck.

A crowd of onlookers was forming as I left the cover of the alleyway, the specter of human misery always a popular draw. The wind had picked up. I pulled my coat tight and hurried my steps.

Want more?

If you enjoyed this and would like to find out about similar books we publish, we'd love you to join our online Sci-Fi, Fantasy and Horror community **Hodderscape.**

Follow us on
Twitter @Hodderscape

and visit our Facebook page at
facebook.com/hodderscape

You'll find news, competitions, video content and general musings, so feel free to comment, contribute or just keep an eye on what we are up to. See you there!

HODDERSCAPE

HODDER